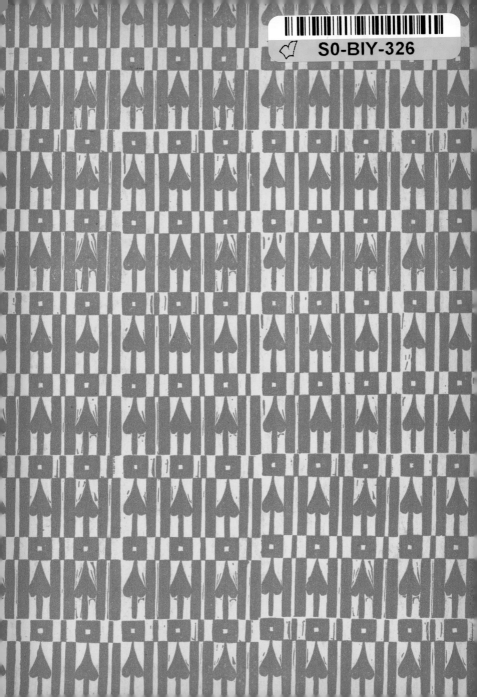

SO-BIY-326

500
808
600
_____
4200

F. Greene

A PRESIDENT IS BORN

by

FANNIE HURST

Harper & Brothers Publishers

NEW YORK AND LONDON

1928

A

PRESIDENT IS BORN

COPYRIGHT, 1928, BY FANNIE HURST

PRINTED IN THE U. S. A.

A-C

First Printing, December, 1927
Second Printing, December, 1927
Third Printing, December, 1927
Fourth Printing, December, 1927
Fifth Printing, December, 1927
Sixth Printing, December, 1927
Seventh Printing, December, 1927
Eighth Printing, December, 1927
Ninth Printing, January, 1928

TO
THE MEMORY OF
HENRY STEPHEN SCHUYLER

The author takes occasion to make grateful acknowledgment to the Schuyler family, and to Senator Bettina Schuyler Sterling in particular, for the privilege of access to the diaries of the late Rebekka Schuyler Renchler.

It has been a task requiring the utmost delicacy to step lightly through the aisles of her pages; and only because of the great interest that centers around even the minutiæ of the life of David Schuyler, has the author ventured to quote from so precious and so private a family-document.

By virtue of this handsome grant of access to the diaries, the public again becomes beneficiary of the Schuyler family.

A
PRESIDENT
IS BORN

ALL footnotes herein appended are excerpts from the private diaries of the late Rebekka Schuyler Renchler and are quoted with the permission of her granddaughter, United States Senator Bettina Schuyler Sterling, in whose possession they are.

A PRESIDENT IS BORN

Twenty-two sat down to dinner on a Thanksgiving afternoon at four, 1903, in the House on Sycamore Street.

It might have been the house in Downing Street so far as its centrifugal significance was ground into the consciousness of the men, women and children gathered about its board.

For thirty years it had stood on the outskirts of a town that lapped out toward it like a constantly encroaching tide. It was then virtually the last house in Centralia. Always had been. As you drove into town, the two-story wooden structure of tower, ell, bulge and gable, marked the beginning of the principal residential street. As you left town, a half mile or so beyond the Schuyler fifteen acres of homestead, a city-limits sign was painted against a whitewashed slab of stone. Later, a large sign the shape of an open book announced:

> YOU ARE NOW LEAVING CENTRALIA. THIS
> SPOT MARKS THE SITE WHERE CELERON DE
> BIENVILLE IN 1749 PLANTED A LEADEN PLATE
> AND TOOK FORMAL POSSESSION.
> CENTRALIA OFFERS UNPARALLELED FACTORY
> AND FOUNDRY SITES AND PEERLESS WATER
> POWER ADVANTAGES. SEE CHAMBER OF
> COMMERCE. WRITE FOR BOOKLET.

Six children and several of the grandchildren had been born in the House on Sycamore Street. The second-story

1

front, a deep room with a bay window formed by a tower that was filled with an indoor vine of myrtle that grew in a flower box, held in its timbers the first squalls of Mathilda (deceased at two weeks of age), Rebekka, Clara, Henry, Phil and Emma Schuyler.

Two of Rebekka's children had been born in that front room. Clara had come from St. Louis for the purpose of having her first-born see its first light of day in that room of double walnut wardrobe that reached to ceiling, hand-painted window shades, washstand with a pink-and-white bowl and pitcher, toothbrush-mug, and grooved soap-dish that had stood dry since the cedar closet had been made into a bathroom.

To open your eyes upon that room was to greet the retinas with a pair of china spittoons on the white hearth; oval portraits of Austrian Schuylers, in oval brooches or square-cut spades of beard; a pair of steel-engravings of "Washington Crossing the Delaware" and "Signing the Declaration"; a horsehair and walnut-backed armchair, in which the Old Gentleman always sat, and that by its shape was to suggest to Henry Schuyler, as long as he lived, the figure of his father crouched into it for his annual cold, a gray-striped blanket across his shoulders, and his feet immersed in steaming foot tub the shape of a kidney and with a tin bottom that plunked.

The solemn double bed with pillow shams the pallor and shape of headstones, was covered with a patchwork quilt of tulip-and-leaf design that Mathilda Schuyler had brought as dowry to Heinie Schuyler when she married him in an Austrian village called Holdstein. On holidays it was piled with the mufflers, the top-coats, the tippets, muffs, baby-leggings, small-boy sweaters, and the little-girl cloaks of the homecoming clan.

It was as if the walls of this house, which had been

outgrown practically the first year of its occupancy, would burst its sides for need of expansion, on that Thanksgiving afternoon, for instance, when the Schuylers, twenty-two strong, sat down to dinner at four.

That meant that Schuylers from as far as Springfield and as wide as St. Louis, with their wives, husbands and children, were home for the holiday.

For two days the rich sweetness of mincemeat stewing in its sluggish juices had wound aromatically through the house. To even stir the colloid mass required Mathilda to grasp the long iron spoon as you would a broom, with both hands, and haul it around and around the pot. Sometimes Trina, who had come to the Schuylers a slim chip of a hired girl and, now twenty-five years later, weighed two hundred and forty pounds, helped. But at the period of this Thanksgiving, Trina was already entering the last seven years of her life, and varicose veins had set in, rendering her chair-ridden the greater part of the time.

And so Mathilda, who had weighed ninety pounds when she was married and now weighed one hundred and one, swung her heavy chores practically alone, importunings of the Old Gentleman and his children to the contrary notwithstanding. As a matter of fact, Henry often said of her that she seemed to take a sort of sadistic pleasure in flaying her endurance; in pulling her muscles at the dragging of heavy objects until she could feel the bones of her arms leave their sockets; in straining the wires of her tough little body at doing the lifting of a strong man. When Mathilda was forty-eight she was shriveled in the way that women no longer allow themselves to grow old. But she could carry a galvanized washtub of hot water or a one-hundred-and-ten pound sheep across a meadow and glory with fierce, straining eyeballs, as her very heart seemed to leave its moorings.

There were two hundred and eighty cookies this Thanksgiving, baked by Mathilda by lamplight before dawn. Pepper drops and cinnamon squares (especially baked because they were Leslie's favorites) and aniseed. The sunshine cake was of a specially-prepared flour, and saccharine instead of sugar (son-in-law Sam Holly was overweight and obliged to reduce when his heart began to flutter), which everyone declared, for purposes of cheering Sam, was even better than if prepared with Mathilda's usual and wickedly-rich ingredients. There were candied yams, candied apples on sticks, sweetbreads in individual ramekins, turkey dressing of citron, chestnuts and walnut meats. Cranberry sauce that had jellied the star-shape of the mold. Cider that stung like all of an autumn outdoors. A pitcher of egg-nog with a fine peppering of cinnamon. Hot biscuit, the size of a silver dollar, that went into the mouth at one plop (the Old Gentleman smothered his in maple syrup). Kale boiled with bacon rind. There were six pumpkin and six mince pies alternating, standing in rows on the pantry sill.

Mathilda naturally alternated them that way. She liked making little patterns of her days and her quiltings and her procedures.

Rebekka Schuyler Renchler had sent over, from her farm, a gallon pail of apple butter, a batch of *zimmt-kuchen* the shape of soldiers, camels, and stars for the children's table, and five bushels of winesap apples, the yield of her own orchards that had come to be known locally as "Rebekka Wines."

The Phil Schuylers, as usual, brought down a hamper of Mullane's Taffy; Phil's annual contribution to his father of a quart bottle of Kümmel, and more cookies, his wife's specialty. Sugar ones with jam hearts.

There was a story abroad in Centralia that one Thanksgiving, Mathilda had sent these jam-hearted cookies to Annie Milliken, who in turn, with a Thanksgiving Day superabundance of her own, had sent them over to a school-teacher friend who had innocently completed the circle by sending them around to the Schuylers as a Thanksgiving Day offering.

Be that as it may, the circle of giving in Centralia was anything but a vicious one. Henry Schuyler used to say, in the dry fashion he had, that more glasses of jelly changed hands in Centralia during a holiday-week; more pies and tarts under snowy napkins; more batches of cookies and mincemeats in Mason jars, than there were stocks bandied back and forth on a busy day on the New York Stock Exchange.

Centralia loved to bite with careful front teeth down on its neighbors' cookies, mince them finely until taste squirted along the tongue. And appraise.

One of Emma's hazelnut tortes, tried and true to occasions of birthday, anniversary, and that chilled moment when the newly-bereaved family returns from the cemetery, stood on the sideboard beside the silver ice-water pitcher with sweating sides, that was mounted like a patent rocker and tilted in its frame for pouring.

Emma had baked it that morning in her white-enamel range, the first in Centralia, that had just been installed in her fine new red-brick Georgian house, that stood on exactly the opposite end of Sycamore Street from her parents. It was made out of double cream, that torte, and seemed ready to burst its steep sides and melt into a viscous pool of its own richness.

There was the kind of superabundance of food that palls before it tempts. That was why Henry Schuyler, who abhorred waste, never came downstairs on these holiday fêtes until after the mumbled grace, the fruit cocktail, the chicken soup, and the creamed oysters in pâté cases.

Just before the fowl was brought in, usually one of Rebekka's eighteen-pound gobblers, with protruding legs in jolly white-paper caps, Mathilda rapped against her water-tumbler three times with her fork.

That was the signal for Henry, whose room was directly above the dining-room, to put down his *Leatherstocking Tales,* Carlyle's *French Revolution,* or Fiske's *American History,* knock his pipe empty into the coal bucket, remove his feet from the nickel-plated rim of the base-runner, and go downstairs to mid-afternoon dinner.

They hung on his digestion like leaden weights, these post-convivial afternoons, causing him to fall asleep later with a newspaper over his face, noxious dreams and the goose-fleshing memory of the sound of steel carving knife and fork, criss-crossing, crawling across his befogged doze.

At the coming of the fowl, the Old Gentleman began his invariable sharpening of the hartshorn knife against the rod, curdling the air in a fashion that gave Henry nervous shudders, and, ever since she was old enough to remember, had sent the goose-flesh flashing along Rebekka.

"Father, please!"

"Puppa, you know how Bek and Henry hate it. Trina sharpened them out in the kitchen."

That was the signal for the Old Gentleman to wield the wicked knife, jerking a turkey leg backward and slithering into the soft flesh, with a rush of juices.

"Here, Mother, you want the part that goes over the fence last."

The family was pretty well reconciled to this moss-grown overture. All except Emma, who would invariably pucker her pretty blonde brows and come out in no uncertain terms.

"Father, that's not one bit funny! It's disgusting! Besides, Mother doesn't really like it. That's her way of denying herself white meat."

The small, bewildered face of Mathilda Schuyler, there in the midst of her five progeny of unusual heft, would begin to pale and wilt under the dicker. Their vitality sapped hers. Her daughters, with their heavy shoulders and strong legs and strong neck-columns. Phil, who in his late twenties was already so rotund as to know his watch pocket by touch rather than sight. Henry of brown brawn, but no fat.

It was a fluttery old face, that of Mathilda Schuyler. Like a curtain in a breeze.

It was a face which the Old Gentleman, sly, wry, bold, and humorous behind his own square trim of white beard, usually regarded with precisely the expression with which he now regarded his grandchildren.

Only, this day, there screwed itself into the old man's eyes, as he observed her from his place opposite her end of the long table, something sly. The old man became a little faunal. A naughty old faun.

"Emma's right, Mathilda! From now on I'll serve you only with white meat. It's good for what ails you."

"Why?" said Phil, who made rapid, cracking noises up the stalk of a celery stick. "Isn't Mother well?"

"I've never seen her look better," said Rebekka into the flash of quick anxiety that went around the table. "Mother has gained pounds!"

Rebekka was five-feet-ten, weighed one hundred and seventy, and had no fat. Level of eye, level of strong, firm bosom. Level of brow, from which she wore the enormously thick brown hair coiled unstylishly on the top of the back of her head. Level of voice, too. One of those low, middle-register people. Without being masculine, there was something rather Socratic about the head of Rebekka Renchler. A brow that jutted firmly over the deeply-molded roofs of eye sockets. A fine, strong, fierce nose. Mouth brackets.

It was characteristic of the family to discuss any one of its members as if the individual under scrutiny were not present. It was particularly a family habit to discuss Mathilda over her head.

"Father!" said Rebekka suddenly, and then again sharply, "Father—what?"

There was no denying it. Above the square white beard that hung like a muslin curtain from the Old Gentleman's chin, were two round dots of color. A shrewd, old, sly face, trying not to look abashed, and humorous eyes, twenty years too young for their weather-beaten setting that kept radiating lines.

That was the Old Gentleman's method of laughter. Behind the beard, that was slightly yellow about the mouth, the lips, heavy and of a raspberry red, remained mobile. It was the sunburst of lines at the ends of his eyes that kept radiating a sort of heat lightning of laughter.

"Once a good strong woman," said the Old Gentleman, letting his naughty old gaze spray over his wife, "always a good strong woman."

"Not at all, Father!" said Rebekka. "Mother's endurance at fifty-three is simply amazing, and see how frail she looks. Every one of us is big enough to carry her off single-handed, and yet she goes on from break of dawn until bedtime, slaving, slaving away as if things were no different now than when we were children growing up."

"Ah, she's a good one!" said the Old Gentleman, winking his two eyes simultaneously at his wife, who fluttered. "She's a good one all right!" And, incredibly enough, made a screwing noise with his tongue and slid his naughty, bright-blue, humorous, twinkling eyes.

"Puppa, don't do that!"

"Don't do what, Mathilda?"

"That! That!" echoed Emma, who could cry from being made nervous by what she considered her father's none-too-subtle sense of low comedy. "With your eyes, Father! It's—it's horrid! What is it, dear, makes you do it?"

"Your Mother's a good one, Daughter! That's all! Don't we sit down to table, twenty-odd of us—Thanksgiving?"

"Yes, Father!" said Emma faintly, and regarded her mother for the moment as if she were going to cry now.

"Pass Mother the gravy," said Rebekka, in her low, rather hoarse voice. It was her way of sparring off for the group of them a moment that threatened to become sentimental.

"No, serve the boys, Puppa."

"No, the Mama comes first!"

"Please—the boys ——"

There was something about the mere idea of her brood assembled, that could send the tremulous wavering along Mathilda's voice. Probably the unbelievable precariousness of it. Six children into the world with perfect sequence except for the infant mortality of the first-born, Mathilda. Nine grandchildren without a casualty. Except perhaps Leslie. And yet Mathilda sometimes wondered, regarding the boy's pale head and his eyes that looked tranced as if with enchantment at what they saw, if he could be classed a casualty.

Rebekka, though, who had borne him, must have thought so. Her eyes, when they looked at this boy of hers, seemed to pour inward, leaving them staring, like empty lake-beds.

Leslie, who was twelve, sat at the younger children's improvised table under the stairway.

At the oval-topped table in the sitting-room, which ordinarily held the four-pound family Testament and a pair of brown porcelain pug-dogs, chipped from being hidden by this or that one of the Schuyler girls, only to be unearthed again by Mathilda, were Rebekka's Steve, who at eleven looked like the young San Sebastian, and who, to his grandfather's delight, could quaff cider like a sailor, licking his lips and drawing his arm across them; and Rebekka's only daughter, a pretty, fair girl, whose dark eyes flashed a curious contradiction to her placid, taffy hair.

It was as if, on holidays, the family thus assembled, the old House on Sycamore Street must fairly burst its weather-colored sides of hubbub.

The Old Gentleman loved the hubbub. It flowed over him with the voice of a world he had peopled. The town, the county, and even the state bore testimony to Schuyler progeny.

Rebekka's model stock-farm, High Ridge, was one to which the entire state pointed with pride.

Phil Schuyler was already, though destined for temporary defeat, a moving figure in what were to be spectacular land deals in the history of Springfield. Henry Schuyler, who coveted no man's office, had twice been approached to run on a Republican ticket, once for Congress and once for District Attorney, and frequently, Cincinnatus-like, had been called from his small environment to his state capital, and twice to Washington, on a point concerning certain legalities of water control.

Yes, the Old Gentleman loved the hubbub of his progeny about him, and today somehow, with the two polka-dots out on his cheekbones and his eyes in that faun-like crinkle—there was something about the Old Gentleman ——

Rebekka, who was fond of saying that she knew her father like a book, and who bartered heifers with him in the open cattle-marts, who housed his sheep for him in winter in exchange for the second crop of his South Meadow of alfalfa, and who carried a pot of her own concoction of cocoa butter in her great leather reticule, for his finger-tips, which cold split terribly in winter, kept sitting more and more stiffly at his right.

Even Henry, who had a way of looking at no one yet seeing everyone, threw his father an occasional glance. Emma was on edge. Ever since she could remember, there had been things her father did that affected her like the scratch of a gold ring across a slate. His way of standing her on the oval-topped parlor table when she had been a child and pointing out her blonde pretti-ness to visitors. "She's a good one, isn't she?" In Emma's opinion, as if she had been so much heifer flesh. The Old Gentleman's insistence, during Emma's second year in High School, of driving up after her in a dirty old phaeton that barely escaped scraping the streets. "The Floozy Flump" they used to call it at school. "Here comes Emma's Floozy Flump," would reach her stinging ears. It was precisely the same way she used to feel later, in the days when her husband, Morton Milliken, had been wooing her and the Old Gentleman would sit on the side verandah evenings in his socks, sucking his atrocious meerschaum, just about the time Morton was due to arrive.

That whole group of grosgrained sensations was on a par with what her father was doing to her now. What made him squint so? The face of Mathilda kept fluttering, in the way it had when agitated.

There was undoubtedly in the air the charged quality of something of note about to happen in the Schuyler family.

A Schuyler must be about to be born. Another impending grandchild? Which of the girls was with child? Or, by a stretch of the imagination, was some one, a Schuyler, on the verge of being rebuked? Who?

The sisters and sisters-in-law felt along one another with their eyes. The bright, inquisitive, rather merciless eyes of women who suspect. Rita Schuyler, Phil's wife, had had her last child. A recent operation had settled that. Well, that left Rebekka. Nonsense! And Clara. No-n-o. Slowly the women's eyes swung to Emma, who squirmed and felt more and more irritated and could have sobbed her denial.

There came Phil's dry little bronchial cough that always attacked him when he felt called upon to defend himself before his father. There had been many such stormy defenses. The troublesome time of Phil's narrowly-averted bankruptcy in a land deal known as the Alleghany Subdivision, against which both his father and Henry had advised. There had been another jam, when Phil, on the inside tip of a street-car franchise, had formed a company to buy up two blocks of Hinshaw Street, only to have the street-car finally run two blocks this side of Hinshaw.

There could be high words between Phil and his father.

And yet the family's outstanding events had had chiefly to do with celebration. To be sure, there had been family conclave and remonstrance when Rebekka had

held out for marrying Winslow Renchler, several years
her junior and a sickly fellow. Clara's marriage to Sam
Holly, a city salesman for the great wholesale firm of
Hamilton-Brown Shoe Company, St. Louis, had also met
a certain mild opposition. Sam Holly was an admirable
young man in the good-as-gold sense of the word. He
had no vices; and his virtues, although they made you
yawn, made you yawn righteously. The name Holly in
St. Louis was synonymous with a large dry-cleaning concern. But it was owned by Sam's uncle, who had never
done a turn for his nephew. Sam and Clara had met
at the St. Louis Exposition. There was something handsome about Sam, who had iron-gray hair at thirty; and
yet, as the Old Gentleman said after reviewing the rather
patient-faced young wholesale shoe-salesman when he
came wooing to Centralia, he had somehow the face of
a man with no future.

Then there was that conclave of a winter five years
previous, when Henry had refused the amazing and
unsought opportunity to run for Congress on a strong
Republican ticket. That had been a blow, even though
the Old Gentleman had valiantly come to see his elder
son's point of view. And besides, even the sting of a
secret disappointment was practically gone now, in the
curious and palmy circumstance of the world finding its
way to Henry's little old one-horse law office up over
Schlemmer's Hardware Store on High Street.

The Old Gentleman had shone of eye like this, upon
the occasion of the engagements of all Schuylers. Upon
the announcement of every one of the impending births
of the grandchildren. The day the honor of the request
of Henry's candidacy was announced. Always around
this very same table. Only, somehow, never before so
much so. This day his eyes went screwing around in
his head. Of mischief. Making the occasion, to his

children who knew him, seem more and more portentous. Of an ultimate solemnity.

Mathilda cut the segments of pie, alternating the lemon and the mince, until the children's table had been served and the Old Gentleman's match held to the suet pudding, so that the thin blue flicker of lighted cognac began to flit along it, and the children shouted and gouged unruly spoons into the fire-dance.

Candied apples, and persimmons for the game of pucker, and home-made taffy still in the greased pie-pans, were passed around to the youngsters, and after-dinner coffee in large cups to the elders. Curtains were drawn and a pail of coal tilted into the base-burner until it roared. A pair of old silver candlesticks on the two little curlicue shelves of the walnut sideboard were lighted by the Old Gentleman, who held each flame in the shell of his hand until the light grew round and steady. Then Henry, who was six-feet-one, and had arms that dangled to his knees, lowered the swinging-lamp that swung on chains over the table, and lighted the Welsbach. It had once been an oil-lamp before gas became everybody's commodity. For thirty years, an old buckeye had dangled from it by a string.

Trina cleared the table, aided and abetted by the Schuyler girls, who were cocksure about withdrawing the additional leaves, passing in and out with stacks of scraped dishes, sliding napkins into their rings, crumbing, folding and laying away the tablecloth in its place under the sideboard, and spreading a red rep one with black fringe in its place. Mathilda had her own way of placing the silver fruit bowl, upheld by three silver cherubs and laden with "Rebekka Wines," in the center of the cleared table. The cherub with the deepest dimple in his chin must always face the South Meadow window.

Then Trina drew the walnut folding-doors, shutting

out the children. Against the plate-glass of the door that led from the dining-room to the small side porch, it had begun to snow. Big flakes that whitened the air, but darkened the sky. The slanting roof to the wood-shed was already lightly covered.

Through the heavy, closed folding-doors, the children could be heard making a scramble for leggings and reefers, and fumbling in the hall closet for rubbers and hockey sticks.

"Winslow," said Rebekka, "hadn't you better bring Leslie in here?"

"Wait a minute," said the Old Gentleman, and brought his hand down on his son-in-law's, pinning it.

"Father!" said Emma and Clara simultaneously, in a sort of bleat, and Phil began to cough in the way he had.

The group about the table tightened into the propor-tions of the table with the three leaves removed. Mathilda with her timid face and her timid lips lifted to simulate a smile that twisted Rebekka's heart strings with its pitiableness. Twelve faces swimming up closer in concentration upon the old face above the spade of beard, at the head of the table, with the sly eyes of a naughty boy screwing in his head.

"Heinie!" faltered Mathilda, calling him faintly by a name she had not used since Rebekka had been born.

"Children," said the Old Gentleman, simulating elab-orate innocence of any realization whatsoever that what he had to say was about to splash over the occasion like a dash of ice-cold water from a bucket. "Children, it is a Thanksgiving Day for every Schuyler to remember."

"Puppa!"

"For goodness' sakes, Father," cried Emma, the bright tears in her eyes drying because her eyeballs were so hot and angry, "for goodness' sakes, Father, the idea of acting—so—horrid. What is it all about, Father?"

"Really, Father, Emma's right!"

"If you'll hold your horses," said the old man on a strangely forced chuckle, "you'll know."

"Well?"

"Well?"

"Puppa!"

"Oh, for goodness' sakes ———"

"Sh-h-h, Em."

"Well, Father?"

"Your mother, children, God bless her, is going to have a baby."

"Winslow," said Rebekka, in a voice that seemed to be running out of her like sands out of glass—"awfully silly—but—glass of water—please—I think—I'm going to faint."

"For Heaven's sakes, Rebekka, don't do that!"

"Of course, I'm not! Give me a drink!"

"Puppa," said Mathilda, and leaned forward to straighten the third cherub's dimple further toward the window that looked out on South Meadow. "It—it is too hot in here, open—open the window ———"

To cross that room, to open that window, was like walking through the buckshot of twenty-two glass eyes, that were looking at the Old Gentleman as if seeing him for the first time.

Chapter One

THERE was a game that David loved.*

He called it Indian in the Corn.

In autumn, in the field beyond South Pasture, when the husks were built into tepees around the cobs of massive, orange-colored teeth, it was his favorite pastime as he bustled up and down the rustling aisles, to slip into a tepee's heart. Lie there. Crouch there. Feel sinister there. And then, deep in his tepee, over the yellow mound of corn that was like a camp-fire, beat his palm against his open mouth and let out yips. Henry, when reading him *Leatherstocking Tales* up in his room beside the old base-burner, used to yodle thus, against slaps at his opened mouth.

Never by chance did a farm-hand encounter the particular tepee that concealed David. Sometimes, to the simply irrepressible excitement of the small crouching figure whose eyes shone like a cat's through apertures in the husks, they rustled perilously near. But never, even though they could hear him breathe, would hired man be guilty of finding out Davey.

That made it perennially exciting. Even if one suspected, at times, an elaborate and almost too consistent immunity to direction of sounds on the part of the field-

---

*. . . they christened this late-comer brother of mine David Whittier. David, a name which Mother had stored up all through the years like a squirrel its nut, bringing it forth each time a son was born to her only to concede it in favor of family-names like Philip and Henry. Whittier was father's choice, after his beloved Whittier County.

workers. Still, one could never be quite sure. After all, in a wilderness of tepees that reached from the sheep pasture to the creek, one Indian chieftain might easily throw puzzlement, even consternation, into the less wily white man.

Tecumseh, Chief of the Shawnees, who had been prominent in border warfare in that very region where the Old Gentleman's corn-field flowed its mellow way, was a favorite rôle.

The War of 1812 could bang in cap-pistol shots among those tepees.

There was a colored picture in one of his brother Henry's books; *The Lewis and Clarke Expedition,* of a solitary chieftain skulking in and out of ambush, and a score of white men from behind a barricade, lying belly low, aiming rifles at just the wrong clump of bush.

Sometimes Jacob, known throughout the valley as the best farm hand in the state (when sober), would throw a fit at these yips emanating from the tepees, and dance up and down on the balls of his feet and rub the seat of his overalls.

That invariably delighted David into a spell of the short, hiccoughy laughter of childhood, and out he came, still yipping, and leaping about in a tribal dance of no authenticity, while Jacob, at sight of the small figure in the yellow khaki-suit overalls, with fringed sides, and the band of porcupine-quills made into a head-crest for him by his sister Rebekka, took to his heels, still rubbing.

Long hazy autumns, the color of an apricot, and of a spanking kind of heat, these years that led up to Davey's being seven. Slow days, even as they grew shortest, that lay in a little yellow mud along the tongue and tasted of pollen.

All of his life David was to remember the taste of those days of his first seven years.

Once, in the full prime of his future, standing on the observation platform of a special train that was draped in bunting, and addressing a group of townspeople who had crowded up around the tracks of a station named Vandalia, the smell of that hot autumn haze, drifting in apricot-colored sunlight from outlying corn-fields, caught him so by the throat, that he terminated his remarks almost on a gulp and retired into the car to the rather bewildered cheers of the crowd.*

Those with him, accustomed to his grim, unrelenting sort of vitality, were surprised at this show of fatigue; and his young personal physician, named Denny Kiskadden, harboring memories of Wilson, Harding, and Putnam finally exacted from him a respite from the whirlwind demands upon his time and energy, and the next few towns were passed with the shades of the car drawn, and the milling crowds about the stations met with a few brief remarks from the Secretary of State.

But it was not fatigue. It was a memory assailing him along the taste nerves of his tongue. The taste of the smell of Indian summer drifting in over soil that was the soil of his being.

The old house on the edge of Centralia was packed with that odor into the very plush and horsehair of its furniture. Hard coal from the base-burners, and the smell of winter apples, and a curious smell that was sweet, like the breath of a cow, mingled with it the year through.

---

*. . . I think some of his most brilliant talks are the unrecorded ones made more or less extemporaneously from the platforms of trains, or I remember once, from the hangar of a roof just as he was stepping on board a plane and a few hundred had gathered to cheer him on his way. The out-of-doors seemed to clarify even that clear brain of his.

For years, during a sustained hiatus in the growth of Centralia, due to certain water-power monopolies that held up a foundry-development which was one day to boom it, the House on Sycamore Street continued virtually to mark the very spot where the bob-tailed town faded back into the placid geography of the meadow, field, and brook from whence it came.

From its square brace of front bay windows, you glimpsed the roofs of the sedentary houses for blocks along the shady length of Sycamore Street. But from its rear; from Henry's window, or Davey's attic one, or Trina's, there uninterrupted, plunged the sheep meadow into the corn-fields, and the corn-fields into the creek; and climbing out of the creek, as if the land were hurrying to be on its way, more sheep pasture, alfalfa, barns and stiles, and so on to the Tarkington Farm, whose buildings, with the exception of silo, were hidden by trees.

In Rebekka's and Henry's childhood, the creek that plunged through South Meadow had wound its way through the town so that every so often, as you drove, clump-clump, went hoofs over wooden bridges. The soft thunder of the loose flooring in these bridges reverberated down into Davey's sixth year, then the town appropriation went through for filling in the creek.

Every Schuyler had reason to remember that rear of flowing pasture and farm-land, and had plunged and shouted away many a somnolent midsummer afternoon in this tramp stream that had, in rare fashion, wandered off the flank of a two-hundred-mile river, to rattle its way over the stones. While David was growing up, practically all the streets that it had intersected were filled in, doing away with the pleasant commotion of the wooden bridges. But like a rash, immediately beyond the town, it broke out again.

The South Meadow ran on beyond the creek to the railroad. A double row of persimmon-trees marked the edge of the Old Gentleman's property. Sometimes, on the afternoons that were mealy to the tongue of the apricot haze, David lay flat on his back under them on the coarse, yellowing pasture-grasses. Sometimes a persimmon came down and spat him in the face.*

Mathilda Schuyler, who sewed a great deal in a large third-story sort of attic-room, with matting on the floor, and large blobs of unused blankets, comforters, pillows, and feather beds, tied into sheets and arranged around the room, could lean out of that window and yodel to Davey when she wanted him, as she had yodeled to the small Schuylers who had scampered before.

But somehow, after the interval of more than the score of years that separated her sixth from this seventh child of hers, Mathilda had taken on some of the nervousness of a young mother with her first-born. And an additional kind of self-consciousness, as if to Davey were owing some sort of an explanation for the circumstance of a curious isolation caused by years.

And yet, after a certain square little fashion, David was the sturdiest of her children, with his father's tight kind of sinew that knitted him down into stockiness, and short heavy legs that were to remain that way until at fourteen they shot up, lean and over-lanky. A brownish little fellow with the blackest of pupils to his eyes, surrounded by the clear gold of syrup. There were three black dots in the gold of the left eye. "Faith, Hope, and Charity," said Emma to him one day, and kissed the eye shut.

---

* A painting of my brother, done from an enlarged snapshot taken one Sunday afternoon in South Meadow by Miss Henriette Simpson, now hangs in Americana House, Philadelphia, the gift of the Midwest Junior Historical Society.

Maybe! But David wriggled. He was pretty constantly being kissed by the three big women, his sisters. And even by his nieces and nephews. It was a favorite pleasantry of Rebekka's eldest son, Steve, who was fifteen when David was four, to address him as Uncle David and then pick him up by the seat of his small trousers and deposit him on top of a mantelpiece.

Emma's daughter Claire was the niece nearest his age. When she was an adorable eleven, a blond Bavarian-looking doll with her mother's bright, plump Teutonic prettiness, and dimples everywhere, knees, wrists, elbows, cheeks and chin, her Uncle David was six. It was the period when he was all square. Square, brown, straight bangs. Square, ragged front teeth. The squareness beginning to lock his chin. The eyes of clear gold syrup with the three brown motes in the left, that looked at you squarely, under the square brow made squarer by bangs.

"He's a Schuyler every inch," would say his Mother, placing cold, oldish hands on his young hair.

"Except the inches that haven't come yet," was the Old Gentleman's chuckle. "Don't count your inches before they're hatched. And there's no telling . . . he may remain a little shorty. . . ."

"No telling," repeated Mathilda, with the thought racing across her eyes that could make them look about to tear. "No telling for us, that won't live to see it."

"We'll live!" said the Old Gentleman, expanding as if to give validity to a remark that had none whatsoever, except what grand manner could contribute. "Never mind, we'll live, to see everything."

"Dave, what do you want to be when you grow up?" was a constant reiteration of the Old Gentleman's, as if to jerk the future closer, so that he might cram some of this late son's maturity into his lifetime.

For the first ten years of his boyhood, with a consistency that never failed to raise the family-laugh, David stood by a selection that was neither precocious nor unique:

"I want to be a policeman."

Chapter Two

THE Renchler Farm stood three miles out of Centralia on a dip of state road that led in a quick, slick ribbon the three hundred and twenty miles across two states.

Two acres of it had been Winslow Renchler's inheritance of his father's small estate.

The house stood to the fore of those original seven acres. In the years since her marriage, and to Rebekka's just pride, those acres had been added to by fifty-eight. The last buy-in had been a coveted acre-and-a-half of old man Algahr's. For years, the Renchler holdings had curved around that plot like a greedy finger. When approached, Algahr, who at ninety had exactly the face of a white, two-weeks-old kitten, tooted around with his thin, high little voice and refused to consider. When he died, a sole relative in the form of a heretofore unknown nephew turned up from Shreveport, Louisiana, and sold it quickly to Rebekka for less than half of what she had been wont to annually offer old man Algahr. The catch was that the young scalawag demanded cash transaction. Even with the advantage to her of cash terms, Rebekka, whose acquisitions were all on mortgage basis, found the raising of two hundred and forty dollars no small matter.

Finally it was negotiated with Ephraim Howey, then candidate for Governor on a Republican ticket and whose stock-farm two miles along toward Middleton was by way of becoming a matter of state pride.

That gave to the Renchler farm a fine, unbroken acreage of flat land. You could stand on the verandah of the house exactly as if you stood on the deck of a steamer, with the surrounding country flowing out from you in ripples toward the horizon.

Gradually, with the years, as Winslow's initial and feeble hold upon the affairs of the farm relaxed and Rebekka took firmer and firmer clutch, High Ridge came to be known as the Model Farm. For no more technical reason, perhaps, than the geometric outlay of its uniformly painted buildings and silos and the well-kept stone hedges, most of them with their top row of boulders whitewashed.

Rebekka's eyes and mouth were grim with the purpose of living up to that appellation. It led her, in breathing space between meeting mortgages, to cast covetous eyes toward installations of machinery and modern devices which were ultimately to justify the term, "model farm."

The Renchler place, with its perfectly square white frame house, its recent addition of wide side verandah, its front of closed shutters and green front door that nobody ever used, stood on a rectangular knoll that was entirely surrounded by sixteen handsome maple trees. In time, with its flock of outlying buildings painted a uniform green and white, its regimental silos, its heated and electrically-lighted barns, its plow-horses of enormous heft, fatted cattle, flowing loam of fields, it was to become second only, as a matter of local pride, to the Howey place, which after all was more of a hobby than an enterprise.

There were those who thought that Rebekka, in her concentration upon the singleness of her purpose, in the sure-footed, deep-throated, high-busted, and wide-hipped kind of magnificence, was too terrific with enterprise.

There was something about a woman—even at the dawn of a day when a suffragette was something that could happen in your own family—stalking about her house at dawn to the clanking of her keys and the swing-

ing of her lantern; mingling in the open cattle-marts with
men who never so much as doffed a cap or shifted quid
when she swung up in flaring knee-boots, with her skirts
crowded up into them, and, at season, standing atop a
threshing-machine shouting orders, her skirts again, for
want of knickerbockers, lashed in the uninterrupted winds
against her great body-curves; well, there was something
about it—a woman and all that—there was something
about it went against many a grain.

It was common say about Rebekka that she could get
more than a third again as much work out of her men
as anyone in the county, because they were ashamed of an
endurance that might not match up with her mighty one.

There was something too ignominious about so minor a
discomfort as a cold, or a tooth- or an earache to be mentioned in the eupeptic presence of Rebekka.

It was not that she was unsympathetic. There was a
shelf in a tool-house on her place filled with rows of
arnicas, headache powders, antiseptics, and various first-
aids, which she personally administered, calm and un-
blanched at the flow of blood, sure and firm at the winding of gauze. Once a boy-around-the-place had tripped
against a scythe during haying time and cut his head
in such fashion that a flap of the flesh hung down
over his face in a great dripping mask, blinding and terrifying him so that he ran screaming through the fields to
the house. Winslow, seated on the side verandah, scooping a very special brand of tobacco from a can into a
rubberized pocket-pouch as the wretched boy ran up,
reeled sidewise from his rocking-chair into a swoon that
threatened, because of its duration, to be more a part
of the emergency than the wounded boy himself.

It was Rebekka who held the flap of flesh in place and
kept the blood stanched until a doctor arrived to sew it,

giving orders the while about the resuscitation of Winslow, who lay like a board.

After it was all over, Winslow, feeling foolish, would have preferred to sit on the verandah until his legs got rid of some of their tendency to wobble. But there was Rebekka, back at her interrupted chore of the setting-out of hundreds of tiny asparagus-plants in frames under glass, and so with bluster, to likewise prove his fitness, Winslow, who detested the smell of lime phosphate, went down-cellar for a bag of it to sprinkle along a border of new-turned earth.

As a matter of fact, Rebekka's legs were wobbling, too. She wanted to cry. She wanted Winslow to come and insist that she go indoors and lie down. She wanted "Doctor Dan" to offer her a quaff of spirits of ammonia, as he had the kitchen-maid and even old Jeff.

He did nothing of the sort.

It would have embarrassed Winslow to show the slightest concern for her. It was not until she was in bed that night that Rebekka let herself have a chill. A long, luxurious one that rattled her teeth and the bed springs.

Chapter Three

THE distance from the House on Sycamore Street to Rebekka's farm could be cut considerably if you went around by the creek and stepping-stoned it in the autumn or waded it in spring. That was David's invariable way, although in spring, pants were sure to get soaked, along their edges, even if he crammed them halfway up along his upper leg.

Rebekka always kept an extra pair of trousers hanging in a closet under the stairs. Knee ones, long since outgrown by Stevey.

They fitted Davey, who never failed to rebel against them, in a comic hit-and-miss fashion, garment and boy seeming to evade each other at all usual points of contact.

A little later, when Steve was at State Agricultural College, his room, up under the eaves, was practically David's, with a closet for extra bits of David's clothing and a nightshirt for those occasions when, for one reason or another, David slept at his sister's house.

Paula, Rebekka's first, was nineteen when Davey was six.

That meant, as in the House on Sycamore Street, here was a forest of grown-ups. Except Leslie. Who had a face that was delicately hung on, like a pear from its branch. A face that quivered with nervous little ecstasies at what it saw.

You could lie on your stomach alongside of Leslie, even though the forest of years was between, and play with lead soldiers and try to make an A-shaped formation with them as Henry had read out loud from Carlyle's *French Revolution*.

But never for long.

Suddenly Leslie would grab one of them out of formation and wrap him in a handkerchief and want to play a game called "Angel in Heaven." Pshaw! That bored David. To him a soldier was a soldier.

Chapter Four

So IT was that David had practically two homes. The
House on Sycamore Street that had to get used all over
again to a youngster clattering through its halls and
nicking into its base-boards and sliding down its banisters,
and his sister's farmhouse with the big square light rooms
of almost too many windows and the bright golden-oak
woodwork and the brass bed and balcony-front bird's-eye
maple dressers and yellow hardwood floors and folding-
doors on easy rollers that divided a dining-room done in
golden oak and leather upholstery of the McKinley
period, from a parlor of dragon-footed mahogany-and-
green-velours, two-tone green rug and Victrola with wax
cylindrical records.

Rebekka was not much on the details of interior decoration. Until Paula grew up and had sharp ideas of her
own that conflicted with her mother's, practically all of
the ordering for the Renchler household was done by
mail-order catalogue. Stacks of bulky pamphlets lay on
Rebekka's roll-top desk in the dining-room bay window
beside a pack of stamped envelopes; and scarcely a day
but what Rebekka, who wrote all letters on pad-paper in
lead-pencil, jotted some such as these:

Please send me as per No. r358762 Two hose nozzles,
brass finish.

Please send me as per No. 238996 One Pet Chicken-
House Oil-Burner. All attachments. No. 60401 One
box 100 sheets 8 x 10 water color paper.

Please send me as per No. 865438 three pair gentleman's black cotton and wool socks. Reinforced toes.

Size 10½. No. 456787 One garden-swing. Striped awning. Green and brown reversible seats.

Please send me as per No. 453973 one pair ladies blue felt bedroom slippers size 5½ C. No. 5925596 One Mother's Comfort Butter-Churn. Accessories. No. 49572530 One box, half-dozen Toothbrushes, Numbered one to six. Number 20e65 Six Sure-Fire rat traps.

Winslow, who squinted over the ridge of horizontal lead-pencils, held out at arm's-length, and who belonged to a Water Color Society, was moved to occasional remonstrance at these catalogic tendencies. Not because they offended, but rather because, as Paula began to remonstrate, and substituted willow pattern breakfast china for the régime of granite coffee-pot, and theatrical gauze curtains for Nottingham lace, something in him, the languid something that made him want to paint, stirred and agreed.

"Bek, that four-tiered wire flower-pot stand is a fright! Thought they stopped making those things forty years ago. You can do better than that right here in Centralia without having to write five hundred miles for it."

"Well, if that's the case, Winslow, it would help a great deal if you would go shopping. Goodness knows, I'm not so in love with the catalogues."

But, as usual, Winslow did nothing. It was easier just to sit and remonstrate, a little gently, a little ironically and with a charm that, as his days almost imperceptibly became more laconic, and Rebekka's more dynamic, seldom failed to fascinate and amuse her.

"Fraud, you!"

But for outsiders, every manifestation of Winslow's lethargies came under the benign heading of temperament. There was something magnificently creative in the way Bek had spun out of the mild figure of a mild man

with a mild flair for water-colors, the variegated figure
of the artist.

No sooner had the man she married developed indo-
lences of mood and spirit against which her family had
vainly tried to forewarn and forearm her during the
period of their wooing, than assertively and unrelent-
ingly, to the community at large, Bek became the wife
of genius.

It was Bek who took out his membership papers and
paid the initiation fees and annual dues to the Water
Color Society. Bek who arranged his one-man show in
the Auditorium of the Tallahassee High School. Bek
who gave catalogue orders for the newest fangle in water-
color equipment. Once Winslow had awakened to find
a black sateen smock across the foot of his bed. That,
as he put it, broke the back of his camel's-hair brush.
Winslow out-and-out refused to wear it. Bek, whose two
feet were said to be on the ground more patly than any
woman's in three counties, put it in a dresser drawer,
where Winslow, going for his shirts, would be sure to
have it ground into his retina every so often.

"These artists!" was frequently a phrase on her lips,
in the form of a sigh. A large, dramatic, sadistic sigh.

Steve's room, where Davey frequently slept while its
rightful occupant was off at Agricultural College, was an
odds-and-ends of a room with half-finished attic rafters
that Winslow had studded with nails for his collection of
pipes. A fine mahogany chest of drawers, a high low-
boy confiscated by Bek from the House on Sycamore
Street, stood between two windows, and a spool bed with
a pine-needle mattress that Stevey had loved and which
David loved after him, jammed the room considerably.
A shelf of books, with an assortment of farm journals,
Henty, Scott, Defoe, Dumas, Hugo, Garland, High
School text-books. A *Julius Cæsar,* with S. S. R. mono-

grammed in lead-pencil along its ragged edges. *Manual of Chemistry. How to Make Your Own Wireless. Literary Digest* for 1902-03, bound. Above it, sprawled across the slanting ceiling, a large yellow pennant, Tallahassee High, '09.

It had cost Rebekka some tears as secret as her midnight chill when Stevey left this boy's-nest of his for State Agricultural. There had been reasons, frantic, private reasons, why suddenly, to the mild mystification of the family, he had been packed off to the first school whose division of semesters fitted in with the hurried arrangement.

Even after four months of Stevey's absence, it was as if Bek could not become reconciled to that sense of the cold, empty room up above the bedroom she shared with Winslow. She loved having David there now, as many nights in the week as she could wheedle him out of her mother.

As a rule, he came over toward late afternoon, with the day's lay of the fifty wyandottes which Rebekka, from an old-time necessity, due to lack of space, but since outgrown, kept on her father's place.

David carried their lay in a chip basket with a cover that lifted from either end.

From one of her cow-sheds Rebekka could see him come up over the wheat-ridge, basket in hand, his stocky little figure mounted in a kind of important isolation against a semicircular wall of sky, his trousers forced halfway up against his upper leg and sure to be wet from the wade.

Rebekka's first question was almost invariable: "Did Mother say you could stay all night?"

Sometimes, in his small, hiccoughy voice: "Yes." Sometimes there were orders for a prompt return.

When he was six, there was already that kind of re-

liability about him.   One October afternoon, when the
apricot haze lay in its inimitable taste and smell along
the child's senses as he crossed the fields, Rebekka met
him down by the cow-shed, where she had been watching
him approach.

"Did Mother say you could stay the night, Davey?"

"There's a little sick ewe-lamb in a basket in the
kitchen, Bek. I've got to get back. You see—you see,
the liddle thing—the liddle thing he's got the shivers terrible. The liddle thing, Bek. Jake's giving him hot milk
out of a bottle. I got to get back and hold the bottle.
He's got the shivers terrible, the liddle thing."

He had the heaving mannerism, not uncommon with
children, of drawing in his breath between words as if he
were hauling up a supply for the next one.

Rebekka loved the childishness of it. She used to regard him, while he spoke, with her teeth gritted as if she
wanted to pinch. She had been that way with her own
children, full of the impulse to kiss and maul at them
when they were babies, for what was adorable to her.

On this gray afternoon, there was a letter stuck up in
the top of her boot so that it stung against her knee. It
was from the dean of an agricultural college. A sympathetic letter, written to a woman known by hearsay
through three counties, informing her that a certain
aspect of her son's deportment was making it impossible
for him to remain as a student. It was a simple, typewritten page, couched in kindness. And yet Rebekka was
seared with it. The letter burned against her knee like
a hot-pack. It was as if she had rubbed flame over her
body, and then in, as you would oil.

She strode down a cinder path that led from the cow-
sheds toward the barns and shouted some orders that
had to do with the backing in of a team of magnificent
dray-horses, with light-brown braided manes and shaggy

forelocks. With that letter searing against her body and her consciousness, she wanted to cry through a throat that was strong and tried from holding back tears. A great, powerful dam of a throat that had never failed her.

And through sickness of soul, she wanted David to sleep at the farm. Up in Stevey's room. It was foolish, of course. But somehow the consciousness of the small, warm nub of him up there on the balsam mattress in the attitude he was to lie all his life, with his knees up under his chin and the back of his hand curled against his neck, could lie to her like a plaster of solace.*

It was his funny sturdiness. The sturdiness of him marching there alongside her, the basket of eggs, about as much as he could manage, always intact. The sturdy kicking of his bare feet into the gravel, making it fly. He lugged with a will and there was a spangling of sweat on his upper lip.

"David, let's go in now and telephone to Mother that you'll stay the night. It's getting along toward dark, anyway."

---

* The morning of the afternoon upon which my brother was to press a button from Washington that officially put into motion the transfer that marked the formal beginnings of the Philippine Free State, I found him lying asleep in his study where he had left orders no one was to be admitted but me. He looked drawn from the rigors of his epochal Congressional address but otherwise strangely the boy. It may have been his position in sleep. One knee drawn up under his chin and the back of his hand curled against his neck—as I remembered him a hundred times in childhood. For a fleeting instant it seemed to me that all the terrific present fell away from us, and there he lay up in Stevey's room—asleep on the balsam mattress. . . .

"But Bek, the sick ewe, he's got the shivers something terrible. I've got to hold the bottle."

"Stay all night, honey. There's hominy for supper." There was not going to be at all until that moment. David loved it with sorghum wound into it.

"He's a poor little, sick little ewe, Bek," began David all over again in heaving intonations, with his voice full of draughts. "Jacob is driving some heifers to Middleton tonight and I've got to be home to feed him his milk in a bottle. He drinks out of a bottle, Bek. Oughtta see. With a rubber nipple like a baby. Ought to see, Bek, he's got the shivers terrible."

"Trina will tend him, Dave. There's nothing much to do for a sick ewe but keep it warm. Dave, Bek wants you to stay! There's some peppermint taffies Winslow's brought."

There was a pucker to David's mouth when it watered. A nibbling little motion that set the flanges of his nose dancing.

"C'n I ride Dodo?"

"He's been plowing heavy all day, Dave."

To ride Dodo, whose back was as broad as a moor, was to sit astride the universe.

"Well then, if I stay, can I flibber-jibber?"

To "flibber-jibber" was to ride the unanchored end of the big ironing-board that unhinged from the wall and then shut up against it.*

---

* My brother Davey used to ride my ironing-board beating his small heels and dancing up and down as he sat astride. Flibberty-jibbeting, he called it, for some mysterious reason of childhood. Friends who saw this home-made device in my kitchen, advised me to have it patented. Later, when reverses struck us and when I saw its counterpart become a general commodity, I had reason to regret I had not capitalized the

"It's Tuesday, Davey, and Tillie is ironing."

"You see, Bek, it's a little sick ewe . . ."

"Little scamp, you. All right, have your way. Go tell Tillie I said you could ride the board."

There was a telephone in the back hall under a slant of low ceiling formed by the stairway, a wall-affair with a handle that you ground around as you lifted the receiver.

The House on Sycamore Street was on a party line. A long ring and two shorts was the Schuyler signal. It was a standing family joke that Mathilda Schuyler unhooked her receiver for all rings. This she denied with great flurry.

But the fact remained that in the little pantry where the telephone hung beside the refrigerator, Mathilda spent long periods a-tiptoe, an eager-listening side of her face glued against the faint crackle of the receiver.

"Well, Mother," was Henry's habit of greeting, as he entered the house evenings, "what's the inside news on the party line today? Any startling revelations? What's the low-down? Is Mrs. Wiley making soft soap this week? Who killed cock robin?"

"Hennery!" She said "Hennery" in a little bleat. She said "Puppa" in a little bleat. She unhooked the receiver, to Rebekka's call, with a little bleat.

"Hello?"

"Mother? Bek."

"Yes, Bek."

"I'll keep Dave all night, Mother, and send him home with the team. Tell Father I'm sending over that load of dirt for filling in the old pig wallow."

---

little idea before others got in ahead of me and made my device worthless.

"But, Bek, Puppa wanted Dave to stop in at Igrotte's on his way back this afternoon for a pat of sweet butter."

"I'll send you a pat in the morning. And Mother, Davey's having a fit about that sick ewe in the kitchen. Wants you to see to it that the range is kept banked all night, and he says to be sure to see that Trina or Jake feeds him from the bottle."

"Puppa wanted him to stop at Igrotte's for a pat of ——"

"I'll see to everything, Mother."

"And, Bek! Hello! And Bek ——"

"Yes."

"Emma telephoned that Claire has a little temperature again and a sore throat, and insists upon going to the movies with her Uncle Hennery."

"White spots?"

"I don't know. Emma seemed right worried. Claire insists upon going out. Thought I'd ask you to call up right away."

"Surely. Father there?"

"He hasn't come in yet from Cottage Corner. He drove out there with Mark to see some steers."

"Tell him I bought those two Holsteins we saw out at Seven Mile last week, at my price."

"Yes, Bek."

"M-m-m-m," said Bek, hung up, and began to grind at the telephone again.

Emma answered, unhooking the receiver of a desk instrument and seating herself at a small kidney-shaped table in a reception hall of highly-colored rugs, small oil-studies in large gilt Florentine frames and shadow-boxes of sheep huddling before a storm; a study of an old man with very many wrinkles and sunken cheeks, and one of the fat monks with the look of pouring mugs of ale down inside their cassocks. A winding stairway rose out of this reception-hall, with a stained window at its first landing and a rubber-plant in a brown-pottery jardinière with warts.

Emma's home had been built at the height of the McKinley indoor period. Her reception-hall boasted an upright pianola, a piano-bench (the stool was over in front of one of the windows, with a rubber-plant on a china plate standing on it). There were lace curtains, sill-high, and, leading into the dining-room, portières of soft chenille ropes that clung to your shoulders as you walked through. On the center mission-table, with its mission-lamp, were such addenda as Owen Meredith in padded leather and, by rather amusing propinquity, obvious to no one in that household, a cloth copy of *The Egotist* that had found its way there by one of those circuitous and anonymous routes peculiar to books. There were visiting-cards on a bronze tray shaped like the Indian head on a penny. Claire's library ticket. A round globe of goldfish threading through a castle. A *Saturday Evening Post*. Morton Milliken's pipe in a white-china dish. A book of family snapshots. A cut-glass pickle-dish filled with salted peanuts.

Emma wore a dressing-sacque made of strips of narrow blue-satin ribbon and Valenciennes lace, and a cream-sateen petticoat with a machine-scalloped edge.

"Oh Bek," she cried to her sister, who stood at the other end of the telephone connection in her knee-high boots and homespun skirt crowded into them. "I'm so glad you called!"

"What's this I hear about Claire?"

"She's got fever again and her throat's sore. She's been so stubborn about my telephoning you. Wouldn't let me."

"White spots?"

"A little one, but she denies it. She's got her heart

set on going to the picture-show with her Uncle Henry and Henriette tonight."

"Where is she?"

"Upstairs, lying down."

"Tell her I want to talk to her."

"Don't let on Bek, that I have said anything, or she will immediately suspect that her father or I appealed to you to.   She's right stubborn."

"Call her."

Claire Milliken, who had a thick, creamy *mädchen* beauty that might have flowed right off her mother's, was lying under a pink blanket on one end of her curlicue brass bed up in a square room of stripe-and-bud wallpaper, bird's-eye maple dresser with dotted-swiss cover over pink sateen, a window-seat of dotted swiss cushions over pink sateen and a ukelele snugged in.

"Oh, Claire—telephone!"

With a lovely sort of languor that was a piece of her mother's, Claire flung off of the bed, and with the pink blanket huddled shawl-wise over her plump and fair shoulders, pattered out into the hall in pink-felt slippers edged in white eiderdown, and leaned over the balustrade.

"Who is it, Dee Dee?"

For some reason, with its beginnings imbedded in the lispings of childhood, Claire was always to address her mother as "Dee Dee."

"It's Aunt Bek, Claire."

Instantly there raced over Claire a tiny rigidity, as her nails whitened at the hold of the balustrade.   There was a letter burning against her body, too, that bore the same postmark as Bek's.   Only hers lay warmly to the soft white flesh over her heartbeat; it rang there as if it were a little electric bell.   It was from Steve, announcing a little too nonchalantly, and binding her to secrecy, the exciting tiding that he was coming home.

Her secret.

"Then you must have called her up, Dee Dee. Oh, I know!"

"Claire, that is positively not so. I was paraffining those Mason jars of damsons when the telephone rang."

"Well, it's *mighty* funny. Aunt Bek isn't going to run my life the way she runs yours and everybody else's in this family—and out of it."

"I can't help how funny it is, and I hope you won't ever have anyone less efficient to run people's lives than your Aunt Bek."

"Well!" said Claire with ambiguity. "Well! I'm not so sure about that by a long shot." And she dashed down the stairs.

There was something about Claire in her teens, her prettiness brightened now with fever, of a petulant child.

"It's mighty funny, Dee Dee! That's all I have to say," taking up the receiver from her mother's hand and seating herself before the kidney-shaped table. "Hello!"

Her aunt was not one to parry words.

"I suppose you know what a sore throat with temperature means if you expose yourself unnecessarily?"

"There's nothing the matter with me, dear! Dee Dee or Father put you up to this. Or Gramaw or Gramp. I won't be treated like a simp."

"Like a what?"

"—elton."

"It is entirely up to you how you are to be treated."

"I tell you I am feeling all right, Aunt Bek."

"Then why are you lying around the house with temperature when it is your afternoon to sew at the Betsy Ross Club?"

"Just because my throat is a little eeny sore and I am taking care of it."

"Yes, that is precisely the way you took care of it when you insisted upon going to the State Agricultural Prom last month and came down abed afterward for two weeks."

"But, Aunt Bek . . ."

"Your mother had your Grandfather Milliken's broken leg to contend with this summer and your father's sciatica. If you feel that you have the moral right to pile more worries upon her, that is a matter for your own judgment. Tell your mother I want to talk to her."

"But, Aunt Bek . . ."

"There's nothing more to be said about it, Claire. If consideration for yourself or your mother does not prompt you, I cannot hope to."

"But, Aunt Bek, I tell you I . . ."

"I'd rather not hear it all over again, Claire. Your mother, please!"

"Oh, very well—of course, if you don't want to listen! Here, Dee Dee, Aunt Bek wants you back again."

"Hello, Bek."

"Yes. Don't answer to what I am saying. But you needn't worry. She's not going. And while it's on my mind, Emma, I wish you would tell Morton to tell his father that I have reason to know that Second Street property is for sale after all."

"Bek, Father Milliken is buying awfully heavy on that Second Street deal. I was telling Morton last night I just don't want him bothering Father again to go his collateral."

"Least said over the telephone about that the better, but if he insists upon being interested, Grandfather Milliken had better let me do the talking, because I handled that same group pretty well the time Phil went in on that Springfield development."

"Yes, Bek. But I'm quite sure Morton wouldn't proceed without conferring with you anyhow."

"Tell Aunt Bek I want to talk to her when you're finished, Dee Dee."

"Sh-h! I can't hear a word you're saying, Bek, with Claire at my elbow. Here, she wants to talk to you again."

"Hello, I'm not going, so there, if it makes you feel any better."

"It does, Claire. Thank you! Good night."

" 'Night."

"Heigh-ho! So much for that!" said Bek's manner as she hung up. Then there was the matter of old Jessup, whose wife Mattie was demanding that his pay be turned over directly to her. Winslow was really the one who should take that up with old Jessup. But no, better do it herself. And those clapboards at the rear of the lower barn needed whitewashing. Winslow could really do that; but no, better to have Jessup do it after the bran was mixed.

There was Davey playing at her heels again, hopping along on one leg after her in a fashion that spun the gravel against her boots.

"Don't, Davey."

But just the same, how curiously pleasant the shot of the pebbles that he kicked up against her boots! He was so snug, David was. So solidly there! A little snug-bug-in-a-little-snug-rug of a brother. And the letter was searing into Rebekka, as she strode down the cinder path toward the lower stables.

Horrible, horrible, horrible, on David's account if no other, that a nephew should stand disgraced in college for drinking. Not but what there were other considerations, more immediate, graver far, than David.

Only you were not always logical about David, as you had been in practically every other aspect of life, even your own children. Except perhaps—your marriage. More than for any other member of the family, Mother, Father, even Winslow, it was most intolerable of all that Stevey should have dared—for Davey's sake—to bring this upon them!

David coming along as he had, in his ridiculous little anticlimax fashion, was an emotion. His diminutive kind of isolation made him somehow—well, special. Born so almost into a forest of grown-up brothers and sisters; knee-high to his universe.

These early years of his were spent among the knees. The knees of his parents, his brothers and sisters, and of even his nieces and nephews. Grotesque world of knees.

It was hard to treat David as anything except an emotion, even if you were Rebekka. His smallness, his squareness, his unnamable kind of solidity. Squat little toadstool in the curiously overshadowing forest of the grown-ups.

Everything, somehow, some way, must be kept right for David. Stevey represented part of that responsibility of keeping the forest of the grown-ups fine for David to grow into.

All the family must have that sense of responsibility to David. To Bek, striding there, it made Stevey's defection seem more than ever a heartburning shame before square, little, stodgy David.

If only he wouldn't stay stocky. The Schuylers were all tall, except Mathilda and Phil. Henry, even with his stoop, stood six-feet-two. Bek herself only slightly under. Funny little old runt of David, kicking the gravel against her boots.

"David, stop that, I said!"

"Bek, will Winslow make me a pea-shooter?"

"Yes."

Winslow must be stirred to set about wrapping those mulberry bushes along the walk in straw against another frost. No, better get Jessup to do it, Winslow's finger-tips split so easily. Besides, must tell Winslow tonight after supper that Stevey would be home tomorrow. Poor Winslow, having to know at last. Terrible! Terrible! Terrible!

"Bek, is there two kinds of crows' nests?"

"No, only one."

"There is so."

"All right." (If Father wants to trade me in those two red calves for the spotted heifer, I take them over. How to tell Winslow!)

"There is, Bek."

"All right." (One must stop the habit of listening to children's queries with only half an ear. Her own children, growing up, had resented it. And now here was David with the most insatiable of curiosities, getting only half an ear.)

"You say there is more than one kind, Davey? Not that I know of."

"There is so. One for crows and one for a ship."

"Of course! How stupid of me! You're right. Bek just wasn't thinking."

"There's a picture of one on a ship in a book up in Henry's room, called 'Our—our—Pac-if-ic Poss-ess-ions.' What's 'Our Pac-if-ic Poss-ess-ions,' Bek?"

(Oh Stevey, Stevey—how could you? Where to turn? How? How to tell Winslow?)

"What are they, Bek?"

"What, Dave?"

"Our Pacif-ic Poss-ess-ions."

"Why—er—islands in the Pacific, Dave. The Philippines."

"There's a picture of a crow's nest in that book. It's got a sailor-boy in it with a hunk of ice hanging on his beard. It's as cold as the devil in a crow's nest on a ship."

"Don't say 'devil'."

"Henry and Father do. How can it be cold on ship in the Pacific, Bek?"

"You must ask Henry that, Davey."

"Bek, I can spell 'Appomattox'."

"Yes."

"Ap-po-mat-tox. That's where Lee surrendered to Grant, April 9th, 1865."

"Good."

"Henry read it to me out of a book full of pictures of flags. Ever see a flag with a skull and cross-bones?"

"Um."

"Why can't you say April 1th like you say April 9th?"

"Because."

"That's no reason. It's a word."

"Well you just can't."

"Tramp. Tramp. Tramp-tramp-tramp. I'm a Confederate Union soldier."

"You can't be both."

"Why? Oh, I know!"

(Poor Winslow, having to be told tonight.)

"Tramp. Tramp. Seventeen hundred and seventy-five, scarcely a man is now alive who remembers that famous day and year. Do you remember that famous day and year, Bek?"

"No." (Lime phosphate for the verbena borders.)

"George Washington would remember."

"Yes, George Washington would."

"Tramp. Tramp. Tramp-tramp-tramp. There's a

picture in Henry's office of Washington crossing the Delaware. Where's the Delaware, Bek?"

"In Delaware, Davey."

"It's in Pennsylvania, too. How can the Delaware be out of Delaware?"

(M-m-m. What to do about Stevey! All the horror of those secret months before he had been packed off to college. The need for more and more secrecy. This thing that had Stevey in its clutch. A Schuyler. Inconceivable. There was something known as Keely Cure. Keely Cure—a Schuyler. Oh God——Oh God—let me wake up and find I'm dreaming. . . .)

"Tramp. Tramp."

(What to do? Poor Winslow, he was sure to turn that green pallor and quiver at the flanges of his nose with the kind of nervous anger that made the backs of his hands sweat and invariably brought on one of his colds. Shame, Stevey! Oh my boy! And David growing up.)

"There's Winslow. What's he painting?"

"Don't holler, Davey, while Winslow is painting that lovely corner of the orchard where all that sumach grows."

"If I was a painter, know what I'd paint?"

(If only Winslow needn't be told! How peaceful he seemed. . . .)

"Know what?"

"Sh-h, Davey, Winslow wants it quiet when he's working."

Winslow was seated in a grassy cove behind a silo on a folding-chair that occupied two levels at a time, and from that tilt kept squinting at a distance of apple trees and fold of meadow-land that were still faintly lit with the most backward spring of many a year. Along a bit of crest ran sumach, red as fire.

He had a pale goatee which shot up with the directness of a pointing finger when he threw back his head to squint.

Rebekka had her own private opinion about Winslow's head, particularly seen thus in perspective against sky-line while he painted. White, high brow, with a blue vein that quivered. Baby-fine hair, a shade darker than beard, lying back from it in a thin, curling roll. Long, delicate eyelids. Almost a womanish neck, the same white as his chest.

To Rebekka, particularly the countless times she had seen Winslow thus at his painting, there was something that suggested the Christ head in the northeast window of the Second Avenue Rock Church where the Old Gentleman owned a pew. Strange that no one had ever remarked it.

There was another blue little vein in the side of Winslow's neck that jumped when he was tired or nerv-ous. His exquisite capacity for pain symbolized to her right there in that bit of neck above the old corduroy jacket. Rebekka was never to realize to what extent her vitality was dedicated to keeping that vein at the side of Winslow's neck from jumping.*

---

*I know that there were those who thought I spoiled Winslow. Brother Phil used to twit me about it good hu-moredly. If I did, it was to try and repay the measure of happiness he brought me. Diametrically opposed as we were in temperament, it was that very antithesis that apparently brought us together. In all the years of our lives together, up to the very hour of his death, I can truthfully say that it was his fineness, his more delicate discernments, his dear un-obtrusive co-operation that brought me the more conspicuous success of the two. As the brother-in-law of the President of the United States, and the husband of a woman whose activi-ties were destined to be more or less conspicuous, Winslow never forfeited one of his splendid qualities to those rather

"Don't disturb Winslow, Davey."

Winslow had already been disturbed. But affably. He came toward them smiling, one long, white hand plunged into corduroy, leather-bound pocket, and his pipe hooked loosely into the corner of his mouth.

How handsome he was and how slim and straight, with that curve at his waist which was almost military. It made Bek, who had not kept her figure, fear that she looked her several years his senior. Except that her skin had the pat, dewy clarity of butter. Winslow's had gutters, and there were long brackets about his mouth. A nervous, dredged face. A face that might have had the same pear-shaped clarity of his son Leslie's, until he had looked into that son's eyes and, beholding their vacancy, his own had become turgid with pain for his offspring.

It was horrible to have to tell Winslow, who sometimes cried to himself over Leslie, at night, as he lay on the pillow beside her, about the letter from Stevey flaming against her knee.

"Hi, there!" said Winslow, and caught David up by the armpits and swung him.

"Quit!" cried David, to whom the gesture seemed infantile, and began dancing on his toes and spitting on his square palms. "C'm on, spar!"

"Shrimp," said Winslow, and placed his long, white

---

spectacular and at the same time enormously difficult conditions. Neither did he ever avail himself of any largesse of favor which might have come to him because of my brother. He sought no favors. He asked precedence over no man. An artist of parts was my husband, whose work, in my opinion, never won the wide approval its gossamer beauty deserved. It was as a revered father, a beloved and respected husband, that he was to come into his own. The day of his death, the greater part of the light of the world went out for me.

hand against David's face in a soft sort of mash that pinned him back against the silo, "where did you come from?"

"Your brother-in-law is going to sleep here, Winslow."

The family never tired of its sense of the humor of David's disparity among them.

"Well, brother-in-law," said Winslow, and tossed him high a second time, "we'll have the Cherokee snake dance on the Victrola after supper."

"Yoo-hoo," yodeled David, and beat his palm against his wide, open mouth.

Winslow, who before marriage had lived in New Mexico over a six-month recuperation from a lung condition, knew some Cherokee lore and had a great silver tribal belt that wrapped twice around David.

"Indian Territory is bounded on the north by South Dakota, and Henry says if you draw a straight line ———"

"Henry says! Henry says! Henry says the moon is green cheese!"

"Now, Winslow, don't go teasing that child."

How peaceful, in the westering light that was lovely across closely-nibbled pasture, to saunter with these two. Externally as peaceful as if a letter were not flaming. . . .

"Henry says ———"

"Henry says!"

"Winslow!"

"Henry says when I'm big there will be a Panama Canal and then he is going to take me to see it. Panama is an isthmus ———"

"Henry says!"

"Panama is an isthmus, Henry says, connecting North and South America. Know what an isthmus is?"

"Good Lord, no. Neither would you if you didn't have a human encyclopedia for a brother."

"Winslow!"

"An isthmus is—is ——"

"Doesn't know what an isthmus is. Henry for a brother, and doesn't know what an isthmus is."

"I do so. I've just forgot. I do so."

"Winslow, stop teasing that boy."

"I did know what an isthmus was."

The sweet, the westering light. It was like a bath to Rebekka, flowing along her flesh. Her pastures. Her lands. Her husband in his lithe, easy way that suggested a remoteness from the soil she wrestled with, ambling along at her side. And her brother David, for whom the family must be kept perfect with integrity. And against the love in her for the peace of the land she was wresting her success from, there burned that consciousness of Stevey, about to be suspended from college for what to her was an unnamable vice. A vice that she had secretly wrestled with in this boy-child of hers for five years; ever since the November dusk she had first stumbled over him below Casey's Cider Mill, lying huddled on his way home from High School, as if an old sack had been lying there.

And now, after she had fought it with him to the finish of packing him off to college, apparently cured, here it was again, the old terror, lifting its head.

The struggle to keep the thing that had happened, and then happened again and again, secret. Just her fight and Steve's. And now that it seemed won—poor Stevey! And there was Jessup. Oh—poor Jessup! Jessup and Stevey were so terribly akin.

"Winslow, you and Davey go on up to the house. I'll be along in a minute and dish up supper. I want to stop and talk to Jessup. Winslow—would you speak to him for me? Never mind." (If only Winslow would! It would be easier somehow for a man to reach a man.)

"What about Jessup, Bek?"

"Never mind. Go 'long. I'll be up to the house in a minute."

Jessup was forking fertilizer from a horseless cart that was backed up against a barn door. A few brown wyandottes stalked about without scarcely the ado of fluttering before her, as Rebekka strode across the clean wood flooring.

"Jessup," said Rebekka, and hit herself on the thigh as she drew up before him, "there won't be any need coming up to the house for pay tonight. I'll be sending it to your wife by Hallie when she comes down for milk."

The watery old face of Jessup swam toward her, milky-eyed, cranberry-nosed. The head of Jessup, long and hairy, was like an old cocoanut, nicknamed "Emmy Sue," that had dangled from the ceiling of the barn of the House on Sycamore Street ever since Bek could remember.

Jessup's was just such an old hairy ellipse of a head, with eyes with red rims that were constantly about to brim over.

She had taken him off her father's hands, for whom he had worked thirty-five years, because the Old Gentleman, as Jessup took more and more to bad moonshine whiskey that filtered over so cheaply from Kentucky, used to fly into his terrific apoplectic tempers and berate and shout at him and scream and curse him in round, sound terms that mortified Mathilda terribly.

And now here was Jessup at sixty-eight, who had never fallen this low, beginning to lay hands on his wife, until pretty Hallie, their orphaned granddaughter who made her home with them in a little old wooden house behind Casey's Mill, had to run out dead of night, calling help for her grandmother, whom Jessup was flaying with an old broom.

"Now, Miss Bekkie," said Jessup, shifting quid, "you

wouldn't be humiliating an old fellow like me in that fashion, now, Miss Bek?"

"Oh, Jessup, Jessup," cried Rebekka, looking into the watering old eyes that were so kindly when sober, "don't try to bamboozle me."

"But, Miss Bekkie—an old man ——"

"It's what you deserve. Shame! And Hallie growing up in your house. Shame! Have you no decency left? No pride, Jessup?"

"I have, Miss Bekkie. Pride for working for the Schuyler family all these years. There's things, Miss Bekkie," said Jessup in a sudden, cautious whisper, and advanced a step, after the manner of one about to reveal something secret and sinister, "there's things can take hold of a man without his knowing it. Devils. Drink-devils that get hold of him and make him what he ain't. Mattie hadn't ought to be told on her old husband. Twenty years of poultices I've laid to her old back, Miss Bekkie. It's a bit of a swig makes a devil of me."

"That's the common defense of the common drunkard, Jessup," said Bek; and as the words came, the memory cut her like a knife that Jessup's words were practically the words Stevey had used to her one dreadful evening when she had found him in bed stupefied. "Something gets a fellow, Mother, like a burning devil over which he has no control." (Oh, Jessup—poor, poor Jessup!)

"It's in every man's power, Jessup, to be stronger than those devils."

"Now, that's because you're so strong, Miss Bekkie, that you say that. The weak has more pity for the weak than the strong for the weak. They know."

How often Stevey had defended Jessup!

"The weak ones are the most sympathizingest, Miss Bekkie."

Was that true? Rebekka, who could scarcely bear to

look into the watering old eyes of Jessup cringing there
before her, knew the capacity of her strength better than
she knew the gauge of her pity.

"Don't take down my pride, Miss Bekkie. That's all
I've got left to keep my old woman from kicking me into
the corner like the dirty old sack I am. Don't deal out my
pay to my wimmin, Miss Bekkie, that's the low-downest
a man can fall."

Jessup, who could be so pitiable in his sobriety and a
lashing kind of demon in his cups. It made it so difficult.
Who was she, with that letter flaming against her flesh,
to judge that watery-eyed old face, horny with its years
of service to her family? Besides, this was a man's job,
by rights. Winslow should be chastising Jessup! Sometimes, a kind of slow anger smote Rebekka at the brand
of her own efficiency, which made it appear there was
nothing she need be spared.

"Miss Bekkie, I'm going to turn over a new leaf.
Watch me!" Stevey had used just those words the night
they had so secretly decided on college. "Mother, watch
me. You won't be sorry we've fought this thing out secretly. I'm going to turn over a new leaf."

"I got a little crazy last week. Fust time this winter.
Don't take down my pride, Miss Bekkie."

"I'm sorry, Jessup. Your wife and your grandchild
cannot continue to live in terror every Saturday night
for fear you are not going to get back from Seven Mile
with your pay."

"Miss Bekkie, I'm going to turn over a new ———"

"Don't—don't—keep saying that!"

"Why, Miss Bekkie?"

"Because. Because. Because. Too many years of
that speech, Jessup!"

"Miss Bekkie—please—I'm an old man. . . ."

If only he wouldn't bleat and roll his eyes like something wounded. Great Scott, a drunk and a wife-beater was nothing to snivvle over.

"Sorry, Jessup."

"Miss Bekkie!"

Why didn't he rise up? Or threaten to quit? Or kick over the traces? Gnarled old servitor, with thirty-odd years of Schuyler soil and toil ground into his pores. The terrible meek. That was what hurt most.

"Sorry, Jessup," said Bek and went out with her firm tread full of emphasis along the wooden floor, and the heart inside of her sick.

Winslow and David were already at table, building wigwams out of toothpicks and waiting for Bek to come in and dish up. When Paula, who taught kindergarten in Cleveland, was home, the little pressed-glass holder for toothpicks was not in evidence, nor the four-caster cruet nor the mother-of-pearl napkin ring with "Niagara Falls" and "Daddy" written across it.

To Bek these things mattered little.* Even as her house became more modernized and furnace supplanted base-burner, and the coal-range, that had made fiery Hades of the kitchen summer after summer, had been replaced with a nickel-trimmed gas one, and the old

* . . . I was never able to take those differences of taste seriously which accept the antimacassar in one generation and ridicule it in the next. As I used to say to my daughter Paula, who before she became State Superintendent of Schools had a small modernistic gift-shop of her own in Cleveland, a good thought for anyone to hold, who was over-impressed by the rightness of his own time as over and above all other times, was Omar Khayyam's salty old observation that tomorrow we may be with yesterday's seven thousand years. I often wonder to what appalling extent my clear-eyed Paula must think me the old fogey.

walnut dining-room set with golden oak, selected by catalogue, Bek's table, except where Paula intervened, remained broadly a farmhouse board. Rich flour gravies to be sopped into with hot biscuit. Fried foods soaked through with flavor. Every homemade conserve and preserve, pickled, brandied, and sweet. Home-killed meats and fowl. Home-corned beef; salt pork; smoked hams.

Even then, Bek had been about considerably. Stumping the state for Ephraim Howey's second-term candidacy; and once a year Bek went as far as East St. Louis to the stockyards and put up across Eads Bridge, in St. Louis proper, at the Planters Hotel instead of at Clara's, who lived in the "West End" of the city and a good hour's trip from the scenes of Bek's activities. Bek had also attended a convention at Louisville as delegate from her state of the Home Growers Association, stopping at the Seelbach Hotel for a week. Every few years she and her father spent a few days in Chicago at the stockyards. The Schuylers, seven strong, had attended the Chicago World's Fair, and Bek and Winslow had honeymooned via Pittsburgh, Buffalo, Niagara Falls and Washington, to New York. And once, Bek and Winslow and Leslie had journeyed to Rochester, Minnesota, to consult a pair of famous physicians there on the matter of brain surgery. Then, of course, too casual for mention, were the trips to "The City"—twenty-five miles distant.

Bek had been about, but she still set her table in red-checked cloths, punctuated with large pressed-glass dishes of preserved and pickled stuffs, and two great white ironstone pitchers of milk with the foam still on. She did the work of an eleven-room house unaided, except for Jessup's wife Mattie, who came down on Tuesdays to help with the rough-dry ironing. The "hands," now that the children were grown, no longer sat at table, but in quarters of their own, rigged up over the summer kitchen, but Bek still did the cooking for them, and at harvest-time, fed as many as twenty from the great copper pots that hung in rows, unused from season to season.

Winslow, whose habit it was to sit down before the meal was served and, proclaiming his hunger, eat in frugal fashion once the food was before him, had pushed back his plate in the game with David, so that knife, fork, and tumbler cluttered up the center of the table.

"Winslow," cried Rebekka, tying on her apron over the heavy cloth skirts, boots and all, "that's no way to clutter up the supper table," and began shoving back objects into place and jerking David into a semi-high chair that she had used for her children, and then hanging his napkin about his neck by a homemade contrivance fashioned out of a discarded pair of suspenders.

"Food! Food!" intoned Winslow, and beat with his fork, which set Davey beating after him.

"Food! Food!"

"Babies!" said Bek, flouncing out into the kitchen, smiling because she loved their being babyish.

Her children and nieces and nephews and in-laws said of her that she could stand in the center of her vast kitchen and reach with her long, sure arms for anything she wanted. That accounted for her amazing kitchen efficiency. This was scarcely true, of course, but fact was, Bek could prepare and dish up and serve a meal in the kind of jiffy that appalled, rather than merely amazed. No one ever saw her "in dough," yet her pantry could steam with pies on a half-hour's notice. Her doughnuts were a matter of community pride and sold at bazaar as "Bek Schuyler Beauties."

Bek could cook!   With the kind of tastiness that

poured itself into the palate and quickened the gastric juices.*

In later life, David was to recall these sleight-of-hand meals of his sister's preparation with astonishment. Her fowls that seemed to run the succulent kind of juices that only Bek could coax out. Bek's bread! She baked twice a week, mixing after the family was abed, and covering the pans of swelling dough with flour-sacks which she cut open and hemmed herself. And hominy! Either you were a hominy person or you weren't. David was. The isolated, taste-packed pearls. Strange, David was to have cause to comment later in life, how few people knew how to cook hominy. Usually, they slopped it together in a mush. Bek's pearls stood each and every one alone. White, perfect globules, inviting the teeth to grind out their corniness. And then, when Bek poured sorghum over it in a great, slow, amber rope from a glass pitcher with a mouth that opened back like a new sparrow's, your own mouth began to water in two expectant grooves.†

There was barley soup tonight, full of the taste of bay leaves and cylinders of ox-tail that you fished out with

---

* David never lost his childish fancy for my cookery. I recall once, the second year of his first term as Governor, his visiting the International Food Show, in the days before the general use of dehydrated vegetables. There he stood before my booth where I was demonstrating, in the name of this great food-revolution in which it was my privilege to act as pioneer, and with cameras clicking upon him, shamelessly devoured three portions of my dehydrated hominy prepared in a fireless cooking-range and served piping-hot under molasses cubes.

† My brother Henry, never too reverent, used solemnly to recite the rosary over my hominy. I can hear him now . . . impaling with his fork, to the rhythm of "each bead a pearl, each pearl a prayer." Dear Henry—simple spirit. Great spirit.

your fork and then flecked with mustard. Sliced cucumbers called "hasty pickles," that Bek peeled first and sliced longwise and then set to boil in vinegar, cloves, and sugar. Pickled beets, grape jelly, pear-and-quince preserves, piccalilli and chow-chow, in the pressed-glass dishes. Hashed brown potatoes with a crust on. Oxtail stew with circles of green pepper swimming in a rich brown gravy that the very biscuits seemed to sop up hungrily as you dipped. Hominy and sorghum. Milk with a half inch of cream on top. And then Bek's fruit pie with the fork-prints on the cover and the lurid juices making it soggy. Cherry pie tonight, out of Bek's closet of hundreds of Mason jars of preserved fruits. How the ruby flavors spurted as the fork dug in. Usually, though, David took up his slice and bit, so that there were two gashes of smear beyond his mouth, into the middle of his cheeks.

There was never anyone, for all her bigness, more lithe than Bek. Presto, change-o, with scarcely more than a rattle of pans, a dart or two through the kitchen door, and there steamed the meal on the table! Winslow's dish of soda-crackers, that he liked to break up into his soup, and Leslie's special soup-plate that had a legend from "Peter Pan" on the rim.

At eighteen, Leslie, who was tall to gangling, pale, and with the identical heart-shaped face of pallor and a certain beauty that had been his, six, eight, ten years before, was not, to members of his family, the mental delinquent that all of Bek's journeys with him to specialists had so irrefutably determined.

Leslie was Peter Pan detained by the lure of perpetual youth. There was the fine hand of Bek for you! Subtly, surely, if gradually, out into the community at large, Leslie became one visited with the strange wisdom of knowing how to stay a child. There was something sly and subtle in the way Bek dressed this borderland boy of hers. Great, slender gawk of a youth with the frail look of a girl, startled by the sound of the fall of a leaf in a forest. There was always an adventurous-looking feather in the soft green-felt hat that he wore, and his jacket was of bottle-green, too, cut Eton, with an open collar and short trousers of the kind of brown stuffs that blend with tree-boles and reveal bare nut-brown knees. Peter Pan.

Bek always led Leslie to table herself, with her arm about his waist, as if they had just strolled in from a somewhere that was as lovely as it was mysterious. Without Bek at his side, food might sometimes have tumbled off his fork and down the white-linen front of Leslie's blouse. That never happened.

It is doubtful if in those first years of his life Leslie was a whit more peculiar to David than any other member of the world of grown-ups into which he had been born. Except that it was so much easier to play pretend with Leslie. For instance, when you told Leslie that the carpet sofa in the dining-room of the House on Sycamore Street was a sea-serpent, Leslie didn't fall creakily to all-fours and begin making pretentious, insincere noises like his brother Phil or Grandfather Milliken when he came over to play chess with the Old Gentleman of a Sunday afternoon.

Leslie really saw the sea-serpent there and tackled it. Except when he got what Davey called the sillies, and just sat and stared or insisted upon draping everything, even the sea-serpent, with a bit of white net from an old curtain that he was forever dragging everywhere with him.

Angel-veil he called it. Of all the silliness! Trina confided a curious reason to Davey why Leslie always carried about with him a bit of net. Because he was born with a caul over his face. Leslie was half angel. Of all the silliness! Angels never came on earth. Leslie had just shoulder-blades. Not wings. Besides, it was said of David himself, that he had been born with a caul over his face. But only a little one, that tore.

Oh, but there was a good one about the bit of net! David could make a naughty little roly-poly of himself and slap his thighs with laughter at the mere recollection.

Once Leslie had pinned the bit of net against Bek's great, thick, cloth skirt, and out she went into the pasture to look over some heifers, with the bit of veiling flapping backward in the wind.

Leslie had been known to deck out pretty nearly everything about the place as his angel. But oh, Bek! Somehow doing it to Bek was funniest of all. In bed, at night, to Davey, who had a habit of coming up out of sleep along past midnight for a wakeful little period of five or ten minutes, that picture of Bek with veil flying off her boots would often set him to rollicking with laughter up and down against the bed springs.

At the Renchler table, Leslie was always served first. Great, tender helpings that he never half consumed. David came second. It had always been Bek's theory that the growing child was the first responsibility at table. David loved to eat there. He ate abundantly. Had a short way of masticating, caught up his food on quick fork-stabs and, unless watched, cracked bones between his ragged, saw-edged teeth.

The barley soup let him in for rebuke, too. He let it wash around his mouth noisily, for that moment when the cunning flavor was most tickling. Tonight there was hot corn-bread, to be pried open like an oyster-shell, and a knifeful of pale, sweet butter slid in.

With Paula off teaching in Cleveland and Stevey at

College, her table seemed immeasurably reduced to Bek.
Just her three boys to serve. Winslow, who always ate
languidly. Leslie, and then Davey, when she could borrow him from the House on Sycamore Street.

Bek, eating quickly, but heartily, herself, up and down,
in and out. Replenishing. Carting out plates. In with
fresh ones for pie. Granite pot of steaming coffee, replaced, when Paula was home, with a Wedgwood one,
with a tricky snout. Leslie had to have his pie cut up for
him, so that he dished it up with a spoon. Often his
hand trembled. Then Bek steadied it from the elbow.

Sometimes David wondered why Leslie's hand trembled.

"What makes you shake that way? Huh? What?"
David had once asked with the directness of childhood.

Leslie, who had a strange vocabulary of nouns joined
together by shakes of his head, was bewildered at this,
and only quivered his head the more. Bek, with a sixth
sense where Leslie's dilemmas were concerned, had called
from another room where she had been rushing muslin
window curtains onto their rods:

"Leslie's all full of secrets, Davey. He's like a leaf
on a tree that rustles with laughter each time the wind
tells it a new one. You and I can't hear the wind like
Leslie can."

Winslow, who had been painting in his attic-studio,
overheard, and took his pipe ruminatingly from where
it hung cold, as usual, on the edge of his lips.

Strange woman, that Bek of his.

Davey ruminated, too. Aw—the wind don't talk.
That was on a par with dressing up a lead soldier and
calling it an angel. A soldier was a soldier. Oh—oh,
the time Leslie had pinned the angel's veil to Bek's skirt!
No siree, wind don't talk. And yet—come to think
about it—if you ran when you crossed a meadow and it

zipped through your hair, there was something quick and rushing in what it seemed to say. Swift, almost uncapturable things. That must be why Leslie trembled. They were not too swift for him to capture. Anyway, Bek knew more than anybody. Except Henry.

"Yum-yum, the cherry pie was good!" Davey made a pyramid of the pits and it tipped over onto the cloth, and he got spanked softly across the back of the hand by Bek.

"Davey, fruit-stains don't come out!"

"Let the youngster alone, Bek," said Winslow, sitting back in a slim, relaxed fashion he had, that made him a restful note in any room, and feeling down into his side pocket that Bek kept replenished with a brand of tobacco she ordered by catalogue. "Gad, but it's good to be tired and fed and warm all at the same time."

Poor Winslow. Logically, now was the time to tell him about Steve. After dinner, with the warmth of inner well-being to sustain him, would be time enough to tell him. Poor dear. . . .

"Davey, run upstairs, honey, in Bek's room. There's an express package from Sears Roebuck on the table. Open it carefully. There's two new phonograph records in it. 'Sweet Adeline' and 'Viennese Melodies.'"

"Bek, hand me my specs while you're at the sideboard. They're in the silver pitcher."

It was so hard to tell him now, with his *Chicago Tribune,* which came on the afternoon mail, ready to be slid out of its folder, snapped open, read. Well—later —upstairs in bed—perhaps.

"Winslow, hadn't you better run upstairs and lay a fire in the alcove? It gets chilly for Leslie."

"Can't Davey put a match to it while he's up?"

"That child, handle fire!"

"Nonsense, he has the steadiest hand I've ever seen."

"Never mind, I'll run up. Have to go anyhow."

"I'd have gone, if you'd have given me the chance."

It was usually like that. Bek already up the stairs and down again, drawing shades, turning on the dome of many-colored glass over the dining-table (Paula's installation), clearing the table, folding the "silence cloth," spreading a fringed red-and-green rep cover, and placing a red-glass bowl of russet apples in the center.

There was Saturday's pay roll to make out, what with two extra hands at work on fencing in the Algahr addition. There was a note to be met, that eked out exactly the last dollar of her bank balance, on a seven-per-cent loan from a shark of a fellow named Joe Quirk, in Middleton, who had advanced her five hundred toward the Algahr buy. Such further addenda as bill-of-sale for two heifers to be drawn up. Trade Hiram Igrotte load of small winter apples for two hauls of cinders. Hog medicine. Mail blue sweater to Paula.

Heigh-ho! Davey and Leslie playing at lead soldiers in the corner. The phonograph turning out the new ones, "Sweet Adeline" and "Viennese Melodies." How debonair, the last melody, in a stately Old World fashion that suggested some of the Old Gentleman's tales of the Vienna he had glimpsed once as a boy. And then Winslow's favorite, Alma Gluck's "In the Land of the Sky-Blue Water." Bek, lower and lower over her accounts at the roll-top desk in between the windows.

The light was bad. For fifteen years, Winslow had been warning her she would ruin her eyes in that corner. Steve, when he was fourteen, had once given her a student-lamp with a green shade for a Christmas present. But that was up in Winslow's studio in case he might need it to browse around his dim store-closet among old canvases.

The unwieldiness of her pay roll, especially during

harvest and periods of extra labor, was pretty constantly worrisome. She hated to have to borrow from her father, as she almost invariably did on those quarterly months when notes of one sort or another were falling due. "Land poor," was the bugaboo phrase with which Bek had constantly to flagellate herself, when her acquisitiveness for more and more acres laid hold of her. Yet everyone, even Stevey, with his agricultural phraseology acquired at college, had approved the Algahr buy.

"Looks like I'll have to ask Father to meet me at the bank, after all, Winslow. I was counting on Heffernan's cash for those three calves, and now he wants to trade in that last year's Ford truck body. Of course, we need it for light hauling, but that three hundred Phil borrowed last week, and now that wire fencing, have put me in a hole."

"Pity Phil couldn't have gone to the Old Gentleman for his loan."

"He must have had good reason, Winslow."

"The very good reason, I suppose, of too high frequency."

"Phil knows how he can get on Father's nerves."

"Well," said Winslow and snapped his newspaper and slumped down more deeply into his Morris chair, "see where Taft isn't going to give in an inch on the Sherman Anti-Trust Act. The Roosevelt Big Stick is still waving from behind the throne. Can't you see those Roosevelt teeth grin?"

"What's a throne, Winslow?"

"A throne, my young brother-in-law, is the chair at present occupied by a King called Edward who rules the greatest democracy in the world."

"Winslow, don't confuse the boy!"

"Teddy's teeth! I know. I know. When I get big

I'm going to be a rough-rider and have the biggest—the biggest teeth in the world."

"Fee, fie, foe, fum, with which to dig your grave."

"Lookie, Leslie, my two front teeth are out in the middle for bigger ones to come in. Let's see yours!"

Leslie opened his mouth obediently. His long, narrow pointed teeth hung almost like a young terrier's and as beautifully white. When he showed them, Bek, through the adding of accounts, turned her head.

Leslie's mouth, when he opened it, constantly reminded Rebekka, with a stab, of a girl named Lotta Hensel, who used to carry her father, who was a housepainter, his tin pail of hot lunch from the Hensel shanty in South Centralia. Lotta had been a pretty thing. Sixteen. And under Bek's very eyes, had run screaming one day into the kitchen of the High Ridge Farm, in flames. Some burning leaves had caught at the hem of her skirt as she was passing along the road on her way to the Algahr house which her father was painting. Bek beat at the flames, but Lotta, in her terrible plight, only milled around faster, fanning them. Later there was an emergency operation and skin-grafting in the dining-room. Bek stood by. There was no anesthetic, only a linen cloth laid across the upper half of pretty Lotta's face, as she lay stretched on the table. At the first incision into her already boiling agony, Lotta's hand tightened on Bek's. But her mouth, where it showed beneath the linen mask, a pretty bud of a mouth, opened as sweetly as a child's. "It doesn't hurt," she said. And died.

There was something about Leslie's mouth that reminded Bek perpetually of Lotta when her lips below the mask had lifted into a little smile to say that.

"Leslie has beautiful teeth, David. You see, his baby ones have never come out. He still has his angel-teeth."

"Angel-teeth," repeated Leslie, who usually picked the noun out of a phrase to repeat.

"I can spit through mine."

"That's horrid, Dave."

"Father does."

"Winslow, I've work to do here at the desk. Go along and take Davey and Leslie up to bed."

"I was just starting to read the Taft inaugural address, Bek. Fellow ought to . . ."

"Henry was reading it to Father last night, but the new mare had colic and Father said Trina was giving him the wrong bran and Father hollered like anything and Henry went on reading out loud just like Father wasn't hollering."

"I'll wager Henry knows it by heart, by now."

"I know what's in it."

"In what, Davey?"

"Pres-i-dent's in-augural. We're going to have a bigger navy. I'm going to be a sailor. Teddy wasn't fat like Taft, was he, Bek?"

"No. Come. Winslow must read. Bek'll take you and Leslie up to bed."

"What if Mother forgets my little ewe lamb? Once Mother forgot to let in Sofia and Sofia froze her foot."

"Won't you ever forget that, Davey? I'm sure, honey, in the millions of Sofia's ancestors, most of them born under the board walk that leads from the house to the kitchen, that not a single pussy of them ever had a frozen foot until that night Mother, for the first time, forgot."

"But if Mother forgets again . . ."

"Mother won't. Come, Leslie, and Mother will tell you for a good-night story how the moon carries honey to the bees."

"For Heaven's sake, Bek," cried Winslow in the key of having said it countless times before, "get it right. The *bees* carry honey to the *moon*."

"Of course. Mother meant that, Leslie. Oh, Winslow, you are so much better at tales than I am. Leslie would rather be put to bed by you."

"All right if——"

"Oh, never mind. Come, Davey. You skip on up to your room and Bek will be there in time to tuck you in."

"Bek, I can recite the preamble of the Constitution. We, the people of the United States, in order . . ."

"For the love of Heaven, muzzle that child, will you? Your brother Henry is going to make a gibbering encyclopedia out of him before he's seven."

". . . in order to form a more perfect union."

"Come, Davey."

"The moon," said Leslie trailing after—"honey—to —the—moon."

"You see, Bek," said David, clamping each small, square foot on the stair as he toiled up after, "you see he's such a little ewe-lamb, and if such a little ewe gets thirsty and there's no one to give him a drink . . ."

"Muzzle that kid," said Winslow, hooking his pipe into the corner of his mouth and stretching out comfortably on the dining-room sofa with his *Tribune,* "s'pose a fellow ought to read the inaugural speech—dry as dust——"

"The bees don't neither carry honey to the moon, Bek. Now the way a bee makes honey is this . . ."

"Muzzle that kid!" roared Winslow, ramming his right ear into a cushion and jamming another on top of his left.

Chapter Five

IT WAS snug up where David slept. Bek's covers were
nicer to snuggle into than the ones in the House on Sycamore Street. Chiefly because Bek used quilts that an old
farmer-woman over just beyond Cottage Corner made
with spud-like fingers out of the choice cotton and percale
scrappage of a county of attics. Blues and reds and grays
and oyster whites. There was one, Davey's favorite,
with a border that looked like rows of intently listening
rabbits' ears. In Bek's attic, it smelled like calico as you
tear it. Clean lint of the loom. There was a window
set in a slant of ceiling and sometimes it was entirely
filled with moon that made everything white except the
shadows and the school pennants that Steve had nailed up
against the slopes of wall.

There was a moon tonight. He had a toothache. He
often did when he came up almost full, one of his cheeks
bulging and making him lopsided. It was nice to be
tucked in bed at Bek's under quilts that did not scratch
like the gray blankets in the House on Sycamore Street.

When blankets got old, sick ewes liked them. If a ewe-
lamb got sick, a very baby one, and you didn't give it
warm milk out of a nursing-bottle, it died.

"Poor e-w-e. E-w-e. Y-o-u. Funny. How could you
always know which of the two meant? If you said, 'You
go downstairs,' it couldn't mean e-w-e. But if you said,
'poor e-w-e,' then which you? E-w-e or y-o-u? Henry
would know even that."

Haw, Leslie thought the bees carry honey up to the
moon to make it clear. Haw!

Now I lay me down to sleep. I pray the Lord, my

soul to keep. If I should die before I wake, I pray the
Lord my soul to take. God bless Mother 'n' Father 'n'
Henry 'n' Bek 'n' Leslie 'n' Winslow 'n' Phil 'n' Emma
'n' Clara 'n' Jacob 'n' Hallie 'n' ewes 'n' Pete McNally
'n' the inlaws 'n' nieces 'n' nephews 'n' Teddy and let me
go to see him march when he comes back from Africa 'n'
make Mother remember to feed the ewe 'n' God bless me
for not swiping Henry's coon-skin cap for my tommyhawk
and bless we, the people of the United States in order
to form a more perfect union ——we ——the ——
people——of the United States, in——order——"

Down in Leslie's room it was moonlight, too. It was
not really a room, but a sort of alcove that adjoined Bek's
and Winslow's so that the moonlight flowed in from
their room.

That was exactly the reason of the alcove. Because
it had no windows. Sometimes Leslie walked in his sleep.
There were bars across the window in the big room.

The moonlight lay in a long patch. To Leslie, in bed,
it was like a river. Of light. It fascinated him as things
that gleamed always did. He sat up in bed to feel the
sway of its bright tide.

Leslie had a song. It went something like "Evoe!
Evoe! Evoe!" His mother had attempted to teach him
ballads, tried and true, but this one was Leslie's own. A
little chant that he always sang with his long, white eyelids closed. Henry, who knew his self-taught Greek, was
wont to observe with mock manner of pious rebuke, that
there was something Bacchanalian about Leslie's choice
of lyric outburst. "Evoe! Evoe!" The call of Greek
youth. . . .

That last was enough for Bek. "Sing your song,
Leslie. The song of the Greek youths."

Leslie, with the droop of his long, pale lids: "Evoe! Evoe! Evoe!"

"Go to it, Leslie! Vine leaves in your hair."

"Don't tease Leslie, Henry. It's the perpetual call of youth in Leslie."

Later, after she had come upon Stevey that first time behind the Cider Mill, Bek had cause to feel her flesh crawl at that song of Leslie's. "Evoe, Mother!" he had shouted to her.

"Evoe! Evoe!" sang Leslie in bed, to the swinging tide of the moonlight. The bright tide down which he could feel himself riding in a skiff made out of a bed. "Evoe! Evoe!" The humming of voices from the big room was disturbing. One of them a harsh, man's voice, that split.

The humming of the voices was Rebekka's and Winslow's. Winslow was lying rigid in bed, with the flanges of his nose quite green, and Rebekka had the light on and was throwing an extra blanket, which she had to stand on a chair to drag down from a closet shelf, on top of him, and finally against his continued shudderings, his corduroy jacket, with the strings of his tobacco-pouch dangling out of the pocket.

"Making yourself sick isn't going to help matters. I suppose I shouldn't have told you, but there are some things I haven't the right to carry alone. Besides, he will be home tomorrow."

"I won't have it!" said Winslow, through teeth that shuddered. "Damn him!"

"Scarcely the most helpful way to set about getting Steve out of this—mess."

"I won't have it!" said Winslow, and began to cry quite weakly against the pillow; and along his brow and the backs of his hands, the tallow-colored, moist pallor sprang out, and beads of moisture, in the weakening fashion that Bek dreaded.

"It's no wonder," said Bek, standing surveying him and wanting to keep her voice cold through her rising concern for him—"it's no wonder I carry everything alone sooner than go through this sort of thing with you."

"Young pup, he'll not drag his family name into the dirt."

"He will, unless you treat this matter like a problem instead of a calamity."

"I won't have it!" cried Winslow, and beat with his hands into the pillows and sobbed like a baby.

"It's not a matter of what you'll have. It's a matter of what you've got to face."

"There's something you're holding back. There's something more to it than just withdrawing him from college at the dean's suggestion because he's loafing. Boys don't get fired for such small-fry offenses. There's been something more behind it right along."

Rigid at his bedside, Bek bit her lips with the truth of this. But to tell Winslow all the facts of his homecoming, she realized now, was as impossible as it had been to tell him the truth of the hurried decision to send him away.

This must apparently remain her fight and Steve's. She had meant to tell Winslow the why; the whole miserable why of the going and the coming of Steve; of the wretched reason of her sudden determination to send him to State Agricultural; of that first time behind the mill— that second—third, fourth time. The deceits. The deceptions. She had meant to tell him all, now that Stevey was coming home, his secret pledges to her shattered . . . Winslow must fight the fight with her and Stevey now. . . Winslow must be taught a quality of mercy and wisdom toward his boy . . . who needed him.

"I'm cold."

Winslow must—must meet this with her ——

"I'm getting a chill. . . . Damn young pup—he'll not drag our name in dirt."

"Winslow, you mustn't get yourself into a state. Are you really cold? Or just nervous? You don't want the hot-water bottle?"

"Young puppy!" sobbed Winslow. "Over indulged. Gentleman farmer. Never quite understood it all, anyhow. No son of mine comes home suspended from college for loafing . . . young puppy . . . won't have it. I'm getting a chill."

"Hot-water bottle, Winslow?"

He was sure not to want it or to endure it, once it was there, but his silence meant acquiescence to her going for it. That meant padding down through the dark, cold hallways, and the slow performance of waiting for the water to boil in the black iron kettle.

"If it will make you feel better, Winslow, I'll go down and heat water."

"Amos Milliken," said Winslow, from his pillow of misery.

That was a localism that needed no interpretation to a Schuyler. Emma Schuyler's father-in-law, Amos Milliken, had long since placed the flavor of his hospitality in local ill-repute, by his habit of asking a guest, "Have a cigar if I go upstairs and get you one?" instead of passing around the box of his own excellent brand that always reposed in the top sideboard-drawer.

It was just as well, though, not to act on Winslow's jab of a reply. It was only his nervous ague. She had first beheld him in the grip of it in the days of their engagement, during a quarrel that had to do with some trivial misunderstanding over the time and place of an appointment.

High-strung! To Bek, whose nerves seemed to run through her body with serenity of veins through marble, there was a preciousness to Winslow. Standing there in her plain, white-muslin nightgown, vigorous, deep-fleshed, her strong, brown hair, that even her own children seldom saw down, hung in two plaits that were almost too enormous for beauty.

There *was* something Christ-like to Winslow's face as it pressed into the pillow that way, with the profile ground against it in pain.

A picture of her father on the night he had screamed and raved about the house when she announced her engagement, rose before Bek.

"You'll get nothing out of a Renchler! It's not in them to give. They're takers. His father before him would take a favor from you like it was coming to him. And the dam'-fool part of it is he got the whole town to thinking it was coming to him. Once a Renchler always a Renchler. The whole tribe of them. Pretty folks. But not in them to earn a penny or keep it, except when they marry money and catering wives. I know the Renchlers. Mark my word, Winslow Renchler will ride a girl like you to death. He's a taker."

Was Winslow riding her to death? Not while the rich flow of her sympathies could well out to him, as he lay there, shivering of the ague of nervousness. Theoretically perhaps, Bek was the giver. Actually, though, she would have clawed for him; fought for the qualities in him that were weaker than she was. There was pain in loving like that. And fierceness and a certain glory. And, strangely enough, reward.

"Damned young puppy!" sobbed Winslow again and again and again . . . "I won't have it!"

"I'll go down and heat you the water, Winslow," said Bek in a lusterless tone. "You *are* chilled."

Downstairs, in her enormous kitchen, spick, span, clean and cold, putting match to the gas-stove to which she could never become quite accustomed, playing its knobs as you would the stops of an organ, and then standing by to watch the water come to a reluctant boil, a lump of misery lodged itself in Bek's throat.

Here she was, confronted with what must surely be one of the grim climaxes of her life. Surely, surely, none grimmer could await her. Leslie up there swinging himself softly to sleep on "Evoe! Evoe!" while to that rather unearthly rhythm, downstairs in the chilled kitchen, needing Winslow if she was ever to need him, she stood alone, faced with the homecoming of a seventeen-year-old inebriate son. Here she stood, as usual, administering solace to the husband who should have been administering solace to her!

How unreal! Steve, who had grown, like a streak, from his adolescence into a young-manhood that delighted her. A curious combination of his Grandfather Schuyler and of Winslow. There was a threat of fine fettle to Steve, which made his profile dance like a blooded horse about to leave his post. A poet, or a peasant, or both. And now this.

Stevey must be helped. Cured. Men were. There was George Birkaway. Carrie Birkaway used to drop something into his coffee. For five years before his death, George had not touched a drop. Backs of magazines were full of remedies. Stevey must be helped. There was yet time. He must be made to have the power to resist. And without Winslow's knowing. Winslow was too high-strung. Without anyone's knowing.

They must again fight it out alone. The Old Gentleman—why, the Old Gentleman might have a stroke if

he knew.   Stevey must promise—Stevey must promise—
on Davey's life!   For Davey's sake!

How good, how strangely comforting, the consciousness of the little nub of him up there asleep in Stevey's
room.   How good. . . .

After a while, the shining tide began to slow—
drowsily—"Evoe! Evoe" sang Leslie to himself, and
singing it, dropped off to sleep.

The hot-water bag, sure enough, lay unapplied on the
floor when Winslow finally dropped off to sleep with his
head resting on the upper part of Bek's firm arm as she
lay beside him, his hair damp and smoothed backward in
long strokes of Bek's fingers, even after he slept.

What to be done?   Repeated drunkenness, the letter
had said.   Solitary-drinking vice, that, unless he left
college at once, must soon leak out among his colleagues.
Solitary drunkard.   It spread black wings over all the
things that mattered.   And suddenly they were not mat-
tering at all.   And they must!   There was so much to be
done.   Tomorrow's workaday was spinning toward.
Everything must matter as usual, if one was to carry on.
That broken plowshare-blade to be shipped back to the
factory for repair.   Rock salt for pasture.   Father to
be broached at the bank tomorrow for a loan.

Old Jessup's eyes.   They had turned at her like the
reproachful eyes of a dog that had served her well.   Poor
Jessup!

Emma's Claire needed a talking-to.   She had worrisome ways with her mother.   Sometimes a vagrant
thought flashed through Bek's mind.   Claire and Stevey.
The eyes of those two cousins when they were together.
Nobody in the world had noticed except Bek.   A dis-

turbing thought that never got more than half-born before she banished it.

Father must be got at before ten in the morning at the bank. If only Phil weren't needing that loan. Why couldn't he have borrowed directly from the bank, instead of crippling her this way? Three heifers due Thursday by shipment from Tom Groady's place. Groady must wait, now that Phil had horned in for this loan. Foolish of her to have mentioned Phil's loan to Winslow. Winslow hated the perpetual financial cross currents. And tomorrow Stevey. Oh, Stevey, how could you? All these weeks of reassurance about him, and now the secret terror lifting its head again. Oh, Stevey! She wanted to cry. She wanted Winslow to hold out his arms that she might creep into them. Instead, her arms were held out to him as he lay there asleep with his head on the pillow of her shoulder.

But good, at least, to feel up there in the room under the rafters the somehow reliable little old nub of Davey.

His being there, absurdly enough, gave a stability to the large white night that was spinning tomorrow relentlessly toward.

The room was so bright. It's shininess finally hypnotized her to sleep.

How bright! Davey waking into it, leaped up with a sense of broad daylight. It was still only moonlight, except that the old fellow, with his slightly swollen cheek, had moved entirely out of the window. Davey, in his flannelette night-drawers that fastened about the waist with large bone buttons, sitting up in bed, gouged his eyes with his fists. Sense of awakening to something not right. What if Mother had forgotten! What if they had let the fire in the range go out. The ewe with the blue eyes and a black slit down their middle.

By day and to the routine doings of people about, there had even been a wrench about it. But now, in the still white drown of a moonlit three-o'clock-of-a-morning, what had seemed fairly all right by day, was dreadfully all wrong.

The little old thing in its blanket beside the stove had pulled at his finger as if it had been the teat of a mother lamb. That little old thing had looked up so and trusted Davey, sitting up there in his cotton-flannel night-drawers, with the moonlight flooding over him, and Davey had not gone back. But Bek had wanted him. That made it hard. Being wanted by two people not in the same place. Ewe-lamb wasn't really a person, but the ewe wanted, just the same. And Bek was so big. In a world full of big things, Bek was almost the biggest. Only Davey and the ewe were small. And the ewe was smaller than Davey, and the ewe trusted David.

Up through the window there was only a slant of sky, the color of a grape. Cold. Terribly clear. If one could run home and back. Bek needn't know. The ewe-lamb had pulled at your finger so!

How cold it was! The cutting cold of a March that comes raw. It made David shiver as he drew on his pants and almost with the same gesture snapped down the little suspenders over his flesh. There was no time for shoes and stockings, besides, shoes squeaked. In the *Book of General Information* on his mother's kitchen shelf, from which Trina could laboriously read, you took the squeak out of shoes by standing them in a half inch of water overnight. "I know how to take the squeak out of shoe-es. I know how to take the squeak out of my shoes." It helped to chant foolishly, against a rising tide of fear. One leg over the sill. Two.

Many a time he had slid the galvanized rain spout that led from Bek's second-story room down into a black-mouthed barrel beside the porch. From the third story, it was another and steeper matter. Ouch! His body made a soft rush going down and the snag of tin that he struck took a bit of the flesh too. Almost the only sounds, that tiny rush and tiny tear, in this great white night that slept with one eye blazing open. It was almost like a sun, that lopsided moon. It made the shadows short and grotesque and a little frightening.

Something made a neighing sound that caused Davey to crouch for a moment beside the rain-barrel. He knew that neigh. It was Flora, the right gray mare of Bek's huge plow-team. Except that in the white night, the curious inverted noonday, it smote him with the strange terror of unreality. The sound that by day made the world seem small and friendly, was by night a thin cry of the mystery of all beasts.

Out across the pasture, toward the creek, there were almost no shadows. Just the greenish grayness and the light-drenched silence. It made Davey's heart shy back so that he plunged his hands into his pockets, and once out of earshot of the house, set up whistling. A pretentious kind of whistling, mostly breath.

How good it was, even with scare at the pit of you, to be going to the ewe-lamb, and then back to Bek, too. All that you had to do if you had to choose between doing two things, was to do both of them.

It wasn't fair to quit the ewe. It wasn't fair to quit Bek. Now you weren't quitting either of them.

Sometimes something crackled and made him scurry.

There was a song Jessup was always singing as he mended harness in the barn.

Ole Black Joe. Ole Black Joe.

There was something out there! Out there where the ghostly pale meadows ran into the grape-colored sky. There was something. A cow?

"I'm coming, I'm coming,
For my head is bending low;
I hear their gentle voices calling,
      'Old Black Joe!'"

Bek's cows slept in rows of long, clean stalls. Jessup's cow? But Jessup had no cow. Tarkington's stray cow? Nobody's cow was that tall! It was hard to continue going toward it, with the tongue a stiff thing in one's mouth, and the throat so dry it would not swallow.

"Ole Black Joe." You couldn't sing with a throat that was parched with terror. You only squeaked like something rusty, "Ole Black Joe. . . ."

Here, now, was the creek to be crossed. At night, somehow, it became a terrifying, bottomless divide, that by day trilled with water that showed the stones it ran over and slid past the brilliant flanks of minnows.

It was hard not to cry, and most difficult of all not to run back. That something on the horizon, that object too tall to be a cow, was coming toward him! Splash! The water came running up about the legs, greedily. Sucking in a way it never did during the day. Pulling downward in a way that terrified. Plunge, plunge went David's knees, so that he came out drenched to the waist, this time, shivering. And there was the thing now almost upon him.

"Bek! Henry! Mother! Go way, you. Big Thing!" sobbed Davey, and began to cry, and back toward the creek. "Go way," screamed Davey and because to really turn back was unthinkable, threw up his arm across his eyes. Henry would not be afraid. Nor Bek. Mother might. If Mother might be afraid, it was not wrong to be afraid. Sur-ren-der, in the histories Henry read from, meant something like afraid. No. Lee surrendered. There was a colored picture of his surrendering in Henry's book, called *General Lee*. Lee surrendered.

But that wasn't that kind of being afraid. Of just a thing. A thing in the moonlight. One didn't surrender to things in the moonlight.

"Go way, you!" screamed Dave, and batted his eyes and plunged forward, so that suddenly the thing swung into outline. An outline that suddenly sent him limp as a bag, of relief.

The thing was a threshing-machine. Many a time his bare legs had kicked its flanks. He gave it a punch as he passed. Corn runts began in rows now, brittle against his feet, and then a bit of fallow land with the turned earth in frozen little peaks that bit against his soles. Jessup's place came up over a ridge, huddling for all the world like an old hen in her shoulders. That must be Jessup's old rooster Cheetie, who would never sleep under roof, perched on top of the hen-house like a wart against the sky.

Dave's six-year-old world, moonlit, flowing there under the feel of his toes. Its reassuring familiarity warmed him clear into his being, like a toddy going down when he had a cold. Lickity-split! He ran and spun the fields back from under him. The gnarled old veteran fields lashed by March that seemed to be resting from their day-by-day burden of the toiling of the men who tilled their faces.

They smelled deeply. Known smells that you could rub between your fingers in a nub of dirt. That was part of the warmth. The great sleeping world that milled and tilled so by day, asleep and docile, with its great bosom swept with moonlight.

When you were no longer frightened, and sick with the impulse of surrender, it was good to be spinning through their March starkness on that mission, between the ewe-lamb who needed you, and Bek who wanted you.

The kitchen window opened from the outside, so that

just by shinnying up a tin water-spout, balancing tiptoe on the sill, and shoving down the upper pane by the ends of your straining fingers, in you were! It was dark inside, not even a red circle showed around the stove lid. Mother *had* forgotten! Trina had failed! No, Mother hadn't forgotten. It was just her way of thinking that with the little iota of red coals over in the corner, there would be enough heat for the ewe. The nickel-plated lifter in the stove-lid, you could raise noiselessly and place on one end of the range. That threw the kitchen into faint glow. Just a handful of red coals, supposed to be enough for one ewe.

The kitchen in the House on Sycamore Street was the oldest room in the house. Full of sags. Sags that might almost have been scoured in. Two white-pine wood tables that sagged and smelled perpetually cool and sudsy. Mathilda ground into them with scrub-brush in grand semicircular smears. A scrubbed floor that sagged. A safe with a perforated-tin front, that sagged. Even the sheet of metal around the range, scoured tin that shone, sagged. A scrubbed, scoured, spotless kitchen, with everything turned to the wall, nights. And there, in a chip basket beside the range, in its blanket, tiny thing, the ewe-lamb. With its snout thrust up.*

---

* I think we had the most beautiful kitchen in the world in the House on Sycamore Street. Old Trina used to tell us how the Welsh love their kitchens. Normandy is filled with quaint, curtained, shining kitchens after every woman's heart. The kitchen plays no mean part as the social center in the entire history of civilization. To the Dutch and the Danes, it is still literally the nucleus of the home.

Our kitchen was that. Father originally built a house of one room. A kitchen-living-bedroom. It ran, of course, the width and length of the building. A long, low room, with oak rafters and an open fireplace with a spit. Later, when the original

There was milk in the pantry in a five-gallon pail.   It was about the same height as David.   That made it dif-

---

room was surrounded and surmounted by more rooms, the enormous fireplace was fashioned into a bricked-in range. And what a range! It had a hot breath that warmed through the fine thick walls. It could roar with a draught the like of which I have never seen since. In winter, even after the house had grown to proportions sufficient to comfortably house a family of five youngsters, that range attracted us like a great flame all the little moths. We toasted corn over its red caves. Baked yams and marshmallows in its fierce oven. Dried our snow-clogged clothing before its Sahara breath. Usually, there was a baby lamb or an ailing calf or a cat with a leg in a splint in a chip basket beside this astonishingly maternal stove.

It was a more beautiful kitchen than Washington Irving's. It had mullioned windows that opened outward. In summer, they were grown over with columbine, that had to be kept clipped in order to allow opening them. There were two long white-pine tables in our kitchen, big enough to seat eight. On a bench, beside one, was a wooden bucket, with a dipper gourd, filled with the coolest cistern-water in the county. A second bucket was filled with well-water. Softer, for cooking. How well I recall the festoons of peppers. The hearth-broom made out of the left wing of a rooster. The great crocks of the various greases my mother rendered from goose and hen and parts of the hog. There was a wooden box in one of the window-sills stocked with twists of newspaper. Firelighters. A rifle, sans barrel, and with a broken cock, said to have belonged to Daniel Beinville, hung over the door.

My mother's pleasant mania for starched ruffles asserted itself everywhere. Along the shelves of the safe. Along the muslin curtains in the sweet old mullioned windows. We used to tease her about these ruffles. Yes, there was a God Bless Our Home sampler over the cupboard door, and a small white ruffle along the shelf that bore it. And a clock, mahogany, with a nosegay painted on its glass door. This clock may be ficult to tilt.   The bottom made a great planging sound as it left the floor.   What if it should awaken Mother or Father?   Or Henry, whose room was over the pantry, and who, winter and summer, slept with his cot drawn up to the window and his pillow on the sill so that his head was out-of-doors.

It was easier to find a dipper, stealthily, to save clatter, scoop down into the pail and heat the bit of milk.   Over the sink, so that he had to climb, was the bottle, with the rubber nipple.

Funny ewe-lamb.   Without opening its eyes, it sucked it all down, in gurgles.   Grateful, sleepy darling gurgles. The pulling against the rubber nipple.   It was like the thing that made the creek move.   And the lilac-bush to bloom.   And worms to ooze up in the lower pasture after rain.   Gosh.   Little thing.   Little old thing.   In a world of big things, it was the littlest old thing. . . . "Getty back there.   To bed.   'Nuff, I said.   Getty back!   'Night, you!"

Scampering back, up hillock, down hillock, lickety-split, over the fallen tree-trunk that spanned a small ditch, up hill, down, around, splash!—the already wet trousers sopping in more water—zither—through cinder-paths. In less than twenty-five minutes, the return was accomplished.

It was deliciously good to be in bed again under the quilt that was gay with rabbits' ears, and with the moonlight, now receding, leaving enormous dark splotches in the room.   Good, except that almost before he could sigh out with the satisfaction of it, plomp! sleep was a bottomless pit into which he had walked, open eyed.

---

seen in the American Institute in Baltimore.   Every Schuyler of us has reason to remember this kitchen with affection.

Not so Henry, who, up in his window, cold pipe lax on his lips, had seen Davey come and Davey go. Such a strangely beautiful steel-blue night as this would not let a body sleep, for pondering and pondering on a bit of everything and nothing in particular.

Chapter Six

IT WAS one of those days like Christmas or Washington's Birthday, or Father's birthday, or Fourth of July, or April Fool. One of those particularly nice days with an underlying current of events to it.

First, Stevey was coming home from Agricultural. "For good," Claire had said and kissed Davey square on the lips and hugged him until his cap came off. Then there was the something pending about Henry. Henry, it seemed, could have had celluloid buttons, with his picture on, that you wore on the visor of your cap. "Vote for Henry Schuyler."

Phil was coming in on the four-twenty-eight, too, and Clara from St. Louis, but this time without Sam or the children.

But it meant meeting three trains practically at a scoop, because they all arrived within three hours. The Old Gentleman never missed being the first to welcome home a Schuyler.

Phil's wife Rita always declared that her father-in-law's basket phaeton, a dirty affair much maligned by the family, which you could see by craning your neck, as the Springfield train drew into Centralia, was as much a part of the landscape as the Capitol dome was to Washington.

The family was given to exchanging amused persiflage with one another, and suggesting to the Old Gentleman, from time to time, that he had better will over the phaeton to the State Museum as a relic of pre-Civil-War transportation.

The Old Gentleman lived under a barrage of winks and nods between his children. He moved calmly among them, oftentimes mimicking their very gestures with his sly old eyes.

David liked meeting trains with his father. They swooped in magnificent, whizzing reality from the world that lay flat and inanimate in words against the pages of Henry's books. Trains dashed into Centralia depot that must have come from Gettysburg where Lincoln made the speech. And from the shores of the Delaware that Washington crossed. Why, there was a railroad called the Chesapeake and Ohio. Chesapeake! Captain Lawrence cried "Don't give up the ship" on board the *Chesapeake*. There was a picture of the frigate *Chesapeake,* in colors, in one of Henry's books.

Yes, it was fine meeting trains. And the depot, a rather grimy, small, red-brick affair, was filled with that intangible and tickling odor of travel. The smell of leather and coal-smoke and pot-bellied stove, red-hot. The baggage and shipping rooms, stacked with crates and bales, trunks and milk-cans and egg-cartons and plow-shares and dynamos and pumps and bicycles boarded up for travel along with shipments of Centralia's not inconsiderable exportations of hardware from the Tools Works, were jammed with the further interest of reading labels. And addresses. Braunson Hardware Company, Terre Haute, Indiana. Mr. Silas Dikey, Johnstown, Pennsylvania. Firbers Mill, Trenton, New Jersey. United States Shipping Company, West Street, New York. It made one tingle with a sense of the outside world. Alton, Missouri. Vesey Street, New York.

Bob Fenton, the baggage-master, who had one eye and a black-cloth flap for the other, gave David gummed labels, which could be spat upon and pasted against all sorts of surfaces. Fragile. Hold. Live Stock. Eggs. Baltimore and Ohio. Farmers Shipping Union. Glass. This Side Up.

There was sure to be talk as easy as the jangle of change in a pocket, around the depot. Talk that ran like this:

"Hi, Schuyler! Got them two red heifers up at Seely's place if you'n' Miss Bek want to drive over to-morrow 'n' have a look. Hi, Schuyler, whose coming home today? Hi, trade you that youngster o' yourn for a red calf. Hi, Schuyler, see that new breed of hogs Lederman is showing up t'fair? White belly-bands. Look good. Wal, sir, see where they're mentioning Henry hereabouts for District Attorney. He's got my vote."

A vote was something you couldn't see. People kept talking about them and offering to give them, but nothing ever seemed to change hands. A vote was something that was not something in your hand. Just the same, if Henry wanted them, he could have them. Henry, who had a head that was almost the shape of the bottom of a foot and a bald, shiny spot where hair should have been, but hair that grew down the sides of his temples into two oblongs on the sides of his cheeks, where hair should not have been, and the very nicest eyes in the world that smiled and did things that most people did with their mouths; it was highly desirable that Henry should have all the votes in the world.

Even on the way to the depot, rumbling along in the Old Gentleman's phaeton, the way was strewn, from the sidewalk and from passing vehicles.

"Hi, Mr. Schuyler. See to it that boy of yourn runs this time. The state needs his kind. Hi. Howdy. Hi. Somebody acomin' home, I take it?"

The Schuylers were rallying for conclave all right. It was fun rumbling up to the depot with the Old Gentleman. It was in the days before his self-importance had shrunk to a kernel. Was in the days when the dirty old phaeton was only a badge of his unassailable well-being like a rich man's shabby hat.

Down Second Street toward the depot was the most familiar ride in the world. When Davey was five, and the Old Gentleman dozed at the reins, not infrequent with him, the small boy held them importantly. Not but what every mare that the Old Gentleman ever drove knew its somnolent, unguarded way through the streets of Centralia. Even when the automobile had practically nosed out horse traffic, the Old Gentleman's mare and phaeton had a sort of right of way.

There was a flat building going up on Second Street. The first in town. A square, two-story, two-family affair of concrete. A "St. Louis flat." The Old Gentleman could never pass it without clucking his disgust.

Further along, though, the street relapsed. The Blue Bird Lunch Room. The Red Trunk Dry Goods Company. Binswanger's Hardware. Hot Lunch. The White Kitchen. Gents' Furnishings. Buddy's Cut-Rate Drug Store. Co-Operative Mill Supply Company.

Beulah Kohn, who wore her left leg in a brace from meningitis, leaned as usual across the picket fence of the dirt-colored frame house where Mrs. Kohn kept a rooming house for mill workers.

"Hi, Mr. Schuyler!"

"Howdy, Beulah! Come out here and shake hands."

"Now, Mr. Schuyler! . . . you'll hurt!" But out she came limping, while the mare drew up, just as if this event did not take place every time the Old Gentleman passed Beulah Kohn's home. The Old Gentleman reserved his trick handshake for the very old, the very young, and the ailing.

You extended your hand. He took it gingerly by the tips of the fore and little fingers, and then, with his free hand, came down whack across the wrist of his victim, causing the bones to make a cracking sound. The Old Gentleman's delight in this was unfailing. Sometimes children cried. Then he plied them with licorice. Beulah knew his licorice-pocket, into which she dove immediately following this habitual chastisement.

Rattly old phaeton. You could jump in and out while it was moving, which David did all the way along.

Second Avenue, as it approached the depot, was myriad with interest.

"What does 'Katy Flier' mean, Father?"

"Katy flies, I reckon."

"B and O," began Davey, bursting for no apparent reason, as another sign presented itself to his amiable gaze, into loud cacophony, and beginning to direct an imaginary orchestra from standing position in the phaeton, as he faced Jenny's unexcited tail, "Bawleymore and O-high-O! B and O. Yip! Yip!"

The Old Gentleman never minded. Sometimes David climbed up his flank as he drove, balancing on his shoulders and shouting aloud as the little panorama of his thoughts came tumbling.

The Old Gentleman never flecked an eye, or for that matter, heeded.

The train tracks cut through Centralia like a diagonal, bisecting a rhomboid. Their grime kept the chestnut trees along Sycamore Street gray. They grazed the red flank of the Five and Ten on High Street by one foot. They skirted the edge of the Old Gentleman's South Pasture just remotely enough to have netted him not a penny when the railroad was out franchise-buying.

It rushed into town like the proverbial lion.

It tore out of town like a howling hyena. Never was the somnolistic tendency of a community more ruthlessly split to smithereens by the bangs, the bleats, the bells, the puffings, and the backings of steam-engines, than Centralia with the railroad trains across its very face, as it were.

Siren-shrieks and plumes of smoke lay on its dead of night. Fee, fie, foe, fum, snorted and rampaged one engine after another at the red flank of the Five and Ten. Freight engines backed-and-forthed up and down the center of Maple Street, baa-ing, moo-ing, and grunting with cattle and freight cars. Fee, fie, foe, fum, I'll blow and I'll blow 'til I blow your house down. Where Maple Street intersected Second Street, the railway's gates were almost always down, Buick and Ford delivery-wagons, farm-teams, buggies, roadsters and family-cars waiting, and often, to save time, backing down and making détour around the viaduct-way.

"Stop, Look and Listen" signs criss-crossed the streets of Centralia. The local Democratic and Republican factions both had a Grade Crossing Abolition plank. Nothing happened.

Centralia smelled with the railroad tracks that entered and intersected her, and erected white crosses upon the scene of every grade-crossing casualty.

Driving along Second Street, not only the Old Gentleman could detect the first remote halloo of the incoming passenger train, but up went old mare Jenny's uncurried ears that were the shape of the perpetual corner tied into the Old Gentleman's handkerchief, and jerk went the basket phaeton that was as full of creaks as of years.

Centralia met its incoming trains with a line of short-snouted family-sedans and open Fords; occasionally the Milliken seven-passenger Cadillac that belonged to

Emma's father-in-law, or the Howey Pierce-Arrow, mixed in. They stood in motley line-up before a row of what had once been hitching-posts.

The Old Gentleman's phaeton and the yellow lorry from Dr. Spaeth's Sanatorium were usually the only relics of a horse-age. They waited side by side in a little brick clearing opposite, where there were no hitching-posts, and their horses wound necks.

Jenny knew her place all right, even when the Old Gentleman dozed, edging herself and phaeton in beside the lorry, or where the lorry usually stood. When David was along, even when he was so small that a shake of Jenny's neck jerked him forward by the reins, he drove her quite grandly into the station, clucking at a great rate.

The Old Gentleman was not dozing today as he drove in. There was a constant screwing noise he made with his tongue, spurring old Jenny to uneven lopes; and above his square, white beard that hung like a curtain, the humorous blue eyes, twenty-five years too young for their setting, kept radiating. Phil's wife was right. He was as indubitably a part of the landscape as the rick-rack outline of the depot against the stubble of corn-fields. In his hip-high reefer, jouncing along in the old phaeton which creaked around him like a rusty ocean, he was an institution for you! He was a silhouette unto himself, in reefer, round cap bound in astrakhan, slightly mangy, in puttees, string-wound where the tapes gave out.

"Old Gentleman's quite a character," someone or other was forever saying.

"Hi! Howdy! Hi!" called the Old Gentleman, driving up.

"Hi! Hi! Ho! Howdy!" said the loiterers.

Almost simultaneously, Emma Milliken drove up in her father-in-law's car, a slick, night-blue affair of shine and snout, with a nickle-plated Discobolus doing a lunge off the hood. Her mother-in-law, Annie Milliken, occupied the rear seat, a sparse, iron-gray woman, with a palsy-affliction that kept her head like a flower on a stalk in a stiff breeze. Beside her, quite a beauty after her blonde fashion, sat Claire, in a brown beaver toque and brown beaver on her broad-cloth coat. Lalite and Kenneth Chipman, children of Donald Chipman, barrister, next-door neighbors of the Milliken seniors, were tucked into the collapsible chairs for the ride down to the depot. They made a carful.

"Mother Milliken, there's Gramp and Davey."

Mrs. Milliken leaned her palsied head forward. "So it is. Your father hadn't ought to come down looking like that, Emma. 'Tain't right. I don't see Mathilda."

Emma wound down the glass window-pane of the car. "Oh, dear! Your Gramp *does* look a sight, Claire. How could he come down to meet Phil and Stevey looking like that! Gramaw didn't see him leave the house looking like that, I'll wager. Fath-er!"

The Old Gentleman shambled over, Davey off to the baggage-room, and Jenny standing without so much as the reins wound around her whip stock.

"Father, come here. You do look a sight, dear."

The Old Gentleman had never ceased to regard Emma, his sixth-born, as a feast for even his sly old parental eyes. As a child, he had carted her among the farmers and had even been known to stand her on the counter of Fred Firpo's bar and appraise her yellow, little-girl loveliness.

"She's a good one, boys. My little Emma she's a beauty! I'm right? Give her a pretzel, Joe."

Although it was Emma's daughter Claire who was now considered the family beauty, Emma herself still possessed a certain cabbage-rose prettiness; and despite the fact that it had always been said that Emma Schuyler did not know how to wear clothes, and was a natural-born "slop," she had realized enough to all her life affect velvet toques to match her eyes, and when she remembered even now, she used a gayly-painted rolling pin which hung in her bathroom, to ward off the pads of fragrant, cream-colored flesh that threatened her shoulders and upper arms.

"Father, Mother Milliken's right. You *are* a spectacle!"

It was rather futile of her to lean out of the car, tilt back his head, and yank at his reefer-collar, particularly since little Lalite Chipman was already at his reefer-pocket.

"Licorice, Gramp!"

"Please, Father, don't give her any. She gets her teeth all full of the horrid stuff."

As if Emma herself, Emma's Claire, and virtually every youngster of the last four decades in Centralia had not, at one time or another, had their milk-teeth blacked from the yield of those pockets.

"Gramp," shouted Kenneth, who was nine and had the straight bangs of a medieval saint, "give me a pretzel."

"Guess which pocket," cried the old man and struck his flanks.

"Both," shouted the boy, and made a dive.

That tickled the Old Gentleman, who dove into a third pocket for more lunch-counter loot.

"Please, Father, Mrs. Chipman won't like it. There's always tobacco in that pocket. You'll make Kenneth sick. Isn't Mother coming down to meet Phil?"

"Yes, Bek is driving her down."

At just that moment, Bek drove around from the shipping-platform in a Ford, with a hooded front and a delivery-body, onto which was loaded a crate of Chester White hogs that she had just picked up from the freight-room. Seated beside her, in a little bonnet with a jet spray and a cape with fitted shoulders, was Mathilda, her hands clasped nervously over an empty shopping-bag of shiny black oilcloth.

David leaped the running-board before she brought the car to a short stop beside the Milliken Cadillac.

"Bek, I c'n bound Ohio. Ohio is bounded on the west ———"

"Davey, don't hop a going car!"

"——by Indiana on the ———"

"Look at Puppa!" cried Mathilda weakly and threw up both mittened hands in a faint gesture, "And I laid out his brown pants on the bed."

Emma and Claire had climbed out of their car.

"It's a shame, Mother!" cried Emma. "I declare, Father, I wouldn't come down to meet a load of heifers looking like that. How do you think Phil will feel stepping down off the express, with you looking this way to meet him. There's always plenty of Springfield and even Chicago business-men on that train. And Stevey coming too. I declare, Mother, I'd burn that phaeton, if I were you."

"Puppa," said Mathilda, a little tiredly, and a little helplessly, "I laid everything out . . . your cuffs with the buttons in ———"

"Poppycock!" said Rebekka. "He looks all right. Let him be."

The Old Gentleman made one of his sly, screwing noises with his tongue and poked an elbow into his wife's hip bone, where the cape neatly covered it.

"I'll dress up, 'Tilda, when we have an Attorney General in the family. I'm right?"

"Does Henry know, Father," said Rebekka, "that you sounded the ram's-horn for conclave about his candidacy? He'll be a mad hatter."

"What he don't know don't hurt him until he sits himself down to supper," said the Old Gentleman, and went off chuckling, with David anchored to his pocket, burrowing for a pretzel, which had looked good to him as he saw Kenneth nibble bites out of his.

"Bek," said Emma, eyeing her sister, with a furrow between her pretty eyes, "isn't it sudden, Stevey quitting Agricultural this way in the middle of a semester? Nothing wrong, is there? Never knew a word about it until Claire told me she'd a letter ——. Nothing wrong?"

"Nothing," said Bek, looking straight ahead over the wheel upon which her square, white hand lightly rested. "His father and I think it best to have him home this winter. That's all. It is good practical experience for him to be around while the state dam is under construction. He'll learn more about practical irrigation that way in a month than in a college year!"

"Funny, though, his coming so sudden," said Emma.

It was as if the slight figure of Claire, standing beside her mother, swayed as a fir tree sways, from its toe to its tip. An almost imperceptible sway, except to Bek, to whom most tiny things were perceptible.

"It's Junior League afternoon, Claire. Why aren't you there?"

"Just felt like running down to the station with Mother and Grandmother Milliken to meet Uncle Phil and see the four-ten come in," said Claire, her pretty, her appealing but faltering blue eyes meeting the absolutely horizontal ones of her aunt.

"And, of course, you wanted to come down to see Stevey too, dear," put in her mother, who was a great putterer in the name of amicability. "You didn't even know Uncle Phil was coming until Gramaw telephoned just before we left."

"And Stevey too, of course," said Claire. Her voice

was as thin as a quail's and her white young throat beat
like one, as she met her aunt's gaze.

"Of course," repeated Bek. Her voice was so level,
to Claire swaying there, like a vast and level plain.

"Bek," said Emma, and leaned close, "Mother Milliken is so sensitive. Hadn't you better go pass the time
of day with her? She gets more and more sensitive as
Father Milliken's notes to Father fall due. Better go
over. . . ."

"Indeed, yes," said Bek. "Come, Mother, you too.
And be sure you don't ask her about her brother in Saalsberg, Mother. Intimate as you are with Annie Milliken,
you cannot seem to remember that he died last year."

"I am glad you reminded me Bek, it does slip my
mind. Saalsberg is so far," said Mathilda, lifting her
skirts neatly, as her two daughters and Claire assisted
her down the step of the car. "I think I'll take her a
bit of that nice, crisp celery; it's under the seat. I just
picked it up at market."

"Hurry, Mother," said Bek, striding across the platform toward the Milliken car.

"Bek," said Mathilda timidly, and put out a restraining hand upon her daughter's stride, "I don't want to
seem unchristian, Daughter, and I wouldn't have Emma
hear, seeing how bad's Annie's palsy, but you and me
riding up in the Ford truck, Daughter, and there sits
Annie Milliken in a Cadillac, them never out of your
father's debt."

"Sense of humor, Mother," said Bek, hooking her
Mother's arm into hers and patting it. "The Lord gave
us ribs so we could keep them tickled."

"Yes, but not jostled, while Annie Milliken rests hers
in an upholstered limousine." Just then Davey, spying
little Dora Tarkington walking primly into the depot

with her hand in her father's, made a megaphone of his hand and shouted to her:

"Stevey's coming home!"

"Stevey's coming home!" Bek's heart, all the time that Claire's was fluttering like a bird's, was heavy within her.

Stevey was coming home. . . .

Chapter Seven

P HIL was the first of the Schuylers to go chubby, as the saying is. So rotund, in fact, that in his middle thirties, his waist-coat, that was usually a none-too-subtle check of plaid, buttoned over a semicircle. He was a tee-totaler, from inclination rather than conviction, but there was something in the veininess of Phil's face and the drape of flesh over the back of his collar that suggested alcohol.

There was an air of too-high blood-pressure about him. His face red and his voice a little breathless. At thirty, Phil Schuyler had twice been almost a rich man. The elusiveness of his quest glittered in his eyes. It was as if in attempting to force his destiny, he had antagonized it.

"Anything very special, Bek?" he said, through the light peck he deposited on his sister's cheek, as she ran considerably ahead of the others to greet him.

"They're after Henry again. District Attorney this time."

"Suspected as much. Well, he's got to take it. If he doesn't feel he owes it to himself, he at least owes it to the family. Man can't go through life turning down one honor after another. Howdy, Father. Well, Mother! Careful! There's some geranium-cuts in this paper bag Rita sent along for your side-yard borders. No, Rita decided not to come. Baby seemed a little croupy last night. Well, Father, am I to ride in the one-hoss shay?"

"Better men than you have ridden in it."

"Dirty crack!" cried Phil, who was accustomed to his father's easy irascibilities where he was concerned.

"Puppa—Phil was only teasing."

"Well then, so was I."

" 'S all right, Father. You're immense."

"So are you."

"Now, Father, don't taunt me for my figure. Who's giving me a lift?"

"I'll drive you home, Phil. I can bound Ohio—Ohio is ——"

"Can you bind my kitten's broken paw?"

"Phil!"

There ensued then the usual family-conclave, Emma bidding for Phil to sleep in her spare-room, where he could have steam-heat, Mathilda demurring that Phil's old room in the House on Sycamore Street was ready and the fire laid. Claire threw her young arms around her uncle's neck and begged him to wait for Stevey's train and then to ride up in the Cadillac, David meanwhile lugging his uncle's valise, and almost toppling backward with effort, toward the phaeton.

"No, never mind anybody waiting for Stevey's train, Phil. Claire and Emma will drop you and Mother at the House on Sycamore Street. Davey and I will wait for Stevey."

As she spoke, Rebekka's eyes, round as two pinwheels, had come to full stop upon her niece Claire.

"Go, Claire."

"But, Aunt Bek," faltered Claire, her blonde skin pinkening furiously. "But, Aunt Bek . . ."

"Run along," said her aunt and laid a firm, a heavy, an uncannily aware hand upon the small, frail shoulder of her niece.

"But . . ."

"Claire!"

"But, Aunt Bek—my own cousin—coming ——"

"A good thing to remember, Claire. Your—own—*cousin.*"

"Oh, you—" almost sobbed her niece, and ran after the others, with her handkerchief pressed against her lips— "you're—terrible to me."

The family shooed off before Bek, with an automatic kind of acquiescence.

There were only Davey and Bek left standing, wind-blown, on the platform, as the five-fifteen, bearing Stevey, drew in.

How handsome Stevey was as he stepped off the day-coach, in his slip-over sweater and a pigskin bag and a tennis-racquet in a case and his cap crammed into his pocket so that his hair, Winslow's waviness and baby-fine brown, blew backward giving him a swift, winged look.

Stevey was really David's eldest nephew. Leslie some-how did not count, as ages go. A lean-jawed young fel-low, with his father's sensitive nostrils and his mother's level mouth. Gray-eyed, with the depth to them that black lashes can lend; as indefinable a tang to an expres-sion, as the flavor of the caper to sauce. Personable, after a fashion, cut along lines rather lighter than the Schuyler heft, wide-shouldered, light-waisted, with some-thing correct about the line from femur to ankle that was not characteristic of the House of Schuyler in general.*

---

* . . . poor kid . . . destined as he was for the exhibition-ism of lecture-platform, rostrum, grand-stand, David had not escaped the Schuyler femur. From the hip to the knee, with most of us, the line was too short, making us a top-heavy-looking lot. We girls managed to hide it. But with the boys, Henry excepted, the effect was stockiness. We used to laugh

"How handsome he is!" thought Bek even when he could not quite meet her gaze in greeting. She wanted to take him in her arms, except that it would have embarrassed them both. For one second it flashed over her, as he made a quick movement of greeting, that the returning prodigal might be going to take her in his. Flashed over her in a warm goose-flesh. Of course, Stevey did nothing of the sort. People did not take Bek in their arms. He did exactly what she gave him the cue to do.

"Hullo, Mother," said Stevey, and flung out for her hand and shook it low, down and vigorously. "Hi, Unk," and caught up Davey by the armpits, as he was forever being caught up.

"Stevey, I can bound Ohio."

"Bound it tomorrow!"

"Stevey, me and Henry have a chart and we followed the American fleet around the world with the red pins."

"—as well as with breathless interest."

"And, Stevey, I know where the American fleet was on February twenty-first. Ha-waiian Islands, and Teddy fired a salute to Mo-lo-kai where the lepers live. If I was a leper, I could get fired a salute at by Teddy. Know what?"

"Dave, you run home now! Bek is going to drive Stevey home for Winslow, and then we'll all be over to Sycamore Street in time for supper."

---

about "the Schuyler femur." It is the answer, I think, to the fact that my brother Dave was what is known as a static speaker, remaining quietly behind his table or stand. It is also the answer to why, with the one exception of the Landsdowne painting, there are no full-length portraits of him. From the waist up, he gave the appearance of towering solidity. The effect of the long waist and slightly too short legs, even in the Landsdowne, was to make him appear stocky.

"Can I have a houn'-dog out of Tom Willet's litter, Bek?"

"No, those Willet dogs are always flea nests."

"The flea is a para-sit-ic animal that lives off ——"

"Good Lord!" cried Steve and tossed him again. "Go tell your Brother Henry to get you bound in a soft-leather edition and sell you from door to door."

"Run along, Davey, there's a good boy, and tell Mother not to bother about the sweet butter. I'll stop by Koerber's and bring a pat. Jump in, Stevey."

How easily as Davey with his short legs spun off toward Sycamore Street, Stevey swung into the seat beside his Mother, not bothering to open the door, just one long lithe leg after the other climbing over it.

"Shall I drive, Mother?"

"No," said Bek, and threw a clutch that jerked them forward.

The town in its cold March drabs was a one-colored affair. Sky the color of the weather-beaten boards that houses and fences and many of its sidewalks were built of, dry wash in back yards half-frozen and flapping stiffly gray, against gray sky, streets merging off, with scarcely a change of gray, from the smoothness of made into the roughness of unmade roads.

Down Second Street, Beulah Kohn still swung on the broken front gate.

"Hello, Miss Bek. Hel-lo, Stevey."

"H'lo. Stevey, that's Beulah Kohn, the one with meningitis. Poor child, speak to her."

"Hel-lo Beulah," called Steve, and tried to smile through a face that, once alone with his mother, had grown stiff-looking and white.

At the wheel, Bek's hand, ungloved now, was large and calm and pliable-looking as a surgeon's. But inside, against the palm, it was throbbing.

"Nobody knows anything, Stevey. Not even your father. The dean's letter came so—sudden, son. Your father might just as easily have been the one to open the mail-box and—find it first!"

Steve moved his lips, but nothing came.

"I—I've explained to everybody that I want you home —while they're building the dam. Practical observation —irrigation, y'see?"

His face only whitened and tightened, and his lips, handsome when in repose, shirred inward now, like a scar. Out of the tail of her eye, as she drove, Bek could see the young face becoming old. Terrifyingly old. A scarred old walnut of a face.

"I'm no good, Mother. Sooner or later you'll have to reconcile yourself to everybody knowing that."

"I'll fight you to the finish," said Bek, on a click of teeth, "before I'll make up my mind that a child of mine is no good."

"It gets me, Mother. It burns me. It makes a human bonfire out of me. There ought to be some cure for it, like there is for ulcers and scalds and hydrophobia. It gets me. Help me, Mother!"

"Help me, Mother!" At that, a cry that suddenly became the cry of the wind in her ears as they sped along; there lodged in Bek's throat a ball of ache, so that it was a block before she could muster voice. Her kind of dead-level voice without flutter to it.

"I'll fight with you, Stevey."

"Help me, Mother!" Why, to Bek, trying not to wobble the wheel, that was a cry in the wilderness. It smote her. It cut her in two. It made her veer so suddenly, as she crossed Second Street, where it intersected Elm, that Skeet Mapey, the sixty-year-old policeman on that beat, shook an unaggressive old finger at her, as they shot past him.

"I'll help you, Stevey, to help yourself. You hear me! No one can help you but yourself."

"Then I'm lost," said Stevey, and quite horribly began to cry, sitting there with his face twisted and his lips a knot-hole, and his chin all tucked up like a weazened little old man's.

"Oh! Oh! Oh!" Bek kept saying to herself. "Help me to help this boy! God, you—help me to help this boy!" She had the rather disembodied feeling of everything within her stopping like a run-down clock. A momentary inability to think or feel or do. A deadness, as if circulation and heartbeat and the universe of her body had ceased.

"You can do everything, Mother. Save me."

That warmed one back, somehow.

"Is it so terrible, boy?"

"It burns, Mother. Not like anything you've known. It cracks one's tongue, and then one's whole body is like a cracked tongue—thirsting. You can't know—ever ——"

"God knows, no, Stevey. Never in our family—any-one—anywhere—or in your father's—no one ever ——"

"It's like being lined with hot steel, Mother, that you want to cool by making hotter. Or go crazy! Or go crazy! It's hell, Mother. You're too strong to understand."

"Too strong to understand." There it was again. The alienating power of strength. Too strong to understand, when the hand with which she steered so surely was of flaming steel. The same flaming steel that tortured Stevey.

"Oh, Stevey—tell me. Tell Mother. Before we get home. Nobody must know. But you, Stevey, and me.

We'll fight it out.   How did it happen again?   So suddenly—you promised. . . ."

"Not suddenly, Mother—for a little while nobody there knew—that was all ———"

"Stevey, Stevey—as a child—as a little boy—you never even saw it around you, and now—now this ———"

"Never—except Gramp ———"

"Gramp!"

"No. No. I mean, first I remember ever seeing the stuff at all—Gramp used to keep a jug of cider in the phaeton for long drives—winter-time. I remember once or twice taking a swig or two out of it if he fell asleep at the reins. Remember, he used to think it amusing and cute for me to do that. Way back there—me a kid—it used to warm me, Mother, in a way I hadn't ever felt before. I've always felt cold inside. Remember how you used to fix me hot lemonades with mint in? . . . that was because I craved it. Even then. Warmth. Remember me always sucking peppermints? That was it, Mother. The burning. The burning."

"Oh, my boy!"

"That time you found me by the mill—that was the first time, Mother—I was—that way. I've sworn that to you so often. You must believe."

"I do."

"And then—and then—after you got me away—the first three months—I didn't—not a drop ———"

"That's why, Stevey, when it came—so sudden—I had thought—you were all right, boy ———"

"Mother, those first months. The torture. No wonder my marks were so bad. Mother, you'll never know. I used to get up at night—and run—Mother—go out and run around the track—until they began to get on—and think me nutty. I tried so terribly, Mother."

"Stevey! Stevey!"

"And then—the fellows—they began to rush me for Beta Beta. That was the real beginning. I hadn't even seen the stuff around, before I began to get in with the frat crowd. And then seeing it—in bottles—on tables —help yourself. The night they initiated me, I—that was the beginning. . . . Ugh. . . . Mother——"

That cry in the wilderness. The rumble of the tinny little car over it.

"Shame, shame, Stevey."

"Oh! Oh, Mother, if you only knew! If I had any guts—I'd kill myself!"

"No. No. No. Stevey, I'll help you. Mother will help you."

"You will, Mother. You will, won't you?" And sobbed, without troubling to cover his face, which some-how was most horrible of all to her.

"Father—what will he ——"

"He mustn't know, Stevey."

"I couldn't stand his knowing, Mother. Father so —so sensitive—so nervous—I—he couldn't stand it!"

"Father so sensitive. So nervous." What was the secret of Winslow, Bek asked herself. Not bitterly, but out of an enormous wistfulness and fatigue.

"We'll make our fight together, Stevey. I'm not afraid, Stevey—if you'll fight with me. We'll win!"

"I will fight, Mother. There's a bottle of—it— wrapped in a green sweater in the bottom of my bag. Take it away from me, Mother."

"You'll win, Stevey, like that! You're a Schuyler, son. There may be families in the state hold their heads higher, but not any straighter. Look at Davey, Steve. I always say he's everything in us summed up. Seventh child, I guess. Sturdy. Square. That's us." *

---

* . . . as I used to say of our Davey, long before he showed the slightest precocity other than a sort of walking-encyclopedia

"Yes, Mother."

"We've got to keep the family fine enough for him to grow up into, son. Ever think of that? Hello there, Supe. Stevey, that's old Lem Dinwater's boy. Speak to him. Supe, you tell your Pap to make me another offer on that hog corn. He's going to lose a good chance not giving me a price on that feed. Good boy!"

"My Pap says you'n him can't do no business, Miss Bek. My Pap says you're a better man 'n he is."

"Hop out here, Stevey, and into the drug-store, and get me a bottle of Sloan's Liniment. One of my new mares has gone right lame in her foreleg. Never mind, I'll hop out myself. I want to see how Granny Koerber's asthma is to-day."

"Mother, won't that keep? How can you—*now!*"

"No, Stevey. My mare's limping. Those things don't keep."

"But, Mother . . ."

"Open your suitcase there under the seat, boy. There's something in it wrapped up in a green sweater. A bottle of something I want to make a present of it to Granny Koerber for her asthma."

---

garrulousness, for which we used to hold Henry to hilarious account, that he was the typical Schuyler. And so he was, embodying in his very babyishness the square, plodding quality of a small war-tank.

Chapter Eight

FOR the half-dozenth time, his mother, through the buzz of grown-up talk, had turned her rather breathless face upon him and pantomimed Davey to go to bed. By mouthing back violently and stretching his eyes and doing somewhat fearful grimaces with his mouth to indicate that he was the reverse of sleepy, it was possible to appease her from time to time.

The supper-table had long since been cleared, and the red-rep cover back in its place, and the silver bowl supported by the silver cherubs, in its center. There were seven apples in it. They shone under the swinging-lamp that had the buckeye dangling from it.

Henry was speaking. The faces about the table swam in light. Mathilda. The Old Gentleman. Bek. Winslow. Claire. Emma. Phil. Henriette Simpson, who never missed her Tuesday-night dinner with the family, and who was a sufficiently privileged old friend to "sit in."

The scene reminded Davey of something. Something too vague to capture. Flat on his stomach on the carpet-sofa in the corner, elbows propped and chin in palms, he regarded it, when he could keep his fascinated eyes away from the to-bed pantomime of Mathilda. Ah, he knew! It reminded him, that circle of conclave, of a picture torn from Redpath's Universal History, that hung in Henry's dusty little old office, up over Schlemmer's Hardware Store on High Street, "Signing of the Declaration of Independence." The solemn array. The women, by half-closing the eyes, could be made to look like men in wigs. Henriette Simpson looked like a horse.

But a nice horse. Such a kind, slender, solemn horse. A brown horse with a braided mane. But she, too, by squinting, could be brought to look wigged. Only the Old Gentleman spoiled the illusion. He was peeling an apple. You could never conceive of so much meticulousness crammed into the peeling of an apple. He held it poised between thumb and forefinger, as a sculptor might carve a hand holding a pearl in that position.

It was impossible, after the introduction of the peeling of that apple, not to keep the eye riveted. Even Mathilda left off her pantomime to watch it, and rose once, tiptoeing to a cupboard for a plate, which she slid under, and which the Old Gentleman kept shoving away. He was removing the peel, after his habit, in a single long curlicue. The thinnest possible ribbon. Gradually the eyes of the entire group, with the single exception of Claire, who kept her gaze fastened on the weaving motion of her needle over the round of a darning ball, became focused upon the intact unwinding of that apple-peel.

Henry was speaking. He had a solemn, monotonous voice and to David, even then, a wise, intoning voice.

"It is unfortunate that Father did not consult with me before calling you all together at this time. I have never been anything but settled in my mind about it. In fact, the party has already had my written refusal for twelve hours."

"Stuff," said Phil, watching the winding of the rind, and his purplish face pursed as he leaned forward across folded arms. "A man can change his mind. I can have Senator Burton on the telephone and that letter in the waste-basket in five minutes."

"You're talking nonsense, Phil."

"Why, any man they put up in your place will be a stuffed shirt! There is not another possibility in the state except you and Scott Baring, who's never going to get out of that French Lick sanatorium unless on a stretcher."

"That may be," said Henry, in his dry way, and strumming with his dry fingers, and his eyes on the slowly unwinding rind. "But my mind is made up."

"If it was me," said Emma, in that airy, cozy way of hers, tapping her darning-ball and holding a red-and-brown-checked sock off at arm's-length, "I'd take it, just to show those horrid old Democrats that this state has never really had a District Attorney before."

This remark was deemed worthy of nobody's rejoinder. Emma was seldom answered. Nor minded.

"Well," said Phil, who kept wanting to shout but after the first word or two restrained it and toned himself down, "if you ask me, and you don't, I'll say it's a dog-gone shame that the party comes into a Jim Crow town like Centralia to pick its man, does a Schuyler the honor to put him on the sure-fire ticket for District Attorney and . . ."

"You're right, Phil, I don't ask you. This is the kind of question a man has to decide between God and his own soul."

"Yes, but what the dickens can your soul and your God find in a proposition like this except honor?"

"Son, take not the name of the Lord, thy God, in vain."

"Excuse me, Mama, but, good Lord, look at the honor for himself and his family. It was enough turning down mayors' committees, trusteeships, school-board appointments, and pretty nearly every honor the town has to offer. But when it comes to a big state job like this— 'tain't fair to us!"

"Sorry you feel that way about it, Phil."

"I do. Mother and Father are entitled to a little something out of this game. I'm bringing up my little family to the best of my ability, struggling along to make good American citizens out of them. Bek's got standing and children. Claire. Emma. Davey's going to want the background of good, sound family-connections. No one person's got the right to deprive an entire family of honor. No, by God, not even ——"

"Phil!"

"*Gad* was what I said, Mother. Wish you'd try to remember that, Ma. No matter what I may happen to say—it's 'Gad' I mean—no siree! Father here comes to this country a poor boy. Not much more than an ordinary farm-hand. Mother here a girl that had never been out of her Tyrol village ——"

"Kufstein, son."

"Kufstein, mind you. Well, what do they do, these two? Practically not a penny to their names. Strangers on a strange shore."

"We were awful strange, son," said Mathilda, and placed the tip of her handkerchief to a reminiscent tear.

"Phil should set this lyric he is singing to 'Hearts and Flowers', Mother," said Henry, and slid one of his sly, wry winks to Henriette, who laid an admonishing forefinger against her lips.

"I think it's beautiful, Phil—I love to hear it over and over—the coming to America of our Mother and Father. I just think it beautiful," said Emma, leaning over her darning-ball, her soft, blue eyes filled with tears of melting dolly sweetness. "How was it, Mother, you and Father stood hand in hand when you got off the old coach at Centralia, all those years back? Tell it again. I love it. Father holding the carpetbag and your two precious quilts wrapped up in a huge sheet, and you clutching onto your great kerchief-bundle of clothing, with a pair of Father's brogans joined by string flung over your shoulder. What a cute, adorable greenhorn you must have looked. I can just see you!"

"Your father was down to his last twenty dollars, son. At Ellis Island they wouldn't let us ——"

"Yessir!" cried Phil, warming. "There's a picture for you. Scared out of their lives. Practically broke. What do they do? I'll tell you what! After managing to eke their way out here just because a fellow named Hans Stengle from their same little village was living hereabouts, what do they do? I'll tell you what ——"

"When Puppa and I arrived greenhorns, and first set foot in Centralia, son, I can tell you, except for some few kronen inside my bodice and ——"

"They come out here practically penniless and with their bare hands, and their courage, and their grit, they build up the name Schuyler to one of the most upstanding in the state. We're not what you'd call a moneyed family, but by Gad, we're as upstanding as they come. The name Schuyler has come to be in these parts synonymous with salt-of-the-earth. Those two little peasants that got off the coach here forty-odd years ago, have put their notch in what's called the backbone of this country. We're the backbone. You've got it in you, Henry, with your head on those shoulders of yours and your reputation for being a sort of Cincinnatus at the plow hereabouts, to make this here name Schuyler not only the salt of this here county, but salt of the earth the country over. I know I haven't always done all the fine things I set out to accomplish, due to no fault of mine. I'm part boob, but you're a big man, only you haven't got the sense to show it. No siree, you haven't got the right to deprive this family of adding inches to its stature. Why, man alive, men with no more brains to them than you've got have become President of these United States of America. Men with no more brains than you've got are sitting on

Supreme Court benches while I'm saying these words. Fellows holding big office and with twenty times your money, and running to you for advice on the laws of the world, aren't they?—No siree, you haven't got the right to deprive the Schuyler family of being as big as its biggest man! No siree!"

Here was Phil, with the little roll of fat above the rear of his collar, bulging and apoplectic with purpose, and his two fists striking against the table again and again, making the apples in the silver-cherub bowl rattle, and all eyes slowly swinging away from the unwinding of the Old Gentleman's perfect one-piece rind, to burn solemnly upon the speaker.

"Phil's right, there," said Bek in her square, even tones. "Leastwise, he's right until we hear what you have to say in rebuttal."

"Why, everybody knows Henry's one of the smartest lawyers in the state. He could be in big-league boots today if—if everything didn't always seem to seem funny to Henry, instead of worth wanting."

Curious how even the occasionally pithy remark of Emma's could go by unheeded.

"Hennery—it would be a fine honor for me and Puppa——"

"You hear now, how your Mother feels! It isn't often she asks what she wants, in so many words. She just sits and eats out her heart."

"Phil's right, Henry."

Here went Phil, soaring again: "Why, with your mind there's no telling how far you can go. You read a valedictory on this here town's high-school platform, when you were sixteen, ought to be printed and put in every boy's hand in this state today."

"Beautiful," said Emma. "I remember I cried. And to cry on a hot night like that meant something."

"You're one of the biggest authorities on international law in this country, only you go holler down a well about it."

"For God's sake, Phil—let up!"

"Hennery!"

"Sorry, Mother."

"Why, men from as far east as Pittsburgh and Washington have found their way to that little old dusty office of yours up over a hardware-store. What do you think it does for the rest of us having a man of authority in the family? Take the matter of a man's credit. Why, just take a man like me. The difference it would make to a man like me in a town like Springfield. Family-standing. Brother of Henry Schuyler. Yes, I'll say it right out. Selfish, maybe, but I'm honest, that's all. I'm not afraid a fact will bite me if I say it out. Yessir, I believe in calling a spade a spade, and a big one."

"Not much sense to calling it a steam-shovel, Phil."

"That's all right, Bek. I'm showing my hand a little bit plainer than the rest of you. Pull. Influence. Power. That's what it will give the family. Not asking anything of him except honor for himself, and, what's left of it, for us. Why, there's no telling how far—gives me the shivers, that's how far a fellow like him can go ——"

"Me, too . . . right down my spine," cried Emma, and did shudder a little quite cozily, between her shoulder blades.

"Know something? Well, if you don't, I'll tell you. Man named Bill Slade down in our town, newcomer from Indianapolis; nice fellow, quite a promoter from what I understand, and bringing some good capital behind him for a garbage-incinerator project he's backing, well, that fellow sat next to me at Business Men's Club lunch other day. One thing brought on another and finally, talking over the Republican state ticket, this fellow says to me, he says, 'You're not by any chance related to Henry Schuyler, down Centralia, are you?' 'No,' says I, 'excepting he happens to be my brother,' I says to him, just like that. Could have knocked that fellow over with a feather. 'Well sir,' he says, 'there's a fellow, they tell me, could have the biggest political plums in this state, if he'd a mind to. Why, I hear, if he wasn't such a queer duck for hiding behind a bushel-basket——why, sir, they tell me that brother of yours, with his slant on things and his reputation for having been the inside brains on everything from water-power to franchise in the state for the last ten years, why, sir,' Bill Slade says to me, 'why, sir, a fellow like that there brother of yours, proper handling, can go far. Why, sir,' Bill Slade says to me, he says, 'What this state needs is more brainy men like him with hindsight, and fore. A fellow indifferent enough to glory to be able to refuse to let his party tweak his nose and lead him. Why, sir, a fellow like that, proper handling, can go far!'"

"Go far!" said the Old Gentleman, on a sudden snort. "It does me a lot of good if I enter a horse in a race that's got it in his legs to win, only he won't leave the post."

The family laugh broke out on that, and Morton Milliken, entering in corduroys and hip-boots just in time to catch the drift, seated himself beside Emma and placed the large sprawl of his hand against her shoulder.

"What Henry needs is a little political catnip," he said with the sort of disinterested amiability characteristic of him.

"Yes," said Henry. "It's a great game, if you weaken . . . enough."

"Oh well," said Phil and pushed back his chair with a toss of his napkin toward the center of the table, which his mother caught up and neatly folded, "I don't see why I am the only one seems to be taking this thing seriously ——"

"No, no, son, we all ——"

"What say you, Henriette?" cried Phil, suddenly finding her out with his bulging eager eyes, where she sat quietly, a little out of the group around the table, her chair pushed a discreet few inches to the rear, as if to suggest that even though she was a privileged friend of the family, after all, even so close a friend must know her place. "Seems to me, if anybody is entitled to a say around here on this subject, it ought to be you! What say you to Henry's making little of everything big that comes his way?"

There was Phil for you! Every time! The family drew in a simultaneous breath of embarrassed dismay. Leave it to Phil to overstep. To go too far. The same bungling tongue that doubtless kept matting up his business affairs. The one wrong thing, here it came. The wrong thing that Phil could usually be trusted not to leave unsaid. Sooner or later he would not fail. The composite breath of the family was a pained and embarrassed one.

All except Henriette and Henry. Strangely enough the long, rather spinster-like face of Henriette was not unlike Henry's in its lantern-like contour. A face shaped somewhat like the sole of a foot, and that even in its twenties had had no particular youth or age to it. At this time Henriette's face was practically what it would be at forty-six, even to the coloring of the brightly brown bangs. Frizzed ones, worn unfashionably above handsome brows. There was about her, and remained even after she had ceased to teach, the odor of the fifth-grade schoolroom.*

Chalk-dust seemed to hang on Henriette's skin, making it pale and brittle. And chalk seemed forever against her finger-tips, which made her brush them together lightly of a dryness that had a tiny harsh sound to it. She wore a shirtwaist dress of dark-blue silk, with polka-dot collars and cuffs; and a round bag made of tiny steel beads hung from her belt after the fashion of the day.

Except for the fact that she fumbled at this chatelaine, there was nothing about Henriette to denote the flutter of heartbeat underneath the blue silk at this spot light of a remark thrown suddenly upon what might be regarded as her equivocal position of intimacy with the family.

"If Henriette Simpson and Henry Schuyler aren't engaged, they ought to be," was about as far as local insinuation could possibly stretch to the apparently impeccable friendship of these two.

To the wrongness of Phil's question, Henriette revealed an illuminating row of slim, beautifully white teeth.

---

* Possibly Henriette was plain in appearance. To know her was never to think one way or another about how she looked. It was what she looked. And what she looked was all the calm competence in the world. Henriette *was* calm competence. A woman with a rare gift of knowing how to bide her time. How frequently and with what success, in the turbulent, stirring years that were to fall our lot, she imbued members of our family with some of that secret of hers, I shall not take time to record. . . . Suffice it to say that what this powder-dry little lady taught us out of her innate culture of mind and spirit, her wisdom-before-the-event, and her incalculable power of patience, no Schuyler can ever repay.

"Seems to me, Phil," she said, "that Henry is a pretty fair master of his own soul."

"Staunch words, friend-ally," said Henry.

"Who am I to match my judgment against his?"

"That's what lots of us would like to know," growled Phil cryptically.

There was a long, stunned moment after that, nothing said, except that over the back of Henry's neck, so that he put up his hand as if to stem it, there rolled a flush.

To David, lying flat on his stomach, heels waving, and his bright, square gaze carefully averted from his mother's fluttering one, that rush of red across the back of his brother's neck was like the running-up of a flag. It was fascinating to have seen it happen. He bored with his bright gaze against the spot, waiting to see what next. When the red that did not belong there faded out, it was disappointing. It just blinked out. Like a light.

". . . No siree—neither Democrat or Republican——" Phil was saying to more stamping of fist—"no siree—neither Democrat or Republican——"

"Nor," said Bek.

"Henry," said Dave in a shrill voice that he threw into the group, "to be a Republicrun, does it mean to run the Republic?"

"Davey, go to bed!"

Henry had a peculiar kind of ingrowing laugh. Davey loved to watch it. From the carpet-sofa, he could see it begin. Had he been silly? Well, to be a Republicrun could mean to run the Republic. Henry's was sure to be a silent laugh, almost an imperceptible one, except for the heaving of the shoulders. There was something furtive about Henry's laughter. There was something about laughter that seemed to make Henry ashamed. He seldom, if ever, showed his teeth. Curiously, again, they were strangely like Henriette's in shape. Long. Only quite yellow and twice the size of hers. A clean old-ivory yellow. When he laughed, he kept his lips down carefully over them; and, as if from the effort, tears sprang into his eyes and the color dyed his face in splotches. It was altogether a sort of a contortion of a suppressed impulse. He laughed now until the tears in his eyes took form and began to roll, and he had to fumble for the rear trousers pocket of his nondescript gray suit and fish out the great square of cotton hand-kerchief which his mother ironed for him into the four large folds he liked.

It impressed the family to see Henry laugh. Because he laughed seldom. There was nothing about Davey's remark that had appealed to the risibilities of any of them. It had only happened to strike Henry's, probably tapping him of nervous strain to let it rumble out in laughter. Just the same, it was the signal for family-hilarity to mount.

"What's the joke?" said the Old Gentleman, who him-self loved to be the one to arouse family-risibilities and then pretend to feel aggrieved. "Here we sit! We've got a fine fifteen-hand trotting-horse, there's the finest pail of water in the state before him. He won't drink!"

"You can lead a horse to water," cried Emma, leaping brightly, "but you cannot . . ."

"Yes," said Morton, and patted her hand.

". . . but you cannot—make him drink," she concluded, on a soprano shriek, and not to be done out of her *bon mot*.

Henry cleared his throat, and with head lowered, set his piercing eyes upon the Old Gentleman's apple. The family knew precisely what the Old Gentleman was going to do about that now nude apple. He was going to plug it with his penknife as you would a watermelon, impale each segment upon its tip, and pop them, one by one, into his mouth, for short, audible mastications. The women hated the grinding sound he made, the men scarcely noticed.

"You're exactly right, Father," said Henry, strumming his fingers, and his eye unswerving upon the apple. "I'm not thirsty. You people make the mistake of reckoning without your host. Naturally enough, I suppose, under the circumstances. Except you, Bek. I should hardly expect this of you, after the number of times we have been over this sort of thing together."

"This is different, Henry. This is big stakes. Not just local chicken-feed."

"It isn't different. It is just another plan to project me into public life."

"Sooner or later, Henry, the world will find its way to your door."

"If what you say is true, Bek, then it must do just that. I am not the man to run out into the public marts to meet it."

"Man alive, who's sending you out into the public marts? You talk like Julius Cæsar or one of those guys in a toga. The party for which you've never turned a hand comes to your very door to seek you out."

" 'Know thyself' isn't just a copy-book line, Phil, that you used to write in Spencerian fifteen times after school. It's about the darnedest good advice was ever packed into two words. I'm onto myself sufficiently to realize that my greatest service to my family, my state, my country, does not lie in the public service of holding office."

"I'll be dog-goned if it don't look to me like your idea of your 'greatest service' is handing out free advice to everybody from a poor-white squatter who has had his hog poisoned, to a state commission which needs expert advice on a franchise situation. And a pin for your pains! That may be service all right, but its damned idiotic service. All that gives a diamond ring any value is the fact that there's a price-tag stuck on. Start giving them away, and see how long they keep their value."

"You're right, Phil. But hang it, for the life of me I can't seem as interested in intrinsic values."

"For the life of you," said the Old Gentleman, "is the best reason a man has got to be interested in values. In-trinsic—if it means what I think it means, is what you try to forget when you're trying to sell a fellow a bronze medal."

"Puppa!" bleated Mathilda.

"Pah!" said the Old Gentleman, dusting his hands free of apple. "Don't worry. I'm not joking, Mother. If Henry chooses to live and die a poor nobody, that's his own business."

"It's nothing of the sort, Father. It's the family's business, too."

"Well, I've never asked any help of my children and I hope to God I'll never have to."

"There's not one of us would fail you, Father," said pretty Emma.

"I know that. But all the same, I hope to God I never have to."

"There are men in life, Father, who belong on the captain's bridge, and there are men who direct the course of a ship, and there are men who build ships, and there are men who raise money to create ships. My job is in the engine-room of a ship. As Phil says, these matters we are discussing are not my own business alone. I have you to consider. But I know myself, Father. I can serve you well from the lower decks of this old boat we're bobbing along in, but not if you force me out of my greasy old overalls into brass buttons and try to proclaim me captain, when I have the heart of an engineer. I want to serve as passionately as you all want me to serve. But in my own way."

"What way is that? Hollering down a well? Hiding behind a bushel-basket? Back-door diplomacy?"

"Phil!" cried Henriette, as if she could endure no more—"You don't understand Henry—none of you—I mean—oh, I mean you can't tamper with the course of a river or the course of the sun—oh, I mean—what do I mean?" and sat back with her knuckles pressed against her lips as if to stem what further might come indiscreetly rushing to them.

"What Henriette means," said Henry, stepping in calmly, as if to build a wall of words between her and her flooding embarrassment, "is that my way is the way of a man, Phil, who knows the limits of his strength and the extent of his weaknesses."

"A man, when the big men of his state and even from Washington look him up in his little office in a small town, don't talk about his weaknesses."

"But, Father, therein lies my strength. I am a spectator. I stand by. I can develop wisdom only by attaining knowledge, and my kind of a brain can achieve knowledge by contemplating from the side-lines. I'm like that old fellow Cincinnatus, Father, in one respect anyhow. I think best behind my plow. And my plow is that little old yellow desk up over a hardware-store. It's the nature of the beast. Surely you must understand."

"I understand that no one with the brains you're supposed to have, would turn down the opportunity to put some of those brains to turning a wheel. I'm not saying the attorneyship in itself is the biggest plum in the world. It's what it can and will lead to. Power, man. That's what counts."

"That's Henry's whole point, Phil, and as usual, you've

gone elaborately out of your way to miss it. He's just finished saying that his power, he believes, lies behind the machine of state."

"That's it exactly, Bek."

"Pah, wouldn't give a nickel for that behind-the-throne stuff. I'd rather have been Marc Antony than Mark Hanna. Believe me, the up-and-coming man of today is the up-and-going one. Get into big business, or politics. Not only get your hand on the lever that controls the machine, but *be* the machine. Huh—if I had your chance ——"

"If ifs and ands," said Emma, and smiled at her brother—"were pots and pans ——"

"You want this town to furnish bond to secure factories and foundries, don't you, Henry?"

"Yes, Centralia's water-power warrants it."

"Good. You believe that the grade-crossing conditions in this town are a menace to public safety and should be radically dealt with! You believe that outside capital should be attracted into the state. You believe, according to an article of yours in some law magazine called *Civic Inventory,* that Elihu Perkins quoted at the Chamber of Commerce, up home last week, that towns under half a million population, Centralia for instance, should be run by about twelve members of a board of estimate and apportionment. Well and good! You believe, according to that article, that in making a budget, the civic organization must be the hub, bringing all the civic interests together like the spokes in a wheel. Mighty fine way you put it, "The spokes in a wheel." Well, you try just blowing off steam about it in a magazine article, and then being in a position to pull strings that can set some of those theories into practice, and see which gets you there quickest."

"I know, Phil. Every man who shares Blue Plate

luncheons with you at the Business Men's Club agrees with that."

"Bet your life they do, because they're the go-getters without your brains to go-get! Yessiree, you disbelieve in capital punishment, don't you? You say Prohibition is bound to come in this country, but you favor a light-wine-and-beer plank, but only one that the people themselves demand, don't you? You're watching that Hague show over there, aren't you? They come to you to get your opinion on the Johnston extradition-matter, don't they? You were the mainspring behind the Centralia municipal-bond issue for sewerage-extensions and additional fire-protection, weren't you? You believe that the Taft administration is in a position to do important things for the country, don't you? Well? Well? From up over your hardware-store, what wheel does it all turn? No wheel! You spend your brain-money like water, and the other fellow cashes in on it. Bah, that's not even good Americanism!"

"Phil," said Rebekka, regarding him with a slow, tired tolerance that made her eyes crinkle, "you're a fool. Perhaps it is Henry, of all of us, who is truly American. Show me a man in this town, in this county, in this state, with enough idealism in him to turn his face away from the marts of men, if he had the ability and the opportunity Henry has. Would you turn yours away?"

"No, by God. *Gad*, Mother. *Gad*, and I'm not ashamed to say so. Maybe Father might. Hanged if I know. With all his shrewdness, I've seen him do sky-larking things in business that you couldn't account for. He'd be a far richer man today except for those blind spots in his dealings, like staying out of the Fulton Market project that time, for fear of having a hand in damaging Milliken's residential property along Third Street when there was a garage already horning in.

That's what they call in the classics, tilting at windmills. Guess you know all about that deal, Morton?"

"I do seem to remember something about it."

"I never knew, Pap, up to a year ago, from old man Grokin in Springfield, that you went flat broke the year Bek was born, trying to save some low-down crook of a cattle-dealer, who had double-crossed you, from going to pen."

"Why, Father, did you really?" cried Emma, her mouth falling open in easy surprise.

"Sure he did. That's fine. That's great. But it was tilting at windmills. Didn't save the dirty little crook from dying in the pen, so Grokin told me, did it?"

"But I didn't put him there."

"Why, take Fulton Market today, what you bet, Morton, that your old man would think even better of Pap than he does, if Pap had jumped in and cleaned up on that deal."

"I've never discussed it with Father, Phil."

"Maybe Henry is a chip off the old block, eh, Pap?"

"Henry is chip off the old block, but the block is not me. It's the block of his own hard-headedness. I don't go into a deal that will shove meat-market business property next door to my friend's residential holdings, and ease my conscience telling it there's a garage already there; but I don't hesitate over the difference between doing something and getting the honor for it myself, or doing it and letting somebody else get the honor for it. If it was me in Henry's place, I would say to myself, you're a fool if you don't take all the honors they pile on you."

"Now you're shouting, Pap!"

"But if I was in Henry's place, and felt like he does about it, then I would tell the whole business of them to go straight to hell."

"Puppa! Davey, go to bed!"

"You're swell, Papa," said Rebekka, winking broadly, brazenly and with an open grimace toward Phil.

That seemed to startle the family plumage. Clara, sitting forward on the edge of her chair, with her china-blue eyes dots of exclamation, and Emma looking like a broody hen that had suddenly been startled off her nest.

"All right, have it your own way, Pap, only I say again, Father ought to be as rich a man today as there is in the county, instead of just bobbing along, middling well-off and putting up what he can lay hands on as collateral to help somebody else get by."

"That's the least, Phil."

"Easy enough, Henry, for a bachelor to look at matters this way, and regard money as only a secondary consideration. Guess if the truth is known, that's the answer to the mystery why you stay bachelor."

There was Phil again with his turtle-shot gesture of head toward Henriette! The family fingers curved inward, of instinct to throttle him.

"Yes siree, easy enough for a bachelor, but there's not a member of this family with his head high enough above water financially to see shore. We're a funny crowd thataway. I'm not here to talk about myself, but take me, for instance. You don't need me to tell you, Pap, that with capital in back of me, I'd be in a position to ride in on a land-boom in my town that would put it on the map."

"No, Phil, I don't need you to tell me you need money."

"There you go, always ready to dig the spurs into me. But look at yourself, Father. Generally acknowledged to shrewdest cattleman in the state, natural kind of smartness to you that can't be learned in schools—

what have you got to show for your years and years of
rising at dawn, trapesing through snow and sleet and
rain while other folks are asleep—what's it got you,
compared to what you ought to have?"

"I've got this much. I don't owe a penny that I can't
show land-collateral for. I've got a name as clean as a
whistle. I've got——"

"Of course you have, Father. That's just the point.
Here's as straight-dealing a family as there is. Father's
word as good as his bond. Misses-out making himself
a rich man in the Fulton Market deal, out of purely ethical consideration for a friend. . . ."

"That'll be about enough of that, Phil," drawled Morton; "nobody's contesting that point."

"Sorry, Mort. No reflections on your old man."

"It's not considerate, Phil," said Emma, and dotted
the back of her husband's hand with little pats from the
darning-ball. "Father's always been only too happy to
go Grandfather Milliken's collateral. Grandfather
Milliken would do as much for him."

"Mort knows his old man stands all to the good with
me. I'm just pointing out that Father's only well-off,
when he ought to be rich. Land-poor, when he ought
to be pocket full. Nothing personal in what I'm trying
to say."

"You are not so wrong there, son. Land sucks the
money up."

"Look at Bek. Best business man in this county."

"I'm just one of the Schuyler boys," said Bek, drily.

"That girl's working the best farm within a hundred-
mile radius. Runner-up to the Howey place itself. With
capital, she could make the Howey place look like a dime.
Capital. That's what she needs."

"Capital is right, but I'll compromise for the moment

on those eight Poland-China sows over at Pemberton's I'm trying to make him take my sixty-day note on."

"Well, be as funny as you like, pigs is pigs. I know the power of money. I know that if Morton here didn't have his inheritance from his grandmother tied up, he'd probably be building bridges instead of laying out the sewerage of the back streets of this town."

"We can't complain, Phil. Morton's doing well, and his father is paying off the house for us."

"Well, just the same, with the right kind of pull, he'd be in on the big plums."

"A fellow can't crash through the politics of this town."

"Exactly, Morton! What this family needs is the kind of political influence that gave the Whittier family the position it holds. You don't think Ephraim Howey would ever be where he is if Zach Whittier hadn't happened to be his father-in-law, do you? You don't think Ryan Whittier cleared a cool million on that Light and Power deal, do you, just because it fell into his lap? Every member of the Whittier family owes where and what he is to Zach Whittier. He went out for political power. He got political power. Long before Howey ever dreamed he could do more than polish the handles of the big front door of the gubernatorial mansion, Zach was throwing this and that municipal and state plum in his son-in-law's way, so that he couldn't get past without stumbling over them. That's how the Whittiers became what they are today in this state. Zach Whittier had talents, and he used them."

"That's exactly what I'm doing, Phil," said Henry, swinging his long, lean lantern of a face toward his brother. "Using my talents, such as they are, to their best advantage. God knows I wish it were in my power to elevate the family fortunes. But it isn't, Phil. I'm not the stuff of which rich men are made. It doesn't worry me, either, except when it worries you."

"I'm not saying it worries me . . ."

"You are, Phil," cried Bek. "You're saying it for all of us. Well, it doesn't worry me."

"Nor me."

"Me neither."

"It doesn't worry me neither, son, so much as the waste of the smartness. Your mother and I have no kick coming. I'm better on my feet today than any loafer I employ on the place. We've got a good administration in Taft. I see good crops and good times ahead, if not this year, maybe next. We've got our health. Our children, God forbid we should ever need it, we have around us in case of need. All we are asking now is honor. Honor is about to come to one of us. We want to honor back the country that took in two immigrants, all those years ago, by giving the best we got."

"And that's you!"

"We've got a little fellow growing up in this family, Henry. It would be fine if he should grow up in a family that has been honored. . . ."

"Davey, go to bed! I knew he'd fall asleep there!"

Bek leaned forward. "Father's hit the nail on the head there, Henry," she said softly, with her face carefully averted from the small, sleeping form on the carpet-couch. "Supposing he were to grow up into a great, successful family like the Whittiers or the Howeys. A family that has an Attorney General in it isn't to be sneezed at."

"Don't worry about Dave, Bek. I'll lay a red chip on him. There's quite a few little fellows have managed to grow up into a pretty fine manhood, in spite of a District Attorney in the family, too. Don't worry about Dave. Dave's all right."

Dave. Dave. Dave. The name kept flickering against his eyes, as he lay half-asleep round and warm, on the sofa, while the carpet-nap ground in against his cheek. He had been dreaming, ever so lightly, in between the little pecking admonitions of his mother and his own mouthings-back. His mouth ached a little from grimaces. The snatches of dreams had a to-be-continued quality to them, like the newspaper comic strips that he devoured from day to day. They were of Minute Men in knee-breeches, and three-cornered hats trimmed with pen-wipers.

Rub-a-dub-dub. There was a line of them, with short, white stiffish plaits of hair, like a sow's tail when you hold it out of kink, marching down an old street in one of the gray-looking pictures that hung in Henry's room. The Minute Men at Charlestown. The two foremost rows of them carried drums and short fifes. Poised against the drums were short sticks ready to r-r-r-rattle. Henry knew forty stories about them. "I'll lay a red chip on him." Now why did Henry want to lay a red chip on him? Tiddlywinks. There was an old set in the attic over at Dora Tarkington's.

The Minute Men in their three-cornered hats marching past an old state-house with columns down the front like Renchler's house—the Minute Men at Lexington . . . don't worry about Dave—Dave—Dave. The name kept flickering like a match before his consciousness. Who? Me? When he forced open his eyes finally, stretching his small body so that it rose in an arch off the sofa, there was the family of grown-ups, down among whose knees he lived, regarding him.

Chapter Nine

Warm gush of spring in spurts of living, bubbling mud up between his toes. Its ooze among the dog-violets and anemones flowed and tickled, and there was still hard stubble here and there that bit up into the soles of his feet and made him hop and screw up his face from the sting.

The soles of his feet, the first day of earliest spring that he went barefoot, were pink, tender things from shoes, heel and ball spanned by a thin strip of white arch that would tan soon enough, and toughen.

The sweet, flowing meadows seemed to rock a little of mud. It was like swimming, to run through the soft splash of grasses.

When Davey was only six, there was a five-o'clock chore expected of him three mornings a week. Carrying a pair of pails of sluggish looking cream over to Jessup's Mattie, who did the churning for the Schuylers, now that Trina's weight was rendering her more and more incapacitated every year.

Lean, agile, and wiry as a cat, and with an endurance that seemed to lodge somewhere in the steel wires of her nerves, butter simply would not gather under Mathilda's churning. Something gray and curdled coagulated instead under her eager, thin fingers.

As a girl in Austria, they had used to chant about her a farm-legend that translates something like this. "Maid whose butter will not churn, do not be downhearted. Unlucky at butter-making, lucky at love-making." *

---

* Curious thing about my Mother. Try as she would, butter

132

Sometimes the rod onto which the pails were hooked cut deeply into Davey's shoulders. Then it was not so easy to swim through the meadows. One plunged, instead, with short, high, stabbing steps, and the cream in the pails swirled and sometimes slopped out.

It was richly sweet milk, that the Old Gentleman had pulled in long even strokes from his Holsteins. Its sweetness was part of the grand, teasing smell of spring.

Usually Mattie, who was all soft bulge of flesh through gray calico, came out of the gray, shanty-colored house in the hollow behind the Cider Mill, and waved to him, with arms that were exactly the shape of the rows of hams that hung in the smokehouse at Bek's.

"Hurry—Dav-ee!"

Ugh! Whew! Mattie must not know how the ridges, where the pole across his shoulders dug in, were blazing, and that something heavy seemed hung onto his heart, making him so terribly short of breath.

There was always that blessed moment of heaving up the last lap of hill before the easy swoop of the descent into the hollow. Mattie lifting the rod out of the blazing ridges and depositing the pails upon a bench that stood against the rear of the shanty.

Mattie's cookies had a spice-taste that came out best when you minced them finely between the front teeth. There came a time for David when, minus two front teeth, those cookies bit up sharp as needles into the

---

would not churn for her. I can see her yet, standing on the flagstones outside the kitchen of our house on Sycamore Street, a plane tree throwing its mackerel shadows across her, and wielding the rod with all her might and main. The result was sure to be a fibroid, stringy mass. In later years, Mother developed a sensitiveness on this subject and sent the milk over in pails, which Davey lugged in on a rod across his shoulders, for Mattie to churn.

gums. But when the flavor came flowing over the pricks, that was a magnificent kind of alleviation.

There was always the smell to these every-other-mornings in the spring, of Mattie's bacon-cracklings sizzling on her range. Sometimes, after the cookies, there was a good tough piece of rind to chew on the way home. It had about the consistency of leather, but flavor that could be coaxed out every inch of the way, even if he took the long route, down past the hedges that skirted the Tarkington place.

Curious, the pungent tenacity of those days of his first years. Apricot haze that tasted and had a slow thickness of smell, like syrup. Bacon-cracklings. Warm, uddery smell of sweet milk. Winding of smoke off burning leaves that writhed like human hands in pain. There were the unforgettable smells. The leathery one of Henry's office, that was to persist through the years. The Old Gentleman's short reefers that smelled of fertilizer. Dora Tarkington's breath when she darted at him from the hedge, if he happened to take the longer road, and stuck out her tongue in a little flame of naughtiness. Dora's breath was exactly the smell of a calf's that had been chewing the yellow life out of a buttercup. Flower-sweet.

Dora's breath scented those days of those earliest years. There came a time when Davey never took any return-road except the longer one that led past the hedge that was apt to conceal her crouching little figure.

The Tarkington place had a red roof that shone through the battalion of maple trees and hedgerows that divided it from the Schuyler South Meadow. There was a new silo, too, with a red trim at the top, that remained pretty much in evidence from any two-mile radius.

Mornings, after the milk-lugging, to Dave's whistle between the "V" of two fingers, Dora Tarkington, who was sure to be playing around the gunnysack-wrapped feet of Old Nemo, a black gardener, would scuttle her plump little body through one particular spot in the hedge. Their opening. Dora's and Davey's opening. It wasn't much of an aperture, just a little dug-out, large enough to belly through.

Sometimes Dora, who started every day in a fresh blue-and-white apron edged in three bands of rick-rack tape, came through the aperture all smudged. That was the signal, even before they raced down the slope together, or started the morning sharply with a "Tag, you're it!" for them to stand scraping at the mud-clot together; nor was Dora above aiding with saliva.

Dora's old Mammy, who kept house for the widowed Tarkington, could be stern about mud-smudge on freshly clean aprons. Besides, Dora had a certain fastidiousness all her own. The dive through the hedge was one thing, but the damp, black earth clinging to her made her say "Ugh!"

Davey liked her to say "Ugh!" The pink cave of her mouth came open, all filled with the littlest teeth. One was missing now. In front. The front of Davey's own mouth was an excavation. Two fingers could pass through the gap.

"Last tag," though, was what set them into flame as if two matches had been struck.

"Last tag!" and off they were through the lush of meadows. Spring-lit mornings of tearing through dirt that smelled softly as it kicked up after them.

Dora Tarkington was a little terror. She sometimes seemed to go liltingly mad. "Last tag! Ba-a-a, you're it! Lickety, lickety-split—I'm a kitten having a fit! Meou! Dare you to catch me! Catch me if you can! Davey's mad, and I'm glad and I know what will please him. A bottle of wine to make him shine, and three little niggers to squeeze him."

"Don't say 'nigger,' Dora. Nemo'll hear. Nemo's got feelings same as you 'n' me." *

---

* In the light of the important rôle my brother was subsequently to play in the destinies of both the American Negro and the American Indian, it is not surprising that, all through his childhood, the boy had a most inordinate sympathy for the black man. In our small town, we had a colored population of about three hundred. Dave was known only to a few of them, and those the ones who occasionally worked about the place. I have seen him listen with a sort of pained quiescence to my Father's flash-in-the-pan outbursts of temper toward some one on the farm. But let it break against a black man, and for some reason, as if he could not endure further humiliation for the race, off he would rush to some self-inflicted chore, such as water-drawing or wood-chopping. Anything to shut out the sound and scene. Once, it must be recorded, when he was only five, he fairly flew at my father and banged him in the stomach for screaming his rage at a negro farm-hand who had overturned a five-gallon bucket of soft soap.

The two Chinese laundrymen in town used to interest him too. He was forever standing against their plate-glass windows, watching them sprinkle clothes by holding mouthfuls of water and spraying it out.

I think one of the finest passages in H. T. Wayne's preface to his three-volume work entitled *The Thirty-five Terrific Years After Roosevelt* is the one Winslow loved, and which I am sure I can write down by heart.

"It was as if the Negro race, once it found its legs, thanks to the divine intervention of a Lincoln, found those legs, figuratively speaking, to be as spavined, as rickety, and as bowed as the children of squalid negroes could be.

"It was left for David Schuyler to lead the American Negro out of the more or less dazed eighty years following his emancipation.

"The Schuyler Housing Bill, as applied to the Southern

That was the signal for Dora to scuttle all the way back through the hole in the hedge and throw her arms around the white cotton head of Nemo, bent low and slow over his task.

"Nemo's mine. Nemo's my old Nemo." That was pretty nearly true. Shaggy old Newfoundland dog was what Nemo amounted to in the affections of the child Dora. She rode him as if he were one, kicking her small heels into his tranquil flanks. "Giddy-app—you can't ride my Nemo—giddy-app!"

"Don't want to. Wouldn't. Get off. Get off, I say." Once David jerked her off so that she fell in a soft, little crab-like sprawl into a strawberry patch, her mouth opening to an outraged howl of wounded pride, and old Nemo floundering after David with a threatening gesture.

It hurt David for Dora to ride Nemo as if he were a pony. And his pain and his sympathy, as always, took the form of impelling him to action.

When Dora said "Nigger" in front of Nemo, or rode his delighted back and pummeled his flanks, when Davey did not knock her off or charge head-first and bump Nemo in the stomach so that she bounced off, he tore off homeward on scuttling legs to hack at wood in the shed, with an ax that was almost as tall as he was.*

States alone, stamps its author as one of the great social liberators of his time, to say nothing of the subsequent intellectual awakening of that race under the benign influence of his three administrations. The American Indian owes him territorial, civic, state and property rights that were to clutch him back from a precipice that overlooked the abyss of annihilation.

"'The Yellow Problem,' as handled in those three terms, will not bear elucidation here. The fourth and as yet unwritten volume of this group will treat of it exclusively."

*. . . except for the unique form of restraint Dave could exercise over his temper, I sometimes think he might have been subject to Father's kind of outbursts of passion. But David

It helped to hack wood after Dora had ridden Nemo as if he were a dumb beast. And Dora, who loved Nemo with a fierce inner ticking of her small heart, took wicked delight in seeming to beat him with her heels, which in reality slowed so by the time they reached Nemo's flanks, that part of his pretense at neighing was laughter from the tickling sensation.

Dora was a tease, all right. And such fun. "Catch me if you can! Whoop—double-dare me to jump clear across the creek without getting my feet wet?" She could stick out her stomach and blow out her cheeks and make herself into a fright. She could somersault without so much as showing more than the ruffled rim of her panties, clasping her hands about her knees, and then, in a little hoop of herself, over! Over! Over! And climb! Dora, who was plump and full of curves, and with the round bisque face of the doll that sat in a small toy rocker in the Tarkington dining-room, could shinny up a tree on her toes and her finger-ends, turning furiously if you gave her so much as a boost from her rounded little legs. Sometimes Dora spiked all of her honey-colored curls on the top of her head with a meat-skewer, and pulled an old stocking-cap down over her forehead. Then it was precisely like playing with a boy. You knocked her down without feeling the foolish crawl of curls across your hand. You shinnied up a tree after

---

literally worked off his rage. I have seen him run out of a room and chop wood or lug something heavy or go curry a horse when threat of anger began to rise in him.

In later life, he had a habit of abruptly leaving the room during a disagreeable conference. Usually, it was for nothing more than to gain control of a rising anger by pacing an adjoining room or indulging in a momentary and completely irrelevant task of stacking books or rearranging a desk, a power of restraint that was to stand him in good stead.

her, prodding her pedaling body unmercifully from the rear. Sometimes, when she wore the stocking cap, you forgot far enough to clench in a wrestling-match, one kicking, panting, struggling little body grinding down the other into the tickling, tender grasses.

Warm, sweet mornings. Davey and Dora seven and six, fleeting through them. Oh, but Dora was nice! There were usually cubes of brown gingerbread in the patch-pocket of her apron. Sometimes still deliciously warm. She let you bite, holding her finger, just so far. Sometimes you bit at the tip of her finger, and she squealed. A warm, delicious squeal that went through you like a corkscrew.

The sheep in lower South Meadow scarcely bounded, as the shouting, running, children darted through the dusky snow-bank of them. The feel of their undismayed, curly flanks gave Davey a warmth at the pit of him. He could swing himself off the ground between two of them by placing a hand on each of their backs. Dora had rather a frightening way of throwing her arms too tightly about the necks of the nibbling creatures, startling them so that they shied back like broncos, in an effort to throw her off.

It was almost the only time she made Davey remember she was a girl. A fellow didn't hug things thataway. "Aw, quit, Dora! You don't do that to sheep. They don't like it. Silly, you don't do that to sheep."

It was the sort of thing that women did. Like having one's face tilted back, by women, for a kiss from a grown-up. The back of Davey's hand was forever at streaking across his, wiping off Clara's and Trina's and Mathilda's kisses. Bek seldom kissed. She had a way of patting a shoulder, that made one feel a man, every inch. Imagine Henry kissing!

Oh, yes, there was something else Dora did that made

him remember fleetingly that she was a girl. Her way
with kittens. There were constantly-replenished litters
of them in the Tarkington and Schuyler barns. Dora
clasped them to her in violent, gleeful hugs that drew
small wails of misery.

Why, the way to handle a kitten, unless you were silly,
like a girl, was to lift it by the scruff of the neck. Silly
of Dora, gritting her teeth and squeezing thataway.

Dora herself was handled pretty much as she did the
kitten. Jerked toward. Squeezed. Pinched. Her
cheeks were so round and plump. The women were always pinching at them. The pinching, gritting women.
Why? And the Old Gentleman used to poke his finger
against the round little ball of her stomach and make a
skewering noise along the side of his mouth.

Frequently, these mornings of Davey having delivered
the milk, Dora turned a continuous string of somersaults
down the slope of the lower South Meadow. David
after. Usually they wound up in a heap at the salt-rock,
staring at each other breathless and disheveled. Then
suddenly, and by some hidden secret signal, up simultaneously, quick, staccato. Last tag! And off again.

Sometimes, by the time they reached the Schuyler
summer-kitchen, Mathilda, at her baking, had already
three pans of fluffy bread, which she painted by dipping
a camel's-hair brush into a teacup of water, making the
loaves sleek and varnished-looking as violins. Usually
there was a coffee-ring, sprinkled with cinnamon and
sugar, and a crescent-shaped bun of the sort the Old
Gentleman loved to "dunk" all steaming and smelling on
the table. The cinnamon, and the sour, hot smell of
dough, cut into the very grooves of the mouth, causing
saliva to flow. Break that crescent in two, and its hot
breath made little fountains of the pores of your mouth.

From the leavings of the dough, were two cookie-cakes

sprawling in a pie-pan. A hunky little girl, with the spread arms of a semaphore, and currents for eyes and a current for a nose, and a mouth done by pricking it with a fork.

Dora, whose little incisors were as white and as sharp and as greedy as a mouse's, beheaded her girl-cookie with a snip. Sometimes Davey, with little more than surreptitious rubs of his tongue over it, carried his boy around in his pocket all day, bringing him out at bedtime a crumby mass, and then trying to put him together like a picture-puzzle.

Long, sweet, innocent days, when Dora was barely turned six and Davey was seven.

Chapter Ten

For sixteen years Henriette Simpson and Henry Schuyler, as the saying is, had been "going together."

They had graduated together from the Tallahassee High School, Class of '91. A framed photograph of that class of nine girls and three boys, with the brick wall of the school-building for background, hung in Henriette's front hall.

Henriette herself, a long-necked, frail-necked girl, supporting a weight of pompadour which she seemed to balance as if it were a vessel of water, while around her feet swirled train, and against her breast beat a gold watch hanging from a gold fleur-de-lis pin. Held firmly upright against her lap, a framed placard bore in admonitive script the class-motto, "Animus. Fides. Successus." Eight more sweet-girl graduates flanked her on each side, interlarded with the three generous-wristed male members of the Class of '91. They were a necky group, Henry's characteristics of more-than-considerable of neck gangling above tall collar and stand-offish ears, holding for all of them. Henry's hair, which at that time gave no sign of the premature horseshoe of baldness which was to beset him, was clamped in straight bangs across his brow. An enormously sober young man with a lantern jaw.

Henry and Henriette used to laugh over that picture. Only six out of the class, what with deaths and removals, were still living in Centralia.

May Kinealy, the third girl from the left, with the yellow Della Fox curl oozing from the center of her pompadour, had married Phil Koerber, the son of Cen-

tralia's most prosperous grocer. The Koerbers had
grown rich. Koerber's Corner, where canned goods
were piled in bins on the sidewalk and sold at slashed
prices, was one of the thriving ones in town. May, who
was fat now, and whose Della Fox curl had straightened
from an interrogation-point into an exclamation-point at
what she had become, had nine children. She still did
her own work, however, and her own green-marketing
at the farmers' wagons, which gathered around Court
House Square on three mornings a week, cramming
purchases into two oilcloth shopping-bags, which bulged
from beet, celery and carrot-tops.

Tom Powers, the exceedingly narrow boy, wedged in
between Bleema Deifenbach and Ella Tarl, had married
Hanna Quick, first girl on the left, and, at thirty, held
what was to be a lifetime position as foundry-foreman
with the Giles Tool Works, at a salary never to exceed
twenty-four hundred a year.

Ella Tarl, the class beauty, with the small heart-shaped
face hanging from her pompadour like a bangle, had
died in a shameful childbirth, and the shooting and maim-
ing of Judge Sloan's son Tod by Ella's brother, who was
acquitted, was one of Centralia's sensations of the decade.

From their first year in High, Henry and Henriette
had paired off. That is, when there was occasion for it.
Class functions, especially the senior year when Henry
was class president and Henriette sergeant-at-arms. In
the debating-society when teams were formed. Com-
mencement hay-ride. The senior week-end excursion to
the Etruscan Pottery Works and the Art Museum.

In the subsequent years that Henriette had been teaching fifth-grade, and Henry plodding his slow and
thoughtful way into his curious sort of muted eminence,
that friendship had ripened; indeed, there were those
in Centralia who would have said, over-ripened—into

one of those cases of courtship that never seem to come
to anything.

" 'Twan't nice."

"Henry hadn't ought to."

"Of course, just as abiding a pair of young folks as
there is in town, but Henriette ought to have more
pride."

"Well, it might be abiding, so far's anyone could tell,
but why didn't Henry marry her or leave off keeping
company?"

"All those years.　'Twan't nice!"

"Surprised the Old Gentleman would stand for such
doings."

"Now that Henriette was orphaned, too. . . ."

"A nice pair."

Centralia had its solutions.　A streak of hypothetical
and absolutely untraceable insanity that might lurk somewhere in the ostensibly nice, clean stock of Beebe Simpson and his wife, who had moved West from Edelweiss,
Maine, years before.　Then there was the old wives'
hypothetical legend of some streak of frigidity that might
lurk in Henriette.　Those high-shouldered, lean-necked
girls.　No telling!　Or was it due to Henry's just out-
and-out failure to live up to his responsibilities of so
long a courtship.　Could that be?　Henry, as fine a son
to his family as ever breathed the county air!

For twelve years, at least, public opinion had wagged
over this protracted courtship.　The idea!　High time!
Here they were, Henry thirty-eight now, and Henriette
possibly a month or two the older.　Not that it mattered,
where the difference was so little!　For at least ten years
of Friday nights, long before her parents had died and
left her alone in the little, frame, two-family house on
Primer Street, sure as fate, Henry had suppered at the
Simpsons'.　Every Saturday for at least the past eight

years of her life, Henriette had lunched with Henry at the Blue Bird Lunch Room on High Street.

For those same eight years, Henriette had partaken of Tuesday suppers, Christmas, Thanksgiving, and birthday dinners at the House on Sycamore Street. The summer that Bek Schuyler stumped the state for Ephraim Howey, Henriette, who usually took summer-courses at State University, had accompanied her instead, distributing campaign literature during meetings.

"High time," was the popular phraseology about it to everyone except those most immediately concerned. "High time" that they did something about it or quit. If they aren't married, they ought to be! Oh, not that I mean it in that sense. Only, it isn't fair to the girl. Henriette's no spring chicken. Not fair to keep away others, if he hasn't intentions. Surprised the Old Gentleman would countenance it. High time. . . .

Fact of the matter was, Henry was not insensible to "high time." At intervals of never less than a twelve-month, he was wont to open up this extremely delicate and periodic discussion with Henriette. Usually at the Blue Bird, where the privacy seemed less concentrated, than in Henriette's own little front parlor, where two equidistant parental Simpsons, in crayon, looked down and bated one's breathing.

Almost invariably at the Blue Bird, while Henriette broke up bread crumbs and squeezed them into dark-gray pellets, they discussed it. The Blue Bird was an ordinary room on a level with the sidewalk. There were two plate-glass windows that looked out on High Street, brown jardinières of artificial and fly-specked nasturtiums in each of them posed before lace curtains that were draped to shield the diners from the gaze of the passer-by.

Pasted against each of the plate-glass windows was

the day's menu. Hektographed. Twelve square tables, each large enough to seat four, formed three aisles.

Since the opening of the White Kitchen, one block down, there were those who contended that the old Blue Bird had deteriorated, to say nothing of the inroads by the Business Men's Noonday Clubs. But all the old group from the Renchler Business Block still lunched there, the Giles brothers of the Tool Works and old Judge Wale, who brought most of his provender in a tin box from home and washed it down with hot coffee.

Henry and Henriette's accustomed table was under a ceiling fan toward the rear.

Every Saturday, Henriette, who usually came directly from teachers' meeting, arrived at five minutes to twelve, and did the ordering before Henry arrived.

Mock-turtle soup for herself; the Blue Bird Noonday specialty, *lamb with mint-sauce and mashed potatoes,* and a dessert also very special to the Blue Bird, known as "Berry Swim," a concoction of noodles with stewed berries (in season) dumped over.

Henry's lunch never varied, either. Poached eggs (eyes closed, please). Stewed corn. Glass of buttermilk (not too cold, please). Bowl of rice, for dessert, to be covered with cinnamon and cream (don't forget his cinnamon, please).

They were, at their respective thirty-eights, a neat pair. Henriette in her tweed suit with fur tippet, or, in season, foulard, that she never wore in schoolroom, sprigged over with a small, coral, berry-and-leaf design. Henry in his gray sack suit of herring-bone pattern that he was never known to vary.*

---

* . . . there was something enormously stable and implacable about my brother Henry, that dates back in my memory even to his first long trousers when he was in High School.

If anything, the years had improved the angular Henriette of the Class of '91 photograph. Her brown hair, graying now, was worn low enough to cover much of the high, narrow brow that the pompadour had flared to reveal. The current fashion of draped clothing concealed a certain spareness of figure. Henriette's good eyes, golden, kind eyes, were capable of all sorts of humorous twinkles behind their pince-nez. The pince-nez, even though they dug in cruelly to the sides of her nose, far from detracting, gave importance to Henriette's face. They shone like a pair of brilliant wings.

As is common enough among girls of her narrow-chested kind of youth, it could be said of Henriette that out of a girlhood filled with the agony of her awareness of her lack of so-called physical charms, in her thirties, a saving sense of humor had sprung full-grown to her rescue.

At thirty-four, Henriette, in her under-bodice, before her mirror, could smile and try to powder out the knobs of bones at the front of her neck, where at twenty-four

---

In spite of the dry cackle of his humor, my memory does not take me back to the time when a gray kind of reserve did not seem to powder over his entire personality. How we used to tease him about his suits! Jevey, our tailor up in the Renchler Block, used to buy the gray, herring-bone cloth by the bolt and put it away for Henry's annual encroachments. Long after Jevey had died and his son, Big Jevey, had rejuvenated the business by catering to the campus-cut of the younger generation, that herring-gray bolt continued to lie on the shelf at my brother's beck and call. I never remember seeing him in a day-suit of any other cloth, color, or design. These suits, made in Centralia, were delivered to him, whatever his whereabouts, arriving by express in a long, brown box, marked JEVEY, OF HIGH STREET.

she had stood and watched herself cry secret tears that coursed down her cheeks and splashed onto these bones.

After the first frightened months of pulling each gray hair out as it appeared, there was the solace of realizing that as they thickened and whitened beyond her control, they softened her face and became her.

The children of her schoolmates, as they appeared from time to time in her classes, had for years been the source of her secret, gnawing pain. May Koerber's ('91) two tow-heads might have been hers, but for accident of—of—everything. Little Jean Powers, child of Tom Powers ('91). Children to whose generation of mothers and fathers she belonged. By right! By right of—of—well, by the same right as the May Koerbers and the Tom Powers. The right of the secret places of her heart.

There had been years when carking yearnings lodged in Henriette.

Those particular years of the race were over now. And, with them, a letting-down. The fingers of the children to whose generation of parents she belonged no longer stabbed her with secret sense of frustration. There was something dry and brittle and no little efficient about Henriette now. Beside her, the May Koerbers looked and felt a little over-blown.

Henriette hadn't let herself go. She attended summer sessions at State University, Morning Choral Society at Middleton, and, one summer, had taken a course in domestic science and English literature at Northwestern University. And why not, with no home ties to bind her? It was well known that Henry Schuyler considered her brainy and for years Henriette's papers at the Saturday Morning Club annual had been outstanding. One had even found its way into print.

Some said they were written for her by Henry Schuyler. Be that as it may. . . .*

The week that Henry's proposed candidacy for District Attorney was being noised about, they met at the Blue Bird, come Saturday, in just the fashion they had been meeting there for the years of Saturdays. Henriette, in brown foulard and a mink tippet with a head that bit into its tail, already at table, and a heavy girl, named Katy, who had served them for all the years, spreading the unvarying meal.

Her orange pekoe tea, strong, the way she liked it, steamed up into Henriette's face, softening the rather angular manner it had of thrusting itself into the light of a High Street midday.

"Are your eggs done enough, Henry?" For these years and years of Saturday noons, Henriette had asked that question. She was an excellent theoretic cook herself, and conducted a domestic-science class in the High School physics-laboratory every Wednesday evening. It was said of her that while she could direct the baking of a perfect cake, her own were apt to fall, sadly. And that whereas a pupil of Henriette's could serve you up with an excellent meal, Henriette's own meals were nothing to brag about.†

---

* . . . and the storm of innuendo it brought down on poor Henriette's head from a local literary circle when she was invited to repeat her paper entitled "Whose Mexico?" before the State Federation! Of course, Henry helped her write it, and Henriette was the first to admit her source. How, I ask to know, could Henriette, with all her nice, bright mind, have been expected to contribute the peculiarly thoughtful and delightfully satirical quality to that paper, which, by the way, was later published in *Reedy's Mirror*.

† . . . funny, but something our town was never to understand about Henriette was the disparity between her own

These solicitous little questionings of Henriette about his eggs, his cinnamon, the desired coolness of his buttermilk, the rightness of his stewed corn, apparently pleased Henry, although he never replied to them, shaking a bit of salt into his palm, mashing his poached eggs down into their toast, and drinking the buttermilk at one sustained tilting of the glass, even while she queried it.

"Here's that Taine's *Origin of Contemporary France* I was telling you about last week, Henriette. Thought you might be interested in reading it."

"That's mighty thoughtful of you, Henry."

"Don't block-read it, Henriette. There may be some of it makes pretty hard sledding, but if you'll read it slowly, you'll be well repaid. I tell you, that fellow had the right idea. Revolution, he points out, didn't destroy absolutism and set up liberty, anything of the sort. France was already a centralized country before 1789, and grew more so from Louis XIV onward. The Revolution merely gave it new form. Don't mean to say I agree with more than two-thirds, but I'd like you to read that book, carefully—there's food for thought in his point of view. . . ."

Years of Henry's intellectual fodder, carefully predi-

---

rather mediocre cookery and her ability to instruct others in domestic science, after she had taken work along those lines at Northwestern University. I myself used patiently to hold forth the example of Miss Lee, our town's music-teacher, who could teach our youngsters to play a Chopin Etude to the note, but was never heard to perform herself. It didn't help, though. In the mind of Centralia, there was something irreconcilable in the paradox of Henriette as a domestic-science teacher and Henriette's own rather dismal culinary efforts. Henriette's brown raisin-bread, for instance, was atrocious. So soggy! Her recipe for making it, on the other hand, won my raisin-bread first-mention at every food-show I entered a batch.

gested by him for her, had strengthened Henriette's powers of assimilation. She owned, quite frankly, that it was a privilege to be dominated by another mind, if that mind was of incalculably better caliber. Therefore she seldom dipped into a book, since he almost entirely prescribed her reading, without the crutch of Henry's preconceived opinion to help her toward his conclusions.

"I wrote down and pasted in the back of my attendance book, Henry, something you quoted me from Taine once. 'Every man and every book can be summed up in three pages and those three pages can be summed up in three lines.'"

"That's me, I reckon, and all this hubbub about the attorney-generalship. If there's any special job that I'm cut out for at all, it's not to be out in the ring, acting out the three pages. I'm the fellow on the side lines, who sums it all up in three lines."

A kind of light came into Henriette's long, lean oblong of a face. A pinkness across the bony mold of it.

With no other person in the world, except his sister Bek, would Henry voluntarily have opened up this subject. Henriette knew that. Something clutched at her, a little excitingly.

"You know best, of course, Henry. Of course, it isn't given to many, Henry, to refuse honors like that—one after another—alderman—assemblyman—mayor—and now this! Why, there's no telling . . ."

Henriette's voice slipped a little, causing her to clutch with an angular hand at her angular throat. It was seldom, indeed if ever, in all the years of their methodical allotment of so many hours a week together, that Henriette ever let slip an emotion. She caught herself up by the slow, measured manner which followed.

"I mean, Henry, you have already refused more honor than comes to most men in a lifetime."

There was something particularly pathetic about her half-illumined face, as if she dared not let the light come, and it was Henry's turn, stung by a consciousness of what she withheld, to make his conscientiously periodic observation.

"I've refused the greatest honor of all, Henriette."

"I didn't mean that, Henry, and you know it," she said without the artifice of pretending not to understand, and colored a wintry, russet sort of not unbecoming red.

"That is what makes it hard, Henriette. You are above meaning that which makes the situation difficult and no less true."

The subject was one which always induced a rush of blood against Henriette's heart. She could scarcely breathe. There were head noises. Secret, raging tragedy of her sparse years beat in blood against her heart. Under it all, she invariably succeeded in speaking in slow, measured tones.

"We understand each other, Henry."

"I could never forgive myself if I for a moment thought otherwise, Henriette."

How solid he was. How stolid. Sometimes, as she cried secretly while she lay in bed nights, that stolidity was almost a presence in the room.

"You have nothing to forgive yourself for, Henry."

"Maybe not, Henriette. You can't blame a man who knows the fruits on the tree are luscious, and yet, by some devilish inhibition, cannot raise his arm to pluck them. He is the loser."

"Nonsense. Life is like that. You've every reason in the world to be in love with me, except you aren't! Now!"

There was an air of surprise to Henriette, as if from what she had just heard her lips utter.

"No, Henriette ——"

"All right then, except you aren't *enough* in love with me. No, Henry, you have nothing to forgive yourself for. Except perhaps making life a pretty wonderful affair for me, with you to throw the light of your mind upon the world I live in. Think of the narrow, groping affair it might be for an old maid in a one-horse town. What would I be without this friendship, Henry?"

There was something of a cry in that question. The cry of a spinster's dread of her loneliness.

"That is the question which sometimes torments me, Henriette. You have let the years pass by, when except for me, you might have been married by now and settled down to a home and children and the sort of life to which a normal, wholesome woman like yourself is entitled."

"No, Henry, we have been over that hypothetical ground often enough for you to realize that in all probability things would not have been different."

"Not even if no such person as me existed?"

"That, of course, is impossible to answer. But the fact remains that I am satisfied, Henry. In a way, quite happy. In any event, completely understanding."

"I wish I were that—Henriette, about myself. Where you are concerned."

"It needn't trouble you, Henry. Ice-cream may be a nourishing and even a delicious food, and yet there are those who do not like it. There is not the slightest reason, merely because we have been friends all these years, for you to feel the responsibility of falling in love with me. Even granting, for the sake of our mutual amusement, that my friendship with you has kept off swarms of suitors, don't fool yourself, Henry. My destiny in this town would have been just what it is, except without my friendship with you. And without it, I would be just one more old maid headed for the pension-list of our public-school system. I know what contact with a mind like yours has done for me. I'm the best appraiser of my own assets and liabilities."

"You're a thousand times too good for me, Henriette. I'm a fool."

"If that explanation appeases you more successfully than any other, we'll let it go at that. What's our programme for the afternoon, Henry?"

"Thought we might drive out by the House on Sycamore Street and pick up Dave. Well, sir, funny thing about that youngster. Never saw the like, the way his mind runs to pretty nearly everything you put up to it. Napoleon, The Three Bears, sheep-breeding, and Gunga Din seem to interest him about alike. Got him all het-up now about his tiger-moth and its color-reaction to temperature."

"I know it. I overheard him telling the Igrotte children about it last week when I took those Mason jars over to your mother. They didn't know what he was talking about."

"Speaking of natural history, other night, sitting smoking up in my room in the dark, along the time, I guess, when any well-meaning citizen should have been abed, thinks I to myself, is that something moving out there along South Meadow? Coyote? Dog? Stray sheep? Man? Turns out to be Dave, sneaking all the way from his sister Bek's, where he was spending the night, to feed a sick lamb down in the kitchen, which, I figured out, he must have forgotten about. As a matter of fact, I had tended the little thing myself before going upstairs, and Trina had minded him too—but for a mite of a kid trudging all that way, dead o' night—right queer, now wasn't it?"

"He was telling me about the ant-hill you've made for him, his little old hiccoughy voice just heaving away and trying to explain their habits."

"I think Dave ought to have a good hound-dog. There's a fellow called Sweeney out along Pikes Road, breeds them."

"Yes, I've had both the Sweeney youngsters in class. Ragged lot."

"Thought we'd pick up the boy and take him out there and let him pick a puppy. Nothing like a good hound-dog to teach a fellow the decencies. A dog's got about all of them—honor, loyalty, courage. Thought we'd take a ride out along Pikes Road to Sweeney's, if it's all the same to you?"

Henriette bit her tippet's mouth into its tail, and rose from the table with a little backward kick of her long, full skirts.

"It will be the same to me, Henry, wherever we go—together."

Chapter Eleven

THE hound-pup was named Teddy. David called him that because, when he came loping out of the Sweeney kennel toward them, his lips tilted back in a flash of white teeth.

Teddy! Everything somehow tied up to the image that name made against the brain. Mark Milliken's old slouch hat on a hall table when he came over for long-closeted interviews with the Old Gentleman. Dora Tarkington's father's ruddiness of complexion. The huge pair of eye-glasses in the optician's window on High Street. The stuffed grouse on the oval plaque in Clara's dining room. The drum Emma had sent him at Christmas. T-t-t-ted-d-d-d-dy! You learned to roll your sticks to that rhythm. T-t-t-ted-d-d-d-dy!

And now the little old hounddog flashing across the Sweeney kennel yard. Showing his teeth. Batting his absurdly heavy paws by jumping up as high as Davey's chest, his tongue dripping-wet, hanging out of the side of his mouth like a rag. If you were the sort of person who likes the trusting leap of a dog, it made you catch your breath, sort of. It did something more. It hurt a little somehow. Not exactly hurt—exactly, but—but kind of. It made you bat back a little too roughly. "Get away—you! Hey—get away, you!"

From that moment, however, Teddy was Dave's, from his dripping-wet tongue to the wag of his tail. A funny old tail, shaped like a beckoning finger, and tipped with white. A curious mixture of Chesapeake retriever and spaniel, this fellow. Squat, long, low, short-haired, brown body, with rag ears and a sniffing, burrowing face.

A vociferous pup with an expression that yearned excitedly and an unquenchable eagerness that kept him wagging from the middle of his broad, low back to the tip-end of his tail.

The last of six, and Henry and Henriette were for holding off for the yield of a next litter. Strictly speaking, there were points to be desired in Teddy.

But too late. Dave and Teddy had already clapped eyes on each other.

It was a job, that night, in the face of admonitive orders from his mother to house Teddy in the cellar, to secretly lug him up to his room by way of the summer-kitchen, water-spout, and to bed with him.

Then, at midnight, didn't Teddy begin to dig with his forepaws into the matting and yap so for the accustomed luxury of his straw bed at Sweeney's kennel, that, finally, nothing would quiet him but to permit him to sit squat on Dave's chest and doze off there.

For eleven years, except for scarlatina when David was nine, these two were never to fail to sleep together.*

---

* When Dave's dog Teddy fell through a trap-door in the upper reaches of the Igrotte barn, where Dave had a secret reading-retreat in the hayloft, and landing on the upright prongs of a hay-fork, had to be chloroformed out of his misery, I think I have never seen so sick and blasted a face as my brother wore for weeks after. Some of that look was to remain. Not in expression so much as in the dawn of that later David to whom all pain was to be something as close to his own capacity for suffering as the nerves in his own body. My brother Henry had the dog's body stuffed by a taxidermist in Cleveland, Ohio. I confess that at first I questioned both the taste and the wisdom of this, until I saw the curiously comforting effect it seemed to have on the boy. Strange thing, but after the death of Teddy, I never heard my brother refer to him in any way, nor did he ever accept another pet, although

dozens of them were offered and indeed sent to him, from the beginnings of his public life.

The stuffed Teddy, however, has always stood in every one of my brother's offices, an unused pen-wiper dangling from his neck, as if to ward off the onus of any implication of sentimentality.

Chapter Twelve

THE summer that Dave was seven was one of a drought; added climax of a late frost, and an absolutely unprecedented scourge of caterpillars had done for several acres of the Old Gentleman's cabbages.

It was a crop that the old man by unusual arrangement had sold two weeks before the first seed of it was sown, on a several-hundred-dollar advance, to a commission company to whom his word was his bond.

It meant not only the loss of the crop, but the doling back, with interest, of the advance payment. In the end it was Bek who managed two hundred of the three hundred refund, Mark Milliken's failure to meet a certain large note squeezing the Old Gentleman pretty terribly on cash. Then the forfeiture of the additional six hundred expectancy on that same crop put a crimp, so to speak, in the entire summer, so far as ready cash was concerned. Not that there was any crisis, it simply meant the old land-anomaly of all outgo and no income. Acres of potential values, but for one reason or another, without yield enough to pay their taxes.

It meant, with Mark Milliken's and the Old Gentleman's reciprocal habit of calling upon each other for loans of cash and land-collateral, that cash was pretty usually at low ebb. Often, indeed, for the Schuylers, at least, it meant an old story of fending off the little crisis of having to sell a parcel of land. The land-acquisitive Schuylers! They came by it honestly. In the Austrian Tyrol, generations of Schuylers had somehow managed to own an acre, even if the only other property-holding was a sow. Mathilda's great-grandfather had owned an acre which was so meticulously tilled that it resembled a colored geometric drawing. That acre had passed immaculately from father to son. Mathilda Schuyler's hands were still horny with her girlhood part in coaxing and tilling it.

The Old Gentleman's battered safe, in one corner of the dining-room, and the drawers of his still-more-battered old desk beside it, and the stacks of deeds and notes, current and canceled, bore documentary evidence of the years and vitality that had been dedicated to trying to make real estate real, in terms of yield.

Bek's love of land was ingrained. So was Phil's. Twice in five years the family's cash resources, scant beyond credulity, had been rallied around Phil's love-of-land ventures, which ultimately were to make local history.*

---

* . . . I suppose it can be said that the years of our childhood (years that of course excluded Davey) were Father's palmy years. If, with our proverbial family-capacity for land-poverty, there were times when Father felt actual pinch for ready money, we children knew nothing of it. Excepting Davey, everyone of us was given the full advantage of a grade and a High School education, to say nothing of Henry, who took his Law and Bachelor of Arts degrees at State University.

Phil was probably the most energetic of us all. Restless, ambitious, impulsive in a dangerous way, up to his fortieth year, he was a source of constant anxiety to my father, who had scant patience with his daring land-ventures, and who came to his assistance only after terrific flares of temper.

At this writing, and while my dear brother lies desperately ill at his country home thirty miles out of Springfield, I suppose he ranks as one of the richest men of the state. I actually remember the day that dear Phil's tide turned, so to speak. The day that my Stevey, with one hundred dollars in his pocket, closeted his Uncle Phil, who happened to be in Cen-

This summer of fright, threat of hoof-and-mouth disease, and general money-tightness, Davey, to save an
extra hand's wage, was put to tending the South Pasture
flocks during school vacation.

Long, slow, sun-drenched days, that vacation after his
first year in public school, with the earth rippling under
him as he lay flat against it until he could seem to feel it
pushing softly, like a breathing flank. Days that moved
so slowly from the east where they arrived pinkly, to the
west where they departed redly, that they seemed to
stand stock-still for hours during their middle, pouring
into him their warmth, their hot lush smells. They had a
taste, too, all their own, these motionless days.

Sometimes, when he rolled over on his stomach away
from the light, as it became unendurably strong, and
all of him seemed gathering the heat like a disk, the taste
of the earth came crawling into his mouth.

The taste of the land rolling, billowing, and riding him
along like a petal upon its current. The toes bit in. The
nostrils breathed in. The body of the boy wiggled down
—wiggled in—close to turf and earth.

At twelve o'clock, Trina, who wore a sunbonnet with
a starched visor that buttoned on, came down to South
Meadow with a tin pail of lunch. Good, square chunks
of his mother's bread, smeared with apple-butter. Strips
of bacon and sometimes strips of the rind itself, tough
enough to be chewed the afternoon through for the last
squeeze of flavor.

The tussle with Teddy, as he bounded up from keeping tidy the edges of the flock, to fasten his teeth into

tralia on the difficult matter of borrowing twenty-five hundred
dollars from the bank, and put up to him a proposition for a
landing-field and hangar that had to do with an aëromail
parcel-post-delivery scheme. . . . Ah me, what acorns of days
those were. . . .

that remnant of chewed-out rind, forelegs squatted, tail
high, white-fanged, eyeballs bulging, ears laid! Then
for the grand jerk! Gorgeously futile jerk. Teddy
with his teeth sunk into the leathery morsel and snarls
mixed up with his breathing, beginning to spin!

The boy and the dog. Teddy out on the horizontal.
Sustained momentum. Terrific momentum. Spinning
boy. Spinning dog. Riot of sunlit afternoon, with the
dirty sheep grinding their teeth in a low thunder and
nibbling their strange-eyed heads off.

They had no sense. Teddy was better at making them
herd neatly than Grime, the eleven-year-old sheep-dog.
All you had to do was to circle the flock once every
hour or so to close them in a little tighter, Grime or
Teddy yapping at the narrow ankles of any straggler, or
Davey flecking at his flock with a peeled switch off a
plane tree.

Otherwise, just hours and hours of his flesh close to
flesh of earth. Lying face-up or on a slope against which
the sun banged. When it rained, and the smells that
had been baked into grass and tree-bole and leafage
came out in cool breath, there was the hay-rick to burrow
into, the sheep gathered pat as a mat beneath the spread
of two maple trees that sort of linked arms.

There were books, too, which he concealed evenings in
a little spring house down by the Tarkington hedge.
Books off of Henry's shelves. Sometimes, if a down-
pour came along, or a quick, thick thunder shower, there
was a scurrying of dogs and sheep and boy to cover of
the hay-rick and interleafing maple trees, and the books
remained out, usually face-up, and were drenched, and
then, as they dried in a quick, repentant sun, warped.

There were books on Henry's shelves twice their normal size. Volumes that bulged from the damp of the
spring house or from hasty showers. *Around the World*

in Eighty Days was as bedraggled-looking as something the cat might have dragged in. *The Voyage of Magellan* had a great blister on its cover; and the most exciting book in the world, that meant everything when Henry intoned it in his slow, careful voice, but meant so little when Dave tried to pick it out for himself, *The Life of the Bee,* had a great rent down its cloth binding. A combination of damp and Teddy's teeth.

Henry never remonstrated as his shelves of books began to wave and careen and warp.

He used to plant himself before them first thing when he came home evenings, regard the new vacancies and inundations with a wide, slow smile lowering half of his face, so that his jaw hung over his cravat.

Curious relationship, when Davey was seven and Henry was four times that seven, and more.

Chapter Thirteen

THE day was like a crystal fish-globe, crammed with
light. On all sides the horizon had a transparency. At
noon, when there were no shadows, it was like lying at
the bottom of the transparency, munching thick, white
bread that you had to tear because it was cut twice as
deep as your teeth. It was like the most perfect kind of
drowning imaginable. It was like the piece Dora Tarkington recited so shyly Friday afternoons from the
school-platform, her skirts maneuvered constantly between her thumbs and forefingers:

> For the moon never beams without bringing me dreams,
>   Of the beautiful Annabel Lee;
> And the stars never rise, but I feel the bright eyes
>   Of the beautiful Annabel Lee;
> And so all the night-tide, I lie down by the side,
> Of my darling—my darling—my life and my bride,
>   In the sepulchre there by the sea,
>   In her tomb by the sounding sea.

Anyway, if it wasn't like that—it reminded you vaguely
—of a sep-ul-chre by the sea. No, not that! This
drowning of the long afternoon was in a sea of blue and
silky air that jammed the enormous fish-bowl with the
nicest kind of universe.

If you slitted your eyes and lay on your stomach, down
on the green floor of the bowl were the backs of the grazing sheep. Dirty foam. And no shadows. Just light.
Light. Light. Light was grand. You wished you were
made of chicken-wire. That was to be all light.

And Teddy, while you lay with your eyes closed, panting short and quick and hot at your side, and taking

164

sudden rough licks at your hands or wallowing on his back, so that without opening your eyes you could hear the nice noise his rough coat made against the nibbled grass.

The days were as long and as slow and as big as the eternity they sang about in the hymn-books of Sunday mornings in the vestry-room where you "had" Miss Lare in Sunday-school. Eternity was full of God. What was God full of? The hymn didn't tell that. Henry would know. Yet, somehow, that was the one question of all you would not ask Henry. God was something private. He wasn't quite that way to Henry. Not that Henry had ever said so. It was something you just kind of knew.

Henry's *World's Almanac,* face-down, rustled when his flung-out hand fiddled with the leaves. Earth pressing warmly into one's face made it difficult to even delve into its panorama that helped so to while away the hours. The Territories. Descriptive. Hawaii—Territory of. Area 6,449 square miles. Capital, Honolulu.—The crossroads of the Pacific—Henry's map showed the mountains and the volcanoes. Hawaii had not the right of statehood—Henry said—the right of statehood?—the brain reeled lazily—life was just a swinging foam of the dirty backs of the sheep. Of the *World's Almanac.* Of a blur of last night's impressions of Magellan skirting the fringed edges of the Philippine Islands, to the guiding waggle of Henry's long forefinger across the page. Of Lincoln on the rostrum, delivering the Gettysburg Speech that hung framed over Henry's mantelpiece. Lincoln's face was the shape of the bottom of a foot. Lincoln made it grand to have a face the shape of the bottom of a foot.

Long, dozy high-noons of munching the deep bread, with your eyes closed, and high-noon lapping over into

afternoon. Teddy squatting himself flat on your chest,
and the two of you, for the briefest moment while Grime
kept watch, dozing off, nose to nose, eye to eye, breath
to breath.

It was in the middle of one of these June-drenched
afternoons of perfect, drowning peace, that Teddy, who
was a terror for detecting sounds, leaped off of Davey's
chest and ran down barking toward the spring-house.

Once before he had routed out Stevey and Claire, who
had been seated down there without Davey ever having
perceived their coming. They must have strolled along
by the creek-banks, where trees, skirting South Meadow,
blotted out a brief moment of sky-line.

That was the time Davey had lain on his stomach at
the top of the slope and shouted to them while Teddy
whizzed downhill.

Poor Davey, in the unwonted excitement of having
human figures walk into the lull of one of those long
afternoons, had tried to lure them, with cat-call and
shouts, to the top of his slope. But Stevey and Claire
had hurried away so strangely, and not friendly at all,
into the concealment of the bush that lined the creek.
And, presently, there were their silhouettes once more,
hurrying homeward.

Now Teddy had found them out again. You could see
Stevey's head coming cautiously out from the other side
of the spring-house and the yellow that showed beside
him was the edge of Claire's skirt. Stevey was stooping
as if for a stone—surely not—

"Stevey! Claire! You—hoo—come on up. Stevey
—come on up—not hot up here. Come on—up—'s me
—Dave!"

Foolish whirligig of Teddy wanting to leap and yap
and dash himself against these friends whom he recog-

nized—pulling at the yellow of Claire's skirt—hurling
his body against Stevey—yelping. . . .

What was Stevey—what was Stevey—doing? No.
No. No!

But it was then that there crashed through the brain
of Davey, shouting from his hilltop, a sort of an insanity. Something locked his breathing so that it could
not get through. A paralysis. Sight became a blur.
Pain became a devil.

Stevey was kicking Teddy. Body-blows. The yelps
that leaped out were kicked out. At first, under the rain
of blows, Teddy had started to run, bellying to the
ground, bewildered, full of pain. But Stevey had followed him up. With terrible, terrifying, careening
strides, that zig-zagged crazily, and now Teddy was
lying on his side against a salt-rock, pinioned there by one
of Stevey's boots, while the other was kicking that soft
spot above Teddy's ribs that made the yelps leap out.
And the world was gashed with those yelps and the dancing horror of Stevey's foot, and the yelps ran into you
and then out of you like blood, and Claire was beating
with her futile girl's fists at Stevey's shoulders and still
Stevey, with his teeth bared back, was kicking—kicking—

Teddy's eyes were being kicked, and the yelps were out
of his eyes—that was how it seemed to Dave in the midst
of the insanity of seeing black.

Twice as he tore screaming and strangling down the
slope, he fell as if into the spinning yelps and the spinning insanity that gave him speed.

How Claire screamed! In high, harsh sleigh bells, and
by now the yelps were like a shower of red-hot butcher-
knives that leaped out of the dog and into one's breathing. And breathing became a delirium that pulled and
roared and exploded in blasts, and you were plunging
through high waters—tears—and Teddy down there, in

a crouch beside the salt-rock, was being kicked into and kicked into.

Then, as he tore up and threw himself across that small crouch of his dog, one of the kicks intended for Teddy went into David's thigh, so that, with Teddy in his arms, he went down flat, winded, gagging, the color of chalk for the moment, jerking Stevey to his senses with a suddenness that seemed to make him, too, the color of chalk.

There were only the wheezing noises Stevey made as he stood looking down at the sprawl of Dave, with Teddy in his arms, and the small sound of Claire as she began to cry, with her face in her hands.

The horrible, pain-riddled afternoon, where before there had been just the peaceful translucence of a goldfish bowl filled with niceness of universe. Stevey, with sweat making his white face glisten with the strange pallor of an arc-light, continuing to stare sickishly down at the sprawl of Davey. His lips kept twitching so, as though they could crawl along through his cheeks and on —away—

Teddy whimpering as though the very yelps had been bruised. That was what kept the insanity boiling, even after the wind had been knocked from Dave. Teddy trying to lick his hands, between bruises of whimpers. Incredible pain of that. It made him leap to his feet. It made him beat with his fists, claw with his nails, batter with his palms against the rather dreadful pallor of Stevey's face, which felt sticky and sickening, with a clammy kind of sweat that was cold. It made Dave, with Teddy swooped up into his arms, run hiccoughing and strangling through the red-speckled, hot afternoon; run blindly, with dust caking his tongue and his tears, and making the world a slime of horror and pain.

The destination of Bek was instinct rather than impulse. Somewhere, in the terror of things, she must be waiting calm and true and cool. Out of the pain and the chaos, out of the hurt world full of the red specks and yelps from a kicked dog, there was Bek! It was like lugging a sheep, his long legs dangling, his head lolling so, that from the open mouth the saliva spun off the tongue in flying rills. There was that red, wet spot against Teddy's side, that kept Dave's hands sticky. It was a pain-crazy world. Crazy world of Teddy's dangling head, as if he were fainting as he whimpered. Crazy world of stones that bit up into bare feet. Of up hill and down dale, through strangulation of rage and horror. Fields that had flowed so placidly about him, all his life, now seemed to rise up, to throw him, to cut him with lurking stones, to stretch and to stretch endlessly between him and the haven of Bek.

Dave wanted Bek. Through the strangling passion, the first he had ever known, that seemed washing away the roots of his small heart, Dave wanted Bek.*

---

*. . . seldom, if ever, did I see my brother in the throes of those rare fits of passion that invariably were to leave him the victim of one of the black headaches to which he was subject.

Of course, there was the unspeakable occasion of Steve and the dog. My pen will scarcely drag across the page that memory of the face of a child torn with anguish. I recall how I trembled for the pain-of-the-world that must inevitably find its way into a heart that was capable of suffering as David was the day he came running to me with a wounded dog in his arms. O Steve—Son—Boy—except for my unquenchable faith in you which you have so superbly justified, I think that would have been the sorriest hour of my life.

In subsequent years, I have, of course, seen David control my Father's kind of wrath, but only with great effort. There comes to my mind that memorable occasion of a state dinner to the Queen of Holland, in the days when visiting queens and

As luck had it, she was striding along the cinder-path to the house from just having superintended the loading of six calves up an incline and onto a truck that was to carry them to Centralia Junction for shipment.

At the scuttling sound Davey made tearing through the cinders, and the low whimpering of Teddy, she turned in time to catch them as they hurled against her skirts, foamy saliva streaming from the pair of them.

"Why, Dave!"

She had never seen passion before. She had never seen tears lash at a face, and that a child's face, and leave it so rigid and bony. He was a knot of strangulation; and, for the moment, the fear smote her, what if his breathing should get too clogged! . . . "David! What?"

"He—he—he!" screamed David, "He—he——"

"He what, boy? He—who—what? Davey!"

"He—he—he——"

"Stop it! You'll choke! He what——"

"He hurted him," shrieked David. "He hurted him." And thrust out the body of his dog so that the side which panted and was moist and red from having been kicked in, was between them. "I'll—I'll run him through with a

---

royalty were still a novelty to us in America. At this function an Italian plenipotentiary constituted himself an ambassador-without-portfolio, and introduced a diplomatic topic at the banquet-table which threw great embarrassment upon the guest-of-honor and drew admirably restrained but nonetheless angry public rebuke from the President. Another time, when my brother's face was my Father's all over again, as it quivered in anger, was when I happened to be seated in his office, and he overheard, with what I always call that curious third ear of his, a secretary out in an anteroom, insolently dismissing a World War veteran, who was presenting what he thought were sufficient credentials for admission to see the President.

pitchfork from the barn—I'll get a pitchfork after him——"

The screaming, childish voice. There was that constant fear that his breathing could not get through. The mounting hysteria of his rage. The tear-lashed face streaked with runnels of mud.

"Dave! Hush, do you hear? Hush, I say!"

"He—he—he—he——"

"Who, Davey?"

"Steve."

"Steve what?" said Bek and closed her hand over her throat. "Steve what, Dave?"

"Kicked him! I'll pitchfork him," screamed Davey and lunged again, this time into his sister's arms, so that she caught and shook him until his small, square teeth rattled.

"David, behave!"

"I—yi—yi."

"Quiet. Not another sound."

"Old Teddy——"

"Lay him out. There, on the grass. Quit your crying. Do you hear? Quit it! Get me one of those window-sponges under the porch. Dip it first. Teddy, good dog. Don't snap, old fellow—I'm going to hurt a little bit—good old Ted."

The long, even strokes of the sponge were enough to set him yelping, and then gamely to subside, with his forelegs held out as stiff as sticks.

"Dip the sponge again. Wash your own face there at the hydrant. Hold it under. There—old Teddy—patience——"

"Is he, Bek—to death—"

"No. Broken rib, I think. Flesh-wounds."

"He hurted him, Bek—with kicks—"

"Sh-h-h! Get me fresh water."

Stevey had done this unmentionable thing. Stevey had kicked in the side of a dog until a bloody tatter of his flank hung down. Stevey, who was supposed to be surveying up around North Dam had been somewhere around South Meadow instead, and had kicked in the side of a dog. And Davey, whose heart was as good as kicked in too, had seen him do it. Had not only seen his dog kicked, but had seen him kicked by Stevey!

The *terrible* Stevey must have done that! The terrible, secret Stevey who must be kept from the knowledge of Winslow and of the family, of the community, of Davey, must be at large again. Stevey, drunk, must have done this atrocity!

"David, run into the house and fetch me my first-aid bag from the hall-closet. And, David, you won't mind if Teddy hollers a little. Looks like I have to yank this bad old rib into place."

"I won't mind, Bek," said Dave, with a smear of pain across his face and started running toward the house.

Between them they held Teddy, while Bek poked at the rib with a forefinger, and Teddy moaned and quivered; and with the dog's head locked down between David's small knees, Bek started winding the gauze. On the first tightening pressure, the frantic muzzle of Teddy slipped Davey's hold and sank teeth into Bek's arm, above the wrist. A long ooze of blood appeared slowly.

"Hold firmly, Dave. Don't move. Teddy didn't mean that. He thought he was biting the pain. Don't mind the blood, Dave."

"I—won't."

"Hold him firmly."

"I—will."

"If you faint or do anything silly, you'll mess things up for Teddy, now that I'm getting him in his splint all righty."

"I—won't—"

"Try not to mind his yelping, Davey. No, No. No. Hold him firmly by the hind-legs—it's got to hurt."

"I will."

Finally, he was bound and laid under the porch on an old horse blanket used for covering bulbs in autumn.

Without talk. Then there was Bek's wrist and arm to be bound. It was hard to hold the bottle of peroxide properly above the wound and pour it on and see it bubble in with the blood, and not begin to feel squeamism all over again. The bottle kept seeming to rise up and down and the blood to be all running through one's eyeballs in threads—except—the shame of feeling squeamish before Bek—one dared not—before—Bek—

"Now, Davey!"

"I'm all right, Bek."

"A little more here. His teeth got snagged, you see." Finally, the blessed relief of the gauze clamping down. The almost instantaneous spat of blood against the white made it hard for the moment, but then the winding covered that—the winding—the winding—and through the winding, the insistent impulse to slip somehow underneath the somnolent afternoon that was suddenly so slashed with the yelps of the kicked dog and the red bands of blood. Then, too, was the sickening background consciousness of forty-eight sheep with only Grime for guard.

And through the swinging sickness of it all, there suddenly was Stevey, with his face like a pat of dough before Mathilda flattened it out beneath her rolling-pin. Stevey standing beside his mother and leaning against a rain-barrel because he had to sway. It must have been the dizziness—the wanting to slip underneath it all that made Stevey seem to sway so.

Just the same, sight of him brought the old impulse

back to batter, except that Bek's hurt arm was trembling, and one must keep on winding—winding through all the red impulse ——

"You're drunk, Steve," said Bek, without the pretense of even so much as turning her face away from Dave hearing. It couldn't matter—now. It was the only way to explain to him that the Steve who had kicked a rib broken, was a Steve outside of himself. Evenly, and with a cold manner of appraisal, Bek repeated it, regarding her son teetering beside the rain-barrel.

There was something of enormous and omniscient calm about Bek, so casual about her gauze-bound arm, with the red spot widening, skirts tucked into boots, feet spread, strong black hair with the bluish light over it, and the enormous levelness of her eyes—the prairie-flatness; the un-undulating squareness of Bek's gaze, pouring against the bloodshot, watering eyes of Steve. It seemed almost to grip him into standing erect, as something loose and boneless can be grabbed by the back of the neck and pulled to its feet.

Steve looked like that. Boneless.

"You're disgustingly, bestially drunk. You've done a cruel terrible thing to a child and to a dog!"

"You—bad devil you," cried David, and began to dance on his toes and make lunging, hysterical throws of his body toward Stevey—"you bad devil you ——"

"Sorry—didn't hurt him, Davey—didn't mean to, Davey," said Steve, trying to fasten his watering gaze upon the white-faced boy. "Sorry, Davey—shorry, Dave ——"

"You bad devil ——"

"Davey—go, do you hear? Stay with Teddy beneath the porch. Go!" Finally he had to be dragged there by Bek, who lifted him by the underneath of his arms. "Dave, stay with Teddy." She left him, a silent huddle beside the silent dog, his lips still sucked back against his teeth and the flanges of his nose sea-green. And Stevey, watching her retrace her steps toward him, wavered as she came, tottering a little, like a scarecrow in a wind-swept field.

"You're a drunken—sot, Steve."

"Well—so was Cæsar—the Julius one—many a time. Excuse me, Mother—didn't mean—that ——"

Her throat ached for him. His young, flawed hand-someness. The black bang of his hair, down over his eyes. Soft shirt open at the throat. Legs slim in puttees as he had worn them on the campus at Agri-cultural College.

Olive pallor. Gray eyes, with black flecks like his grandfather Schuyler's, behind the too-quick batting of black lashes. A slim, handsome, insolent drunkenness. A fastidiousness to Steve, even in his cups.

"Where did you get—it?"

"The stuff? For God's sake, Mother, don't catechize me like a revivalist. Where did I get the filthy stuff? Ha! The gin mills have got your fair-haired boy. The dens of vice. The cesspools of iniquity. Dens of vice and cesspools of iniquity. Where is my wandering boy tonight—oh, Lord ——"

"I can't fight it alone much longer, Steve. Your father will have to know. The family, too. It is getting beyond me single-handed."

"What they don't know, old-dear Mother, won't hurt them. They're safe in sobriety. They're so damn safe in sobriety."

"Where did you get it, Steve? You promised to come to me when—when you had to have it."

"Yah—yah—with my throat on fire, with the lining of me on fire—begging a thimbleful from the bar of the holier-than-thou."

"Where did you get it?"

"Em's."

"You mean—Claire—gave it to you?"

"Yes, I mean Claire."

"You got Claire—innocent, unsuspecting Claire to dole you out drink from her mother's cellarette?"

"Betrayed the hand that quenched me," cried Steve, and threw out a mock gesture.

"Steve, look at me. You and your cousin have been meeting clandestinely for a month. Ever since you're home."

"Interesting way to meet. Hadn't thought of it that way before. Clandeshly—clandesthly—clandesh—ly——"

Suddenly Bek's hand leaped out. The one with the red-stained gauze.

"Hurt your hand, Mother? Been indulging in one of your feminine pastimes like hay-forking, I take it. Poor old Mum's hand." He started to carry it to his lips on a grand over-balanced bow—and teetered.

"Steve! Steve! Pull yourself together. For God's sake, Steve—poor little Claire—you like this——"

"What do you mean, poor darling? She's as fine and as sweet as gold—if gold is as sweet as I think it is, seeing's I've never been on close terms with enough of it. What do you mean, poor?"

"I mean, Stevey—I've seen it happening day by day. You two. Grown-up and cousins!"

"What do you suspect, my dear mother Bek?"

"Suspect?"

"Yes, old dear—you have been suspecting—now haven't you?"

"Change your manner to me."

"Sorry, Mother. But you have been suspecting?"

"Only with my eyes. Not with my heart."

"Well, she's a darling!"

"Steve!"

"Yes, I've been meeting her. Actually seeing my own cousin—how would you call it in movie lingo—er—ah yes, clandeshtinely. Safternoon. Many safternoons. Yessir—when everybody in the world, except the canniest person in the world, known as my mother, thought I was at the dam, and that Claire was at her this-ing or that-ing, or whatever it is small-town, young-lady schoolteachers do with their late afternoons. We, we—the darling—guess I'm pretty drunk for admitting it ——"

"Guess you are, Steve."

"Guess I'm pretty damn drunk for saying so."

"Guess you are pretty—damn drunk ——"

"Well, I like her. She likes me. Dammit, a fellow's got no right to stay sober. Makes a mollycoddle out of him. Saps his courage. But I'm not afraid. Of you. Of the family. I'll march her up to Thanksgiving dinner in the House on Sycamore Street and face the whole battalion of you. I'll tell the family. I'll tell the world. She's a darling—even if she does come from the horse-faced Millikens. She's a darling. I want her!"

"Steve," said Bek, in her foggy voice, and went up to him and took hold of his teetering shoulders to steady them, and tried to pinion his eyes with her own. "You don't know what you're saying."

"I'm drunk enough to have the courage to say what I'm afraid to say when I'm sober. I want her. She wants me!"

"You're drunk, I tell you. Listen, Steve, Mother understands."

"Mother doesn't. Mother's too damn strong to understand."

"Steve!"

"Mother's not human. I am. Claire is. Mother's

noble. From the too-damned-noble, deliver me. Sorry, Mother. Excuse. Mother's always shielding. Mother-the-shielder. Nobody's got to be shielded from me. If Father's going to have hydrophobia over me, let him have it. If Gramp is going to yell—let him yell! Won't be the first time. If the whole holier-than-thou house of Schuyler has got to be protected from me, dammit, I'm not going to do the protecting. To hell with this salt-of-the-earth stuff. Where does it get you? Suppressions. Repressions. Listen, world, I'm in love with my cousin, my first-cousin, even if it gives Father hydrophobia and Gramp the screaming yammers. It's a grand idea, Mother, walking through life and keeping it as calm as Dickery-dickery-dock, the mouse ran up the clock, for the whole family. Grand, if you want to make yourself the go-between—and take the buffs for the whole clan. Strong. Strong. Noble. But here's one blow the family's got to take square in the solar plexus. I'm in love with my first-cousin. She wants me. I want her."

Bek took hold of her son's arm with her own blood-stained one and shook him until his teeth clicked. "You're a drunken fool!"

"Tell me that again, darling. Didn't hear it the first time. Claire knows it too. That's part of the infernal glory of a woman in love. She cannot help forgiving. Mother-love. Sex-love . . . both pretty much alike, when it comes to the quality of mershy."

"Steve!"

" 'Course. Forgot. Sex is unmentionable in a respectable world that has been created by sex."

"You and Claire wouldn't dare to do a thing like that to the family. Your silly little yellow-haired cousin. Of course she thinks she's in love with you. Always has. I've known it, only don't you fool yourself, she's too much of a Schuyler to be guilty of ——"

"Guilty of what?"

"Guilty of dangerous social behavior like marrying your own cousin. That's—almost what the Bible would call ——"

"That's vice! I know it all before you say it. You're in the intellectual backwoods, same as the others. You're no different except in strength. Intermarriage of cousins. That old myth went out of date with antimacassars. Ask Henry! Everybody who's even half-abreast with the times knows that the horrible thing we used to call inbreeding needn't be horrible at all. You've seen it among your own cattle. Can even strengthen the breed. Ask any biologist. Pff! That for the first-cousin myth. If I marry Claire, you let biology, not the family, worry about progeny."

When Bek spoke next, standing with her feet in their wide plant, her hurt arm gripping her son's, her face almost touching his so that he could feel the shape of her low, intense words in breath against his face, it was as if, through her son's fogged brain, her force were blasting itself and staggering him sober. "Biology, piffle. Isms! Sophomore-twaddle. You're not dry yet behind your ears!"

"I won't be made ridiculous!"

"Too late. You're already very that. Biology. It may be all right theoretically, and from the laboratory of the guinea-pig. I don't pretend to know even your half-baked science. What I do know is that there are too many examples of its wrongness right here in this town. You know Jean ——"

"Yes, yes, I know. She'd have had imbecile offspring if she'd married all of Harvard College."

"All of which is beside the point. The point is now, that you're drunk. You're standing there reeling in the way of my lifelong ambition for my family, in this community, in this state, in this country. But so far as I have anything to say, this family is going to remain the salt of the earth, clean straight through."

"What you going to do with the salt? Sprinkle it on a sheep's tail?"

"No, I'm only going to maintain the traditions that those two old people in the House on Sycamore Street have started for us. Your grandmother and your grandfather literally worked the earth you are standing on, teetering on, to make it fit and fruitful for you."

"Yah——"

"Yah! And your aunts and your uncles represent the decent, law-abiding, upstanding citizenry of this country. We have that heritage to carry on. And you!"

"Heritage of middle class."

"Heritage of decency! Decencies that you, as you stand here before me now—a drunk—are dragging down. As you inveigle a sweet girl, your cousin, into clandestine meetings with you, because you dare not be open and aboveboard. Because you know the wrongness of it. You're loafing on your job! Betraying my confidence in you. You, insulting by your dishonor, your grandmother and your grandfather. You, imperilling your father's health. And lowest of the low, you kicking dumb brutes. Offending every decency, and then, when there are none left, you turn beast yourself."

"Mother——"

"I've lied for you. I've protected you against the punishment of your father and the terrible wrath of your grandfather. If you haven't any decency left for me, then, for God's sake, have it for them. For your Uncle Henry. For your Uncle Phil. Your aunts."

He began to cry a little, licking off tears with the tip of his tongue as they straggled loosely toward his lips.

"That child over there. He's handicapped as it is,

growing up down there by himself years and years away from the companionship of brothers and sisters of his own age. I want this great big growing family of ours to be the finest imaginable for a child like that to grow into. He deserves it. You can't smash his heritage. Not while I'm your mother and his sister."

The crumpling-up of Steve was more of a collapse than a faint. Perhaps a little of both. His mother caught him as he tottered.

"Steve. Please. Sh-h-h. There's your father coming up from the orchard. He's been painting. He must not see you this way. Steve, I want you to walk! Erect! Up to your room. With me. With Mother—Steve—don't you dare to stagger ——"

"I——I——can't——make it ——"

"You will. You must."

"I will—I must ——"

With the support of her left arm against him, as the figure of Winslow came up above the rim of slope that led from the orchard, they walked up the steps, across the verandah, unwaveringly, into the house and on up to Steve's room underneath the eaves.

One hour and forty minutes later, Bek came out again. Alone.

"Where've you been, Bek?" asked Winslow, who was working away at his pipe-stems with "cleaners" she kept him supplied with by mail-order.

"Putting my house in order, Winslow," she said.

Chapter Fourteen

THE Mark Millikens, Senior, lived in a twenty-two-room wooden house, with a tower at one end where Annie Milliken wintered her geraniums and rubber trees; a millwork "gallery" ran clear across the front of the house, with two hardy perennials of rocking-chairs, that in summer wore linen slip-overs and most of the winters a light ruching of snow.

Originally, the Milliken homestead had stood in the center of a square block of ground. Now the Opera House nudged it from one side and a gasoline station from the other. To complete the insolence of this last, an iron negro boy, with a hitching-ring in his fist, stood resting at the Milliken curb that was nearest the gasoline station.

Once, some town-wag, (Aloysius Chipman probably,) had hung a pasteboard tag about his neck, "TAKE A TUMBLE TO YOURSELF, JOE." But Mark Milliken had unsmilingly broken the cardboard across his knee and crammed it into his pocket, to avoid its cluttering up the lawn.

It was estimated that Mark Milliken had made a quarter of a million, when suddenly the two next-to-the-principal streets of Centralia had elected to run along two sides of his property.

One of Annie Milliken's great trials as this situation began to manifest itself, was the soot-balls that fell from the chimneys of the three-story brick office-buildings, so that the Milliken wash could no longer flap itself sundry on clothes-lines stretched between two fine plane trees. In fact, one of the trees had to make way for the

Opera House and the other was jammed up against the gray-brick rear wall of a Woolworth Store.

So a steam-drier had to be installed in the Milliken basement.

"I know the days when her washing wasn't fit to be seen on the line for her laziness about mending," said Mathilda Schuyler, whose tongue could be trenchant where Annie was concerned.

A Schuyler had married a Milliken; there was a thirty-two-year-old staunch, if tempestuous friendship between the Old Gentleman and Mark Milliken, Senior. The two men, in fact had been business partners for eighteen years, and even after dissolution were more or less in constant negotiation; children of the two houses had grown up with the closest of interrelated interests, and yet, the thirty-two-year-old antagonism between Mathilda Schuyler and Annie Milliken remained just about intact.

An anniversary, an illness, or even a slight mishap in one or the other family was sufficient to bring about tearful reconciliation, after estrangements of sources too trivial to recall. The marriage of Emma and Morton had tided them over years of suppressed misunderstandings; but, at heart, both of them, women of tough endurance and patient noses-to-the-grindstone of large families; at heart these two old women were anathema to each other.

The drop of a hat could send them flying asunder. They could quarrel over the relative blondness of their children, the respective excellencies of spouses, the clarity of their respective apple jellies, the complexion of daughters, the fidelity of hired-hands, the relative consistency of the soft soap stewing in their respective iron kettles, methods of chicken incubation, the selling-price of butter, the buying-price of unbleached muslin, the this and the that of quilts, poultices, grandchildren, resemblances, giblets, sons, pip, county fairs, cheese-bags, and growing-pains.

Their men tacitly ignored these ructions, their own overshadowing them in proportion, if not in frequency.

High and terrific words had from time to time raged between these two. As a cattle-trader, the Old Gentleman despised the methods of his erstwhile partner. Secretly, Milliken had a contempt for the Old Gentleman's virtue in the Fulton Market deal, which he regarded as virtue only because it had been applied to him. They were ultimately to disrupt partnership. First as cattle-dealer, later at those real-estate operations that were to alternately make Mark rich-man, poor-man. There was never a time when, at the bottom of his heart, the Old Gentleman did not doubt the Milliken integrity.

And yet, not entirely trusting intuition and the rather insufficient evidence, even when Milliken was in a position to buy and sell him, he was constantly in the Old Gentleman's debt.

The Old Gentleman had been known to sign notes for Milliken that were up to the hilt of his holdings.

Mathilda cried bitter tears over this. It riled her to see Annie Milliken ride out in her surrey-and-two, and later in a Cadillac sedan, on moneys that she knew were made possible by financial cooperation and maneuverings of the Old Gentleman.

It was a tumultuous feud between these two houses. The women at their small bickerings, the men waging bitter if more infrequent wars of deeper portent.

On the day that the Old Gentleman's sheep were wandering at more or less loose ends in the pasture that had been so precipitously deserted by David and Teddy, Mark Milliken, with his long, lean, leather face showing a peculiar pallor through its tanbark, was huddled opposite the Old Gentleman in a small room to the rear of the Whittier County Bank, where depositors were allowed privacy for conference and opening of safety-deposit boxes.

They were two stricken old men's faces. Milliken had a long, lean, Yankee figure and a white goatee that turned up like a Turkish slipper. The Old Gentleman, looking actually atrophied, seemed to wither as he stood. Eye to eye, the two of them. Pretenses down. Lean, primitive fears out. Something vast, and all that vastness stupidly spreading across the Old Gentleman's face, turning it into a rimless plane surface of widening and widening incredulity.

"If—I thought you meant what you are saying, Mark, by God—by God—I'd ram—your teeth down into your heart."

The figure of Milliken, with the wattled brown throat throbbing like a peafowl's above the soft, low collar, crouched back against the wall, after a fashion of a figure hugging for shade on a desert.

"I'd sooner be struck dead than live to see this hour, Schuyler."

"You mean," said the Old Gentleman, whose head was lowered like a charging bull's, and whose breathing came up through his chest as if it were dragging heavy chains with it, "you mean—you can't—ever!"

"I can't, Schuyler! God forgive me! I can't——"

"Can't!" said the Old Gentleman. "Can't!" He seemed to gargle the word around his mouth as if it were a dry old marble. "Can't."

"I could cut out my tongue rather than have to say it, Schuyler," said Milliken in his whisper, backing and backing against the wall as if he would force it to yield and swallow him.

Suddenly the Old Gentleman let out a sort of yell of realization that banged into the quiet morning.

"No, no! Tell me I'm crazy! Damn you, tell me I'm crazy!"

"For God's sake, Schuyler, hold yourself together! Don't shout—don't let them—know—yet—out there ——"

"I am crazy! I must be! He stands there and tells me I am a ruined man for going on his notes. I've gone on his notes for the last thirty years. For bigger amounts than I would trust to my own blood and kin. Every cent between me and ruination lies in his hands," cried the Old Gentleman, and began to dab, in the rather horrible fashion of the frenzied, against his face and his throat. "I am crazy. I am crazy! I am losing my senses. "It can't be true!"

"Schuyler, for God's sake, hold yourself together. Don't shout. Sit down, Schuyler. Don't take on, Schuyler. It's enough to give a man a stroke. Sit down, Schuyler. I—I can explain ——"

"Explain!" cried the Old Gentleman, clasping and unclasping his hands. "Explain! What else is there to explain? I come to a man, that man my best friend, I come to him weeks ago, the day my notes are due. Not an hour before. I'm not worried. Only under a strain. Like a man will be when it's the biggest loan he's ever made and everything is in one basket. Only under a strain. I must have had the feeling in my bones. I see it now. Even this morning, you remember I said to you out at Dittenhoeffer's farm, 'Mark, you don't look so well. Is anything wrong?'"

"I haven't closed an eye for eight nights, Schuyler."

"It is true, then? I can't believe it. By God, I can't believe it—if you're fooling with me, I'll make you regret ——"

"Schuyler, you have sons."

"Yes, I have sons. Clean-livered ones."

"You'd have done as much for yours."

"You-mean-to say-that you-placed collateral—my collateral—in the hands of that scalawag of yours in Toronto?"

"You would have done the same for one of yours!"

"Not with my best friend's money. Not to save a thief!"

"Don't say that," cried Milliken as if pleading not to be goaded, while the right was not his to strike back. "Don't say a thing you'll regret, Schuyler."

"Regret? What in God's name is a man to say? Maybe I didn't get it right, Mark. Tell me I didn't?"

"I'm afraid you did, Schuyler."

"What else—damnation—what else, then, am I to call him? Scalawag, good-for-nothing thief!"

"Schuyler!"

"Ran away from home twelve years ago to get into one scrape after another—and now—a thief—on my money—on everything in God's world between me and ruination."

"It's the old story, Schuyler. But you've got sons. Think, if you found yourself in my terrible dilemma."

"A son of mine who embezzles, God forgive the thought, would have to—I can't think! I'm going crazy. I can't seem to think."

"Like a hundred boys before him, he meant to put it back. He saw great real-estate possibilities in Toronto, just as your Phil——"

"By God, take that back! Don't mention my Phil in the same breath ——"

"I only meant, Schuyler, the same impulse was behind him. He meant to put it back. Frank's been a good boy, Schuyler. Wild in the early days, but married and settled in Toronto these ten years now and cashier in the town's largest bank."

"I see now. I see now. God! Good God! I denied it when Alf Dreffous told me he saw Frank Milliken and you walking along the railroad tracks night before last.— He must have stolen down to see you—sneaked into his home town like a thief in the night—a thief it took my lifetime of labor to save ———"

"He's desperate—Schuyler! Desperate a boy as ever kept himself from shooting his brains out to hell ———"

"I see it now—I see it now— God! God! God! What is to become of me? Every cent I can count my own, put back into a Toronto bank to save the hide of a thief."

"He meant to put it back. He kept drawing out good money to send after bad. A land-investment deal. He says he's sure to realize on it in time. I'll be able to meet things in time, Schuyler. But they wouldn't give him time. They were watching him three months before he knew it. They closed in on him, Schuyler. If I hadn't let him have it—mine—and your collateral—it would have meant—penitentiary! His mother—your daughter —and my son—me—my family—yours too, Schuyler— much as mine—your daughter bears my name—I had to let him have it to save your flesh as much as my flesh.

"Why—" said the Old Gentleman feebly, this time like water spluttering onto a hot stove-lid, "why, I'm ruined. I'm a penniless old man with a family—my hard-earned—my life-earned thirty-five-thousand collateral— I'm a penniless old man with a family."

"So'm I, Schuyler."

"My woman, who helped me to scratch it together— she's ruined—my children—who count on me to help them—cheated—my seven-year-old boy cheated out of his rights—growing up into a penniless future. God damn you!" cried the Old Gentleman, and lurched and struck with his knuckles into Milliken's forehead above the left eye so that a spurt of blood jumped out and ran down warm and thick under the Old Gentleman's cuff.

The red glue of it in the smear across his arm and his eyes made him rear back squeamish for the instant, and in that instant old man Milliken had fallen to his knees, and hooking himself to the table-leg, lifted his face with the blood on it and said:

"All right, Schuyler, hit!"

"No you don't!" screamed the Old Gentleman. "You don't get me thataway." And as the figure hooked to the table-leg lopped forward a bit, the Old Gentleman's arm shot out again and again, and they locked, the long, lean, Yankee figure of Milliken and the thick, squat one of his adversary. Locked. Swayed. Tottered. Panted through the noises that chairs made, scraping as they staggered themselves a path through the room.

And suddenly the Old Gentleman felt the flesh of his knuckles break and spout blood from hard steel into which his fist had crashed and there clattered from Milliken's breast-pocket something shiny, the something the Old Gentleman's hand had struck.

It was a cumbersome old model of a Colt .32, with a black hartshorn handle and a long pull-trigger of a twenty-year-old make. It made a clatter falling out of Milliken's pocket. It struck against the table-leg and went off with a loud report and a shower of plaster began snowing down from a new scar on the ceiling.

"Shoot me with it, Schuyler. I hadn't the nerve to do it myself ———" In the confusion of feet running over the tiled floors of the bank, of the opening of doors, bustle, hustle, two old men, on the floor of the small room reserved for depositors, were sobbing arm in arm, the bleeding face of Milliken dragged up into the embrace of the Old Gentleman, whose spade of beard was riding up and down like a latch.

"It's all right, Mark, it's all right!"

"Finish me, Schuyler. Shooting's too good. I'd have done it myself. I hadn't the nerve."

"It's all right, Mark! Everything's all right—crushed to earth—all righty—but by God—rise again ——"

Chapter Fifteen

WHEN Mark Milliken went down, it was a case of the tent-pole toppling pretty nearly everything with it into a muddle.

And there were more Schuylers to pitch into the maelstrom than there were Millikens. There were only Mark and Annie and Morton Milliken. But Morton, who had never known a day's financial independence of his father, was, after all, married to and therefore half a Schuyler. So there it ended for the Millikens. Except, of course, for Frank in Toronto, who was ultimately, some twelve years later, to build a twenty-room Tudor mansion on a Toronto boulevard, with a wing for his parents, who, shortly after the crash, left Centralia to take up residence with him.

There was, to be sure, an old maiden-aunt Rebba, who had lived with the Millikens for half a century in dual capacity of cook and poor relation, but who died half a year after the crash.

In the shadow of quick, cataclysmic events, there crept into furtive existence a rumor about this old woman. She had really been Mark Milliken's half-sister. She had moved with them to the county forty years ago, under the guise of distant relation. There were certain stocks and holdings in her name. Rebba, who during her life had no significance, came, upon her death, to have a sinister one, builded on rumor that was never to be either justified or discredited.*

---

* . . . once I remember hearing Phil make a slurring reference to what he called the stocking National Bank of old

With the Schuylers it was a matter of interrelation-ship of affairs that pulled them all down into a heap, a sprawling, bewildered heap, that for a time could not be jerked to realization because of the dust of collapse.

When the Old Gentleman went down, practically to the last acre of his holding (counting some grazing-land up behind Middleton), every plan of Rebekka's, land-acquisitive ones, and the paying-off of mortgages on her present holdings that were chiefly dependent upon loans from her father, went up in a puff of appalling smoke. Overnight, as it were, the Model Farm and hopes for its future slipped out of her hands.

With Phil, for a moment that struck terror to the house of Schuyler, it looked perilously as if his only way out of the crimp his father's catastrophe had put into his affairs, was to let himself slide non-resistingly into a state of bankruptcy.

For weeks he had been tuning up his courage to ap-proach his father for the loan that would forestall that already impending event. And then on the very day that he had steeled himself for what was sure to be a bitter wage of war with the Old Gentleman against speculative land-methods, the crash!

Rebba, which was supposed to have helped retrieve the Mil-liken fortunes. He was sternly rebuked by my father. In all the years of stress and strain which were to follow this catastrophe, no member of our family was permitted to refer at all, much less slightingly, to Mark Milliken. If my mother rankled when she heard of the twenty-room house in Toronto, she rankled silently. If my father owed the twist that had come into his face since reverses due to the betrayal of a friend, he bore it silently. Probably out of deference to Emma and Morton, who were to come in for bitter times. And just as probably out of the fine, high pride that was part of Father's many-sided, but always inviolate personality.

The peregrinations by which that bankruptcy-act was ultimately avoided bear not the telling here.

It was said around town that the Old Gentleman attempted the incredible device of trying to sell his son Phil's next five years in clerking-service to his old friend, Tom Wexler, who ran the Red Trunk. And on the same principle, his own services to Wexler, capacity and remuneration to be determined by Wexler.

That news of the Old Gentleman thus peddling about five years of his son's and his own future spread like wildfire.

Henry Schuyler, upon hearing it from young Simon Wexler, who retailed to him the fantastic and embarrassing proposition, was reported to have cried out, shortly and sharply, as if some one had struck him, and then, without a word, to have walked over to the peg for his hat, unhooked it and walked out of his office, leaving young Wexler to his somewhat stupid self.

In any event, it did not come off that way. Smudgy account-books of Henry's saw the light of day. Bills were rendered to clients for legal services that dated five, six, seven, eleven, even twelve years back. One statement sent to a Solomon Hilp, Esq., Middleton, Whittier County, for legal services tendered in the successful settlement, out of court, of an involved damage-suit, was returned to sender with "party dead four years" scrawled across the envelope. An expert accountant was called in to dredge into the dusty, profitless tomes that had lain moldering along two shelves in Henry's office for year's end on year's end.

The Howey estate alone was rendered an accounting of six thousand dollars for legal services extending over years, and because of its incredible moderation, was paid with alacrity. The Giles Tool Works met a similar presentation of statement with similar alacrity, for similar reasons.

All in all, Henry collected a little less than one-fifth of his claims. And he went about it shamefaced. Not as a man claiming his due.

It netted him out of the twelve years, something less than sixteen thousand dollars. It made a single purchase. It bought Phil out of impending insolvency.

Even Clara, off in St. Louis, had for years been looking warily to her father to make possible that two-story, pressed-brick, seven-room, Georgian house in University Heights that she had begun to desire from the day her children crawled their way out of rompers.

The plans for the house, a fanlight over the front door, hardwood floors throughout, and a bit of formal garden with a bird-bath, were to repose in Clara's top dresser-drawer until they curled and yellowed there.

The Holly children were also expecting a Shetland pony from their grandfather. A brown, with a cream-colored mane and a basket phaeton with side seats, like some of the youngsters in Vandeventer Place went bobbing about in.

Last, but not least, something that had sprung eternal in the narrow breast behind the spotted foulards of a lean and earnest little lady engaged in teaching the sprouting minds of Centralia that "we, the people of the United States, in order to form a more perfect union . . ." died that year the Schuyler fortunes were swept asunder.

Henriette, who had hopefully told herself for years on end that there was no hope, stopped hoping.

To the boy, David, trudging his way in winter to a one-room country school, instead of the two-story brick structure on Second Street, herding the sheep in South Meadow through the long, baking, fructifying summers, only no longer his father's flocks, but those of a new-comer from Middleton, named Gus Kelsoe, who now occupied the House on Sycamore Street, the change had come sharply at first, but certainly not in the nature of a catastrophe.

Indeed, to the unrooted nature of childhood, there were thrills and the adventure of disorganization in the move from the House on Sycamore Street to the bald-faced frame house where Judd Igrotte used to live.

A bald-faced, packing-case of a structure, with its windows distributed in the pattern of two eyes, a nose, and a mouth, that stood flush to the road in a one-acre patch one mile and a half south of South Meadow.

Pictures came down during the weeks of that move from the House on Sycamore Street, that left great pale squares against the walls. Window-shades, the front ones with painted ovals and lace edges, dropped rotting right off their rollers, when it came to removing them. The mahogany sofa of great floriated curves had sunk so deeply into the parlor-carpet that there were four caster-shaped holes in it; and since the sofa could not even be moved through door or window of the Igrotte house, two of those holes, arrange and rearrange as you would, were to sprawl themselves out, mended two tones too dark, into the center of the small, square front room of the Igrotte manse.

They were a pair of friendly patches. You were for-ever aware of the presence of the two dark objects to trip over, and the consistency with which you did not trip was something to be perpetually surprised about.

The Igrotte house, as a matter of fact, faintly within David's memory too, had once stood on the Schuyler property as a sort of auxiliary summer-kitchen. Hams, bacons, peppers, packs of dill, hanks of raffia, drying mushrooms, hung in its upper story; and the downstairs, entirely laid out in benches, was a wilderness of jars, crocks and casks of meat salting, corning, and pickling. Cucumbers in brine. Pigs' feet stacked into cool jars of vinegar. Brandying peaches. Spiced pears. Stuffed mangoes. Blackberry-cordial. Grape-juice.

Len Tarkington had finally bought the little building from the Old Gentleman, and moved it bodily onto his own property, to be used as a granary.

All that week of the moving of the building, as it had ridden grotesquely and in scarcely perceptible jerks along the open road, causing horses to shy, tiny Davey had ridden in its upper-story window, shouting, grimacing, and wild with the novelty of it.

Then Judd Igrotte, known thereabouts as a squatter down near the Cranberry flats, up and purchased it from Tarkington, and moved it still another two miles down that same road, using it as a dwelling until his daughter Helga had married out of it and into a prosperous Iowa farming-country, and taken old Judd to live with her.

It was to the Igrotte place, then, that the Old Gentleman, disdaining every proffered scheme of combination-living with his children, moved with Mathilda, Henry and Dave.

The rehabilitated old box, with Helga Igrotte's choice of wall-paper plastered to the wooden partitions, and with neither plumbing, nor gas, nor electricity, had a set-on-to-land look, as if it had been deposited there very gingerly, like some one sitting on the lap of another, without letting his weight relax.

There was a bony look to the land, probably from the way the rocky ledges ran through it, breaking the flesh of earth and showing in mica-streaks. A lean, meandering acre, for which the rental consisted of the yield of its potato-crop.

The day that Mathilda arrived to stay, riding in a

rocking-chair to the rear of the van that bore her household chattels, she just sat on in that chair, frozen from misery, long after the last of the objects that surrounded her had been lifted down and carried into the house.

It was hard to begin life in the wooden box. The rocks surrounding it gleamed up so through the earth. To a woman who loved shade and the benign, grand bosom of fruitful farm-land, the scene before her was as lusterless as a lead nickel flung out there under the sun. Not so much as a maple tree or a plane tree or an arbor to relieve the glare.

What a move it was! The yield of that attic in Sycamore Street. It spoiled it a bit to have Mathilda sit most of the days with odds and ends and bits on her knees, crying over them. And the girls too, poking in among chests and trunks and hampers, and then sitting down to let a tear fall onto an ordinary afghan or a bit of unearthed muff, all mangy and moth-eaten, or one of the Old Gentleman's buffalo-robes from sleighing-days, or a thread-lace baby-cap, stained yellow.

It was strange. The wet kisses that were suddenly mumbled against his neck, or the quick embraces into which they caught him, as he darted in and out of the wealth of those chests brought suddenly to daylight.

Smell of old harness. Rifle with a rusty lock, that hung broken. Pleasantly-chilled pungency of camphor-balls. A brown gavel that had been Henry's in the days when he was president of the High School Debating Society.

"Ladies and gentleman!" cried David, when he came across it, banging against the window-sill that opened out from under an eave out upon the chicken-yard, "—out there—world, you! Listen! Listen, world!"

"Stop that banging, Davey!" said Emma, who was

shaking dried rose-leaves out of the foot of an old white-lace stocking she had worn to Clara's wedding.

"Let him be," said Bek from the depths of two huge feather-beds crammed onto the top shelf of a closet. "That's right, Davey. Make them listen. Gracious, listen to the quiet—even that big, gray rooster stopped crowing—I do declare he's made all outdoors listen."

"Bang! Bang! Bang!" went David with his gavel, from the pulpit of his window-sill overlooking the world of summer farm and fowl, and then paused again for the fancied silence, "Bang! Bang! Bang!" *

"Davey, stop! That's my old golf-cape. Oh dear! Remember, Bek, when they were wearing golf-capes and rainy-day skirts? I'll never forget, Mother, how I prayed for rain the first day it came all the way from

---

* How well I remember a day in June, when David was about seven. A bitter, heart-aching day, as days go. I was over helping Mother move from the House on Sycamore Street. I can see us now. Emma, Mother, and I, in and out among the boxes and chests of that priceless attic, so filled with memories for us all, and Emma hot and blowy and perturbed. Poor dear, it was to be the beginning of many a hot and perturbed year for her. Mother full of tears. Davey, a squirrel in and out among us. Here. There. In hamper. Out of trunk. Little nuisance. Suddenly, pouncing upon an old gavel that had been presented to Henry by the High School Debating Society, David leaped to the window, hammering with all his might. "Listen, world!" he shouted—"listen here, world—out there—to me!" and 'pon my soul, it suddenly seemed that through the drone of that June afternoon, lowing with cattle, crowing with cocks, buzzing with insects, there did descend a silence. Fantastic, of course, and yet in the light of subsequent events—that child hammering his gavel up in the little window that overlooked his universe, was not just any child hammering his gavel for the world to heed him.

Montgomery Ward and then because it really did rain you wouldn't let me wear it, for fear of spoiling it. Oh dear——" cried Emma; and because tears were too close to the surface, the three women worked in silence, among the yesterdays.

To Dave it was like Henry's picture of "Washington Crossing the Delaware" to stand in the center of the billowing old horsehair sofa, wrapped in golf-cape, and peer off into a corner that contained the stooped figure of Mathilda dragging gunnysacks of hickory-nuts out from under the old washstand that used to stand in the girls' room before they married and left the House on Sycamore Street.

There was another cape, a black-plush one, with shaped shoulders and chenille ball-fringe, that Emma cried into. Then came along a boxful of albums, with tin-types of the girls, their panties showing, and Henry and Phil, with their ears very large, standing on either side of a small table, with a toy steam-engine on it. One of Mathilda, when her face was much rounder, holding the infant Bek against a black-brocade basque. There was another of her, when her face was rounder still. ("Mother dearest, in this daguerreotype you're beautiful!") a small, black-velvet bolero spanning a swell of timid young bosom. Mathilda, in her teens, in the Tyrol.

More and more clothing tumbling out of trunks and bags. Every possible graduated size of trousers. Little-girl frocks. Yellowed. Two more rifles with rusty locks that would not budge. A fine old hand-carved musket filled with shot. A carpet-bag crammed with the identical costume of an Austrian peasant-girl that Mathilda wore in the picture. That was the day pretty Claire plaited her taffy-colored hair into a braid over each shoulder and slid into the voluminous skirts of her grandmother's dress, and Mathilda laced up the black-velvet bodice; and when she stood there with something of Mathilda's gone prettiness to her, Mathilda began to cry feebly, and then Emma, and finally Bek, who did not cry, but held the two of them in the fine width of her embrace.

Strange days to the boy David, when even through the incomparable thrill of the move, his throat was somehow aching most of the time . . . mostly when he looked at his mother. She ran hither and thither so. As if doors had been closed against her and she wanted to go in.

Those were the days of a suddenly-promoted sense of importance and a sturdy sense of standing by. Days home from school to help hammer cases closed, rip off the tops of barrels and boxes for the adventure of seeing them yield their strange content of feather beds in striped tickings. Family albums. Plush panniered dresses. Basques.

Boxes of the Old Gentleman's papers. Deeds. Bills of sale; bills of lading. Packets of canceled checks. Notes. Stubs. Cattle-pedigrees. Henry's high-school diploma rolled in a tubular tin case. Clara's certificate of election to the Girls' Good Deed Club, dated 1891. A group-photograph of the family, when Bek was in pigtails and Emma was in arms, taken against the side of the House on Sycamore Street. A riding-crop. A small pair of antlers, unmounted. A half-finished piece of embroidery, on linen, of Betsy Ross at making the flag.

There never were such days of loot. The unpacking of the cases of Henry's law-books and miscellaneous collection, and of sitting beside him in the clouds of dust while he solemnly sorted them over, pausing for full half-hours at a time to pore. Once he read aloud, sitting there in shirt-sleeves, hunched under an attic-eave, part of *The Letter to the Sheriff of Bristol*. It was blunt

reading, the words like hammers from a sledge. Some
more of Burke's books Davey had spelled out on a shelf
in Henry's office, a labeled *History of Political Philosophy*. Sometimes, in his room, evenings, Henry had
talked to David of Burke. Thinking out loud, Henry
called it. When Henry told you about Edmund Burke,
or read parts of the conciliation speech, his eyes,
under their deep eaves of brow, brightened. "Here was
a man [Burke] pass-ion-ately and un-theatri-cally for
freedom and justice." That was a heavy phrase Davey
had memorized from Henry. When Henry read Burke,
as he unpacked him in the attic, there was something fine
and rolling in his voice, that even, when David did not
understand the lugubrious text, held him fascinated.

Henry must be like God. Henry knew everything.
It would never do to say that out. Henry would begin
to laugh. Silently. In the way that rumbled through
him. And laugh. And laugh.

There were hundreds of these books of Henry's to be
pounded free of dust and stacked, tied with twine, into
sixes, and then carted down to Henry's office in Bek's
car. There was not room enough for them in the
Igrotte house.

When Henry explained this to David, he kept his eyes
averted as if he were guilty of something. There was
not to be room in the Igrotte house for books to live
under the same roof with them. Why, in books there
lurked some of the great thrills that had come into seven
short years of a life. It made Davey feel the elusive sort
of tightness at his throat. For himself, but mostly for
Henry, who handled books as if they were live things.

The Old Gentleman was the stoic of this move. He
stalked among the upheaval of things, some of which
had lain quiescent under thirty-five years of dust. There
was the ax, rust crusted, with which he had hewn the

first timber for the roof over his head. The roof that was no longer his. There was a large carpetbag into which his sole earthly possessions had been crammed the day he first set young eyes on Centralia. An old lantern he had swung through the dawn-darkness of the terrific winter of '88, when his cattle sickened and froze in his barns, and his credit gave out about the same time as his winter-supply of feed. Bitter days that had crawled in wrinkles across the Old Gentleman's face, to remain there. And now that the chimera of those old, lean days was lifting its head again, the Old Gentleman was unbroken, or so nearly simulated it, that there was something a little terrifying about his stride. The women dried their eyes and made wide détours at his approach. He barked with his manner, and the members of his family, eager not to seem to notice his over-emphasis, barked back. He was full of bluster, those days, moving men scurrying up and downstairs to his order. Bek's light two-seated Ford, laden with such intimate chattels as chip baskets filled with dishes, boilers, crammed with percolator, awl, clothes-wringer, soup-tureen, hose-nozzle, vinegar-cruet, lamp-base and coffee-mill, rattled under the Old Gentleman's orders, back and forth along the rutted three miles from the House on Sycamore Street to the Igrotte place in Pessimines Lane.

The Old Gentleman clung to his huge baize-top desk that had to be forced in through a window and placed under the stairway in the first-floor hall where the sole light and ventilation came from the transom above the front door. It was more of a closet than a room, scarcely larger than one of those under-stairs affairs for goloshes and wraps. In vain Mathilda expostulated, and Henry proffered the room over the rear porch that was to be his.

No siree! There, under the front-hall stairs, the Old

Gentleman caused to be installed this baize-top desk of
his that had stood for thirty-odd years in the window-
embrasure of one of the towers of the House on Sycamore Street, adapting himself at once, by the vehement
gesture of hanging above it a colored lithograph of the
1901 Cattle Fair at Sandusky. And if it must be admitted, providing his usual cuspidor of a cigar-box filled
with sand, and hammering-in his pipe-rack of nails, which
he drove into the wall himself at carefully-calculated dis-
tances to correspond to the respective sizes of the bowls
of his meerschaum family.

It was a dingy hole of an office, that was to immediately become foul with smoke that permeated the entire
lower floor. To the Old Gentleman, who for the years
he could have afforded better, had swayed through town
in the mangy phaeton and the chewed-looking old reefer
with the dangling lining, it might not have been so much
of a hardship. Except now, suddenly, and with a pathetic
streak of the psychology of the needy, one of the first
acts of the Old Gentleman, under the new régime, was to
furbish up the phaeton, paint it a livid ochre, jack up old
Jennie's twine-tied harness, and venture forth into town
in the brave trapping of a man who could no longer afford
to be shabby.

That almost broke Mathilda's heart. Her needle repeatedly jabbed into her fingers as she sewed up the
reefer over which she had vainly expostulated during the
well-to-do years, and which he now voluntarily handed
over to her for repair.

The Old Gentleman was sprucing up to meet vicissi-
tude. Not one of his adult children but what nursed
secret heartache over the pathos of that.

Once, when she came across the refurbished reefer
hanging in the hallway, Bek secretly smeared it with some

dry dirt out of one of the potted geraniums Mathilda scrupulously kept on either side of the one front step that led to the hallway. Foolishly enough, she admitted to herself, the Old Gentleman's reefer, mud-streaked, made her ache for him a little less.

And yet, to Davey, fickle with youth, filled with the wild, shy imagings of a mind vigorously and unprecociously beginning its unfoldings, the bald-faced house took on almost immediately, all the aspects of home.*

David's room, where originally the garlic and peppers had hung drying, was little more than a pocket up under the slant of roof, that you reached by ladder. A snug enough little pocket, with a soda-pop bottle on the table beside the cot, and a candle stuck in. The candle in the bottle always ran down over itself in elaborate blisters. It was a flickering light to lie on one's stomach and read by. It gave the page a crazy, breathing quality.

---

* It was about a six-month after the move to the Igrotte house that my brother Dave, a quiet and rather thoughtful child up to then, asked me a question that surprised me with its observation. There had been a labor-strike among the men who were laying the new-paved road between Centralia and Middleton, and one of the so-called scabs had been struck by a rock thrown by a union man. When old Jessup told me of this happening, I was salting out weeds between the bricks of a garden-walk. Helping me at this task, Davey, digging away, looked up to remark, as ants scurried from the path of his trowel, "Ants run their world better for themselves than folks do, Bek. Bees too. Bees and ants all work together. Why are folks always trying to crowd each other out?"

I sometimes wonder if right then and there was not planted into his heart the unconscious resolve that much of his life-effort must be waged against man's inhumanity to man.

That day he was just a kid, faintly perturbed with his first awareness of injustice. . . .

Down in Henry's room, with a reproduction of a bronze bust of Benjamin Franklin by Houdon on the bookshelf, and a steel-engraving of a naval engagement between Paul Jones's *Bon Homme Richard* and the English man-of-war *Serapis* against the wall, there was a student-lamp and a gouged-out armchair and a carpet hassock upon which to squat while Henry read aloud. There were long hours spent thus at the feet of his brother. But even longer and rather curiously dreamy ones spent alone in the room with the walls that were scarcely taller than he was. Teddy, who slept at the foot of the cot, usually snored through the flickery gloom. It left the boy alone to the crocheting shadows which, as the book in his hand might suggest, were armies, or navies, warriors, maidens or red-skinned Hiawatha, who was full of wrath when he came into the village.

The printed page loomed with him and stalked, and the soft hiss of the candle was the roar of Marathon over the plain where Miltiades saved Greece.

Henry's telling the saving of Greece by Miltiades! It was something to listen to, and then, word-for-word, to store away like nuts, and later, up in the privacy of his attic, take out in the flickering shadows into which Teddy snored, and lo, the attic was the plain and the plain was Greece! A blazing Greece, because, in summer, the tiny room up there gathered heat unto itself like a sun-glass. Evenings, with the rolling meadows breathing out as if in an enormous sigh of relief, the room could seem to spin of the heat-waves. But the roll of the heat over the small nude body of David as he lay on his cot was, mysteriously enough, life-giving to him. He loved the thick and plushy quiet. The pulling mysterious sense of growth through the hot, black silence. The sun-soaked, vast outdoors of meadow-land and field, fructifying. Sense of squirm of life.

All of his life he was to carry that immunity to heat.* Those summers, drenched in the heat of that attic-room, were baptism of fire all right, his square boy's body, as he lay there, pouring from every pore.

Yes, it was smaller and meaner in the Igrotte house. Even Davey, while the sense of novelty and adventure were still high, sensed that. It was something else, too. Something sad in the Igrotte house. And yet, within a month, every stubble in the lean little pasture, every lark's nest, every winding of Pessimines Lane, every hidden spring, every rabbit-patch, was home to him. A home into which his adaptability fitted him with the same perfection that his bare boy's body slid into the swimming-hole.

---

* On his tour of the deserts of the world, in behalf of his reclamation-theories, it was said of him that at noonday, when the natives lay scattered about the tents like so many meal-sacks, he remained at his desk throughout the siesta-period, reviewing in map and diagram the morning's observations. Midsummer campaigns across desert-country in the close density of sleeping cars, when members of his party succumbed to actual prostration, were not to faze him, nor for that matter, the terrific onslaught of mosquitoes the year of his famous Alaskan tour in behalf of his long-sighted domestication and cultivation of the ovibos, when the eyes of the dog-teams were literally bitten closed, and the motors of the aeroplanes, as they left the ground, were clogged with these pestiferous insects.

Author's Note: See David Schuyler, the Man, the Statesman, the Geographer. *Athenaeum* Vol. XXX. Timothy Tyker, M.A., B.S., Ph.D., Fellow Magdalen College.

Chapter Sixteen

THE most radical changes seemed to come so imperceptibly, that within the year it was as if there had never
been a time when the spacious front verandah of his
sister Emma's, at the far end of Sycamore Street, had
not been cluttered with boarders seated on round straw
mats. A Max Juss, overseer of the Tallahassee Tobacco
Factory, his wife, and two children. Old man Clotillo, a
county-clerk. The Misses Breen, Daisy and Sachet, mil-
liners, with a shop in the Renchler Block, and Miss de
Lisle, who taught violin and guitar, a sign in Emma's
right parlor-window to that effect.

Even the disintegration of the outward appearance of
the house had been too gradual to disturb the perception
of youth, to whom years are long. The scarred, nicked
places on the verandah-paint, where before the white and
green had shone. Starchy lace curtains had become
strings. Weeds and dandelions had cropped up between
the bricks of the sidewalk, to say nothing of Emma's once
famous reception-hall, the first in Centralia, now always
agog-looking with boarders' letters stuck into its mirror.

In no time at all, it was as if Davey could not remember when his sister's house was not the rather derelict-
looking affair with the front shades all at cross-purposes
and the Misses Breen's handkerchiefs drying against
the window-panes.

Claire, who taught kindergarten, and frequently came
home with her tired, pretty hands filled with colored-
paper mats and putty pigs, used to spruce bravely, after
school hours, at the littered rooms, with the dining-table
always half-set now, Mr. Juss's bottle of iron-tonic and

Miss Sachet's box of Kay's Komplaint Pills huddling around the catsup-bottle. But it was not much help to putter. The Millikens' was an out-and-out boarding-house now. Emma served five prunes to the dish, and the sign over the bathtub read: "Please scour. Do unto others as you would wish to be done by."

Poor Emma. It was hard to be a Milliken and a Schuyler. Morton's mouth was bitter with it, too. The name of his father or of his brother never left his lips. Secretly, he wrote occasionally to his mother. After a while, what was practically inevitable happened. Morton, whose business connections had been solely with his father, lost his position as agent with a local realty company, and then one that Henry procured for him as collector for the Ice and Coal Company. Not through anything more than just mild inability. Gradually, Morton became just a putterer around home. Oiling locks. Mending rugs, fences, china, rain-spouts and pocket-book clasps. A handy-man-about-the-house. The Schuylers quailed over that; and as he lost subsequent position after position, just of mild inability, every time, they became extra nice to him. Emma most of all, who meticulously ended all household disputes and difficulties with boarders by stating that she would talk the matter over with "Mr. Milliken." As a matter of fact, Mr. Milliken, as time marched on, could more and more frequently be found sitting in a basement room that had been fitted up as office, whittling on the wooden toys that Claire had brought home from the kindergarten, for some mysterious reason known only to himself, whiling away his time by making them leaner.

The change at Bek's had come perhaps as more of a shock; and yet, in some ways, it had probably the least perceptible change of all.

Bek still strode the farm somewhat terrifically, with

her skirts tucked into her boots.   The perfection of cattle
still stood in rows in her model barns of asphalt gutters,
running water, and electric light.   The clean-clipped
acreage of yellow mustard, alfalfa, and grazing-land,
scattered with salt-rock, silos, red roofs, stone hedges,
flowed out to the horizon.

Winslow still smoked his pipe on the side porch and
sketched his afternoons away down in the lower meadow.
Steve strode about the farm now, doing such solitary odd
jobs as breaking a colt or drilling for artesian water.

The great difference that was not on the surface was
what changed the aspect of Bek's farm so that about the
entire place there was the feeling of something having
died.

A dream had died.

Ex-Governor Howey now owned the Bek Renchler
place.   For the modicum of one hundred dollars a month,
Bek remained on the farm as overseer, occupying the
house as formerly, except during September and sometimes part of October, when the Warrington Howeys,
from Washington, came on for their annual visit.

Then Bek and the family moved into the rooms over
the garage.   They were four, firm, square, bright rooms,
with running water and clean new paper and yellow
floors.

The Howeys were extremely nice about this, and urged
Bek and her little brood to remain in the left wing of the
house.

This Bek refused to do.   The Howeys and Schuylers
had never been on that sort of social plane.   The Howey
girls had been away in the East at school while the
Schuyler girls were growing up.   The Howey boys had
been scattered since their days of Military Academy.
Then, too, the family had lived in the state capital for
eight years.   The enormously wealthy old Ex-Governor

himself, a widower for twenty years, spent two-thirds of his time in the East or abroad, negotiating all the while, by proxy of agent and telegram, in land and cattle deals back home.

Frequently, during his two terms, the Governor had called Henry to the capital for conference. Bek had stumped the country in behalf of his second campaign. The Ex-Governor, through his agents, had negotiated mortgages and sale of cattle and land with Bek.

The families mingled in this fashion, except, come to think about it, a Howey had never crossed a Schuyler threshold on social visit bent, and *vice versa*.

It is doubtful if Bek ever thought about it consciously. But the idea of remaining to occupy the left wing of the house, while Warrington and his French wife and three little girls flooded in, was unthinkable. She never batted an eye about the annual performance of that move into the flat over the garage; but from the first time that it took place, when she had sat up all night, placating Leslie, to whom the new sleeping-conditions were terrifying, some of the light went out of Bek's face. The pages of her diary, into which she wrote with consistency, are blotchy in through here.

All this, the year that Davey was eleven and the World War broke out with a clap over what had seemed to all thereabouts, except Henry, the clear noontide of Peace on Earth.

Chapter Seventeen

AT FIRST, Mathilda cried secret tears over Davey's having to attend the county school.

She cried secret tears over pretty nearly everything these days. That was why her face seemed to wear an almost constant smile stretched across the surface of her glassy teeth.

It was as if she had erected that smile on a stick and carried it about before her face as you would a lorgnette.

They were slightly larger than the life, these artificial teeth of Mathilda's, with a dazzling-white lifeless glaze to them, and pink-celluloid gums that had an air of detachment from the unsullied porcelains.

The girls had remonstrated for years against this blazing dentistry, and once, on one of her visits to Springfield, Rita had decoyed her mother-in-law to the office of one of the town's most eminent dental practitioners. But it was no use. Mathilda would not so much as mount the chair.

The great strip of smile, cutting so blatantly through the lean, bony structure of her cheeks, was a barrage behind which she could cry more secretly. It hurt her so terribly for the Old Gentleman, almost as much as for Davey, considering the school taxes her husband had paid into the town of Centralia. Davey, because of the move, obliged to receive his schooling in a little one-room county structure that was no larger than a shed!

Second Ward School in Centralia, where David had enjoyed only three months of primary grade, was a three-story brick structure, as regular-looking as a biscuit-tin. Henriette Simpson taught in that school. Every Schuyler youngster had at one time or another carved initials into its desks. Second Ward School was somehow David's right! sobbed Mathilda, bitterly, to herself. David's right. The Old Gentleman's right!

Of course, there would have been a way to obtain special dispensation by establishing Davey's residence, nominally at least, with the Morton Millikens in Centralia. Mathilda was all for that. Dave could leave with Henry each morning and return with him at night. But the Old Gentleman would hear to no such arrangement. No favor of any man! His back and his head were up, so far as his habits in adversity were concerned.

Besides, with the early-morning and after-school chores that were now falling to Dave, county school, only one-half mile distant, offered advantages.

At six o'clock, as early in the spring season as March, Davey used to help Tarkington's old black Nemo drive a herd of about sixty Tarkington cattle to pasture, and then drive them home at dusk. Winter mornings, long before the stars were gone, with a black crocheted scarf of his mother's tied over his ears, which he removed well before coming in sight of the lantern hung in Nemo's barn-door, Dave used to lickety-split over to the Tarkington place to help Nemo mix bran.

For this he received eighty cents a week. Sickeningly often, the winter that Davey was eight, Mathilda, secretly from the Old Gentleman, who even though knowing its inevitability would have yelled about it, was obliged to accept from the boy this eighty cents every Saturday night.

He gave it so blithely and yet a little furtively. No spoken word between him and his mother, and yet guarding the transaction from his father, even as Mathilda guarded it.

"I'll make it all right with you some day," Mathilda

was in the habit of saying to him, as the coins slipped hands.

"Make it all right!" Why, as it was, the days were packed with being all right. All-too-fleet days, for the doing of the many, many things to be crammed into them. Even the ones of rising in the chilled dusk to the light and heat of the candle stuck into the bottle, or to perhaps a bit of gleam thrown in from a last great isolated star showing through the frosted design on the window-pane.

The names of those last stars of the cold dawns were "Procyon" and "Sirius." "Castor" had a green fire in her. There was a way, with Henry alongside, to figure the distance from the earth of certain constellations. They had run across an old volume of Henry's during the move, called *The Geography of the Stars,* and another old text-book, *Handbook of Astronomy*.

When it was not too cold in the room to have an arm out from the cover, there were volumes to pore over. *The Relations of the Planets*. Pictures of them. There was a precision about this business of the stars, once you were able to figure it out a little for yourself. There was beauty in precision. Soldiers had precision. Stars. Funny, even Dora had precision. The way her eyes made you want to look and look, because they were set at exactly the right equidistance and were just the precise blue of perfection.

There was an array of books which Davey had routed out of the attic for himself. *Canterbury Tales. David Copperfield. Around the World in Eighty Days. Black Beauty. A Condensed History of England. Peck's Bad Boy. Golden Treasury. Forestry and Fisheries Report for the State of Maine,* 1901. *Dr. Jekyll and Mr. Hyde. Treasure Island. Essays of Elia. Franklin's Autobiography. Æsop's Fables. Burke*

*on Taste. Boy's Æneid. Voyage of the "Beagle."
Gilbert's Voyage to Newfoundland. Don Quixote.
Gil Blas. A Study of the Diseases of Chickens. Circus
Tim. The Jungle Book. Hoosier Holiday. Course in
Telegraphy. Jesse James—The Boy The Red Badge
of Courage. The Five Little Peppers and How They
Grew,* with "From Henriette to Bek, with best wishes for
a Happy Birthday, June 6, 1889," in angular script on
the fly-leaf.*

A jungle of books picked hit-or-miss. For the lure
of a title. Or because, as in the case of the *Boy's Æneid*
or *Burke on Taste* or Charles Lamb, Henry had paved
the way. Or just because.

The Red Badge of Courage. Spelling out the title
under its coating of dust, it came through at one so! *The
Red Badge of Courage.* Years before he was ready to
read it, that book was always lying around somewhere in
his room. For a long time it propped the unsteady
fourth leg of the small white-pine table. Once it was
used for pressing mint-leaves and left on a window-sill

---

* I remember walking across the Tarkington pastures one
day and encountering Davey, with Teddy and Grime minding
his sheep, lying stomach-flat on a rock, reading an old book of
mine which he had dug out of gracious knows where, and which
seemed to be causing him some bewilderment and no great
entertainment. "Five Little Peppers and How They Grew?"
he said, looking up at me with his small, square, intent face,
and a quality of eye-strain in his gaze that was later in life
to cause him bad headaches, "Gee—I thought this was a story
of the way pepper grows—and here it's nothing but the name
of a lot of folks." He had picked the book on the assumption
that it was on botany. There were years, watching Davey
grow, when I sometimes thought of him as becoming a
horticulturist.

all night to be rained on and warped.   Motley of books, chosen for a motley of reasons or lack of them.

No, these were not days and nights to mope over, or to have Mathilda dry her eyes over.   Each and every one of them was a key-hole to which you glued your eye and saw something of the great, grand, alluring tomorrow.

The schoolhouse, a one-room frame building with a fine-bellied stove on a tin mat in the center, adjoined the pasture where Davey helped old Nemo to herd the Tarkington stock.   One of the fascinating aspects of the Tarkington pasture was that the city-limits imaginary line ran through its middle, cutting a salt-rock in two.

The school windows overlooked all this.   There were blackboards around the four walls, and carved and whittled desks in sizes sufficiently graduated to accommodate seven grades.

Small Miss Hassebrock, who the winter that Davey was eight was beginning to sicken of a bone-disease that was to almost ossify her and keep her ridden to a slanted bed for the next eighteen years of her life, carried across her narrow shoulders the burden of that ill-equipped schoolhouse.

There was a handful of children, seven grades and first year High School entrusted to the tutelage of the gallant, ill-trained, underpaid and undersized little person who seventeen years before had graduated from the equally inadequate High School of a town called Ideola.

In the course of her seven-hour school-day, Miss Hassebrock taught two-plus-two; Ohio-is-bounded-on-the-North-by; James-Monroe's-Administration-was-the most-serene-and-yet-one-of-the-most-important-periods-in-the-life-of-the-nation; $\left(\begin{array}{l}2x+3y=8\\3x+7y=7\end{array}\right)$; This-is-the-forest-primeval; The-battle-of-Bunker-Hill-all-things-considered-is-the-most . . . ; Listen-my-children-and-you-shall-hear; Friends, Romans, Countrymen; How-many-yards-of-50-inch-linoleum-are-required-to-cover-a-floor-27x34; all interspersed with drawings of geometrical cubes, spheres; rhomboids in red chalk; and antiquated relief-maps of Europe and Asia.

It meant that in that small room of graduated desks and conglomerate subjects, there was allotted to each child about twenty minutes of direct instruction out of the day.   Twenty minutes of Miss Hassebrock tilting her little brain, like a spinster at the old gesture of tilting her teapot, to let trickle the stale, small array of academic facts and near-facts of the vintage of Ideola High School Normal Course, 1897.

The schoolroom squirmed with this ill-assorted conglomerate of children, waiting or dreading their turn for the trickle.   The mornings were riddled by their spitballs, hacked up by their penknives, whispered into; hissed into; scraped into by their restless feet.   Often, during the drone of these days, with his mind sliding and shying away from the chief exports of the Argentine Republic and "In 1066, William the Conqueror invaded England," David would become part of a fast and furious spit-ball barrage taking place beneath desks.

These occasions could reduce Miss Hassebrock to a state of helplessness that sent her rushing and dodging pell-mell about the room, usually ending in tears, the poor pug of her hair lopsided and every pupil in the room suddenly subsiding into a state of repentant and aboveboard beatitude.

There was something a little horribly pathetic about her, as she stood there defeated.

Once Davey, who sensed that more strongly than was comfortable for him, let a few of the spit-balls lie conspicuously in his open palm, thereby offering himself up as victim to take the edge off her somewhat disquieting defeat. But if Miss Hassebrock saw them, she did not let on. It was simpler, somehow, just to take up her pointer and indicate on the map the point where the Suez Canal becomes the north outlet of the Red Sea.

That meant the spit-ball barrages must to her seem something appallingly outside her control. As a matter of fact, she used to cry over them after school, bitterly and privately humiliated by the realization of her lack of disciplinary powers.

Davey sensing that, kept out of future spit-ball encounters rather than endure what the sight of her, standing there with her hair sliding, did to him.

There were nine pupils in all. Ross Tawkett, a great lanky sixteen-year-old fellow in the seventh grade. How he could confuse and bully and intimidate poor Miss Hassebrock with questions specifically designed to trip her up. Thus:

"Now Ross, name three of the eight planets of the solar system."

"Mercury-Venus-Earth !"

"Excellent. That will be all, Ross."

"No, now you name the rest of them to me, Miss Hassebrock, 'n' then I'll know them all eight for next lesson."

"Why—Ross, that's not in our today's lesson. Be seated."

Poor Miss Hassebrock, sufficient unto the day were the facts thereof !

Once Davey found himself in the position of prompting his teacher.

"How can Thomas Jefferson have died on July 4th, 1826, Miss Hassebrock," sneered Ross one day, "when you just told me John Adams died that same date?"

"Why, Ross—did I? Now did I? How come?

Let me see—guess I must have meant—now how come
I made that mistake?"

How well Davey knew that they had both died on that
date exactly fifty years after they had signed the Declaration of Independence. Henry had read him that long
before he had ever entered a schoolroom.

"They both died on that same date," mouthed David;
hissed David to Miss Hassebrock behind Ross's back.
And then when she continued to regard him helplessly,
held up two fingers in emphasis. "Both. Both—died.
Same—day!"

"Of course," said Miss Hassebrock, rather coldly.
"It is a well-known historical fact that both Thomas
Jefferson and John Adams died on the same date. David,
come to order or take a demerit." Ross was a class
terror, all right.*

Six out of the nine pupils were primaries, besides
David, who fitted into third grade because of certain
precocities resulting from the long evenings with Henry,
and a girl named Flora Wohlgemuth in fifth, whose
father ran a flour-mill. A great flax doll, with the loveli-
est lips, that adenoids kept rather breathlessly apart.

Knowledge of that educational boll-weevil, the ade-
noid, was not part of Miss Hassebrock's teaching-equip-
ment. She daily instructed little Flora to keep her mouth
closed, and struggled to crash the principles of long

* . . . Honorable Ross Tawkett, who was probably responsible, more than any other individual, for my brother's first
candidacy for public office, made the introductory address.
He did not, as many believe, first come into David's life when
they were fellow members of the International Board of 1937.
On the contrary, Ross had lived in our county for one winter
when he was sixteen, then his father, who was a dairy-farmer,
moved to the outskirts of Springfield.

division through the two greatly enlarged adenoidal impedimenta to Flora's alertness.

Later, still without benefit of surgery, Miss Wohlgemuth was in turn to teach school, through those same two, even more deplorably enlarged, impedimenta.

There was something about Flora's round little smudge of a face that one day impelled David to yield to an old temptation to wash it roughly with a snowball. There was an hour after school of writing "The Good That Men Do Lives After Them" fifty times down foolscap; and Mrs. Wohlgemuth, who ran a butter-and-egg stand "at market" in Court House Square, complained to the Old Gentleman in Low German.

For it, the Old Gentleman stood David up on the edge of the kitchen table and gave him three wallops against the seat of Henry's cut-down trousers.

It was almost a pleasantly reminiscent chastisement, recalling the satisfaction of feeling the snow squash up against Flora's boneless-feeling little face, which had to it the feel of mashed potato.

Years later, from the vantage of a private hospital room, made possible by the annuity of her one-time pupil, Miss Hassebrock used to strain her tired old hack of a brain for anecdotes of Davey. She was too conscientious to invent, even where anecdotes would have been treasures, but as she used to say, there was just nothing to be said about Davey as a youngster, those primary-years, that could not be said of the average run of them who had shuffled their small-boy days across the routine pine floor of that schoolroom. Nothing, except the certain precocity traceable to the home-opportunity of reading with an older brother, and the intent quality he had of listening and sucking in, well in advance, the work of the classes ahead of him. And then the funny additional precocities that contact with the older man's

mind had given him.   Rag-tags of odds and ends of information that clung to his mind like fuzz.   At six, he had
already begun to hoard books in the secret library of the
spring-house.*

---

* I think that David's library, begun, I always say, back in
the days when Father accidentally stumbled across a whole
nest of books he had secreted in the spring-house, is probably
the greatest commentary of all, upon his kind of intellectual
curiosity.   On two important occasions, it has fallen to my lot
to superintend the moving of his library.   First from his
home in Springfield to the State Mansion.   There were then,
as I remember it, about fourteen hundred, exclusive of law-
books.   Many years later, in the move to Washington, there
were over again as many to be recatalogued and boxed.   Nor
were these volumes books with uncut pages.   A book never
reached his permanent shelves until its contents had been either
read or "duly noted."   Insatiably curious, the headings under
which his books fell into catalogue were as grotesque as varied.

He loved and revered lyric poetry, although modern verse
was on his shelves.   The only soothing agent ever discovered
for one of his blinding headaches was curiously enough, Dora's
low and rather sing-song voice which she had cultivated to a
monotony that could fairly drone him to sleep on the word-
rhythms that he loved.

His personal collection was catalogued under such headlines
as Horticulture. Electronic Theory. Soil Chemistry. Parasites
in Central American Tropics. Geographies. Organic Chemistry. Evolution. Psychiatry. Aeronautics. Physics. History. Greek, American, French, Russian, Scandinavian Litera-
tures. Drama. Sociology. Church History. Heredity. De-
terminism. Behaviorism. Anthropology. National Parks.
Deserts. Travel. Genetics. Shorthorn Cattle. Morphology.
Race. Essays. Philosophy. Waterways. Radio. Theater.
Birds. Chess. Dogs. Population. Fundamentalism. Astronomy. Public Health. Theory of Relativity. Fisheries. Astronomy. Furniture. Architecture. Journalism.

Senator Harmon once said of my brother, that he knew so

Once at Friday afternoon platform-exercises, when a
small boy named Ike Mintz, the son of a dealer in old
iron, began to sniffle and shuffle of inability to remember
his allotted recitation, Davey volunteered with the
following:

> Heaven lies about us in our infancy!
> Shades of the prison-house begin to close
>   Upon the growing boy.
> But he beholds the light, and whence it flows,
>   He sees it in his joy;
> The Youth, who daily farther from the East
>   Must travel, still is Nature's Priest,
>   And by the vision splendid
>   Is on his way attended;
> At length the Man perceives it die away,
> And fade into the light of common day.

Henry frequently read this poem aloud to himself,
evenings. It is doubtful if, at the time, Dave took in its
meaning as much as its music. It is certain he did not
know its source. Neither did Miss Hassebrock.

No, he was scarcely a memorable pupil, except for his
sturdy little personality thumping in so dependably every
morning. Never tardy. Seldom unruly enough for more
than a passing reprimand. Seldom brilliant. Never
remiss.

There is this little incident, which has to do with
Teddy. All of the school-day Teddy lay in the vestibule
that led into the small section where the children hung

---

well the secret of surrounding himself with brilliant minds on
every subject, that he had only to press a button marked Coin-
age, Immigration, Mexico, or Techno-Psychology, and lo, a
specialist on that subject appeared before him.

That, of course, is an amusing exaggeration. It could more
truthfully be said of my brother's library. Books were literally at his elbow by the thousand, on call for almost any
reference.

their hats and coats, or wandered the countryside of the vicinity, usually showing up at recess or lunch period for the droppings from Davey's lunch-basket.

There was an old feud between Punt, a fox-terrier that belonged to Red Kelsoe, and Teddy.

Their masters had bitten the dust together more than once over the mangled ear or the torn flank of the conquered. Teddy was half Punt's size, but an eye-to-eye fighter. Punt, on the other hand, had a trick of hurling himself from the rear, taking his adversary unawares. Teddy bore scars that had been inflicted by a rearward adversary.

One day, just as the children were filing out of school, a series of yelps split the tired, four-o'clock air.

Teddy's moment had come. At the very threshold of the building, his teeth into the rear of the terrier's neck, Teddy had Punt pinioned in the bloody dust.

Through the cries of excited children, as they formed a tight circle, the air thickening and blurring with more dust and yelps, there mingled the squeals and the high admonitive tones of Miss Hassebrock.

There was a red trail across the school-yard and with his teeth all of their depth into the terrier's throat, Teddy was shaking him like a rat, releasing him only to prove further the glory of his sure vantage, by leaping at him for fresh clutch.

It was a one-sided struggle this time, and David had finally to pull Teddy off by the scruff of his neck, while he still leaped and yelped for more Punt-flavored blood.

It was Davey's and Teddy's moment, as Punt, limping, slunk off tail-down past his master, the children applauding the turning of the tables of this old feud between dogs and masters.

It was Davey's moment all right, when Red, instead

of leaping at him with his usual taunt of victory, stood grinding his toe in the dust.

Except that Davey knew what Teddy knew! Teddy had conquered his foe with his foe's own despised methods. Teddy had leaped on Punt unawares! Davey knew, in his heart, that was the only way Teddy could ever have gained that particular first strangle-hold over an adversary twice his heft and cunning. Teddy must have leaped at Punt as he lay sleeping at the threshold, waiting for Red. It was in the half-slink of his tail, as he crept up to his master. It was in the fawning lick of his tongue. Davey knew! And Teddy knew what Davey knew, and victory was as dead-sea fruit.

And in that instant, as Davey stood looking down at his dog, and shame of shameful conquest lay in the eyes of both, the belated flash of understanding was transmuted to Red.

"You're a dirty little sneak!" he shouted, and batted David sideways on the head, so that he saw things in waves. "He sneaked up on Punt—yer dog's a dirty little sneak, too!"

"Red," said Miss Hassebrock sharply, stepping forward into the ring, "that blow was a cowardly act. Either you apolog——"

"No," said David, a little dully, "Teddy did sneak up. His winning don't count."

That evening, after the supper-things had been cleared, Mathilda, who had pains in her legs from having done a day's washing in the damp Igrotte cellar, set about the unsavory task of stewing up some asafœtida in an old tomato-can.

This she sewed up into a small bag and hung about David's protesting neck, for what she termed his right peaked look.

Chapter Eighteen

A MAN down at Wohlgemuth's mill was enlisting. He was a fellow with a receding chin and a reddish birthmark seared across his cheek, who had drifted in on a freight-train from Kansas City, and who claimed to have walked it overland from San Francisco.

For over a year he had been working about the neighborhood. First as herdsman at the Howey farm, for a while doing chores for Bek, and finally running a truck for Ed Wohlgemuth.

He was a gangling, big-jointed fellow, full of the lore of the open road, and with a quid as big as a nugget protruding from one cheek or the other. He had fought in the Boxer Rebellion and in the Spanish-American War, and "guerilled," as he put it, in Mexico and done six years' navy-service. A soldier of fortune in the literal sense of the word. Anybody's fight was his fight.

The boys, for miles around, clustered about Pete (the only name by which he was known thereabouts) along about sunset-time, on the row of barrels that flanked the Wohlgemuth Mill. He had the knacks that delight boys. He could spit straight, and twice any competitor's distance. He could lure a rabbit out of a hole by a jargon he knew. He could also, by another mysterious jargon, entice grasshoppers to the back of his tattooed hands and make them spit tobacco there without so much as touching them. He could tie a sailors' knot with one hand, cause hairs from a white horse's tail to stand straight on end at the tip of his nose, pull a cork from the inside of a narrow-necked bottle with a bit of twine, bring down one blackbird to every shot and do a snake-dance that he had learned from the Pueblos.

And now Pete, who was an Australian by birth, was about to set off for Montreal to enlist under his own flag. It was the closest that remote thing, the World War, had penetrated the uninterrupted rhythm of Whittier County.

To David, racing home that dusk, from having sat about on the row of cider-barrels with Pete and his cohorts, the fuzz of the day's heat was a taste up against his tongue. Cattle lowed. The winding of smoke from his father's chimney curled languidly against a torrid sky, and out of all this gentle trance, something a little terribly alien seemed suddenly to have come to life off the printed page of a history-book. War had come to life.

Pete, some one who was as casual to the countryside as—why as the very barns, the meadows, the silos, the hedges, the farmers themselves, was going to war. War had come up off the history-pages into reality.

Pete was going. The tidings made Dave's bare feet send pebbles spinning from under them. He was panting when he reached home, from the dual consciousness of being late, which always grated against the Old Gentleman, who was more easily irascible than formerly, and with the burden of his news.

His mother and Henry were just about to draw up around the supper-table.

Supper served as near as possible to the range, even in summer, made dishing-up an easier matter for Mathilda, who no longer kept help. Trina, poor distressed creature, at the catastrophe of the family-move from the House on Sycamore Street, had been obliged to accept another position in Centralia, for the support of the two invalid old sisters she cared for.

Besides, it was cheerier in the kitchen than in the little aperture of a room off the parlor that was jammed, except for a narrow rim for slithering around with the dishes of food, with the heavy, grape-and-leaf-design, walnut dining-room set from the House on Sycamore Street.

There was no prevailing upon the Old Gentleman to let go of that ponderous "set," even to the antique-dealers from Springfield, who came sniffing.

There was a lamp with a green-paper shade burning in the center of the kitchen table; and Henry must have been reading *War and Peace,* by Tolstoi, because it was hung now, to keep his page, over the lower rung of his chair, and his place was rumpled, and his unused plate pushed center toward the sugar-bowl and castor. The exuding heat of countryside, mingling with the blazing breath of the range, was like steam, and had the cling to it of a hot, wet blanket.

"Father, Pete's going to war!"

The Old Gentleman, seated on the kitchen porch, with his shoes and socks on the floor beside him, and his hot feet dangling to the ground and soaking in the dew of the small surrounding plot of grass, screwed around a face that had been jerked from the intent observation of his dozen or so wyandottes taking roost.

"War?"

"What war?" asked Mathilda and began tilting a skillet of steaming okra-and-tomato stew into a bowl.

"Why, Mother," said Henry gently, and rising to take the dish from her, "you know what war. We've discussed precious little else at this table for weeks."

"Of course I know, Henry," snapped Mathilda, and turned toward him with a flick of her cup-towel. "Don't speak to me as if I were a baby!"

"I'm sorry, Mother!"

Mathilda's memory was beginning to lapse on her, more and more. Sometimes in stretches that were impossible to ignore.*

In the beginning, the family met these lapses in pretty much Henry's wise fashion, usually succeeding in jerking her back to an injured, if resentful air she always employed to cover up these hiatuses that bewildered her and made her constantly afraid of the next.

"Of course! Of course! And what's he going to war for?"

"He's going to fight for his country, Mother. His

---

* . . . even though, as old Jessup used to say, "I says it who shouldn't", if ever a mother was blessed with children who adored her, that mother was ours. Not only Davey. My sisters were her obedient little girls to the end. I can still see Phil, on the very evening that a business venture with which he was concerned took on, overnight, as it were, proportions that caused us all to gasp, sitting in the drawing-room of his new Springfield home; telephone jangling, messengers arriving, reporters and friends in and out, trying to make Mother, whose memory, as time went on, became paler and paler, comprehend the dramatics of the thing that was happening all around her.

Dear soul, her dim eyes wanted so to understand what it was caused his hand to tremble as he told her the same thing in every imaginable form, trying to penetrate the thick, cruel fog, beating about in his brain for ways and means to help her.

As for David—I cannot write it clear-eyed—long after he had passed out of our family jurisdiction, so to speak, and had become the property of the people, he was at her beck and call. I have seen him sit beside her for hours on end, patiently trying to answer her feeble and insistent questions. Tides in the affairs of state and nation beat up around the very room in which they sat with a terrific imminence, but they never budged him from her side while she wanted him there.

Poor Mama—yet who am I to pity her!

country is—the Brit-ish Empire. A fellow's got to fight
for his country, Mother, if his country's gone to war."

"Stop talking like a parrot, Davey," said Henry with
rather an unheard-of-for-him kind of brusqueness and
jerked his chair closer to the table.

The Old Gentleman was pretty apt to become excited
and shout at his mild-mannered son, if these supper-table
controversies led to certain political topics that had particularly to do with the situation in Europe, and upon
which they differed.

Conscription was one of them; and here was Dave
running home with a subject perilously sure to lead up
to it. Be it said for Henry that he made a gallant effort
to divert it.

"While I think of it, Mother, here are those washers
you've been asking about for your faucets. Ed Ryan,
whom I defended way back in a horse-thieving case, gave
me a pocketful."

"Thank you, Henry. I can do with them nicely. Seven
washers for defending a body against a horse-thievery
charge. Ah me, that's why you'll remain a poor man all
your life, son. Fine a lawyer as there is in the state,
and taking washers for fee. 'Tain't dignified, son."

The Old Gentleman ambled in then, his attention
persistently snagged by the subject Henry had tried to
divert. "Who should stop talking like a parrot? It's
high time the boys of this country should begin talking
like parrots, from the look of yesterday's *Enquirer*. Wilson can't any more keep this country out of wa ——"

"Puppa! Now Puppa!" trebled in Mathilda, herself
tired to death of these supper-table reiterations between
father and son. "Taste, Puppa! Bek sent Stevey over
with this okra special for your supper. Stevey's not
looking well, Puppa. Sometimes I think he must have

caught some kind of a slow fever up there at Agricultural School, where he was last year for that spell."

"And if talk don't do the work," bellowed the Old Gentleman in immediately argumentative key and starting to swirl the coffee in his cup with a gouging, angry spoon —"if talk don't do the work—then I say *conscription!* And the man who don't favor conscription for the salvation of his country in time of need, don't deserve to have a country to defend. If you've been through what I've been in a country where they demand the best years of a young man's life, war or no war, a little conscription in time of need shouldn't be necessary, and if it is, by God, I'm for it."

"You are talking the phraseology of militarism, Father. You're the parrot! Go out and train cigar-Indians on such flimsy logic, but not men who think. Besides, if it is your patriotism that is so aroused, the modern doctrine of neutrality is an American idea that Washington conceived and Jefferson phrased in 1803. You can be equally American by adhering to them."

"Doctrines of neutrality don't change the natures of men. Men are men ——"

"Except when they are hyenas."

"Even a hyena will fight for his ——"

"Only a hyena should ——"

The Old Gentleman began rapping the table with his fork. "I won't have sedition talked in my house, where I've got a future citizen growing up to fight for his country, right or wrong."

"When Decatur said that, Father, he was in love with the magic of a phrase, not its meaning."

"He was a brave man and a patriot."

"He was both, Father. But there is a valor born of hysteria."

"I talk facts. Not high-sounding phrases."

"Just the reverse. You talk phrases. The phrases of the immemorial cant of warfare. Embroidered banners of phrases, made to cover up the stinking realities of greed and war."

"Hen-ery! Use nice words."

"I'm sorry, Mother. Please, Father, there is no use going over it all again. Whom do you think I ran into on High Street today? Remember Al Hopkins ――?"

"There is this much use," shouted the Old Gentleman, working himself more and more into the luxury of an orgy of rage, "I won't have a—pacifist in my house! I haven't raised two sons, and a third one growing up, to say nothing of sons-in-law and grandchildren, to have sedition in my house in my old age."

"Puppa!"

"Let him rave, Mother. My hope for him is that he will never have anyone in his house with more seditious thoughts against country than I."

"I don't know about that. When a man questions another man's right to fight for his country ――"

"I question every man's right to fight. To shed blood. To splatter out of a man's heart, with bullets, the life that women go down into hell to bring forth."

"Hennery!"

"And I say a country's honor comes even before that!"

"Puppa, your biscuit is getting cold."

"And I say no country's honor can be raised or lowered by shooting the blood out of human hearts."

"Such talk is traitorous. I won't have it talked before Davey. You're a traitor. Damnation, you're a ――"

"I won't be talked to like this, Father."

"Hennery! Puppa!"

"You don't deserve the benefits of the country you live in. You don't honor it. You don't know what it is to come like I came, penniless, and after years of an empty belly, into the country that gave me my everything. You don't honor the country that honored your parents and gave you a full belly. A country whose cobblestones you should kiss as I kiss them. Traitor!"

There shot along Henry's slowly mobile face the first quick flash of heat-lightning David had ever seen cross it. Small areas around his nose turned jade-white and quivered. Sweat sprang out across the considerable bulge of his forehead. His lips moved as if trying to moisten themselves and his neck began to beat. Regarding him, Mathilda sprang from her chair. Once, in his childhood, she remembered a paroxysm like that. His sister Bek had dared him to fight a debt-of-honor over a slate-pencil, in the yard of the House on Sycamore Street, with a town-boy named Cutty Ditweiler, who had been killed a year later by the accidental side swipe of his father's scythe.

Henry had stood by and let himself be bullied, sooner than fight. Bek, unable to endure it longer, had sprung on Cutty, raining blows, until the weaker man of the two went down before her. It was then that Henry had turned sick and run indoors to Mathilda, his face locked in the same kind of paroxysm that his mother beheld there now.

"Hen-nery!"

His whitish lips were pulled across his face like strips of adhesive tape, and Davey could not keep his fascinated eyes off them.

"We won't go into that, Father," said Henry and swallowed with such an effort that you could hear his throat click.

Mathilda, frantic at what she saw gathering in her husband's face, tilted the whole of the okra-bowl, noisily scraping the last of its viscous contents to her husband's plate.

"More okra, Father. Bek sent it over by Stevey. She

raises the best I ever tasted. Stevey isn't looking so well. Sometimes I think he must have caught a slow fever ——"

"We won't go into that, won't we!" exploded the Old Gentleman, his face a darkening blur, through which he could not or would not see the darkening face of his son. "We won't? We *will* go into that. I'm an American citizen, grateful for the benefits such a country has given me and my family, and even the bad times I am in now can't change that. I'm an American citizen, willing to give every grandson and son I got, if, God forbid, the country gets into war. When you talk as you do in front of your brother, even if he is only a child, I say it again, you are a traitor. A traitor to your country, sir! A damn traitor!"

The Old Gentleman was launched into his rage now. He shouted. He screamed. His voice came leaping over his lips, plunging into choking incoherence.

"God strike me—down—before I should have a son—a—damned traitor!"

It was then that Henry rose to his feet. He had the look of a man whose blood might have stopped in his veins, and he walked over to his father and took him up by a loose handful of the shoulder of his coat, and, for an incredible moment, it looked as if he were going to strike him down. Only he did nothing of the sort. He just began to shake, gently at first and then a little more furiously, until the Old Gentleman was half-off his feet.

"Don't you dare say that, Father!" To Davey, it scarcely seemed Henry's voice. Only something thin, as if some one were clapping two tin plates. "You—with your bombast! You don't know what love of country is. You only love your country enough to die for it, on a battlefield, the martyred death that gets monuments to it for the spilled entrails that have fertilized the earth in the name of Hate. You don't love your country enough to crucify yourself for it in the name of Love. You hear me, I do! Yours is the easy patriotism. The patriotism of the band-wagon. The patriotism of the self-flagellation of feeding the red dramatic jaws of war with the flesh of your flesh. Of feeding your sons' entrails to the bawdy, uncontrolled passions of men of power. Yours is the easy patriotism. The patriotism that gets its name smeared across tablets in public squares. I—oh God—what do you know about love of country?" said Henry, and suddenly, incredibly, released the bunch of his father's coat-sleeve and went sobbing from the room.

Davey crept after, but then only after long minutes had elapsed. Minutes of a silence that was punctuated by the great, unnatural-sounding ticks of the kitchen clock, with the nosegay painted on the glass door before its pendulum.

After a while, Mathilda began to cry softly into her apron, and the Old Gentleman began to swing the low contents of his coffee-cup and drink it down in slow, untasted gulps.

When Davey crept into his brother's room, there was the bulk of him across the red-and-white Paisley quilt of his cot, his head buried in his arms and his body as felled-looking as a tree.

"Henry," said Davey, and touched him timidly on the arm, "you're not a—a trait-or."

"No," said Henry, and jerked himself up and walked to the mirror to run a runty old hartshorn brush over his baldish spot. "I'm only a damn fool, Davey."

"You—you're great—Henry——"

"Yes, a great ass, Davey," said Henry, and lifted his small brother by the armpits and set him down again and walked down into the kitchen, where his father, in a wilt, still sat in his chair beside the table, swinging the last dreary contents of his coffee-cup.

"Forgive a fool, Father," said Henry, and walked up and held out a hand.

"Forgive an older fool," mumbled the Old Gentleman, taking the hand without glancing up.

"Hennery," quavered Mathilda, "will you eat your corn pudding now?"

"A big helping of it, Mother."

The lamp burned like a round and gracious eye into the thickening gloom of the kitchen. There were a dozen and one after-dinner chores to be done, the two men and Davey scattering for them after the meal, and Mathilda lifting the dishes in clumps and carrying them to the pan of hot water on the stove.

Out in the hen-roost, where Davey scuttled to count up his wyandottes, first stars could be seen through the square little window in the roof of the chicken-house. Lovely Vega, which Davey knew by name, popped out even as he stared. Curious, that men could bicker unashamed beneath the placid enormity of stars. . . .

There was water to be carried. On the crest at the back of the house where the pump stood, the billows of the miles of meadows, peaceful under the whitish night, ran out to horizon, the occasional farmhouses, barns, silos, and hay-ricks, looking like frail boats riding a gentle sea.

The pink patch of kitchen window, against which the hooked figure of his mother moved now and then, swam disembodied from the rest of the dark house, and might have been a window to the sky.

Across the silence, a figure, dangling a lantern, moved more deeply into the gloom. It was the Old Gentleman stalking past the barn down toward the pig-wallow.

It was deep night. Almost as if the evening were

holding its breath before exuding a deep sigh of satisfaction.

Curious, that this peace had held the turmoil of men's
passions that had raged in that little room down there
behind the pink patch.   Passions that must even now be
whirling in its timbers.

The pump squeaked as Davey leaned his lips to the
spout for the first cool gush, Teddy standing by to lick
the overflow with more greed than thirst.

How cool it was!   It seemed to Davey he could feel
it run along his throat down into a spot against his chest
that hurt.

The country stretched out before him as he lifted his
head and ran his tongue around his lips.   Tides of
country that seemed to emanate from the spot on which
he stood, appearing to rise and fall, even as his own
breathing, and making the flesh of earth feel almost the
same flesh as the soles of his feet.

"My country," said Davey, in the recitative voice of
Friday afternoons, and standing there with his bare
toes oozing into the cool, thin mud around the pump—
"my country—my country, right or wrong.   Mr. Hennery—you!—smartee—'tis anyhow!"

Chapter Nineteen

No, IT was not the same at Bek's any more.

The family was only visiting itself, so to speak.

For instance, Davey never returned home from the Model Farm any more, bearing big, yellow-toothed ears of corn, or pats of Bek's inimitable sweet butter, or an occasional squab, all picked and plucked and wrapped in cheese-cloth for the Old Gentleman's supper.

The squabs on the farm now belonged to Ex-Governor Howey, and so did the sweet butter that came out of Bek's churns just a little sweeter and creamier than any butter Davey was ever to know.

In some respects, Bek's scruples seemed a bit beside the point. According to her interpretation of what was actually a rather loose arrangement with the Howeys, board and lodging had been allotted to herself, Winslow, Steve, and Leslie. Therefore Paula, on those few of her vacations that she spent at home instead of doing summer work at normal school, slept on a sofa in the dining-room at her aunt Emma's in Centralia.

Davey never slept at Bek's any more, either. His old room at the top of the house was once more occupied by Stevey; and besides, the old, easy generosities of being permitted to straddle bareback the pick of Bek's stables, or of scuttling into the cool, dark cellar for dill-pickles stewing under juices and vine leaves, were of the past.

They were Howey property now. Even the pail of huge dills that had gone annually to Clara in St. Louis was a thing of the past, although Bek still did put up one private crock of the dark-green beauties. And a dozen for old Senator Allen, a gentleman farmer forty miles to the north, who admired Bek and always referred to her as the finest woman in the state.

Howey property! The very side rails of porch upon which Winslow loved to prop his feet and tilt back for hours with his eyes closed and his pipe drooping, were Howey property now. Feet off. Hands off. The old, easy household, with the enormous bounty of Bek, her largess, her come-hard but go-easy, were of yesteryear. Even Leslie, who liked to dig holes and bury such inconsequential addenda as bits of wall paper, empty spools, playing-cards, was now confined to a fenced-off little bit of dirt that Bek nightly spaded back into place. Howey dirt.

The overseer of the new Howey holdings, up with the first streak of dawn, stalking the barns of prize-cattle, riding on the running-board of trucks, as they rumbled out to field where the threshing-machines loomed, superintending the installation of new Howey machinery, inspecting feed-troughs, cattle-hoofs, water-drains and chickens for pip, had the hard precision of one of the new machines themselves. Ephraim Howey could have rented out the main house at good profit, and installed an overseer in the flat over the garage. Bek knew that. It kept her mouth straight and a little bitter with her scru pulous sense of obligation.

Anybody's foot on the rung of a Howey chair, even though that rung were hidden from sight under the the dining-table, grated a message to her alert nerves. Winslow, who used to paint on a Windsor chair which he toted about with him from one to the other of his five or six landscapes, tried and true, had to lug a stool instead now, which Bek herself built him out of pine-wood and a strip of canvas.

It was a tight, constrained household of conscientious economies.

It is doubtful if the Howey family ever came into much realization of this fanatical conservation of their interests.

It was ground into Winslow, all right, whose meek inefficiency under the rigors of the régime seemed to blow him out, like a candle. Bek no more realized this! On the contrary, she tried with every ounce of her grim energy to conserve him against the impact of their reverses.

Largely through her insistence that his work be served first, Winslow still painted throughout the long mornings of Bek's drudgery, puttered at picket-fences or lawn-mowing as his share of the farm chores, trembled and got ague at the mounting problems that had to do with Steve, and started to execute Bek's occasional request for further assistance in a low-geared fashion that almost invariably caused her to brush him aside and accomplish the task herself, with a power which never failed to amaze and further reduce him to impotency.

They never ceased, these two, to hypnotize each other by these temperamental divergencies. They made him precious to her, in the way that her children, in the first years of their life, had been precious. As Davey was still precious to her.

She liked to hurl the bulwark of her body between Winslow and the workaday things that would somehow have made him less dear to her, had he been able to cope with them.

She lifted from his shoulders, or rather never permitted to descend there, the burden of so much as the responsibility of choosing the color of his suits or the weight of his underwear, never realizing that she doused him with every breath she breathed, as she had done from the first day she met him and wooed him and married him.

She kept from him as much of the truth about Stevey as she dared. Not even Bek knew all of that truth. Davey did.

In the crammed routine of his workadays, he used to be sent twice and even thrice a day, scurrying over from the Igrotte place with a batch of his mother's muffins or a fowl for broth, that winter that Stevey was half-sick most of the time, with pains throughout his body that made even the light work outlined for him by Bek more than he could drag himself about to do.

Davey knew the furtive thing about Stevey. He had known it since the day that Teddy had lain before his eyes with a kicked-in side.

To Davey, in the fretful, pulled, nervous face of his grown nephew Steve, there was no longer mystery. Only a certain horror that not improbably played its part in what was to be a life-long aversion to the taste or smell of spirituous liquors.*

---

* Following that 1920 prohibition-fiasco of America's, I often think that my brother's enormous influence as author of the famous Modification Bill, which is already beginning to sweep the civilized world in its application, stands as a particularly fine example of his unparalleled capacity for balanced middle-man's judgment.

His personal aversion to drink, dates back, I feel sure, to an incident that had horribly to do with my own son. Throughout Dave's boyhood, it existed to such an extent that I have seen him turn pale from squeamishness at the sight of someone drinking a cup of cider.

As Police-Commissioner, as Senator, as Governor, he was consistently austere in meting out punishment to the man whose family suffered of his intemperance.

And yet, almost marked from childhood, as it were, with an aversion to drink, this was the man who ultimately was to draft out a compromise bill that was to save the face of the ridiculous America of the Volstead Act.

Not that anything in David's experience had prepared him for realization of anything that had to do with Stevey's plight. To be sure, he had seen old Jessup drink, and the Tarkingtons had once had a gardener who used to come staggering home from periodic Saturday-night trips to Middleton, to sit under the springhouse and crazily play a mouth-harp.

But the slaked throat and the burning eye of a member of the family, that was another matter. Davey knew that, with his intuition.

One dusk, coming across from the Igrotte house with a pan of his mother's clabber for Winslow, who yearned for it, now that Bek meticulously either fed it to the Howey hogs or sent pails of it over to the Howey farm, Davey came across the strange spectacle of Stevey standing in some knee-high grass beyond South Meadow, with the figure of a girl in his arms, one of her hands hanging limply into the grasses and her head dangling back and showing a great arch of white neck.

"It's Claire," said Stevey almost with relief at seeing David, whom he was given to avoiding since the incident with Teddy. "She's fainted. Can't seem to revive her. Help me home with her, there's a fellow."

Davey had known of these meetings. Two or three times, on that short-cut across the lower rim of South Meadow, he had heard their voices and skirted a rockledge to avoid being seen or heard.

One somehow did not run tattling to elders about knowing this—and yet—more than once, waking into the quiet of his room underneath the eaves, something that was not entirely right about his remaining silent smote Davey with the kind of depression that can overtake in the small hours of night.

It was quite a job getting Claire to the house. She was in the dead weight of a swoon from which she did not seem to want to emerge.

Chapter Twenty

THERE were seldom family-conferences now, at least not in the old sense of the word. Except when Phil came down, (never with Rita or the children, because of lack of space to put them up) he spent the night on the curlicue sofa in the Igrotte house.

When Paula came home, she stayed at Emma's and slept on the day-bed in the dining-room alcove, and always left her board-money under the fruit-bowl on the sideboard, over which Emma wept.

Phil worked for an automobile concern in Springfield now, on a commission basis, and lived in a little two-family bungalow at the opposite end of town from the one where the boom was taking place.

Every month or so, Phil sent the Old Gentleman a check for ten or twenty dollars. These, knowing to what extent the Phil Schuylers were reckoning to the penny themselves, his father never cashed, causing confusion in Phil's small banking-matters. Incredibly enough, however, on the margin of income that forced him to reckon in terms of car fares, he was already manipulating on the side again, and one month along with another automobile salesman, had turned over with profit, two hundred dollars in a speculative land deal.

But the gathering of the clan, even for the festal purpose of Thanksgiving dinner, was no longer comfortably possible in the little house in Pessimines Lane. Eight people would have jammed any room in the house to capacity, and the kitchen range, bought from old man Igrotte because the one from the House on Sycamore

Street would not fit in, had a top scarcely large enough for a pot, a kettle, and a skillet.

Mathilda, who was accustomed to six and eight pots seething at once!

And yet, by the mysterious sounding of some sort of a clan-cry, there did crowd into the stuffiness of the little old Igrotte packing-case, more Schuylers than had convened together since that evil day brought down on them by one Mark Milliken.

A little over a week after Davey had helped Stevey carry the limp and fainting body of Claire from the edge of South Meadow to the Model Farm, there gathered, in rather muted fashion, most of the family.

Even Clara, who made a great ado about leaving Sam, who was sure to play penny-ante poker in her absence, arrived this time from St. Louis.

A good baker's-dozen, counting Dave and Leslie and Stevey and Claire, were crowded into the Igrotte dining-room that Sunday for the plate-lunch that Mathilda, with the aid of her daughters and Trina, who came out to help on her every day off, passed in and out among the company.

The smattering of grandchildren on an occasion which ill-befitted them, complicated things a bit. Leslie was there, mild and patient, but a little timorous even among his own. Grown to the great gangling height that had not yet reached its full development, it was difficult—it was grotesque, to seat him among the children. And yet. . . . Finally Bek, with the most drawn look anyone there had ever seen on her face, placed him on a chair between the open folding-doors, so that from every vantage, as she hastened about with a coarse, white sort of butcher's apron the Old Gentleman used to wear into the smoke-house on Sycamore Street, she could observe him.

Indeed, this austere occasion revolved around grand-children. A dark, defiant-looking one, who sat out on the stoop, smoking cigarette after cigarette, and throwing them away only half-puffed. In a corner of the dining-room, seated white and silent and absolutely impassive, sat Claire. A flaxen-haired snow-maiden of imperturb-ability.

It was a wretched "lap lunch" of restraint, ill-balanced plates, and buzzing noonday heat that crowded into the little clapboard house. The Old Gentleman, whose face could be so sly with humor, clamped-looking and grim now, seated like a troglodyte at the end of the table.

There were no preliminaries. Before Mathilda, fol-lowed by Emma, had carried out the last plate of Brown-Betty-with-hard-sauce, the Old Gentleman came out like a cannon at his grandson, pointing him out as he sat twirling his spoon around an untasted dessert-plate.

"A Schuyler," he boomed at him, "has disgraced us!" and began shaking his pointing finger and beginning at once to rise to the dreaded climax of his dreaded wrath.

"Oh, Father," called Bek, "don't begin it that way! Not before the children ———"

"Dave, run along."

"Leslie, darling—come, Aunt Emma will take you out and get you a pail and let you pick some string-beans for grandmother's and grandfather's supper."

"If Grandfather does begin that way," said Steve, rising and kicking his chair back savagely, "I'll walk out of the house in the very beginning and stay out. I was a fool to let myself be dragged here anyway, like a head of cattle."

"Stevey," said Bek, and walked over and placed her palm against his forehead, "what did you promise me?"

She was a mountain of calm, standing there between

her son and Winslow, who had receded into his chair as if it were sucking him in.

"I won't be bullied, Mother."

"You won't be bullied," shouted the Old Gentleman. "You *will* be bullied! Into honor."

"Father," said Bek, "I won't be bullied, either. This situation has got to be talked out in calm, or Winslow and Stevey and Claire and Emma and I will walk out."

"Oh, dear!" sobbed Emma. "Oh, dear! oh, dear!"

"For God's sake, Pap," said Phil, "can't you keep your head on your shoulders?"

"At least," cried Mathilda, in her fluty, dry-lipped tremolo, "Davey don't need to be here. Shoo, Dave!"

"Davey," said his sister Clara, who had a futile, rather antagonizing way with children, including her own, "run out with Leslie and play."

"I want to stay," said Davey stubbornly, and sat with his hands clinched into the sides of his footstool.

Suddenly Claire, collapsing from her imperturbability, began to sob violently, her aunts forming an immediate barrage around her.

"This is an outrage, Father!" said Henry, rising in disgust from the window-sill where he had been sitting looking out upon the bare patch of chicken-yard and puffing at his pipe. "Good Lord! they never did it this brutally, I'll wager, when they used to settle tribal disputes by torture! What is it, Father, now that you have the tribe around the fire? On with the council-meeting."

Poor Claire! At her uncle's words, she crouched and sobbed the more, Emma fanning her with one of the Old Gentleman's tape-bound, palm-leaf fans.

The Old Gentleman began to cry then, in dry sobs that split his voice. "A child of my family. A child of a family that has not so much as a speck upon its honor. Two children of my family."

"Two children of your family what?" snapped Henry. "Swept off their feet by a law of life stronger than they are.   Well, what's to be done about it?   Crucify them? Quit your crying, Claire.   Come out here and face the situation.   Come to a sane conclusion and end all this unnecessary and nauseating clan-panic.   What's on your minds about it all?"

"Answer Uncle Henry, dearest," said Emma.   "Oh, dear!   Oh, dear!   Open the window a little, Morton. I don't feel right well."

To Claire, whose worshipful admiration of her uncle Henry had long been a family-joke, the moment was simply not to be borne.   Her lips shuddered up and down like window-shades sucked inward.   Sobs came that made the noise of a window-shade flopping in high wind.

"I ——can't!"

"The thing in a nutshell is this, Uncle Henry," said Steve, stepping forward and shaking the hair back from his sheet-white face.   "It seems I've been a rotter."

"You've been a low life," screamed the Old Gentleman, breaking loose again from his daughter's detaining hands.

"Father," said Henry sharply.   "One more outburst like that, and I'll join Stevey and Claire and walk out, too!"

"Nobody's to blame in this, Uncle Henry.   But if the family insists otherwise, I'll take it all."

"You used to have her meet you secretly, Stevey," sobbed Emma, "you know you did.   I see it all so clearly now.   My Claire away from home so much after her teaching-hours.   You encouraged her to meet you secretly.   Claire was not the girl to ever ——"

"Oh, Mother, please!   Please!   Stevey never made me do anything I didn't want to do."

"Let's not go into that now," said Bek. "Whether Steve encouraged Claire is not the issue here, Emma."

"But Bek—he did——"

"I take it that the point is," said Henry drily, "Claire is going to have a baby. What's to be done about it?"

At the brutality of that presentation, a series of bleats and short cries rose about the room.

"Henry," said Clara, and made a dive toward Dave, "at least you might realize that a child is in the room. Davey, go out and help Leslie pick beans."

"I won't," said Dave, and sat with his large, dark eyes on his nephew Steve, and his hands clinched tighter than ever into the footstool.

"Let him alone!" said Henry. "Good Heavens! why start out making shameful to him the most fundamental fact of life!"

"Oh! Hen-nery—son—shame—oh! oh!"

"You mean," cried Emma, "you want to hold up to him the example of his elders as something noble!"

"No, I don't mean a damn thing except that all this mewling makes me sick, and I don't want to saturate the fact of birth for him with nastiness by being furtive about it."

"Oh, Stevey, Stevey! Oh, Claire! How could you?" cried Mathilda suddenly, and began to clasp and unclasp her wisps of little hands, and to regard them with the tears running, "How could you?"

"Grandmother," sobbed Claire, easily susceptible to the pitiable spectacle of the sobbing Mathilda, "we know it's no excuse but we didn't mean to—it's not anything you think out, Grandmother."

"God knows it isn't," said Steve, his pallor suddenly aflame, "or do you think we would have let ourselves in for this!"

"By Gad, if I weren't hand-and-tongue-tied by women-folks," shouted Morton Milliken, suddenly, the Morton who was so strangely subdued where a gathering of Schuylers was concerned—"if I wasn't hand-and-tongue-tied, I'd horsewhip the cur who's responsible for this—my daughter ———"

"They get married," shouted the Old Gentleman, wresting free of restraint this time, "before another twelve hours passes over the heads of this family. So help me God!"

"Father," intoned Bek, standing like a mountain, "they're *first-cousins!*"

"That's what makes it so terrible, Father," whispered Clara, to whom the situation was as fascinating as it was horrible, and her face with the scallops of chin seeming to shrivel into loose bags of flesh, "even if they want to do right—they're *first-cousins!*"

"Cousins or no cousins, one sin has got to invite another this time. A grandson of mine who does wrong to a girl marries her, if she is cousin ten times over."

"That's terrible, Father," said Bek. "That's terrible."

"It's a sin, Puppa. A sin on top of a sin!"

"Cousins beget dwarfs—and monstrosities, and—and —oh, I don't know what," sobbed Clara.

"And hop-toads," said Henry with solemnity. "And pollywoggles."

"Henry!"

Seated once more in the window-frame, one knee high, the smoke he blew toward the kitchen yard curled off curled lips.

"Good Lord," he said, and rapped his pipe empty, "one would actually have to sit in on this scene to believe it could happen. You people cling to a worn-out old superstition, when you could have a brand-new truth in exchange for it. Cousins! Suppose they are cousins!"

"Hennery!"

"Don't you know that much of that is just old-wives'
tale! Go into any library and read even a fairly modern
book on biology. Good Lord, what is so reluctantly
accepted by the human brain as truth! Study your sta-
tistics on the progeny of cousins. Face facts. For a
woman as up-and-coming as you are, Bek, and who's had
as much ordinary stock-breeding experience as you have,
you amaze me. Poppycock, that's what you're all talking! I've no patience with old-wives' science. Apparently the two youngsters love each other. It probably
would not all have happened this undesirable way if
they hadn't been kept apart through ignorance and prejudice. Let them marry. There's your problem solved.
Come, I move that this unnecessary painful session ad-
journ."

"But, Uncle Henry," said Steve and shot to his feet—
"but Uncle Henry," his eyes rolling, like an ox in terror
toward Claire—"I mean," he said—"nothing"—and sat
down.

"Why, Stevey, what?" cried Claire, her sweet, moist
eyes roving and probing his face—"why, Stevey, what?"

"I—I—" said Steve and began half-rising again and
wiping his dry mouth with the palm of his dry hand, in
a way that was somehow horrible—"why, I'm nothing.
I don't want—I mean—we—not that!"

"Exactly," said Claire by this time, whose blue eyes,
as she regarded Steve, had grown suddenly black and
round and flabbergasted, "if Stevey doesn't want it—I
mean if I—I—. If he doesn't want it—I don't want it
either."

"Doesn't want what?" roared the Old Gentleman.

"Claire knows I'll abide by any decision she reaches
in this matter," said Steve, standing very straight and
very calm beside his mother. "And if Claire for one

reason or another doesn't want it—she—knows best. I understand ——"

"Why, Steve," said his mother, regarding him with her level eyes and her voice incredulous, "are you trying to let it appear that Claire is the one who doesn't want—when—it seems to be you?"

"No, no, Aunt Bek. He isn't. You see, Grandfather," cried Claire, turning to him, her blue eyes very dark under the light tinge of her flaxen hair, "I—of course Stevey will go through with it if he has to—but, Grandfather—isn't there some way—please—couldn't I just go away? I could, Grandfather, if the family would only cut out the dramatics about it—us. Stevey doesn't want—I mean I—I don't love Stevey any more, Grandfather. I'm not afraid—alone ——"

"You don't what?"

"It's a lie!" said Morton, rising with a stride toward Stevey. "She's trying to save his damn hide."

"It's not a lie, Father!"

"She means, Grandfather," said Steve, deadly white, "after all that's happened—oh, what's the use beating about the bush. Claire would rather go off and have the thing over without marriage, because—because—oh, I'm not hedging, Uncle Morton! When she came to tell me about it—I guess I—did feel pretty sick. I guess that scene down there in South Meadow the day she first told me about it—is what cured her of me—I'm a cad."

"No, no, Steve!"

"I'm not the marrying sort, but not for a cad's reasons ——"

"By Gad ——"

"Oh, hold your horses, Uncle Morton! I'll go through with it. Simply trying to explain my position. I hadn't wanted it to happen this way. Claire's sake, more than mine. Mother and Claire know what else I mean—I'm not fit to marry any woman. Tell them, Mother."

"Stevey! Stevey! I can't bear it!"

"Aunt Bek," cried Claire and beat her hands, "don't you tell them *that!*"

"Yes, Claire, the time is here," said Bek, in tones that were as monotonous as hoofbeats on wood, and pinioning Winslow, with that powerful, level gaze of hers into a huddle which might have been a faint. Whatever it was, it kept him crouched in a deathly pale silence back into his chair, until the scene wore itself out and Bek was daubing cold coffee on his forehead. "Steve and I have been fighting out something. We'll win all right, but—in the light of events, best—you should know. You see, when Steve came home so suddenly from college —well, I guess a better way to put it is ——"

"Oh, Mother, come out with it. I was fired from college for drunkenness, Grandfather! The dean stumbled across me under a bench on the campus one night— gollywogged. Spifilicated. Soused."

"Steve!"

"First taste I got of it at college set me wild. Couldn't lay off the stuff. Can't always—now. Right here— practically under your very eyes, Mother has walked the floor with me night after night."

"Bek!"

"Sister!"

"She's written to Cures for me. She's dropped the stuff into my coffee. I'm a rotten no-account drunk. I am. Now throw me into the gutter, if you've a mind to. I don't care. At least, you must see now—Claire and I—can't ——"

With a cry that had been gathering in his throat as if to crack it, the Old Gentleman made a flying leap across the inert form of Winslow. "I'll show him!" he shrilled, struggling again and again, only to be rudely pinioned backward by Phil. "He's trying to think up a sniveling way out!"

"Good God!" said Henry, and rose slowly from the window-sill and stood looking at his nephew.

"Grandfather," chimed Claire faintly, "if you go on like this—I can't stand it. I've known that all along. It's a fight he'll win some day. I just can't explain it, Grandfather, only—except that if he doesn't want it— I don't want it either. I just can't explain."

"I can!" shouted Morton. "I can explain. She's showing him a way out. The damn white-liver. He's resigning and she's sheltering him behind her skirts— the God-damn ――"

"And I tell you," screamed the Old Gentleman, strangling, "that if he is fifty drunkards and fifty times more the low life that he is, no grandson of mine wrongs a girl and doesn't right it!"

"And no son of mine!" sobbed Winslow, half under his faint, as Bek daubed on the cold coffee.

"Before another twelve hours goes over his head, he rights it!"

"Are you mad?" cried Henry, "every blamed one of you!" his beetling brows drawing together like portières. "Here are two young people. One of them confessedly an alcoholic. And yet you want to tie them together under revolting circumstances to beget children that stand ten times the chance of being maimed that they would were they merely born of first-cousins. You dare to want to tie these two unhappy young people together for life?"

"Yes, by Gad, yes, just that! So help me, I'll see them both dead, if they don't make it right."

"Then, Father, you and the entire family that countenance it are crazy criminals."

"No Schuyler born out of wedlock comes into this world. We're a family with strong honest roots down into the soil of this country. . . ."

"Yes, yes, Father, we've been over that before. Don't scream."

"Let Father alone, Henry," said Phil, trembling. "He's right."

"I *will* scream," screamed the Old Gentleman. "I know I'm right. Those two have got to marry. I don't want to hear the ins and the outs. I don't care that they love each other any more, or don't love each other. They should have thought of that first. That's something that they've got to work out after marriage. You two marry! You two marry! You don't pull the name your Grandmother and I have built out of our blood and our sweat down overnight. You two marry! You two marry!"

"I guess Father's right, Steve," said Bek, standing pale as a statue. "If you've lost your nerve, that's your misfortune. It's all too late now."

"Yes," echoed Emma, Phil, and Clara, "Yes."

"Yes, by God!" said Morton, who was all sweating, and then over and over again, "Yes, by God! Yes, by God!"

"And I say," barked Henry, "that to make these two children marry under these conditions is just as criminal as if you took their lives in your hands and broke their necks for their mistakes. Break their spirits. Break their morals. Break their hearts. By God, you get away with that! But I say you are just as criminal as if you broke their necks."

"Those two marry!" yelled the Old Gentleman, whose shaking finger never stopped pointing. "You with your new-fangled notions that don't fit in with the world you live in, are responsible for where you are today. A one-horse lawyer in a one-horse town, where you should be first in the state. No new-fangled notions here now! Those two marry, if I have to drag them to it through the streets of Centralia to have the ceremony performed."

Through the tenseness something snapped into the expression of that circle of faces. Relief. As if a verdict, dreaded, had none the less brought solution by the very virtue of being pronounced.

Even Claire, slipping back almost as nerveless as Winslow, seemed to relax to the sentence. Even Stevey, who stood facing his grandfather without blinking.

All except Henry.

"Well," he said finally, knowing how complete was his defeat in that circle of acquiescence and giving out one of his short, sardonic laughs, "maybe it's for the best. Doubtless you two are sufficiently cowed to the yoke of the fear-of-living to adjust yourselves to the servitude you have just had sentenced upon you today. But this fact still remains. The scene that has taken place in this room today in this year of our Lord, is as mediæval as hell ——"

"Hennery!"

"Excuse me, Mother."

Suddenly David, most undramatic of youngsters, who had been seated crouched to his footstool like a bit of lichen, ran toward his nephew Steve, and pulling him by the wrist toward the languid figure of Claire, crouched back in her mother's arms, tried to weld their clammy hands in a clasp.

"See!" cried Bek, struggling to keep her voice dead-level, and regarding Henry a little triumphantly, "even a child would lead them—together."

"And a little child shall lead them," said Phil, on a snigger. He had not meant to snigger. The sound had

just jumped off his lips.   Tension, perhaps, but to horri-
fied family-ears the room seemed to roar of that snigger.

From his long, lean height, Henry stood regarding his
small brother, a slow laugh shaking his shoulders.

"Maybe you're right.   The kid's got the trick-combina-
tion of leadership.   Imagination tempered by a level head
and a level heart.   Man-of-the-people stuff!"

"What's man-of-the-people stuff, Henry?" piped Dave.

"You!"

Chapter Twenty-one

THE winter America entered the War was a lean one on the farm, even in a neighborhood where foundries were changing their tunes from the production of safes, tools, and castings, to the grim grinding-out of arms and ammunition.

Young men were being conscripted or leaving the farms to enlist. A hoof-and-mouth disease was rampant among the horned cattle. Old man Igrotte, from the vantage of Iowa, raised the rent one-third on his mangy little place at the expiration of the first year of the Schuyler tenancy.

Frequently now, and with a bitterness that rankled him into constant and aggravated irritability, the Old Gentleman was obliged to cash one of Phil's less and less frequently-sent checks.

He even accepted, with none too much grace, the gift of two sacks of corn flour from the Howey farm, which one of the overseers rumbled up with on a truck one afternoon with the compliments of the Ex-Governor who was wintering in Florida.

The Old Gentleman realized, with the terrible, gnawing bitterness which ate so at his heart, that word must have leaked, even as far as Florida, that the Schuylers were hard-put. One of the Howey girls, on a visit to the paternal winter home, had doubtless let slip that the Schuylers had fallen on bad times.

There was etched in acid into the Old Gentleman's mind a picture of the portly figure of the Ex-Governor and the largeness of manner with which he must have given the orders for the distribution of the occasional offerings at the Schuyler door.

Every month, after a time, with galling and yet welcome regularity, there arrived these offerings. The impersonal kind of gift that stuck in the Old Gentleman's craw, as he put it. Gifts that almost savored of charity. Commodities like a fat goose. A twenty-five-pound sack of coffee in the bean. Ham, smoked on the Howey place, sometimes the cuts off the very killings Bek had that same week sent over to the Governor's place.

It helped. For instance, the barrel of corn flour meant that every morning, when the lanterns were swinging in and out of the barns for miles and miles around, Dave, as he started off on his lonely hike over to the Tarkington place to help Nemo with the chore of bran-mixing did so with a big, hot square of pone under his jacket for the heat it poured against him, and that later was to slide down into him in warm, grateful chunks.

Sleet came down many of the black dawns of that winter, slanted against him in long javelins, and made the roads and the roofs and the hedges to shine. Mornings filled with the glass music of hitting ice. Sometimes everything took on a crystal coating, making it a fairyland of white, stretching arms of trees, the glitter of hedges, and the splendor of frozen breath.

Great, crystal chandeliers of morning, like the big one that hung in the Howey front parlor. It was warming to turn around, now and then, for a glimpse of the lighted kitchen window of the Igrotte house, against which he knew his mother to be moving at the business of preparing Henry's breakfast and the collapsible tin box of lunch he now carried in with him to his office in Centralia.

Those were the shivery, silvery mornings all right, when the ice formed in a mask against his face, and the gleam of light from the Tarkington barn was something to stumble gratefully toward.

Old Nemo drove a close bargain as a taskmaster. It was scarcely ever before ten minutes to nine when he released the boy from his chore, allowing him exactly ten minutes to cover the mile to the schoolhouse. He had never failed, however, to arrive there before the first tick of nine, with his heart seeming to beat against his neck and up into his ear-drums.

There was a pride about never having been tardy, even though Miss Hassebrock knew the condition and offered to grant him fifteen minutes' indulgence in the matter of arrival, as she did to other of the farm-boys.

That was the winter, too, of only half-day sessions for Dave. The class of Colonial History came in the afternoon. Dave was eager for that. It was one of the classes he was sure to shine in, the result of long evenings with Henry. Geography, too, came in the afternoon. Gee!

But the Old Gentleman fell ill about then of a sciatic torture that kept him chair-ridden all of that winter and that meant having to call half a session a day, in order to be home by noontime for the accumulation of chores.

It required a letter to the county superintendent for that special half-time dispensation, which Mathilda patiently, and to Dave's dictation, penned through her tears.

Later, in that first month of the Old Gentleman's disability, when, against every admonition, he was hobbling about sooner than his sciatica permitted, down he went on a slippery runway that led to the hen-house, and twisted a ligament in his thigh. That virtually laid him up the remainder of the winter.

Then Dave just remained out of school the entire session, secretly a little exultant over some aspects of it, and again hankering after the panorama of the Geography, the Colonial History, and the Physiology courses.

Poor Miss Hassebrock, sciatic herself, once and sometimes twice a week that long, dark winter managed to get a lift in the Ford truck of the farmer-family where she boarded, as far as the Igrotte house; and while the boy who drove her, great shy boob, waited in the kitchen, she would coach Dave in a gallant attempt to keep him up in his classes.

But usually, the boy was tired. So deadly tired that once, during a problem in square-root, he fell asleep with his cheek down against the page upon which her hand happened to be resting.

Bird-like little person, she sat there over an hour, with the Ford truck waiting and chugging at the door, before she could force herself to shake him awake.

Twenty years later, and in the most far-fetched, accidental fashion, David Schuyler was to learn that the little woman paid the farm-boy who drove her twenty-five cents for these trips and fifty, the evening that Davey fell asleep against her hand and kept her waiting the hour overtime.

It was the very next day that Miss Hassebrock's annuity began. Poor dear, she lived only bed-ridden years to enjoy it.

That was practically the beginning and the end of any sustained schooling for Dave, those scant, war-ridden years, when Henry put up a partition down the lean-enough length of his office, and rented the other half to an osteopath, and the "Furnished Rooms, With or Without Board" sign flashed all too frequently in Emma's window, and when Bek sat in Henry's office, talking over Phil's troubled affairs, every time she brought Leslie to town for osteopathic treatment in the office next door.

Lean, hard days when, somehow, the faces of the Schuylers seemed to grow longer in actual bone-formation.

But with the end of the sustained schooling for Dave, Henry still read to him, and with him, through the long, quiet evenings. The great embroidered legends of King Arthur. *Canterbury Tales,* of a Knight there was; Abou Ben Adhem who awoke one night from a deep dream of peace! *Letters of a Self-Made Father to His Son; Boy's Iliad; Wreck of the Hesperus; The Ancient Mariner; Bird Lore; Deserts of the World; Arabia Deserta; Faust; Our National Parks; Prisoner of Zenda; Compleat Angler; Golden Treasury; Peck's Bad Boy; Canalse Interpretation of Perjury; Land of the Midnight Sun; Bee Culture; The Philippines, What of Them?* Months of evenings, and years of months of these hours of Henry's intoning beneath the green eyeshade. It was his way of resting. His way of relaxing. Sometimes the boy on the stool at his feet nodded and slept against his knee, as he carried him along beyond his depth. But more often, Dave, who was a good listener, sat with his small, square chin propped in his hands, staring off over the shoulder of the reader. Those were the years of magnificence, all right. Napoleon gazed from Elba in the small stuffiness of that room in the Igrotte house. And the island of Elba was an atrocity of a hearth-rug with the figure of a dog woven in. Leander swam the Hellespont of that room, and the Hellespont was Henry's single cot, with Teddy usually asleep at its foot, with his nose tucked into his fore-paws. A knight there was shivered the timbers of that room. Don Quixote tilted lance there. Through its eight-by-ten, the desert flowed into parched vastness, and William Tell stalked, and Catherine the Great.

These evenings stacked up into practically all three

hundred and sixty-five days of the year, except the semi-occasional ones when Henry remained in town to attend a Bar Association banquet, or to escort Henriette to the rare musical event that found its way into Centralia's Opera House.

His Ford runabout, along with the House on Sycamore Street, was a thing of the past, so that the evenings, in town, Henry spent on a leather sofa in the back of his office.

Twice a day for two years until he made an arrangement with the owner of a dairy-truck to carry him to town and back, he walked the three and one half miles from the Igrotte house to High Street. The actual distance could be lessened a half-mile by a détour that led past the House on Sycamore Street. But from the day he left it, bag and baggage, chattel and what not, Henry could never bear to look at it again.

Never once, in all the years he was to live in the vicinity, first in the Igrotte house and later back in Centralia, was he known to have been seen within seeing-distance of the House on Sycamore Street.

In Davey lurked no such ache. There came the day when the first contingent of Centralia boys marched the entire length of Sycamore Street, then back again half-way, to swing into Court House Square.

In the hours of waiting for the parade to take place, Dave, astride the cupola of the old front porch he knew so well, perched himself like the figurehead of a ship, directly in front of the window of the room in which he had been born.

The Kelsoes, who occupied the place now, were easy, good-natured folk of ready welcome. Tony Kelsoe had a large and paying wholesale fruit-store on Miami Street. The day of the parade, the lawn and the front of the House on Sycamore Street were thrown open.

The Kelsoes had improved the place, although Emma said it made her "positively sick" to pass its pinwheel flower-beds, its splotched old iron deer painted a bright chrome-yellow, and a triple coat of white paint on the house that smote and smote the eye.

For the merest second, it seemed strange even to the child, shinnying up the front porch that had been home to him, but a strangeness immediately to be forgotten in the strangling excitement of the spectacle of the boys in khaki marching down-street under the spreads of the elms of Sycamore Street. Bare elms now, with branches that rattled in the light wind like bones.

Why, those boys out there, practically every fellow of them, he knew by name. Spike. Minty. Jeb. Off to war. There was Joe Lowenstein, with his puttees wound crooked. And Ed Slayback who sold screw-eyes and rubber-tubing in the hardware-store under Henry's office. Paul Koerber. Lynn Chipman, who lived in the largest house in Centralia, and whose younger brother, Kenneth, just two years older than Dave, had a whole wireless-set on the roof of his home. There was a long-legged fellow named Tad, who used to drive a dirt-cart out Bek's way. He was much heavier than the run of the boys, and seemed to mind the weight of his pack. There was Gum Lewis and Bennie Cohen, and a fellow whose name used to be Berlin and who had changed it to Brayley since the War.

And there was Steve! He and Lynn Chipman carried themselves the straightest, and somehow with the most bearing of them all.

"Hi, Steve!"

From the vantage of astride the cupola, they seemed like so many pairs of animated scissors tramping down the street with a hollow sound that was crashed into

every so often, by a small brass band that sent the spec
tators along the curbs into cheers.

It drove Teddy, down on the lawn, wild with excite
ment, and kept him yapping up at Dave and imploring
his descent from the cupola.*

Every inch of the march down Sycamore Street, after
the boys had passed Kelsoe's the second time, Dave ran
alongside.

There was Stevey, second from the end, with his white
face set immobile to the front, and his shoulders flaring
and his waist receding, and his puttees wound the tightest
and the rightest of them all! Not a glance to the right
or the left.

Hoh, and how Minty kept darting his head and neck
in and out like a turtle. Not a glance from Steve though.
Stevey marching off to war. The boys of Centralia
marching off to war.

War was waste, Henry said. War was Nature's
bungling trick for weeding out the over-production of
the race with the blindest kind of non-selection. But just
the same, tramp-tramp-tramp, to sit as Henry was sitting
up in his office, with his eye-shade on and his fingers
pressing against his forehead, while the boys marched
beneath his very window, was impossible, if that curious
rhythm of tramp-tramp-tramp had you by the throat

---

* The day that my Stevey marched away, we drove into
town for a point of vantage from Emma's front windows. As
we passed the House on Sycamore Street, there was our Dave
astride its cupola, just like he still belonged there. I can see
him now. Small and square and firm, as if the old house were
a mare, and he were riding it, straight and sure and calm, into
the maelstrom. And yet how little he suggested to any of
us, as he sat there gazing thoughtfully into the confusion, that
one day he *was* to ride out into that maelstrom . . . a leader
of leaders.

Tramp, tramp, tramp . . . my country, right or wrong —Stephen Decatur was a hysterical woman. My country, right or wrong. Well, anyways—anyways—it was! No matter even what Henry said. It was a fellow's country, right or wrong.

And Stevey, right or wrong, was going! "My nephew, right or wrong, is going to war," shouted Dave to himself, as he ran on his short, squarish legs, breathlessly, alongside. Cæsar had crossed the Alps, Washington had crossed the Delaware, in the name of War! Well —well? Henry hated war. And Henry was always right except when—except when the tramp-tramp-tramp made "my country, right or wrong" sound right! Right, you bet your life!

Stevey was too front-face to know that Davey ran alongside, almost, it might be said, too stern-faced to care. Minty darted his head sideways and said, "Hi, Kid," to Dave. So did Bennie Kohn, Beulah's brother, who finished his words in "ink" instead of "ing." "Hi, Kid, we're goink!"

Tramp! Tramp! Tramp-tramp-tramp. Even in the cold, damp air the moisture formed rivulets and ran down Dave's neck in his effort to keep up with the adult strides; and along toward the end Teddy, too, began to lope with his tongue hanging out sidewise.

My country, right or wrong! You betcherlife, Henry, you! To be as smart as Henry was to think too much and not to feel enough.

At the other end of Sycamore Street, in Emma's house of the peeling paint and the "Music Teacher" and "To Let" signs in the window, were grouped most of the lodgers, and Mathilda, and the Old Gentleman, with a Paisley shawl draped across his remonstrating shoulders against the sciatica, and Bek and Winslow, and Leslie waving a banner, and Henriette Simpson, and Paula,

home for the week.   There they were all, out on the
porch and along the steps.   And in the parlor window
with the stringy lace curtains pinned back, was Claire
looking as white as a flower, clutching her beet-red nub
of a baby, which she held up and dandled, as the autom
atons, hay-foot-straw-foot passed the house.

Long after the footsteps had died down, Claire stood
there, waving her baby aloft, for the husband and father
Steve, who had not looked, to see as he passed by.

When they all came in, a few moments later from
the porch, it was hard to coax Claire away from the
dandling of the baby before the window that looked on
the now-deserted street.

His perfectly-formed, beautiful baby that, as he passed,
Stevey had not turned his head to see.

It was in vain that poor Emma, whose flaxen hair had
developed wide gray streaks, tried to comfort her.   A
good soldier would not, could not, turn his head.   Just
see, there was Lynn Chipman's little brother Kenneth
crying after him and sobbing, and not even a glance from
Lynn.   And see, old lady Mintz, poor old dear, reaching
out empty arms after her boy.   Shame, Claire—for
shame!

Keyed to a pitch of pride that made him bumptious,
the Old Gentleman stumbled about the house, with the
Paisley shawl forgotten and dangling and tangling about
his feet.   Stevey was justifying some of the torment he
had caused the family.

Stevey was going into war.   For country.   It was like
paying a debt of gratitude with a coin that had been
minted from the living flesh of his own side.   Ecstasy of
self-flagellation, as it must have burned in the eyes of
early Christian martyrs, illumined the Old Gentleman.
He stood by and watched, glorying in pain.

Besides, Steve's going to war would make a man of

him. Or as the Old Gentleman put it, would break him, by Gad! And even the latter was no worse than the mess he had made of things up to now.

A Schuyler was in the ranks that were marching from Centralia!

Bek's eyes were blazing with that, too, and Winslow's and old Trina's and even Mathilda's, whose, however, like Claire's, were at the same time crucified.

And while Dave was running breathlessly alongside the moving phalanx of the khaki, up in his office, over the hardware-store, to the rat-a-tat-tat of the marching of feet, sat Henry, with his dry fingers pressed against his eyeballs.

Chapter Twenty-two

WHEN Dora Tarkington was on the threshold of her 'teens, she was about an inch and a half taller than Dave, with long honey-colored curls that lay in a wide fan across her shoulders and a curved fringe of bangs. These bangs, old Mammy, whose hand quivered, invariably cut a little crookedly, because she kept one copying eye glued to a lovely daguerreotype of Dora's mother propped on the washstand beside her.

Dora used to study that daguerreotype herself. The sweet, straight eyes, the elaborately high, honey-colored hair with the curve of bang that Mammy tried to imitate. The fitted basque, with the heavy festoonings of gold chains and brooches. The tapering waist, supporting the little, urn-shaped swell of bust and shoulders.

Dora was of sturdier heft than this mother who had died at her birth. There was more of her father in the molding of her longer, lither legs and torso. But at eleven, the bright gold prettiness of the mother, who had dashed through her youth on the spirited horseflesh of a Kentucky farm, lay over Dora like pollen, conjuring memories before her father's eyes, in a hundred ways.

Every year Dora had a birthday-party and a cake with pink candles and colored-tissue caps that popped as they were pulled open. For these occasions old Mammy, relic from the days when the girl in the daguerreotype had ridden bare-back through Kentucky grass, made large batches of cup-cakes with pink icing; decorated the round birthday-cake in "red-hots"; froze the vanilla ice-cream in a home-made contrivance of galvanized bucket and chopped ice, and then set about fluting Dora's neck-ruffles and cuff bands, as well as the edges of her own cap and apron, with a hot-point iron.

Dave had attended these annual events, up to the time the Schuylers moved to the Igrotte house.

He had been meticulously invited to every subsequent one, in fact so meticulously that to Mathilda, unreasonably enough, the courtesy savoured of patronage.

Dave was never to attend one of these functions after the move from the House on Sycamore Street. To begin with, he had a particularly fierce kind of pride where Dora was concerned, and besides, his mid-afternoons, those subsequent years, were scarcely a matter of girls' birthday-parties and candles.

Then, too, since the crash, the Old Gentleman had taken on what amounted to an unreasonable animosity to Len Tarkington. A resentment that the gentleman-farming methods of his old neighbor should lead to the gradual growth from the scrawny acres Len had inherited from his grandfather, to the present more than triple and vastly prolific pasturages.

It was the Old Gentleman's contention, never beyond his own fireside it is true, that Len Tarkington was "God's laziest white man," working three hours a day as compared with his own fifteen.

Len's doings rankled in the Old Gentleman. His politics! He had never forgiven him for voting Bryan in 1896. Len was a negligent farmer, an indifferent judge of cattle, and notoriously slow pay. One of those devilishly likable fellows who get results out of two-thirds personality and one-third efficiency.

Beware of a man who lets his rail fences go; who votes a mixed ticket; who will borrow your pipe off you; who could sit on his side verandah and whittle a clothespin into a doll for his daughter, with his hay still outlying, and clouds lowering.

It rankled to have Dave help at Tarkington early-morning chores, except that the deal was one strictly between old Nemo and the boy and there was no getting around it—that eighty cents a week helped!

That, probably more than any one other thing, was the realization that used to cause the Old Gentleman, lying beside Mathilda in the ponderous old bedstead that filled their room, to hide his screwed and suffering face into the crook of his arm and lie with his toes climbing over each other with the pain of frustration, until the crack of dawn, when he rose. Eighty cents a week mattered!

At the first of her birthday-parties that Davey did not attend, Dora had clouded up and cried tears all over her birthday prettiness, while Davey, with a throat that hurt him the long afternoon through, went about the business of leading a foal, for a consideration of fifteen cents, from one pasture to a two-mile-distant one, for a petty farmer known as Rocky Toe.

It was the following week that Davey, emerging from the Tarkington barn on Saturday morning, from helping Nemo at currying, beheld her making grimaces, by darting her little pink adder of a tongue in and out, as she stood on the safe side of her hedge, and struck outlandish attitudes at a boy called Desmond Riley, whose father was new superintendent of Giles Tool Works and who had just moved into the neighborhood.

There was, about Desmond, a precision both of manner and of dress that was antagonizing. That verdict, after his first weeks in the Centralia Second District School, was the cruelest of all for a child to bear.

What antagonism Desmond excited was the kind to relegate him to oblivion. Desmond became what you might call permanently unnoticed. The children shunned his selfish little moon-faced complacency. Not a boy offered to fight him.

The awful failure of obscurity was his.

Not so passive, however, was Dora's animosity. His sleek, brushed, brown ball of a head sat in front of her throughout the school-day. He chose the best pen-points and wet sponges, just before the monitors reached her. Desmond had fat, soft little cheeks that quivered like jelly; and that too, infuriated her.

She was sticking out her tongue to the jell of those cheeks the morning that Dave beheld her across her hedge-top and paused, as if to study the facial contractions by which she achieved her magnificent effects.

"Dare you to wallop him!" cried Dora to Dave, as the small, square figure hove in sight. "Land him one for me! Dickery, dickery, docks, his mama makes him wear socks!"

So she did. Tan ones, with plaid tops that reached just below the knee!

"Dare you, Dave—wallop him! One for me and one for good measure."

The wallop had its time and place. Somehow, Desmond, standing there hypnotized and not belligerent, offered neither.

"Aw—no!"

"Scared? 'Fraid-cat. If I was a fellow and afraid to wallop another fellow!"

Bitter. Bitter. Standing there, barefoot, his fingers curling into palms, anger smote Dave. A slow anger. Not at Desmond. But at the shrill little voice of his tyrant. If she were a fellow and afraid to wallop another fellow. What kind of talk was that? Why wallop Desmond? His animosity would not rise to it.

"'Fraid! Snidey! Poof! 'Fraid. Poof! Poof! Poof!"

Suddenly Dave's arm shot out and banged Desmond one in the stomach so that he doubled and ran.

The wallop had not been for Desmond at all. But for the circumstance of naughty, adorable Dora up there, meting out injustice. That was the dreadful part. The blow had been for Dora.

And before he could rush to Desmond, to right it with him, there was the wonder and the glory of small Dora screaming upon him from her vantage. Having goaded him on to attack the stranger, and now turning on him with a fury that had probably never had counterpart in her small breast.

"You didn't need to hit him thataway. In the stomach. Oh, you! Oh, you! Why didencha listen—I only meant—just to hit something. Not him. I meant—hit out against what's no good—oh, I don't know what I meant, but why didencha listen?"

Suddenly, in the blind rage of relief and the shock of the identical quality of their impulses, he was over the fence and pummeling Dora until her teeth shook. Until her eyes popped and saw twice.

"You—you!" she said on the breath that was jerked out of her, and sat down flat, like a doll-baby.

And yet, in the end, that scene confused David.

Dora had a mind of her own only where trifling things were concerned. She would wrest from him an inch of concession, and then, with her matchless capacity for sweetness, give him back an ell.*

---

* One afternoon, on my way home from an auction of short-horns, I came across the two of them seated on a sort of stile that divided the southeast corner of Tarkington's from the Rileys'. Even then, the future little first lady of the land was giving voice to some of those amenable qualities that were later to make her the most unrivaled of helpmates, as well as probably the most dashing hostess of the longest and most glittering régime in the history of the capital. Scraps of the

The second time that Dave did not show up at her birthday-party, it was almost six of the hard and wearying months since they had met.

She had run out one lovely clover-smelling summer

---

overheard conversation across the stile, that day, ran like this:

"Lookie, I've got a Martin Schraft button to wear. Papa says vote for Martin Schraft."

"Puh, Schraft nothing. Vote for Tom Connors for mayor. He hates mono-poly."

"Wouldn't vote for a mayor that hates mono-poly."

"You would, too. Mono-poly's not fair. My brother Henry says so."

"Mono-poly's not fair. All right, Davey, I'll not vote for mono-poly."

"Say, Dora, know what?"

"What?"

"Not so very far away from here, know what?"

"No, what?"

"The Wright Brothers flew the first aeroplane at Kittyhawk."

"Kitty-who?"

"Kitty-hawk's the name of a place. Don't you even know that?"

"Davey, you know everything."

"Not everything. Just nearly. Woodrow Wilson, huh, he won't let Teddy go to war and fight."

"Huh, he won't let Teddy go to war and fight. I won't vote for Wilson neither, if you don't want me to, Dave."

"Huh, Henry says he wants to make the world safe for demo-cracy."

When my small brother mouthed the phrase then current the country over (I can see him yet, straddling that stile!) his words were absolutely devoid of any of the sardonic import Henry's older lips gave them.

"Safe for demo-cracy! Yip! Yip!"

"Safe for demo-cracy," repeated the blessedly sweet Dora, to whom they were just words. "Let's make the world safe for demo-cracy!"

dawn, while Davey, in denim jumpers, and Nemo were currying down a filly which Tarkington sometimes still drove before a light gig.

She was in her nightgown and bare feet, and she and another girl, named Minnie Ryan, who had been spending the night with her, were tearing out toward the clover-field for the early-morning lark of a dash through the dew.

> Walk, fair maiden, through the morning dew,
> If you crave beauty and a sweetheart true!

That was the phrase Dora had drawn from a fortune-telling gypsy girl, whose green parrakeet on a stick had plucked the slip of paper from a box.

> . . . crave beauty and a sweetheart true!

Dora and Minnie craved beauty and a sweetheart true.

At the sight of Dave, currying away there at the near flank of the horse, the two girls turned squealing and scurrying back toward the house. Dora last, her lovely long curls flying back in a banner, her body flashing, and the rosy soles of her feet repeating themselves again and again as she fled.

This was the most disturbing thing that had ever happened to David. His heart seemed to fly out of his chest, leaving him standing like an empty meal-sack. Then the rest of his body seemed to rise to his throat. To congest his breathing and blind him so that the currying became merely a series of strange motions over which he had no control.

Once, on that run down Sycamore Street beside the boys that were marching down it into the lanes of war, the blood had beaten that way in his ears. But to the roar of drums and of hoarse throats shouting.

It was probably the beginning of the normal adolescence of his awareness of Dora. Suddenly, just Dora, who was undoubtedly the nicest of all girls, but who could stick out her stomach and make ugly grimaces and slide belly-buster down a hill, was something as lovely, as remote, as an angel on the merit-card you received in Sunday-school if you were Desmond Riley. Flash of Dora in her sweet muslin nightdress, with her hair flowing and the lovely insinuation of her rosy young body flickering through.

And yet she was not as remote as one of those picture-card angels with trumpets and soaring bodies that rise on a slant through ether. Dora was warm and beautiful and naughty in an adorable way that was not angelic.

Dora was beautiful. The soles of her pink, flying feet that you saw over and over again as they flashed, were beautiful. There was something sweet and rosy about them. They were Dora's.

That was the way his adolescence came in. A fastidious worship of the beauty that flashed to him that dew-drenched clover-smelling sunrise. It was to remain that. A curiously delicate and perfect love-life for a man born to a destiny of tempestuous and dramatic and world-shaping events. But withal, a man born into his time as snugly as a bug into his rug. Forward-looking. Backward-heeding. Un-neurotic. Normal.

Cross-currents aplenty were to riffle the course of the true love of David and Dora, torturous ones, but from the day that he was thirteen, and had looked upon that flash of the innocent sweetness of Dora-in-nightdress flashing from his sight, she was installed and remained the woman of his love and his life and his reverence.*

---

* I wonder if in the history of the presiding couples at the White House, from Dolly Madison who so brilliantly heightened the dark days of that régime to Angelica Van Buren, and on down through the devotion of the McKinleys, if one of them ever approached the beauty of the ideal love and com-

For a six-month after this morning apparition of her, with her loveliness across his eyeballs as he went to sleep nights, and his first waking-thought of her, he did not so much as again clap eyes on Dora face to face. Dodging her, if he happened to be errand-bent in Centralia and saw her coming down a street, avoiding the lanes she frequented and attending the little Sunday-school at Seven Mile, sooner than run the risk of encountering her in town.

Countless the asafœtida-bags that Mathilda hung about his protesting neck these days.

Dave, with the immemorial gesture of young love, paled, and secretly observed but outwardly ignored by Henry, retreated uncommunicative within himself. Took on a pinched look about the mouth that prompted Bek to comment privately and worriedly to Winslow, and acquired a nervous habit of cracking his finger joints that was enormously irritating to the Old Gentleman.

The change of Sunday-school was a matter of some argument, since, on fair Sundays, the Old Gentleman and Mathilda rode into Centralia in the phaëton, hitched to a pasture horse rented from Rocky Toe for fifty cents the morning, to Second Avenue Rock Church. For thirty years the Schuylers had paid pew dues there, and even now, when those dues were no longer sent by check, but sparsely dropped into the contribution plate, they occupied the same seats by the insistent courtesy of everyone connected with the church.

But Dave, privately conscious that his shoes, even when blacked, were nicked, had reached the stage where for want of long trousers, his legs felt long and gawky. Besides, Dora with her hair in the spread of curls and a red cap that had a pompon, rode to Second Avenue Rock

patibility that existed between my brother Dave and my sister Dora.

Church, either in her father's light spider-gig, or in the new Chevrolet roadster.

That in itself, made one feel more of a gawk than if she too had just walked.

So in the end, every day of the six-month that intervened, Dave, with the torment of the desire to see her hot within his heart, carefully avoided her.

Then one day, crawling out from under a runway in the hen-house which he had been whitewashing for Nemo, bespattered, even his heavy thatch of hair with a white smear across it, he came upon her, face to face as she came out of the kitchen door with a small pan of fine white-bread-mash for her sick pet of a hen, a prize leghorn "Smooty," which her father had once brought her from the Lexington County Fair.

It was ignominious beyond anything he had ever dreaded, her unexpected dashing out in this fashion from the house. Scarcely a day that he did not reckon with the possibility of her happening to rise at five of a morning, timing his appearance meticulously to avoid its happening. And now here he was on all-fours, calcimime-stained, daub-faced, crawling out from under, like a rabbit from a hutch, into the very path of Dora, so fresh in her blue percale with three white bands of tape around her slim waist and the hem of her skirt, and all the morning-light there was, caught in the curls that lay along her shoulders.

"Smarty, Smarty, gave a party, and nobody came," was the incredible, the panicky phrase that flew from his agonized lips, while Dora, with the pan of warm mash in her hands, toppled a little forward, of naughty, simulated surprise, as if she had not expected him there.

With what was more of a reflex than a desire, she shot her tongue at him in reply to this, and her stomach too, in the old absurd contortion. Dora, who was almost thirteen now and would no longer shinny trees, for fear of showing her panties.

"Smarty, Smarty, didn't want you nohow at my party."

There was a stunned flash of silence between these two, to whom David's absence from that party had been, to each, a little agony; a flash of silence filled with the noise old Nemo made pouring water into a pig-trough, and with the floating fragrance of Mammy's breakfast bacon, and with the echoes of Dora's mockery. For six months she had been slowly gathering courage to burst this way upon David. And now, the whirlwind of that ruse accomplished, there she stood puckering, and trying not to cry.

"Out in county school, where I used to go," said Dave, "you skip stocks and bonds and then go right from algebra to geometry."

"Honest?" said Dora, as if his remark were relevant to her innermost thoughts.

It was a master-stroke. He was never to know, delving into his psychology later, just how he achieved it. This bit of floating information, springing full-grown to his rescue at the moment of his almost complete immersion under lime and humiliation.

It broke the ice. It broke the ice of Dora's startled, frozen lips. It broke the ice of the long months that had lain chilled, without the sun of her presence, against his heart.

"We're on the Monroe Doctrine," said Dora.

"The Monroe Doctrine," began David, his eyes focusing as they always did from his trick of visualizing the page from which he memorized, "is the principle of non-in-ter-ven-tion of European Powers in American af ——"

"Oh lookie, Davie, you're all tangling yourself up in Queen Anne's lace handkerchief."

Wretched David. It was his ruse, standing there spouting his erudition, to kick, as if casually, the frail, pale stuff growing in profusion outside the barn door, in an attempt to cleanse his bare legs of the lime.

Who could have thought, after the years of childhood they had played through together, Dave most of the time in a single garment of blue jumper and Dora with her neat skirts flying to reveal her little pantie-clad legs, that lime spattered across Dave's legs could matter so to him. Matter so that his tongue began to dry and swell in his mouth like a rusk.

"I work."

"That's nothing."

" 'Tis, too."

" 'Tisn't."

" 'Tis."

"Puf!" She was still flushed with shame at the atavism of having stuck out her tongue and her stomach.

"I know something I could tell if I wanted to."

"What?"

"About ants. Me and Nemo watch ants same as you and Henry."

"Me and Henry have a red-ant-hill now! You know what, there's a species of ——"

"There's ants in our pantry. Mammy can't keep sugar there any more."

All this, savoring doubtless to the uninitiated of slight irrelevance, had bearing upon hours they had spent in the days of the House on Sycamore Street, lying belly-flat, with their noses close to the performance of ant-hills. Sometimes Henry, who had a magnifying glass that stood on a little tripod, had come down under the

grape-arbor and observed with them, and read aloud out
of a book called *Communism Among Ants*.

Davey knew those ants to the habit, many a time remaining stretched on his stomach long periods after
Dora had danced away home. Now it was her little
device for wriggling her away back into grace on this particular one of his hobbies.

"The little ants in our sugar haven't got any an-ten-næ
at all."

"They have so, Dora !"

"Well, anyway, none that you can see without Henry's
manifying glass."

"I work," resumed Dave, stubbornly, and still kicking
into the Queen Anne's lace handkerchief.

The reiteration scarcely penetrated her conciliatory
zeal.

"We're on frogs in physiology, Dave. If you pull one
leg, the other thinks it's getting pulled too. Toads give
warts, frogs don't."

"I work."

This time, her sweet eyes glittered at him, making
his eyes seem to smart, as they did when he stared at
the sun.

"I work, or I'd 'a' come to your party."

"I'd rather had you at my party, Dave, than anybody."

"Would you?"

"I cried."

How sweet she was in the early morning of that beauty
of hers; a freshness of beauty which the years were to
find absolutely unquenchable. The sparkle of world-
sweetheart was over her that day.*

---

*There hangs a portrait of my sister Dora, enlarged from
a photograph of her, taken when she was about twelve, in the
drawing-room of the beautiful house, Phi! Schuyler, Junior's, in
East Sixty-sixth Street, New York.

"I cried, honest."

"Dora! I—oh—last tag!"

Presently they were tearing through the Queen Anne's lace handkerchief, as if into foam.

At home, in the Igrotte barn, a half dozen rather scrawny rams were pressing their none-too-finicky noses to the crack of a door, bleating and waiting for their young shepherd to release them to the joys of pasture.

Finally, the Old Gentleman, who was weighing a heifer on a scale, had to hobble and do it himself.

"Drat that boy, where is he?"

Davey was wooing.

It is a favorite story of my nephew's, that the first day it was hung, Dora herself, who was on a shopping tour in New York for the week, entered the room and exclaimed, "What a lovely portrait of Mary Pickford."

Chapter Twenty-three

FARM-HANDS were scarce, that winter of 1917. By 1918, with ten thousand troops a day, for over a period of five months, being transported, it was practically impossible to get men to handle the heavy chores.

It was said of Bek Schuyler, and she did not deny it, that for want of herdsmen, she personally drove as many as a hundred head of Howey cattle to Ivorydale, which was within a dozen miles of The City, by night, appearing tailor-made and in the stern habiliments of the kind of togs she affected, at the Statfield Hotel for breakfast the next morning.*

Dave had accompanied her on several of these night-drives as far as Ivorydale, taking a local train back to Centralia, after he had given over his horse to one of the men who came from the Yards to meet them. Then Bek, and the small wicker suitcase which she had carried like a pack on her horse, continued *via* an early-morning trolley for The City.

Nothing to suggest in the big, tailored woman having a generous breakfast in the spacious dining-room of the Statfield Hotel, that she had ridden horseback the night through behind a drove of cattle.

They were memorable rides alongside his sister, those winters when the farms were stripped of men and the foundries were humming to the strange, new tune of the manufacture of munitions. Her great figure was like

* . . . we never referred to the great metropolis within thirty-one miles of us, in any terms except "The City." It is surprising, even after the automobile had jerked us to its very flank, how seldom we visited it.

some heroic study in bronze of horse and rider, as she loomed behind the dark, moving cloud of the cattle.

She taught him to swing his whip lariat-fashion, and to curl, with a quick turn of wrist, the rope over the horns of a steer. She taught him the secrets of good points in cattle, how to estimate within a pound or two the heft of a sow or a bull, and some of the laws of breeding her observation had taught her.

It is doubtful if she had ever heard of the Mendelian theory, or of de Vries, but she expounded with beauty and accuracy to Davey, as they rode through those strange and often resplendent nights, to starlight, distant baying of dogs, lowing of cattle, and the dim, etherealized outline of farmhouse, hedge, and tree. Expounded, in the terms of her own observation, of certain pure breeds of live-stock; of mutations in the peach, the chestnut, the strawberry, the sweet potato, without her ever knowing, probably, the meaning of the word mutation, much less of its technical application.

Asparagus-cutting, reproductive cycle in the rabbit, analysis of certain pure breeds of live-stock, heredity and milk-yield, cross-pollination, inbreeding of dairy-cattle, inheritance of black-stripe in China-Poles, inheritance of shorthorns, elementary evolution, dairy-cattle, breeding, genetics, were the tune to which some of these night-rides were taken.

It was out of these long discourses with his sister, that his early inclination veered first toward biology, then natural history and for a brief while, medicine.

The great natural fount of Bek's unerudite but accurate first-hand observations poured itself in long, lucid strain through these nights. Some of the glory that was the old Bek's might have disappeared with her pride of ownership, but none of her kind of mental magnificence. She sat on her idea as squarely as she sat astride her horse. It was generally said of her, and always refuted by Henry, who would never grant you that mentality had sex, that she thought like a man.

Be that as it may, restricted to the penny, stripped of every freedom of action that might have corresponded with the scope of mind, her mind's eye continued to sweep the horizon in the manner of one who reckons in big stakes.

"If I could lay hand on five hundred or a thousand acres, Dave, then I'd show you a thing or two about stock-farming!" Or, "See old Conrad Gronauer's place over there? Falling to pieces of dry-rot. I wrote in my diary about him last night, and I'll say it to his face. Gronauer stinginess and lack of vision are to blame."

"Does stinginess mean lack of vision, Bek?"

"Most of the time. If old Bek Schuyler had Gronauer's place, mark my word, it would be a going concern in three years. I'd have five thousand bushels of potatoes off it the second year." *

"Gee, all that in potatoes?"

"Never play small stakes, Dave. The reward is pro-

---

* Long years before the existence of the Lucy Stone League, which upholds the right of a married woman to still use her maiden-name, I continued to be known after my marriage as Bek Schuyler, except where it came to signature.

My brother was always to the fore in giving his sanction to the unrestricted legal privilege of woman to decide for herself the matter of name.

Theoretically, I agree that a married woman should have the legal right to the use of her maiden-name. But law me, it is one of those questions difficult to feel keenly about. As I always say, for the professional or business woman, whose name is her asset, well and good and fine. But for a plain country woman like me—don't know as it makes much difference what they call me.

portionately small, and a small loss hurts as much as a big. Play the game high and straight."

Those were strangely exhilarating rides. Pearly, quivering horizons. The sense-of-power of his mount under him. The cloud of the cattle thundering softly to the crack of his whip and his will. Bek, seated so squarely on her enormous sixteen-hand-and-a-half chestnut.

It was as if the soil had its beginning in the heart, and then flowed through one, and then on out from the horses' hoofs and became meadow and dale, hill and meadow.

Something in Dave, kinship of the flesh of his body with the flesh of the land that was warm with the thunder of their passing, would seem to unlock, and out of the secret and reticent places of his mind and heart would march the desires and unsaid things, made suddenly sayable.

"Geeminee, Bek—the stars! Those little fellows up there are as big—as big as anything! And we little things are more wonderful than they are, because they can't think and we can."

"That's right, Dave. The stars never make me feel little and insignificant the way they do lots of folks. They just make me feel wonderful, for being made by the same divine hand that made them. Do you ever think of God, Dave?"

"Aw—yes. Sure I do. Say, if I could be a star, guess what star I'd want to be?"

"Don't know as I even know the names of enough of them to venture a guess. Morning Star? Evening Star? North Star?"

"No, Vega."

"Vega. That's a new one on me."

"She's not out now. Vega's the one toward which the whole solar system is supposed to be traveling."

"Great human qualities, like strength and courage and

loyalty and wisdom, can be lights that attract humanity just as much as Vega attracts the solar system, Dave."

"That's what I mean. I want to be wise. Henry's wise."

"Yes, but Henry is a little too wise for his time, Dave. To be a little too wise for the times in which you live, is as bad as not being wise enough. They crucify you for being too far ahead of your time, Dave."

"Henry says most fellows would rather face the machine-guns over there than face a new idea."

"It's all right to be wiser than the fellow next to you, Dave, but just enough so as never to let him know that you are wiser."

"Is Woodrow Wilson wise?"

"I'm afraid he is one of those whom they crucify for being too wise, Dave."

"Is Teddy wise?"

"Just wise enough not to let the other fellow know how much wiser he is than the other fellow."

"Know what, Bek?"

"No, what?"

"I'd like to see an elephant-stampede."

"Kipling says it's one of the sacred sights of the earth."

"Know what, Bek?"

"No, what?"

"I'd like to be a policeman at Loop Square in The City."

"What on earth put that into your head?"

"He stops everything with a lift of his hand. That's more than Woodrow Wilson is doing. He can't stop the War."

At the mention of war, Bek's throat had a habit of beginning to beat.

"Wish to God, dear, he could."

"Stevey is in the Argonne."

"Yes, Steve is in the Argonne."

"There's five Schuylers in the War now, counting Uncle Phil at training-camp."

"That's the law of war, Dave. To give."

"If I was old enough, you'd give me."

"Thank God you're not."

"I'd give myself."

"Surely."

"Is there a law of war?"

"It seems so."

"Who made it?"

"Human nature."

"Is it better to know the laws about human nature— or the kind of law in books, like Henry?"

"That's one of Henry's difficulties. He knows more logic than human nature."

"Ain't human nature—logi-cull?"

"You cannot build up theories, like Henry does, on the assumption that it is, because it never comes out that way. Everybody agrees with Henry that war is sin and evil. But there's one big element in the way of making it practicable."

"Human nature?"

"Yes."

"Henry says . . ."

"I sometimes suspect your brother, Dave, of being a great person with his eyes gazing too far ahead of the ship to see the immediate reefs. Those kind of people don't get anywhere in life."

"How do you get yourself anywhere?"

"By being true to yourself, of course."

"Henry's true!"

"Yes, but don't you see, Dave, Henry happens to have the kind of self that he can only be true to at the utmost pain and suffering to himself and those who love him.

Henry lives in one kind of world and behaves as if he lives in a much more idealized one.   A true leader of men, Davey, must be just far enough beyond the foibles and weaknesses of the average man to understand, not to despise him."

"Say, Bek, you know what?"

"Don't begin every sentence with that, Dave."

"Well, *do* you know what?"

"What?"

"When I'm big—I—when I'm big ——"

"Yes?"

"Aw, I can't say it."

"Say it, Dave."

"Well, when I'm big, you know what?"

"Didn't I just tell you not to begin every sentence that-away, Dave?"

"Well, you know what?   You know the way Ulysses rode at the head of the Trojan War and all in Henry's *Odyssey?*"

"No."

"Didn't Henry ever read it to you?"

"No Davey, your brother never reads to me out of the *Odyssey.*"

"Well, anyways, when I'm big. . . . Oh, I dunno, I can't say it—but when I'm big. . . ." *

---

*. . . one of these rides in particular stands out in my memory. We were six hands short on the farm, all of the second winter of the War. With the cry going out everywhere for conservation, forty head of my heifers were eating their heads off waiting for market, to say nothing of hoof-and-mouth disease, and shipping at a standstill, owing to quarantine.

Dave and I drove these forty in as far as Ivorydale one clear November night.

I can see him as plainly as if that night were before me now, astride his paste-board-looking filly (one that usually

"Go on, say it, Dave."

"When I'm big—I—aw—can't. Lookie—oh, lookie, quick! There went one of those 'possums I was telling you about, Bek. That's one of those woolly kind that have no pouch and carry the little ones on their backs. I think that's pretty funny, don't you? You know what, Bek? A 'possum is a marsupial. Know what a marsupial is? Well, Henry says ——"

"Curve in those heifers, Dave. Here's Ivorydale."

The dawn began quivering up above the horizon in a fancy little shimmer of silver.

---

did sister work at the plow beside a heavier chestnut), loping through the milk-and-pearl fore-glow of a dawn about to break. Head back, the wind before the dawn lifted his bangs to reveal squareness of brow, and his shabby heels dug into the patient old horseflesh with the fervor of the vision he could not get said.

Chapter Twenty-four

To David's generation of boys, the World War was little more than a remote, a magnificent circus, toward which perpetual parades were pouring the older fellows but which never, as a big tent, came within even brass-band distance of town.

All of the circumstances of life were to be altered by that war; and yet, to the generation who were children through the years of its duration, khaki, and gold-star mothers, and Huns, and Big Berthas, and hysteria belonged to the scheme of things, as waterfall belonged to Old Mill Road. Here was a generation born into a phraseology that was new only to the adult. Imperialism of Central Europe. World Safe for Democracy. Over there! Hoch der Kaiser. Russian Revolution. The Poppies Grow in Flanders Field. Conscription. Liberty Bonds. Argonne. Doughboy. Buddy. Transport. Treaty of Versailles. Patriotic cant of this and that propaganda-source, calculated to raise the nap of the flesh of a nation, even while the only palpable results were an impoverished and desolated world.

Many who marched down those languid streets of Centralia as Dave and Teddy ran after, were not to come back; but even that, to children who had seen it consistently happening, did not bring the catastrophic reality of war closer.

If a fellow came home with one leg—well, fellows were always coming home thataway. And still the circus of war remained strangely removed, except one day Pete came home, and a small and suddenly rather sickish-feeling boy, who was lugging a pail of sour clabber from

Bek's place to the Igrotte house, came face to face with him in the open road.

The lower half of Pete's face had been blown away and replaced with sort of a nickel-plated jaw. And his eyes were still looking as if they had frozen there of what they saw.

"Davey, b'God! Hi, Kid!"

"Hi!"

For the first time war became a horror then, stalking with stiff eyes and rigid jaw through those lanes of peace.

David was sick that night, and feverish. "Upset stummick," diagnosed Mathilda, and plied him with castor-oil.

Every Schuyler came home. Phil, who saw ambulance service. His eldest son, who drove a truck under bombarded skies for sixteen months. Clara's boy, who lied about his age to qualify for enlistment and who saw service as far front as Amiens. Paula, who did canteen service in France. Stevey, who fought at Argonne, and whose eyes had seen the horror of the splashing of human entrails across fields.

The war, which had crashed with such terrific interruption into the more or less organized scheme in which David had spent the first few years of his life, came to its portentous conclusion, the world held the brief pose of a chastened, spiritualized humanity that had gone down in blood that it might be cleansed, and then relapsed.

In later years, there seemed to David to be a certain subtle demarkation in human beings. Those born before the Great War and who stood astride the chasm of it, as it were, with one foot in each world, and those born to the curious, old-eyed youth of a post-war world.

It was a fantastic phase of human experience to have lived through, even as a child.

Around Davey's head, while he was a youngster, Russia cracked her shackles, France bled white, the Near

East, the Far East scrambled and squirmed free of chains
that carried the rust of centuries. His own country flung
a faltering gesture. A man named Mussolini thrust his
hand down into the throat of Italy, gagged and then
rode her, magnificently. Czars and Kaisers galloped out
of the human scene like Sancho Panzas on mules. Foren-
sic peasants came into world-power, their followers
crawling like armies of worms out of darkness to live
in the Kremlin. One fine day in Davey's boyhood, Great
Britain handed portfolio to its first labor-government.

Supper-table discussion between the Old Gentleman
and Henry made the light along the lamp-wick buzz and
flare in the gale of explosives. Tariff. Woodrow Wil-
son. Lloyd George. Reparations. Rasputin. Rheims.
Stanley Baldwin. D'Annunzio. Irish Free State.
Colonel House. Henry Ford. Prohibition. Joe Can-
non. League of Nations. Mexico. Trotsky. Jim
Reed. Muscle Shoals. Eugene Debs. Borah. Senator
Moses. La Follette. Nicholas Murray Butler. Wells'
Outline of History. Fascisti.

Time and time again, off the rather weary sill of
Henry's lips, there dropped sparks that set the dry
tinder of the Old Gentleman's conservatisms leaping and
flaming.

This was a curious tenacity to Henry. It bothered him
to see the Old Gentleman darken and redden in apoplectic fashion. Sometimes it even terrified him. But for
the life of him, he could not remain silent and let one
after another of his father's reactionisms die into the
quiet of the evening meals.

"Well, sir, something ought to be done about this
here Red situation. The Boston police-strike, the steel-
workers' strike, the soft-coal miners' strike and now this
here railway-strike in England starting up. Race-riots
out in Chicago. Bomb-plot trying to smash up Attorney-

General Palmer's home. Only way for a self-respecting government to handle anarchy is call out the troops. Shoot 'em down. That's the way to cure these scalawag anarchists. Cowards at heart!"

"Father, every manifestation of social discontent is not necessarily a form of anarchy."

"Like to know what else you call a lot of lazy fellows up-and-revolting against the finest government in the world."

"Revolt is the soul of progress."

"By Gad, not to my way of thinking. If you think a lot of lazy louts of fellows that think they can milk a living out of the Government instead of working for it are the soul of progress, then, by Gad, progress has got a rotten soul that I wouldn't lift a little finger to help save. You and this here Emma Goldman they're giving a free boat-ride to are the kind they drive out of this country and keep out! I. W. W. crowd—I-won't-work-ers!"

"Father!"

"Puppa!"

"Well! I won't have no anarchy talked in my house, where there's a boy growing up to listen to it."

"If it weren't for that youngster, Father, and my desire for him to learn to look temperately at both sides of this troubled old world, I wouldn't even argue the matter with a biased person like you."

"I've worked hard all my life, earned an honest living, and I never had time to sit and criticize the government that ——"

"Oh, Father, Father—won't you try to think with your brain instead of with your prejudice? I hold no brief for anarchy, any more than you do. I'm merely trying to differentiate between ——"

"You hold brief for shenanigans of I. W. W. fellows, who don't mean no good by the country."

"Don't shout, Father!"

"Puppa!"

"I will shout! Anarchists! Anarchists—that's what they are—by Gad, if I thought a son of mine was one, I—I——"

"I quit, Father! If you think I'm going to try and argue capital and labor with a man who sees red the moment a more equable living-scheme for humanity is broached, you're mistaken. You see, Dave, what I was trying to say to your father is not that this strike or that riot is right or wrong. The point, David, I'm trying to make to your father is that without revolt against oppression, ignorance and illiteracy, there can be no human emancipation. Submission, throughout the history of the world, has begotten autocracy."

"And what have such lazy-lout strikes begotten? I. W. W. anarchists. Anarchy——"

"You win, Father. I quit! God only knows how anyone can be so hidebound."

"Hennery!"

"Excuse me, Mother."

"You should have quit long ago, son. You know how excitable your Puppa is."

"I know what Henry means. If the rich ones wasn't so rich, and the poor ones wasn't so poor, then there wouldn't be so much to fight about, would there?"

"Exactly, Dave. But you can't make your father be——"

"Can't make—can't make—I'll break every bone in——"

"Puppa—Hennery—please."

Turbulent evenings. Supper-table disharmonies that

were to set into motion atoms in the boy's brain that might never have stirred otherwise.

Off Henry's sardonic lips were to glitter phrases of curious and significant prophecy. As if against the retina of his lusterless eye was imprinted the ultimate significance of empire toward which all these catastrophic events were scurrying a bewildered world.

World-unification. Annihilation of distance. Propinquity of races. Tolerance. Fraternity. Lonely phrases in a land that presently was to pursue its policies outside the League of Nations.

Presently, these phrases, dinned by Henry, came to be the only reality of war left against Dave's brain.

The boys were home and settled now.

Even Pete's mask was no longer terrible.

Here was Stevey as if he had never marched away to the rolling of drums, living in a semi-attached two-family house out on Tallahassee Street, within walking distance of the Giles Tool Works, where he had a desk job in the shipping department.

Something in the nature of one of those freak tornadoes that can seem to appear in a crazy spiral of fury out of the blue had happened to Steve. The craving for drink had been literally shot from him.

In all the hubbub of the prohibition which a returning army found awaiting it and with the nation lying prone upon its stomach and kicking its heels and squalling over a right that had been wrested from it, the mere sight of a bottle of Scotch on a shelf was enough to stiffen Steve, taut and squeamish with revulsion.

A kind of cure not without its rare precedent in medical annals.

The smell, or for that matter even the sight of spirituous liquor in any form, was to bring back to Steve the odor and smear of a human face in the act of becoming pulp.

One night, crouched down under a hill of wet mud, and guzzling from a flask with two companions in the trench, he had seen the face of his "buddy" literally torn off by shrapnel as he tilted the bottle Stevey had just handed him, to his lips.

The mess and the splatter were to remain irretrievably mixed in Steve's mind with the taste of alcohol, the mere sight of it to recall the terrible sight of a friend's face in the act of being blown to pulp.

Here was Steve, almost through no volition of his own, swept into the scheme of the little two-family house on Tallahassee Street, Claire, plumpish by now, awaiting him evenings, a normal youngster at her skirts, in a doorway that had his monogram embroidered in its lace curtain.

The Steve Schuylers at Number 1569½ Tallahassee Street, rent-payers, water-tax payers, seat- and presently pew-holders, had fallen into pace. The Schuyler escutcheon had remained unviolated; and the Old Gentleman, as time went on, came more and more to cast prideful eye upon his first great-grandchild, Pauline, as she toddled out to meet him on his less and less frequent visits into Centralia.*

---

* . . . that was the winter Stevey's eldest child Pauline accompanied her father and me to Washington, and the young Marquis de Fressac fell so immediately in love with her. From the very first, her interest in politics was to run neck and neck with the social lures her beauty and personality created about her. It was characteristic of Pauline that she should choose both. Considering the part she played during her senatorship, and the influence she exerted both in France and in America as a social force, it is difficult to estimate in which field my granddaughter is succeeding most brilliantly. As my son-in-law

Another Schuyler rivet had tightened the impeccable family-machine. Respectability. Conservatism. Republicanism (consistently up to this time!). Law-abiders. Voters. God-fearers. Rotarians. Masons. Policyholders.

Two years after his return from the World War, Stevey was carrying fifteen-hundred-dollars life-insurance, depositing one dime a day in a toy bank toward his daughter's Vassar College education, lunching once a week at a Blue Plate Booster's Club in the Renchler Block, voting the straight Republican ticket for Harding, and spending his Sunday mornings flat on his back under the Ford five-seater in the corrugated portable garage which he shared with the second tenant of the two-family dwelling.

In the shy coming-together of Stevey and Claire after the convulsion of their flying-apart, the bone, true to physiology, seemed to have cemented more firmly than before the break.

Years after, when the name of a Schuyler was up before the state for the highest honor bestowable upon one of its citizens, someone in opposing political ranks did attempt the moss-grown device of trying to probe out an irregularity in the social history of David Schuyler's nephew Stephen. A far-fetched gesture at best, and one, even had it been successful, that was almost sure to have proved futile.

But to try to penetrate the Schuyler armor of social integrity was like trying to wound the flank of the Himalayas with a bow and arrow.

It was the year that Stevey, with what he considered the hindrance, rather than the advantage of an uncle

de Fressac puts it in his delightfully French manner, "Eet ees een both."

the governor of his state, and a mother the first woman alderman of the town of Centralia, was elected second vice-president and treasurer of the Giles Tool Works.

Someone's faint scent of something hurried connected with the marriage was too faint for even the political vandals to fasten upon. To be sure, Steve Schuyler and his wife were first-cousins. Scarcely a fact to unmake governors.

When Bek Schuyler heard of the feeble intrigue, she smiled. A skeleton, and not much of a one at that, and whose bones by now were soft with decay, could scarcely be expected to rattle for the political gentlemen.

So far as Dave was concerned, Claire's little house on Tallahassee Street was to become the center around which an assorted set of his adolescent emotions were to dash themselves.

When Dora Tarkington was sixteen, and wore her curls in two round, flat mats against her ears, she attended what was then known as the South Tallahassee High School.

It was after a sharp attack of influenza, during one of the frequent epidemics that swept the country those first years after the War, that an arrangement was made for Dora to have her lunches hot at the Steve Schuylers', instead of the cold snack she was obliged to carry with her the two miles from home.

Nowadays, when Steve returned from the Works for his midday meal, there was Dora, whom they had known since she could toddle, to swell the little family circle that drew up to table.

It pleased Claire to have special little daintinesses in her honor; and since Len Tarkington had bartered in vain for some kind of a financial arrangement to cover these lunches—Stevey withdrawing offended from the argument—every day Dora, who was incomparable at handiwork, arrived with some bit of surprise. A woolen chicken for Claire's eldest little girl. A sheer pink under-thing for Claire herself, or a plover-egg with a hand-painted face for the small boy who could crawl, and a tiny crocheted cap for the baby.*

Claire's little house in Tallahassee Street had to it the agreeable untidiness of high, unevenly-drawn window-shades that admitted sunlight in glaring streams across the rooms, youngsters crawling through them and litter-ing the floors with toys, building-blocks and noise-devices.

She was perpetual motion at stooping, snatching, ad-monishing, warning, a wisp of her pretty, taffy hair con-stantly blown across her flustered face; and in just such proportion as her activities seemed to increase, her pretty kind of plumpness crept up on her.

Sweet Claire. She had feathered her nest. At noon and at evening, Steve turned to it eagerly. Sometimes, at the corner, he consciously slowed his step, to seem, from some perversity in him that gave him periods of self-detestation, to enter the home she had made for him, a little less enthusiastically.

Like her mother's before her, Claire's ineffable sweet-ness was like a drug. It swam into the senses. It was into Stevey's senses long before he knew it. It had him quelled, caught, stabilized. It made a Rotarian out of

*. . . growing up, as she did, in a generation of girls to whom handiwork was practically an obsolete art, loving gay-ety, filled with a social instinct and with a brilliant gift for popularity, Dora, in a curious way, was not quite of her time. She rode horseback and crocheted all the edgings for her un-derwear. She won the local golf-championship the year her piccalilli took first prize at the State Fair. Never in his married life did Dave wear a shirt or a tie that was not per-sonally selected by her.

the rebel in him. It was sweet to submit to the little tropic he had married himself into. The tropic of warm, sun-drenched, or lamplight-drenched home, griddle-cake breakfasts, with the aroma of little-pig sausages; the cleanest, deepest of beds; the warm, sweet body of the woman who bore him warm, sweet children. Her intellectual languor was part of her sweetness, just as it was part of her danger. Along with the sweetness of those first years, there was just a little terror of them. Submission. Old rebellions dying. Cravings—old inchoate beauties—finally, just the sweetness.

The lace curtains in the front parlor of the house on Tallahassee Street came to have for Steve the living, breathing quality of Claire herself. She was so warmly behind them, at his coming. At his going. They stirred faintly of her breath. They were a badge of her.

Sometimes Claire, who was even then locally and affectionately known as a congenital match-maker, used to stand behind these lace curtains, tiptoe, to watch for the noonday approach of Dora, usually in the company of Kenneth Chipman, who was junior partner in his father's law-office, just across the street from Tallahassee High.

Kenneth was a campus-looking young fellow, with the first thatch of patent-leather hair that had reached Centralia, and one of those figures shaped like the map of South America. Heavy, flaring shoulders, tapering off into slim, flat hips. He was a graduate of the State University, a winner of a state oratorical contest; pounded a wicked ukulele and already, his second year out of college, had his name on the ground-glass door of the offices of Chipman and Lare, Patent Attorneys.

His brother Lynn, killed at Amiens, had been the white hope of the two white-haired senior members of that office. After his death, the legend grew rapidly that Lynn had been the most brilliant young legal mind to ever take up practice in Centralia. Nevertheless, even with the precedent of this older brother, a capable enough young fellow, whom time and a warrior's death were to canonize into genius, Kenneth, ukulele-pest that he could be of an evening, was regarded as one of the up-and-coming younger men of the town.

The third time Claire stood behind her lace curtains and beheld Kenneth raise his straw cady and walk briskly down the street with many a backward glance at Dora as she danced upstairs, and another lift of hat, and another, Claire remarked to her husband that night, as she was rubbing tonic into his hair before they retired:

"You know, Stevey, looks to me as if young Chipman is smitten on Dora."

"Rub a little toward the center, dear. Getting right thin, there."

"Today's the third time he's walked from Tallahassee High with her, noontime."

"The way to massage the scalp, dear, is with a circular motion of the fingers. Don't shove."

"Henry says he's a chip off the old block, and already handling some of his father's cases, single-handed. Dora's one darling girl."

" 'Fraid that'll put Davey's nose out of joint," said Steve, hitching his collar open.

"What do you mean, Davey?"

"Well, haven't they been smitten with each other ever since they were crawling?"

"Why, Stevey Renchler, what ever put that idea into your head? Those two children! I was saying to Aunt Bek the other day, bright as Davey is in some ways—you know sometimes—I—you know, Stevey, sometimes I—think, in other ways, Dave's not so bright."

"It's his manner, Claire. He's either the smartest

or the dumbest kid on earth. Hanged if I can make out which."

"The way he lies out there, day after day, herding his little old handful of sheep, stretched by the hour on the flat of his tummy, reading or mooning—I guess that's what some folks call bright. He *is* smart, of course, in a school way. Henriette says he's 'way ahead of any boy his age that's had schooling regular and all—but in general—for Davey's age—oh, I don't know—just kinda funny, loony-looking sort of kid to me. Him and Dora! Why, poor Davey, I'll bet he hasn't more than laid eyes on her since the family moved from the House on Sycamore Street."

"Why, you know better than that, Claire. The days when—when we—how often did we use to see Dave and Dora playing around south of the Igrotte house together. Kids, of course, but that's all I'm saying. He's been sweet on her since he could toddle ———"

"I wonder," said Claire, and sat down thoughtfully, in the middle of the act of unfastening the tiny pearl buttons of her pretty little home-made house-dress. "Davey *is* more her type—I guess."

"The kid puzzles me," said Steve and yanked hard at the rear button of his collar. "Can't make up my mind about him."

"Oh, I don't mean I really think he's queer, Steve. I didn't mean that. It's all of you nagging him, I think, that confuses him, as much as anything. After all, he's only seventeen. Dave happened to come along in bad times. He's never had the chance of mixing and schooling the rest of you had. First came the family-crash and then the War and all. After all, he's only a youngster."

"Old enough by now to know his own mind, you'd think."

"Not a mind like Davey's."

"If you aren't the greatest girl! Here you've been wondering why Dave didn't get a move on and take a real job, and the minute I agree ——"

"But I mean, Stevey, lots of times a boy growing up —alone-like in a big family—nobody much to talk to except Henry, who's a pretty queer darling duck too—a boy like that gets to feeling around with his mind in every direction, and for all we know—some day—he may come out all right."

"Something in that. Shame he's had the least schooling of us all. In his way, Davey's bright enough. Dave's deep."

"Maybe. Only it's my observation that still water doesn't necessarily run deep. Maybe it doesn't run at all."

"Things just didn't break right for him, or for the family, about the time he came along."

"'Course, he's had Henry."

"That's something."

"Something! Henry's not appreciated in this town. A fellow like Henry can have a far finer influence over a fellow than all the schools put together. Look how thick they are. Always puttering together over books and anthills and maps. Let me tell you, Henry's a liberal education in himself."

"Yes, if he doesn't go putting crazy ideas in the youngster's head. You see how far his brains have gotten Henry, don't you? Look at what his ideas on war got for him."

"But there's just one beauty about Dave. You can't topple over that youngster. He's that square on his feet."

"That's true enough. Remember that time, over at Bek's, Henry was lecturing on the wrongness of making war possible, and up piped that youngster from a corner where he'd been lying on his stomach with his chin propped up in his palms, and says: 'But, Henry, you can't end war by not fighting in it when the war comes. It's folks you've got to change beforehand, so there won't be any war.' Jove, I thought that about said it in a nutshell. That kid's got the kind of mind believes in preventive medicines, so the world doesn't get the measles. Not what to do about it when the measles have come."

"That's too deep for me."

"Other evening, when I went out to the Igrotte house to help Grandfather and Dave lay those shingles, I was looking around for the kid, and finally I find him lying barefoot, in his overalls, up against a hay-rick, star-gazing. 'Say, you're getting pretty well along for this barefoot-boy-and-cheeks-of-tan stuff,' I said to him, 'How do you get that way?' And what do you think he answered?"

"What?"

" 'You know, that fellow Malthus,' he says. 'Who?' I asked. 'Malthus.' I thought at first he said Methuselah. Mathus, it seems, was a fellow who worked out that the population of the world doubles every twenty-five years!"

"My!"

"Well, Davey must have been lying there thinking about it."

"Henry's doings."

"Because he said to me—'Just suppose for argument, Malthus was over-stating, and the population only doubles every fifty or a hundred years. Where are we going to get food after a while? Eats and stuff. Where are we going to have room enough to grow enough grain and graze enough cattle, if the population crowds up the earth like that?' "

"Why, Stevey—working his brain on such stuff when we've plenty of pasture-land around here can be rented for a song. Of all things . . ."

"That's the whole point, Claire. There's a kid with a long head on him. That youngster, lying there, had thought out something for the future, where most of us only have the brains to see what's right under our noses, and then only maybe."

"You mean, Henry's like that, and he's making Dave like that?"

"No, sir. Henry had been reading to him about Malthus, all right, but darned if the youngster hadn't worked the rest out for himself."

"Well, he's either right smart or right dumb."

"A dummy doesn't work things out for himself. He got me thinking, too. Just as the youngster said, if we can harness the air and electricity and water and sun to work for us, why can't we get busy on the waste places of the world and make them produce for us. Hundreds of thousands of miles of desert and prairie and sand are waiting for man's ingenuity to reclaim them—darn shame, Dave has seen leaner days than any of the rest of us. I think it's put age on the Old Gentleman and Grandmother—just worrying about it." *

---

* . . . looking back, I can see now, how early this idea was boring itself into Davey's brain. In her monograph about him, the late Eda Eberhardt, Centralia's librarian, relates how she was obliged to deprive him of reading-room privileges one week because of his habit of poring over maps and pencil-marking the deserts, mountains, and prairies.

He once related to me, word for word, the doctrine of Malthusianism, as it had been passed on to him by Henry, drawing

"Well, you know the saying, Steve, you can't keep a good man down," said Claire, with her mother's rather dreadful amiability, and mouthing her decrepit observation in the key of having discovered a truth.

"Well, I hope to heaven 'good' is the word. Certainly does seem a fellow his age ought to have a preference for something by now. I offered six months ago to chip in to pay the wage of a hired-man for the Old Gentleman, in case Dave might be wanting to scratch around for a job in town. The Old Gentleman himself keeps trying to oust him out of the nest."

"You know, I think Isaiah Clark would be willing to give Dave a job in his Seed and Feed Store, seeing how Dave's so interested in making things grow."

"Oh, Lord, honey, you see the point about as readily as Grandfather's old blind mare sees oats. Besides, Isaiah hasn't had a boy in there since Joe Mintz was killed in the War. I'm not in strong at the shops enough to be asking any favors, but it looks to me as if I ought to be able to get Davey in at the Works. There's a future there for a boy who's willing to work up from the foundry. Look at Sime Giles!"

---

his own critical deductions, and evidently thinking about the relativity of population and land.

He could never bear to see idle land. Even the stony little nooks and corners surrounding the Igrotte house gave up odds and ends of the most heterogeneous yield. Mushrooms under the back porch. A potato-patch he had somehow scratched into being, on a rocky little ledge of land behind the barns. Even out of the powdery, dry front yard he had eked beets and carrots.

Much of my own later success with crop-rotation I owe to his helpful co-operation in those days when his significant back-to-the-farm policies must just have been taking shape in his mind.

"So you think," said Claire, still sitting in the huddle of her half-open dress, her pretty pink mouth a little open, "so—you—think—Davey's sweet on Dora!"

"I don't think!" said Steve, and went shushing off to the bathroom, in bed-slippers hand-scalloped by Claire, "I *know!*"

Chapter Twenty-five

THE following afternoon, at the Igrotte house, where Claire had enticed an inert Stevey for a five-mile walk through the somnolence of a Sunday, Claire remarked to Dave, who came up on the back porch looking sweaty from having rubbed down a mare:

"Did you know Dora Tarkington has her lunches at our house now, Dave? She's in her second year at Tallahassee High."

"No," said David, breathing very softly as if by that device he could restrain the fact that, at Claire's remark, every pore in his body seemed to leap to attention.

"Yes. Ought to see her. Right young-ladyfied. Gets herself escorted to the very door by Kenneth Chipman, if you please, and is going to take the kindergarten course when she finishes Tallahassee."

"Yeh," said Davey. He was sitting on the railing of the back porch, Claire on the topmost step, hulling a pan of peas for Mathilda. They made little tin-dripping sounds, as they clattered from under her fingers. To Davey, sitting there, swinging one bare foot, and trying to watch them casually, his eyes felt as if they were smeared across his face.

Claire felt rather than saw them, and with the blurting lack of tact, worthy of sweet Emma's sweet daughter, shot out an eager, friendly arm.

"You're twice the fellow Kenneth is, Davey, if you pull yourself together and get yourself started."

"Aw!"

"Dora's smitten with Kenneth because he's sort of what you would call an up-and-comer. Naturally, he's so

306

much older than you, but she'd throw him over like that, for you, if you'd give her half a chance, Dave, by sort of striking out and making your start in life."

A rush of words, of remonstrances, of shame, clogged into Davey's throat, so that he turned toward her a flaming face, which finally decided to save itself from tears by a flare of anger.

"What's Dora Tarkington and Kenneth Chipman got to do with me?" he shot out. "I'd like to know that! I would! What's anything about—anything got to do with me. Pumph! as if I care!"

"Oh, then, Dave, you do!"

"Pumph!" When David was just turned fifteen, his face was still almost the child's face of square, unset-looking contour, and bangs that he was just beginning to train backward, but which still persisted in drooping square-cut over his brow. A lean, childish-looking face, with eyes that seemed all out of proportion, because the cheeks needed filling in. Straight, friendly, brown eyes, level as Bek's, and square white teeth against tan. It was a young face, even for the lean, gangling, childish body. A body of the most astonishing sinuosity. Tough as fibre.*

At seventeen, his arms, knobby at the wrists, seemed

---

* I cannot recall my brother ever having a sick-abed day, with the exception, of course, of the nervous headaches to which he was devastatingly subject, but which did not develop until along about his sixteenth or seventeenth year. He was extremely sensitive upon what he considered this physical shortcoming, and would endure somehow through a day of the most appalling duress and responsibility, with only the tight-drawn muscles around his mouth to indicate to those of us who knew him best, that one of the raging headaches was upon him.

endless, and his legs, knobby at the ankles, seemed longer than they were to appear in his full maturity.

The farm had put its print on David. Drawn him out long and lean and brown, so that store-clothes struck him mid-arm-and-leg. Even overalls hit him too high at the waist, and petered out considerably above his ankles.

Straddling the porch-rail, swinging bare heels into the side of the house, there was something wounded and cloudy about him and something of absurd adolescence.

"Pumph! Good gosh! Dora and Kenneth. 'Sthat to me! Good gosh, can't a girl and a fellow walk from Tallahassee High to lunch? Good gosh! Good gosh!"

Poor Claire, on the thought that she was about as subtle as spinach, Steve could sometimes kiss the lobe of her ear, a little ashamed that it endeared her. So now:

"I just thought, Davey," she said to the ring of the quick peas dancing down into the pan,—"I just kinda thought—you and Dora—growing up together—maybe you—maybe she—it's nice to see girls and boys that grow up together sort of go on together—that is, if—of course, only, that is, only if ——"

"Well, 'tain't," said Dave, and jumped down off the frail rail, and walked with a casual whistling toward the barn, and crawled as high into the hayloft as he could, burrowing in and in and in, like something wounded that wanted to lie hurt and alone.

Chapter Twenty-six

MORE and more frequently, now that Dave was seventeen, usually at supper-time in the small kitchen that Mathilda kept spotlessly clean and decorated in shelf paper of a scallop-design that she snipped out herself, the Old Gentleman came out flat-footed at him.

It held the little group of four around the table tense from the start of the meal. Mathilda, who kept breaking in with her futilities of pass-this-and-pass-that. Henry, whose gaunt, lantern face would darken and scowl, and Dave, whose toes would wind themselves around the rung of his chair.

In summer, the dusk crowded into the small stifling kitchen like a merciless hot smoke, and a clematis vine leaned in at the window and withered on its indoor side. In winter, the range was full of the small roar of flames chewing coal, but there was usually hoar-frost on the leaky windows.

Dave's place at table faced the window. When the Old Gentleman began a fusillade, his tormented gaze would dig into the clematis vine or follow the wild and beautiful outlines of the frozen panes. The Old Gentleman, without any realization of it, could be relentless in his taunt. Could poke fun with a pitchfork.

"Well Mother, what do you think I heard over at Seven Mile, where I drove two heifers this afternoon? There's a greater scarcity of farm-help today than there was during the war. Can't get the men to stick to the land."

"It's a fact," said Henry, obtuse for the moment. "Labor's restive. Flattered by the attention it received

during the war it is now watching the proletarian success in Russia. The Adamson Act fixed the basic
eight-hour day, but failed to keep pace with the rising
prices. Trouble with the back-to-the-land propaganda
is this ———"

"Well, as I told them over at Seven Mile today, I've
got one hand on *my* place don't have to be coaxed back
to the land, because he's never left it. Can't seem any
way to get him to leave it."

"Puppa—some hominy," fluttered Mathilda to the
Old Gentleman, who was quivering with silent laughter.

That was the signal for Dave, who was about to quiz
Henry about the Adamson Law, to wind agonized toes
around the rung of his chair. It was the signal too, for
Henry's face to darken at his own gullibility and for him
to rise to Dave's defense.

"Say, Father, that's pretty raw."

"Pretty raw? Well, facts are stubborn things, as
stubborn as some growing and grown boys that won't get
a move on for not knowing what they want."

"Davey, little more sorghum on your hominy?"

"I'll take my chance, Father, on the mind that decides
slowly, over and above the one that is quick and ready
on the impulse to which it doesn't stick."

"Quick and ready? It's the second summer now, Tag-
gart made promise to me he'd take him on at the bank.
Sawdust-sprinkling has made many a road to the cashier's
cage for the honest, industrious boy. I'd like a Schuyler
in a bank."

"I don't like banking, Father. In a cage—all day—
thataway."

"You worry about keeping spittoons clean first, young
man."

"Puppa!"

"By golly, what *do* you like? I am waiting to hear

what you do like besides doing around here, on the place, chores that you could help me to hire a boy for, on wages you could make in a man-size job."

"Puppa!"

"Now, Father, look here, be fair. It is true Dave's old enough now to ——"

"I don't need you, Henry, to dictate to me to be fair. I don't see that you know how to be fair with yourself, much less instruct me how to be fair with my youngest. How fair have you been to yourself!"

"Puppa!"

"Hiding yourself under every bushel-basket you could find. Refusing honor after honor, like that fellow Cincinnati was named after. Only that fellow finally left his plow. I don't want another Cincinnati fellow in the family."

Anathema to the Old Gentleman were Henry's shoulders heaving in the silent kind of laughter that he expressed in every fashion except the vocal. Red dyed his face. His body quivered. Up under the eaves of his brow, his eyes watered and drew themselves up tightly, like bird-claws, and tears oozed at the corners.

"I wish it could seem so funny to me!"

"I'm sorry, Father."

"Henry, don't aggravate your father."

"He don't aggravate me any more, Mother. That's all past. I've long ago reconciled myself to the disappointment of seeing the son that could bring big honor, satisfied with being a country lawyer. It's bitter to have to see it, but, by golly, I don't sit back and see it happen over again! Dave, content to be just a hand on a one-horse farm!"

The bare toes clamped to the rung again. The Old Gentleman was right. Of course. A fellow didn't stick around a farm no bigger than the Igrotte place, if he was worth his hire at doing anything better. The Old Gentleman was right. But the torturous indecisions! The torturous, torturous indecisions. . . .

"You see, Father, a fellow like me in a bank-job—wouldn't—make a go of it."

"What about that job with Seth Pritchy on his dairy farm?"

"But, Father, the trouble with that . . ."

"The trouble with that," suddenly shouted the old man, his irascibility rising and spluttering, "is *you!*" . . . .

"I know, Father, but I don't want——"

"Then what in Heaven's name do you want? All right, Pritchy's out. The bank's out. Clerking's out. Dairying's out. Farming's out. Now, young man, you tell me, by Gad, what you've got on your mind. That's what I've got a right to know. Moon-herding at seventeen. Belly-reading. Star-gazing. Well—now what?"

"Father—when you yell that way—fellow gets confused."

"Fellow gets confused," mimicked the Old Gentleman. "Fellow gets confused. By golly, what do you think your old Pap is getting, sitting by and having to see a young fellow stagnate for want of the gumption to know what it is in life he's cut out for. Day-dreaming. Night-gazing. Star-hunting. And the world going marching on! Fellow gets confused. . . . Like to know what you think I get!"

"Yes, Father, you get the boy confused, and you get me confused too. Pretty darned confused. The wonder to me is that the whole Schuyler outfit isn't down in medical annals as Exhibit A of nervous dyspeptics, from a lifetime of meals eaten to your howling temperament."

"Puppa—you haven't touched your dish of rice. Pass your father the cinnamon, Davey."

"I'm only asking him to tell me what he's got on his

mind that is better than anything we have to offer him!
A father is entitled to that right. A bright boy, his age,
can't turn down everything that will help to get him off
a shanty-farm without having something better on his
mind than he lets on. What have you and him been
cooking up together all these years, if it don't give him
enough gumption to come in out of the rain?"

"Give the boy time, Father, to find himself."

"To find himself, Puppa. Henry, you sprinkle a bit
of cinnamon on your father's rice for him. He just won't
eat his rice plain. Puppa is the greatest one not to eat
his rice plain."

"To find himself! By his age, you were already in
your second year law-school."

"Yes, Father, but I had advantages that—we haven't
been quite able to give Dave."

On that, it was as if you had jabbed a pin into the
balloon of the Old Gentleman's rambunctiousness. He
lopped over along his spine. His chin fell to his chest,
his hands sought the table-edge, and the red ran from
his face, leaving it the blanched smoothness of an almond.

"Don't hold it against me that he was born into the
years of my reverses."

"Puppa . . ."

"Nonsense, Father, you know precisely what I mean."

"I know what I mean. He hasn't even had a gram-
mar-school education. A man like me, who has wanted
for every one of his children what he could never have
for himself, and who has been able to give it to every one
except his last ——"

"If there is anything to be said on that subject, Father,
I'm the one it might be said to. Not you. I've had out a
lawyer's shingle ever since Davey was born. I've been
the one who should have managed to make his education
and his advantages possible. You've the right to expect

that from us—but, somehow, the blamed war—the general slump—the sum total of war, even for those who fatten off it, is loss. You lose if you win."

"Henry's been a good education to Davey," quavered Mathilda. "All education don't lie in the schoolhouse, Puppa."

"If only you wouldn't keep picking on me, Father," piped up David. "I'm earning my keep, thisaway. I'm helping you, and I'll help you more."

"Earning your keep!" shouted the Old Gentleman again. "Earning your keep! Is that all you're fit for? Like any hobo-hand who rides in on a box-car."

"Dave's of a peculiar and cautious temperament, Father. I've noticed that about him. Slow to act, but decisive, once his mind is made up. Give him time."

"Time! Time! Time for what, that's all I want to know. I've got a right to know. A man like me who banks on his children down to the last of them, making them citizens a community can be proud of! What's in the back of this young one's head? My other boys got out. Got themselves started—what's in the back of this one's head?"

"For Lord's sake, Father, quit ragging the boy!"

"Don't keep asking me that, Father!" cried Dave, goaded until he sprang to his feet with his face so drawn that before he even opened his mouth his mother was crying for him. "Don't keep asking me that. Nothing's in the back of my head. Nothing except— everything. I guess I'm not cut out for much, but if you'll let me alone—if you'll only let me alone. *You let me alone,*" shouted Dave suddenly, in the same key of his father's raucousness, and then by an effort that pulled his mouth all out of shape and made his mother sob more with hurting for him, got his voice back again into a curious, hard level that slid up at the end into a ridiculous change-of-voice squeak. "Don't hound me, Father! A fellow needs time. . . ."

"He does that, Puppa. Davey was never a quick child. He's not so strong as he looks, Puppa. He's not looked so well lately."

"Oh, Mother, for goodness' sakes, Mother. I'm well."

"A boy that's too proud to wear his asafœtida-bag—can catch sickness."

"Don't hound him, Father," said Henry, his brow heavy with scowl.

"Don't, Father!" cried Dave, and, leaping up, suddenly ran toward the doorway, as if evading the pursuit of more words. "Don't hound me. You see, with a fellow like me—with a fellow like me," he kept saying through the tight dam of his tonsils, "I've just got to have time to—to—I've just got to have time. Don't I, Henry? Don't I, Hen-ry?" And then, to his unspeakable agony, began to cry. In sniffles. And wipe at his face with the grimy back of a hand.

There was something particularly feeble about the Old Gentleman, as he shuffled in the quick contrition that was sure to follow one of his outbursts, over toward his son, the pyrotechnics of his emotions dying down into broken and pitiable utterances.

"I'm a bad father, Dave. I can't do anything for my children, and then I turn around and blame them."

"Cripes," said David, "what's all the row about? I got to go for those two heifers."

"Mind you close that south gate," shouted the Old Gentleman after him. "Don't you leave that south gate open, this time of night, again, or by golly, I'll ——"

"Puppa!" quavered Mathilda, standing in the open window with a stack of dishes in her hand. "Look! Isn't that a rainbow out over Middleton way?"

It was. Three-quarters of an arch that stopped suddenly in the middle of the pasture, as if broken off.

"By Jove, it is, Mother!"

The delicate thing hung with the curve of a descending skyrocket over the evening countryside, sun-pierced rain-clouds breaking into great chunks and sending down spokes of light.

Into the light-sprayed arch ran the loping figure of Dave, headed for pasture.

"By golly," said the Old Gentleman, blowing at his pipe and rousing the old, cold smell, "that's fine! What's it a sign of, Mother?"

"Run under a rainbow that comes up over your left shoulder, and you'll get a pot of gold at its far end and never suffer a bunion all your days."

"There goes Davey through! No bunions for him!"

"I'm glad. Bunions is mighty painful things," said Mathilda, and limped on her own over to deposit dishes in the sink.*

---

* Time and time again, I've heard my Mother tell the story of Davey running through the rainbow, that prophetic evening that Father took the boy to task for his habit of the slow decision. A trait that ultimately was to become his surest asset, this ability of his to think slowly and surely toward a conclusion, and then act with leaping swiftness. I have it from my brother first-hand that although he signed the Air Lane bill, then known as Schuyler's Cyclone Act, at the conclusion of his last term in Congress, actually he had given the matter six years of detailed premeditation.

Chapter Twenty-seven

ALL that evening, long after the heifers were in, and the last bolt drawn, and Mathilda's last cup washed, and the dishpan set gleaming against the drain-board, Henry sat in his room, as if waiting. The sound of his parents moving about their adjoining room at the business of going to bed, died down, and then the drone of their fitful remarks to each other, falling light as rain upon the silence, before they dropped off to sleep.

Every so often, Henry's pipe, on its way to his mouth, paused, as if to listen. Or suddenly, he slid forward on the old leather Morris chair to cock an ear. The student-lamp had a slow hiss to it that no amount of puttering with the wick would correct. To listen for a creak on the stairway, you had to strain a bit through that soft commotion.

After a while Henry fitted back his copy of *The Martyrdom of Man* into its familiar place on his bookshelf, lowered the wick until its flame slipped into its slot, and then dragged his heavy Morris chair over toward the open window.

An April night, with the cool, filtered taste to it of spring water, lay over the moonless scene. A dark night, but not black enough to erase silhouettes. A soft, lovely, motionless night, dotted with myriads of small stars, and through it, like an arpeggio scale, the minute, silver, hurrying sounds of a runnel of spring water animated by recent rains.

After a while, the sole light on the landscape, one that burned in the remote window of a shanty-dweller named

Joe Batch, passed out into the darkness, and then Henry did what, for him, was an unprecedented thing.*

He tiptoed out into the hall, and with his slippers hanging off at the heels, wound up the ladder that led up into Dave's room.

The candle in that attic of slants and shadows was guttering low in its green bottle; and, fully dressed on his pallet, with his cheek down against the page of an open volume of *Henry Esmond,* and his eyes wide awake but staring off, lay David.

He sprang up at the appearance of his brother's head above the ladder, shamefaced for no reason he could have formulated. Teddy leaped, too, from his doze, bellying across the floor in a recognizing frenzy of wagging tail.

"It's hot up here," said Henry. "Whew!" and walked over to the undersized window and threw up the sash. The gust of it blew out the candle into a darkness for which they both seemed grateful.

"I guess I'd 'a' been coming down to you soon, Henry," said the boy and moved along, so that they both might sit on the side of the cot.

It was only the second or third time Henry had ever been in that room. They sat silently, Henry stooping away from the rough boards of the slant ceiling.

"Down, Teddy!"

"What's what, Dave?" said Henry, and caught up one knee between his hands and began to rock.

"Why—that's just what I dunno," said Dave, and gulped so, that in the smooth, dark silence, it was almost a click.

---

* It was characteristic of Dave, that on his world-tour he should find time to personally see to it that Denny Batch, the son of an old squatter out home, should be included in the secret-service corps of that memorable trip.

"Feeling well?"

"Sure."

"Any more those headaches?"

"Just kinda. Some days."

"Often?"

"N-no."

"Bad?"

"N-no."

"Today?"

"Nope."

"Eye-doctor."

"Aw!"

"What Father meant this evening, Dave, only he's got a rotten way of saying it, is ——"

"I know."

"I figure, Dave, that in your case, you're just a little slow off the trigger. Am I right?"

"You see, Henry—I can't say it to Father—but what's the use a fellow choosing something to do, just because he's got to be doing something?"

"Something in that."

"Now, you just take the way the bees work it out in that book you gave me about them by that French fellow."

"Maeterlinck."

"And the ants in that other fellow's book."

"Wheeler."

"You don't catch one single one of those chaps down in the bee-world and the ant-world doing something just to be doing. No, sir. You don't catch a worker in bee-town putting his bee-shoulder to the wheel, unless he knows that wheel's going to turn something. A fellow's got to have his eye on building up something—even if it's only a honeycomb. Say, Henry, you know what? This

month's *Farm Journal's* got a story in about bee-raising
—maybe if I was to try my hand at that ——"

"Yesterday, it was ovibos-raising, wasn't it?"

"Yeh! That fellow Stefansson you gave me to read.
Northward Course of Empire. That's what I mean,
Henry! Just the name of that book says what I mean.
What's the use sitting in a cage in somebody's bank, or
keeping count of somebody's Holsteins, or raising a little
old patch of alfalfa, when there—when there's whole
empires lying about us, waiting for men; and new worlds
that the airship is going to link onto us, so that the North
Pole isn't even North any more. You know what,
Henry? That land up there isn't dead. Hundreds and
thousands of miles of it. Fellows have lived off that land
up there for years, without having any provisions with
them. That means there's whole new worlds lying
around us. Don't it? Funny everybody don't get excited about it ——"

"Well?"

"Well—well—like it says in one of the biologies,
man's pro-duc-tiv-ity of the soil has got to keep pace with
his fertility of the soil. See? Know what I mean? I've
worked it out. It's thisaway."

"This way."

"Thisaway."

"This way."

"This way. Well, take when a country like ours gets
too many people in it—well, the northward course of empire means that country up there can be used for growing
more meat and more wheat to feed the over-population—
see what I mean?—what's the use fiddling around in a
clerk's cage, when—when there's empires lying around
asleep and waiting to be worked up."

"Well? Go on."

"There's nowhere to go, Henry. That's the trouble.

A fellow just thinks and thinks, and then—he's so busy thinking where to begin—he don't begin—at all."

"Doesn't ——"

"Doesn't."

"Henry, why did you give me that book called Spencer's *First Principles?*"

"To make you think."

"Do you believe in God?"

"Not as he exists in Testaments."

"As he exists in these here *First Principles?*"

"Does he exist there?"

"Sure he does. Who made the First Principles?"

"I like your looking at it like that."

"Was Ingersoll a great preacher?"

"A great orator."

"Who was a great preacher?"

"Demosthenes."

"But he couldn't preach. He had to have a stone in his mouth."

"His wisdom percolated through the stone, and even the stone heads of his public."

"You know what? A good way to make people listen to what you've got to say to them, is to be a preacher."

"Aha! *Now* it's the Church! This is the era of the decline of the Church and the rise of the State. Don't climb a sinking ship."

"You can't ever sink God."

"Wait and see what happens when human beings attain the perfect mind."

"Then they'll be God themselves."

"Exactly."

"I believe in God, Henry."

"Of course you do. Even when you jump the track, your trolley stays on."

"What?"

"Nothing."

Up there, in the gloom of the room that came down on both sides like a book closing, they sat side by side on the edge of the cot, Henry hugging his knee and rocking, Teddy stretched flat on the strip of matting beneath the window, and the cool, washed night-air coming in boldly.

It was a habit of these two to sit in silence, out into which their thoughts could creep, timidly at first, then boldly, like mice at night.

"What's the matter, boy?"

"Huh? Why?"

"You're sighing like an exhausted pipe."

"Roll over, Teddy. It's him, snoring."

"Oh!"

"Henry?"

"Yes?"

"Were you ever—kinda licked?"

"I've been licked from the start, I guess, Dave. In a way you'll probably never know anything about."

"Shelley, the poet, died young. Did you know that? In a boat. Bay of Naples. Sad—and grand—that-away."

"That way. M-m-m. Not my style. The advantages of dying in bed can't be overestimated."

"Have you ever thought, Henry—is life worth living?"

"Depends a good deal, I guess, upon the—-liver."

"Y'know, if it wasn't for Mother and Father, and you and Bek, of course, 'n' all—it would be sad for them. Gee! But I don't know as I'm so crazy about living. I could snuff out just like that!"

"Well, taking it all in all, guess there's pretty much to be said on both sides."

"You're laughing."

"Forsooth, no!"

"Well, I don't expect anybody to understand ——"

"Who is she?"

"How did you know?"

"I'm like that, sometimes. Intuitive."

"Has anybody ——"

"Nobody."

"Has Claire?"

"I tell you, nobody."

"Then how ——"

"Oh, after a fellow has lived as long as I have, he comes to know a few things for himself."

"You see, Henry, I wouldn't mind it so terribly—yes, maybe I would, but maybe I wouldn't, if it wasn't one of those patent-leather lizards like him. That's what's eating me. His walking down Tallahassee Street with her every day."

"Patent-leather lizard like whom?"

"Don't you know?"

"How the dickens should I ——"

"Kenneth Chipman."

"What's the matter with Kenneth? Nice enough fellow s'far as I know. Son of as nice a fellow and as good a lawyer as this county boasts."

"He's a lizard. Tea-hound. Sits in the St. Charles Hotel any Saturday afternoon around four, and drinks it with girls, with his little finger sticking out off the cup."

"What in Heaven's name ——"

"I don't care what he is, so long as he doesn't hook his arm into hers walking along Tallahassee. Guess I'm what you call a single-track fellow, Henry. Can't think of anything else but—but his walking down Tallahassee thataway—what's the use of anything—with his walking down Tallahassee thataway."

"Sounds like an acute case of the girl. Who is she?"

"You—don't—know——"

"Half-dozen nice kind of girls hereabouts that you might get smitten with."

"You—mean—you don't know—everything?"

"Of course not, except a curl on a neck or a pair of blue eyes could be responsible for er—a—well, for your acute—er—a . . ."

"You're laughing at me!"

"No, no, David!"

"You are! I can feel you—shake!"

"Well, if I am, the joke's on me."

"What joke?"

"Life."

"It's not like I was a moonstruck fellow, with eyes for every girl. She's not like other girls."

"I'm sure of that."

"I—I'm not like other fellows."

"I'm sure—of that——"

"You *are* laughing."

"Don't be an idiot."

"With me, Henry—oh, I know how fellows get moonstruck. Fellow can't help hearing. The boys. The way they talk—around the barns. Girls. Fellows and girls. I'm not thataway. I hate that—talk. Ugh! There's only one girl I could ever want to—to—to—touch, Henry. I—oughtn't say it, I guess—but—I do want to touch her beautifulness, Henry. To be the first—the only—is that rotten?"

"It's the soundest thing in life."

"Gosh—I—just do! Other fellows get moonstruck. I'm not like them. With me, it's just Dora. Always!"

"Ah, Dora, old Tark's daughter! That does complicate things. Our Old Gentleman and he have about as much use for each other as two cocks in a pit."

"That's nothing to Dora and me. Nothing's nothing."

"I see," said Henry gravely, fumbling to relight his pipe, the match, in that fitful second, revealing the face of young David smeared with strain and pallor.

"She's kinda outgrown me now, Hen. That's the trouble. I don't belong to the Centralia crowd that she's gone to school with—and then that dancing-school business. We changed schools and Sunday-schools so long ago. She's the prettiest little thing. If Kenneth gets Dora, he—I—dunno. I just dunno——"

For an overwhelmingly difficult moment, Dave's tussle was chiefly with his Adam's-apple, the puffing of Henry's pipe helping to make the noise of the gulping seem less colossal.

"A first love-affair, Dave, is like the measles. A good thing to have and have over."

"That's what you say. You're—old. But I know me, all right. She's—why, she—she's ——"

It was intolerable that a jaw that was about to prick into its first beard should tremble!

"Where does Dora stand on all this, Dave?"

"She—where would she stand? Where could I—come in with her. Beautiful her. With her High School and dancing crowd and patent-leather-hair lizards crawling all around her. Where do I come in? Me? Huh, I don't come in at all! Why—I haven't even seen her, face to face, since—since one morning in her barn—I—where do I come in? Not at all."

"Why?"

"Why do you keep asking me *why?* She don't know I'm on earth—any more."

"Ever asked her?"

"Don't ask a girl that."

"Why?"

"If you don't quit asking me 'why'——"

"Blamed little fool, why don't you go get your dander up with her, instead of me?"

"If you—if you don't quit shaking—if you don't quit shaking—you're laughing——" screamed Dave, suddenly, in a low, tight kind of agony, and hurling himself against the bulk of his brother, landed sobbing there. Tears that laid him low on the rack of humiliation. Deep, wrenching sobs that he flung himself down into the mattress to muffle, and then, because they shamed him intolerably, began to beat and try to tussle with his brother.

"You—what do you know about—about—caring——"

"You're right, Dave," said Henry. "I don't seem to know how to care—enough. That way. That's what I meant by being licked. If I—somehow—cared—more, I wouldn't be missing everything. Quit pounding me, boy!"

"I tell you I can't live in a world where somebody—else —has her. I can't think of anything else. No wonder Father says I'm no good. I want to do pretty nearly everything there is to be done, and nothing's worth doing, because—I'm like a fellow that's bleeding to death, Hen. All the life's running out of me—and I don't care who knows it!"

"Have you talked to Dora?"

"Talked to Dora? What'll I do? Go to her and say, 'Looka here, you're going with a patent-leather lizard, if you ask me, but just the same, a fellow that's up-and-doing, owns his own flivver and can take care of you and get you somewhere?'"

"Got to admit that about Ken."

"Well, I'll say to her, you drop him for me. I'm a farm-boy on my father's place out on Pessimines Lane. Everything that I want to do, or be, is locked up in my head and can't get out. But you go and throw over Kenneth and get yourself engaged to me. That will unlock me and I'll start out to be something. That would make a hit with a girl like Dora, in that gay town-set she's in, wouldn't it? A girl that goes to Saturday-afternoon teas at the St. Charles, and holds out her little finger from her teacup, I'd make a hit going to her with these calluses on my hands, and forty cents in my pocket, and saying, 'Dora, I'm the fellow.'"

"That's about the only way you'll ever be the fellow."

"What do you mean?"

"Go find out. Maybe you are the fellow. If you aren't, take your licking and shut up about it."

The first light trembled over them, as they sat in the long after-silence of that. Henry, with his thin legs crossed, sitting on the edge of the cot and sucking at his cold pipe. Dave on his stomach, with his feet against the warm fur of Teddy and his eyes on the glimmer of dawn.

Chapter Twenty-eight

ON A hot September day of apricot haze; crush of family-sedans along High Street, and a white-clad woman's figure in the show-window of the Five and Ten, shooting hot scones from a patent machine into the acquisitive hands of a sidewalk-jam; a gangling boy's figure in long trousers that stopped as if affronted above the knobs of his ankles, and a short, black coat that hiked, strode along through the thick human treacle and turned down into Second Street toward the Blue Bird Restaurant.

He had just been fitted in the spectacles that are by now indissolubly associated with the square pallor of face, the wide, clear, slightly beetling brow, and the strong, high-bridged nose; a nose difficult to span with a good fit of eye-glass frame.

That was the difficulty this Saturday. There was an inflamed ridge across the top of Dave's nose, and the spectacles themselves were newly wound with cotton to relieve pressure against the abrasion. It kept him blinking his eyes and shrugging his nose. Every so often, he stopped before the mirror of a chewing-gum machine or his reflection in plate-glass, to ride them up and down into place.

The Old Gentleman's youngest was not so well known on the streets of Centralia as the older children had been back in the days when the family lived in Sycamore Street.

The Centralia scene had changed since then. High Street had been widened, and there were double car-tracks now, and hourly omnibuses started their cruises from Court House Square along a route that included Adalia, College Corner, Seven Mile and Middleton. The five-story Equity Building had replaced the old red brick Renchler Block; and the new St. Charles Hotel, with a florist-shop, haberdashery, and Western Union office flush with the sidewalk, occupied the old site of Wabischer's saloon, that had been burned to the ground a few years after Dave was born.

Rows of parked cars stood in a long line down the center of High. A white-granite soldiers' monument, twice as tall as a man, and with a pair of fern-fronds crossed on its inscribed bosom, stemmed the tide for a brief détour around it, as traffic flowed over the viaduct toward Middleton.

Spratt's Dental College now stood on the saloon-corner where the Old Gentleman, in pre-Volstead days, had leaned many a clay-crusted convivial boot and swabbed down bock-beer, cramming his pockets with pretzels and Saratoga chips for young pilferers.

But the Old Gentleman's phäeton and mare had long since ceased to sway their daily way down High Street, and Bek's heroic figure seldom strode there now except on shopping-expeditions, when she carried two large oil-cloth bags that she fed straight from the counters without benefit of wrappings. Henry still occupied his office up over Schlemmer's hardware-store, but his deacon-like figure hurried along close to walls these days, and then mostly between the office and the Court House, with its sooty bunting-draped bust of George Washington over the imitation Greek-proscenium entrance.

So "the Old Gentleman's youngest," except to a few of a generation that still lingered in front of banks, feed-stores, and the sole livery-stable that survived, was scarcely a known figure.

Just another gawk of a farm-boy, attracted by the

Strand Movie Theater, Clabby's Billiard Parlors, half a dozen drug-store hang-outs, and Linden Amusement Park, which, in summer, plastered an artificial lake with swan-boats for hire.

High Street, of a Saturday, was pandemonium. Children with flat, eager tongues for the sticky pleasures of the lollipop. Window-shopping women, spry with the sense of surcease from the rigors of dishpan and diapering. Rattle of tin flivvers, mud to the hub. A graphophone in front of Smilley's music-store braying to the din. The bright clutter of sunshine. The Tallahassee baseball-team doing a lockstep out to Linden Park. The occasional horse-drawn farm-wagon, with chairs in back to accommodate the family. The Chamber of Commerce windows on the second floor of the Equity Building, wide open, and filled with the click of typewriters. Women with net marketing-bags, crammed with spinach and sprays of dill, pearl-fleshed spring onions, and an occasional live wretch of a chicken. Constantly recurring flashes of young girls, with long, revealing, flesh-colored legs, and bold lips, frankly penciled into orange and magenta bow-knots. Centralia's telephone-directory list out in good store-suits, and the first of the new season's straw cadies on their heads, and the fleshiness of canned foods, canned ideas, canned ideals, and canned music, in spangles of light sweat across pinkish faces.

A corn-fed-looking populace, which this boy, ambling slowly through that hottish Saturday, was one day to help swerve from the dangerous complacency of ultimate defeat.

Long before he was consciously aware of it, the quick antennæ of those perceptions which were to win him the ultimate sobriquet, "Leader of Leaders," were at work.*

* "Leader of Leaders" clung to my brother from the occasion of his single-handed crashing through the Reedy Fili-

Every manifestation of crowds such as this "home-brew humanity," milling, toiling, playing, was to sow seed in a clump of his fertile brain.

But on this particular Saturday, the crowds jostling him were just so much superfluous universe spinning around his egocentric figure.

At the Blue Bird Restaurant, the erstwhile brown little waitress, gray now, drew out his chair and handed him a stained menu, flicking it first with the napkin she wore at her belt. Here was a young man, now!

The strong light of the furiously sunny day, streaming in through the plate-glass front of the Blue Bird, showing up mercilessly the cotton palms, the cigar-counter with the waving blob of flame on the cigar-cutter and lighter, the oblongs of fly-paper sucking their toll into glue, the square white tables, with their slightly used cloths and geometry of silverware, made his eyes, still smarting of belladonna, blink even more, and burn.

The Rotary Club now held its weekly luncheons in an upstairs dining-room of the Blue Bird. Business-men, larger retail merchants, petty wholesalers, men whose names were written along High Street's signs and show-windows, officials from the foundries, a banker, a merchant, a lawyer, a chief, began to drift in, practically every one of them wiping at an inside hat-band as he entered.

Five or six of the main dining-room tables were already occupied by single figures, most of them with the

---

buster, which threatened to destroy the Schuyler Alien Bill.

Personally, I have never felt the phrase a felicitous one. While it is indubitably true that David from the start was a man to win the confidence and respect of the mighty minority, as a Man's man, I know of no public figure, yes, including Theodore Roosevelt, who inspired a more deeply-rooted love in the masses than my brother.

Saturday Evening Post or the *Centralia Gazette* propped up against the sugar-bowl. Even though they were unknown to Dave, and he attracted not their slightest attention, these sparsely scattered figures set him writhing. It was difficult, if you had previously been in a public restaurant only one or two times at best, to sit alone at a table under which legs felt too long to fit. The spectacles bit down into the inflamed place on the bridge of his nose, making it feel heavy and round as a potato. His collar twitched, and his eyes; and sidelong glances into a panel-mirror suddenly revealed the long, lean rods of his bare wrists.

It was not easy waiting alone in a public place, particularly since his legs would not seem to fit under. They had fitted under, the last time! Finally he did cram them in, but the edge of the table bit into him; and, when he moved, the table tilted.

Henrietta came first. The years had been at her in what seemed a rather subtle process of dehydration. She had dried, the skin powdery, a little tougher, a little tanner. Succulence all gone, but a brittle, bony, brightened look to her of nervous vitality. Rotarians, whom as boys Henriette had taught the rudiments of long division, passed on their way to lunch, some of them pausing for a good-day with an air of self-conscious juvenility that was never to wear off where "teacher" was concerned.

Even the brown foulard, with the gold bird-claw pinned onto the écru-lace yoke, had but slightly changed in cut. There had never been a time when to Dave, Henriette had not been precisely the cut-and-dried and kind Miss Simpson of that Saturday. A narrow, high-shouldered little person, indissolubly associated in his mind with the odor of arithmetic and the light powdering of chalk-dust across her flesh.

If her heart misgave her for a moment at sight of Dave there at the table, to break in upon the sanctity of her lunch-hour with Henry, she covered it immediately with the same small, kind smile that had coaxed hundreds of the youth of Centralia along the rocky road of the three R's.

"Well, David, isn't this a surprise?"

"Henry said I was to come here for lunch, from the oculist's."

"Spectacles? Let me see. Turn further. Astigmatic?"

"Guess they look kinda funny? Huh?"

"Not at all. Sensible!"

"Not—not so good-looking, though, I guess. Huh?"

"Anything that denotes common sense is good-looking."

"I mean—you see, I just wanted eye-glasses. Not these old spectacle-things around the ears."

"The foolish kind that wobble and inflame the eyes and fall and break at every provocation. Ah me, 'Vanitas vanitatum, et omnia vanitas,' or is it 'vanitates?' "

"Do they look all right?"

"Sensible."

"I don't have to wear them for reading. I'm nearsighted, you see. Guess this cotton wound around looks kinda snide, don't it?"

"Most of my boys have that trouble the first few weeks."

"Would you mind looking," said David, uncircling the frames from his ears with a writhing difficulty, and his face emerging with the peculiar swollen look of the suddenly-unspectacled, "which way does it look best? With them or without them? Huh? With or without?"

Henry entered then, dabbing at his derby hat-band, and paring off the edge of a group of Rotarians.

"Hope you don't mind the boy, Henriette. He's been to the oculist, and I thought he'd want a bite of lunch afterward. How's the eyes, boy?"

"How do I look, Henry? He said the frameless ones would only cost ———"

"Nonsense. These are adequate and sensible. Feel all right?"

"Yes, but you see, Hen, he had some frameless ones there that looked great on me, only you said I couldn't ———"

"What'll you have, boy? Quick!" said Henry, and regarded the speckled menu with gusto. His family was fond of saying that a prodigal host was lost to the world when Henry fell short of becoming a rich man. Himself a sparse eater, he loved the largesse of hospitality. Mathilda always maintained that his eyes were larger than his stomach. He loved to bestow. He was reckless and overabundant. If he stopped at the meat-market, at his mother's bidding, to send home a leg-of-lamb, all her admonitions to the contrary notwithstanding, he was bound to select a far too expensive and extensive whole side of lamb.

Of late years, these commissions had been rigorously denied Henry.

"What'll you have, boy? Quick!"

"I'd like some of that chile-con-carne and some of that cherry pie à la mode."

"Not so good, I should say, for a boy with one fair-sized pimple and a couple of incipient ones."

At that, David hauled back from the table, crimson.

"Don't want anything," he said and gulped.

"I'm sorry, Dave. Raw as the dickens of me. Here, Katy, chile-con-carne and cherry pie à la mode for the boy, and make it a double portion of ice-cream and a portion of that strawberry short-cake thrown in if his capacity is sufficiently elastic. Couldn't tempt you to a bit of that short-cake, Henriette? Come, we'll all three have strawberry short-cake."

"Your rash, Henry!" said Henrietta gravely.

"We can afford to be rash for once, Henriette. We don't have the young bloods of the town in on this party every Saturday."

"You, strawberry-rash was what I had reference to."

"Yes, I suppose that sort of rash is more my speed."

It was exciting lunching with Henry and Henriette. The clatter of dishes rose with the noonday din. Sounds of applause clattered down from the Rotarian dining-room.

Lonnie Haskel, Middleton's foremost lawyer, paused to consult with Henry for a few moments on a point of tariff-law in relation to a long-drawn case of his involving the Giles Tool Works and a firm in Sheffield, England, and then moved along.

"What's tariff, Henry? I know what ad valorem is. Ad valorem is ——"

"Tariff is the barbed-wire fence between nations, that keeps man's activities nationalized. If you're really interested, we'll talk it out Sunday. The first four hundred and twenty-seven principles of tariff are the hardest."

"Henry, I think it's right remarkable, Dave's interest in a subject like tariff. I find my boys just don't seem right bright on the subject."

"Dave's got a good, healthy intellectual curiosity, and a good long head on him, when he chooses to use it."

"Aw. My head—my head's no longer 'n yours."

"Your brother was speaking figuratively, Dave."

"Yes'm."

"Which reminds me, Henry, I very much want your advice. At the Saturday Morning Study Hour Club today, I was elected a member of the debating-team of the Political Science Section. At the October meeting, our subject is to be, Resolved: That Prohibition is the greatest good for the greatest number. Of course, I shall choose the negative side. Yes?"

"Not 'of course,' Henriette. I'm afraid you are by way of becoming a disciple of my wild, strawberry-rash radicalism."

"Nonsense, Henry! You have never won me over to a point of view with any coercion except the coercion of logic."

"Good! Resolved then, that prohibition is the greatest poppycock for the greatest poppycocks."

"Be serious, Henry! It's for the October open meeting, and it's our most important event. I hope you'll come."

"I may be serious at it, Henriette, but I could not possibly be serious about it."

"Now, you've said yourself, Henry Schuyler, time and time again, that however vacuous and pretentious and presumptuous the American club-woman may be, at least she's the bearer of a culture-banner that, except for her, would molder under moth-balls in the cupboard, along with the tired business-man's Knights of Columbus uniform and Masonic apron."

"Oh, there's something to be said for the uniting of fair hands across the tea, hot-biscuit, and chicken-salad tables of the country, in the name of learning the difference between Owen and George Meredith."

"I notice that two of your own sisters are active and helpful members of the very Saturday Morning Club in question."

"Now, Henriette, the hatpin-jab is a method not worthy of you."

"Well, then, Henry, do stop your fooling."

"Give 'em light wine and beer, Miss Simpson. The greatest good to the greatest number."

"Good for you, Dave. That's precisely what I intend to do. Don't you think so, Henry? Davey's just said it right. You know, Henry, much as I've always regretted never having had Dave as one of my boys, I don't know but what he could pass his High exams. I'd have to work with him on his mathematics, he's never seemed right strong to me on square root, but——"

"You see, it's thisaway. It is just as well to take everything away from them in the beginning. Then, when you give half of it back, like light wines and beer, they'll be so glad to get it, they'll forget the other half that's been taken away."

"Excellent points to make in my paper, but, Davey Schuyler, you're reciting something you've heard!"

"I'm not. Henry, didn't I work it out for you that night you said the Volstead Act was—was—aw, I don't remember how you said it, but I remember what it meant and that's what I said back."

"I said, that if you judge a civilization by its laws, the Volstead Act will send us down to posterity as a nation of galley slaves, delinquents, and nincompoops."

"Well, and I said that the Volstead Act wasn't as dumb as it looked, because if you give 'em back the light wines and beer after you've taken everything away from——"

"No, he's not reciting, Henriette. Leave it to him to reach just that safe-and-sane, greatest-good-for-the-greatest-number kind of conclusion. The boy is uncanny in his ability to jump to the one safe-and-sane spot on the trestle, if he hears a train coming."

"If I was running this country," began Dave, digging his eye-glasses out of the trench across the bridge of his nose, "I——"

"Think you'd better not tackle that second piece of

strawberry short-cake after all, Dave. It looks right vicious after the cherry pie and ice-cream. Well, folks, what say to the baseball-game?"

"Splendid, Henry! Tom Connors, one of my boys, takes his place on the bench as substitute pitcher this afternoon. You know Jim Connors' boy, Henry, from Third District?"

"Good! Come along, Dave! We'll have to miss the last inning as it is, if we're to catch the milk-truck home."

A kind of purplish red, like the fruit-juice that dyed his short, square teeth, swept David's face, giving his bella-donna-enlarged eyes the look of being slowly choked out of his head.

"The sun on the bleachers—and all—these spectacles kinda—glare ——"

"Nonsense! We've a lady along. We're going grand-stand."

"My eyes—I—I—better not ——"

"Look here, when you refuse a baseball-game, there's something wrong! Aren't you feeling tip-top?"

"Sure I am!"

"Well, then, if you don't want to come along, why not come out and say so?"

"Just thought I'd loaf around town as long as I'm here ——"

"Leave the boy be, Henry. He's worked out his own way to spend his holiday."

"Just thought—Saturday—loaf around—specs feel kinda new—squint—thought I'd just ——"

"Sure," said Henry, suddenly diving into his pocket for a coin purse and opening it by its little metal catch, "I understand. Saturday afternoon. Just loaf around. I see."

There was something about Henry when he said, "I see," through lips that clicked almost like the little coin-

purse, that sent the red in David's face racing deeper and
deeper.

"Just kinda thought ——"

"Certainly!"

"Thanks, Henry, for the fifty cents. Just kinda
thought—loaf around. These here specs. Give a look,
will you, Henry? Now I've got them on. Now I've
got them off. Quick! Which way looks best? Off or
on?"

"Don't know as one way doesn't look just about as—
er—a—well as another. I—er—mean—strikes me since
you've got to wear them, strikes me they look more comfortable on."

"But for this afternoon. If you were me—on or off,
Henry? Look again. Now look. On. Off. That
there cotton wound along the nose-piece. Gosh, that's
a fright, isn't it?"

"What say you, Henriette? If you ask me, I'll say
he looks pretty intellectual."

"Sensible. Sensible, I'd say."

"You don't think, Henry—just for this afternoon—
look better without 'em? Guess that there red ditch
across my nose shows up pretty strong without them.
Huh? Yes? Look, when I turn thisaway."

"I think the specs win, don't you, Henriette?" said
Henry with unwavering gravity, and covering her shoulders with the string of fur tippet.

"Sensible, I'd say."

"Well, then, folks—so long. Guess I'll er—stroll
around town for a bit. I'll catch the milk-truck out too,
Hen. Or walk. 'By, Miss Simpson! S'long, Hen!
Guess er—I'll just stroll along—and all."

With a gravity that continued to maintain itself until
he was out of sight and hearing, they watched him, long,
lean, and gangling, slip into the tide of High Street.

Chapter Twenty-nine

ONCE off the hard, white-paved clamor of High Street, the shady somnolence of residential Centralia set in.

At the corner of Sycamore Street, on the steps of the square white mausoleum of a "gift library," a band of Boy Scouts was assembling for a hike. David knew some of them, slightly. His eyes flashed away from them in embarrassment. With a sense of ostracism. They were, for the most part, the boys with whom he would have grown up, had the family continued to live in the House on Sycamore Street. He was as conscious of them as they were unconscious of him.

Clabby's confectionery-wagon was at the curb of the old Whittier-Neal mansion delivering a quart of peach-and-pistachio ice-cream for Mrs. Whittier-Neal's bridge-party.

Donald Neal was one of the fellows who took girls to five-o'clock Saturday-afternoon tea at the St. Charles.

Donald had taken Dora on two occasions. David knew.

That made the Neal house seem part of the sense of ostracism. Four girls, all with intertwined arms, and in the bright sweater-coats and small knitted caps of the fashion, formed a solid phalanx down the shady street. The center one was Odette Juss, the eldest daughter of Max Juss, who boarded at Emma's.

They were coming. They were coming toward him. With a mounting agony, David watched them approach, his tongue doubling in his mouth, and his hand clenched for the doff. Some fellows could do that naturally. Doff a hat. With Dave, it was like doffing his heart. Some fellows had a way about them in matters like that! *

At the very moment of his elaborate détour to let them pass, Odette, who was sixteen, let out a spurt of a giggle, into which the other four exploded through tightly-pursed lips.

It was horrible. It was so undeniably combustive, the outburst of restraint. They had burst out laughing. They were laughing at him. His glasses must be awry. They *were* awry. He could see a wisp of that horrible winding of cotton, as he gazed down the bridge of his nose.

Horrible! Horrible!

The impulse to turn around and look after them swept; overwhelmed him. Perhaps they were not laughing at him. At the craning backward of his neck, there were the four girls craning too! And then came another outburst of laughter that splattered the silence, like buckshot.

---

* I can recall little in Dave's boyhood that pointed to what was later to become his capacity for public life. On the contrary, he was a peculiarly diffident lad, never thrusting himself to the fore, unless impelled to do so by the violence of the urge of an idea.

He was stiff, even gawkish with girls. His encounter with Kenneth Chipman, Dora Tarkington, and the dog, told elsewhere in this willy-nilly journal of mine, gives some idea of his adolescent aplomb where the fair sex was concerned.

In a lifetime that was to be crowded with public addresses of the most portentous kind, he has repeatedly told of himself, in the privacy of a family-dinner, and to our reminiscent merriment, that he never approached any rostrum with drier throat or stiffer tongue than he experienced on a certain Saturday afternoon, when he directed his footsteps toward the Tarkington place for his first formal visit to Dora.

It was too horrible. A hot wave of nausea swept him. To have looked back! To have been the butt of their gibes! What was it? Why should the girls splatter into laughter at sight of him? The shortness of coat? Well, what of it? A new one would have had to come from Henry, in whose pockets the clink of the coins was so pitifully light. What else could it be? The yawn of the pair of Henry's gray-cotton socks between his trousers and heavy-looking shoes? Wrists? There *was* something not quite right about them. They seemed suddenly like great, misplaced ankles, dangling.

Why had they laughed? These girls, who were only slightly younger than Dora. Dora, toward whom he was now directing faltering steps. Cold sweat sprang out through the fever of his body. The dry-rusk sensation of mouth screwed tighter still. It was the most devastating thing that could have happened, knocking his painfully-mustered self-confidence out from under him like a pole from a tent.

Why had they laughed? Odette Juss was a shy girl, who stuttered painfully, as he remembered seeing her about his sister's boarding-house. What was there in him to arouse this bold mob-hilarity? There had been moments, too, at lunch, when it seemed to him that the dry lips of Miss Simpson had been compressed against laughter. The same quality of suppressed merriment that had burst involuntarily from the lips of these girls.

Was it the spectacles? In the shadow of the Neal garage, he removed them, examining the frames, and feeling at the inflamed rut across his nose. The street swayed a little, and his belladonnaed eyes were quick to tear. Hooking them back on felt steadying and cool.

Why had they laughed?

What if Dora should laugh! Henry should have warned him if he looked ridiculous. Yet the spectacles

hid the ridge. Better the spectacles than the inflamed
rut across the bridge of his nose, especially now that it
had cracked open. It was the cotton must have created
the outburst. Spectacles might even seem interesting
without the blamed cotton. The oculist had warned him,
though, that the frame against the open sore might infect.
And yet, to be made ridiculous by cotton! Standing
there in the shade of the Neal garage, he unwound it and
fitted the bare frame back across his nose. The metal
bit in with a sting. It was a counteracting pain for which
he was almost grateful. It made the ordeal ahead, that
of calling on Dora, secondary for the moment. Tears
of irritation blistered his eyes and kept him popping at
them up under the spectacles.

What if Dora should still laugh. She was so pretty.
The sides of her nose, rosy little flanges, had a way of
quivering slightly before she laughed, like a small white
rabbit's over a carrot. If Dora were inclined to laugh,
those pink little flanges would become signals. If Dora
should laugh. Lord, don't let Dora laugh! Amen, Lord,
don't let her!

The street stretched on to its leafy conclusion. A
whirling hose spun fragrance from the clematis vines that
clambered over the side of the Neal garage.

Down at the very end of Sycamore Street, the old
Schuyler homestead, with a painter's scaffolding swung
across its face, suggested the one-time short cut to the
Tarkingtons', through South Meadow.

But all that was changed now. The present owners
had sold off South Meadow in parcels of building-lots.
Rows of bright, peach-colored semi-bungalows, with blue
trim and false shutters, lined the new, treeless streets
with the blurring rapidity of a deck of cards zipped
through the fingers. They made you blink. The same-
ness. The hotness. The umbrella-shaped clothes-line

racks in each back yard. Bright corrugated-tin garage, after bright corrugated-tin garage. Miles of granitoid gutters. Blue front doors. Even geometry of criss-cross streets, the new gravel uncrunched. Made streets intervened now, between the old Schuyler place and the Tarkingtons'. And of all things, a square, new cereal-factory, set in a swirl of railroad-tracks, annihilated completely the site of the precious old spring-house and hoarding-place of books.

There were blocks of hard, white, treeless asphalt now; and the creek where it used to flow dark and rich and plum-color, was under the streets now, filled in.

This district, just inside the city limits, was gravely known as Venice.

The encroachment of this "development" of the prosperous factory- and foundry-workers of the peach-colored semi-bungalows, one-Ford-car garages, and umbrella-shaped clothes-driers, up to the very edge of the still-bucolic Tarkington place, was another source of Len Tarkington's resentment toward the Old Gentleman.

Fully acquainted as he was with the details of the enforced evacuation of the House on Sycamore Street,* there none the less smoldered within Len, each time a new smokestack splintered the serenity of Tarkington skyscape, or a row of workingmen's paradises went up along the slick asphalt strips of ready-made street, the feeling that except for the Old Gentleman's weakness of the flesh, the Tarkington Place would still be flanked by the beautiful serenity of South Meadow.

The farm itself, however, did succeed in keeping out a sense of invasion. The same rich undulation of hedge

---

* AUTHOR'S NOTE.—The House on Sycamore Street has since been taken over by the state, and is open to the public three days a week.

that had once divided it from South Meadow, now protected it by a full two feet of additional height from the geometric outlay of Venice.

Approaching it from down the long length of a mercilessly bright and surveyed street named Mark Place, it almost seemed to David that the old aperture through which he and Dora had bellied many an entrance and an exit, was still there. But actually the little body-worn tunnel, dear, warm, funny little turnnel, was filled in now by tight growth. That small, gone paradise of yesterdays.

It was a good three-quarters of a mile down to where the double rows of elms formed entrance and shrouded the old house in an enormous kind of shade that made it possible for Mammy, turned eighty by now, to still keep her newly-churned butter cool in a crock under grape leaves on a back porch.

Tarkington loved this old place with one of his only two fierce passions. The other was his daughter.

His acres flowed redundantly, because even with the indolence with which the Old Gentleman never failed to indict him, they reflected a certain absorption, on the part of their owner, in the grandeur of soil. The rotation of his crops was a rotation that implied thought. Trees on the Tarkington place were carefully forested, and their wounds filled in with cement. The sole bookshelf Len's bedroom boasted was crowded with weather-colored volumes on the habits, the chemistry, the workability of the local soils that flowed in his state. In one corner of the dining-room, a fine old ceiling-high wardrobe was stacked with farm journals that no amount of house-cleaning seemed able to reduce in number.

They were good acres. The taste of them was to be part of the warm-pollen sweetishness that was to lie on David's tongue throughout the crowded years.

At the foot of the road of elms, Nemo was screwing weeds out of the path. For five years, come rain, come shine, come winter, come spring, these two, Nemo and Dave, had curried, churned, calcimined, lugged, plowed, milked, through the dawns.*

There was a curious taciturn friendship between the old white-kinked black, and the boy, but at the sight of Nemo now, out in the light of a broad, soft day that made him seem unaccustomed, it was as if something inner, like David's tonsils or his heart, had plunged suddenly down into hollow legs. The body seemed only a shell to contain breathlessness. Here was old Nemo, who had been in the actual, the corporeal presence of Dora that very day! Doubtless that very hour. It gave Nemo a luminosity that hovered over his kinks.

Well, here he was at the Tarkingtons'! By opening his stiff lips and emitting three words, he could find out from Nemo if Dora were home. As if, with his expert knowledge of her habits, he did not already know. On Saturdays, except for the occasion of a matinée or the once-a-month dancing-tea at the St. Charles, she did not go to town at all. The Opera House was dark that week. It was not dancing-tea Saturday.

What if—if Kenneth Chipman were to be there, with his long legs, in white flannel, drooping over the edge of the porch-hammock. On Saturdays, David's furtive aching observation had taught him, Kenneth pretty regularly remained in the office, while his father, under peremptory doctor's orders, went to the Middleton Country Club for golf. Except two or three times, along

---

* . . . when Dora's Nemo died, the Tarkingtons held funeral for him in their own parlor. David, who was then "spittoon and sawdust boy" for a wholesale-grocery firm in Springfield, sent six carnations.

toward mid-afternoon, Kenneth had closed office and sped in his roadster out to Dora. Dave knew that! With his strained, sick heart Dave knew pretty nearly every external there was to know about these two.

Yet all odds considered, Dora was terrifyingly certain to be at home. And alone. Abysmal emptiness continued to clutch at him and cause the day to sway.

"What you doin' roun' this time o' day, boy?" asked Nemo, scarcely glancing up from his weeding.

"Nothin' much," said David, breaking into a run and afraid to ask the question that might, by its reply, dash the fervent prayer within him that Dora be not home.

That was absurd, and once out of sight of the old black huddle of Nemo, he stepped off the cinder path, behind the bole of an elm, and shook himself. Shook himself literally and with a characteristic clamping of his square teeth. Struck an attitude. A sort of declamatory attitude, with his right arm plunging, as if he were striking down something.*

---

* So far as any of us seem to remember, David as a child did not display propensity for public speaking. I do recall time and time again seeing him, under strain or nervousness, use his famous arm-plunging gesture. I particularly recall once, his running to me, over a really terrible incident that had to do with his dog Teddy and my son. His dramatic pantomime, as he tried to tell me that story, matches up with some of his subsequent performances from the platform. But as a growing boy, it is fair to say that my brother gave no prophecy whatsoever of the oratorical force which was to penetrate his country to the core.

It was with an amazement that bordered upon actual incredulity, that Phil and I sat in the little spectators' gallery, the first year of his election to state senate and heard him deliver a ringing and inspired plea for a lowly sewerage-bill, that somehow, by his presentation, he made magnificent in its scope.

He was. The rising sense of his nervous frenzy.
That rusk of a tongue cleaving so to the roof of his
mouth. The body a vacuum for breathlessness. He was
striking down, all right. Terror! After all, through
every hour of the last twelve, the procedure had been
so intimately, so privately, so fervently rehearsed.
Nothing for a fellow to feel skittish about.

All there was to it. Calling on a girl. Look here,
Dora! Look here, Dora! Gee! All there was to it.
All you had to do—why—easy's anything——Look
here, Dora! Looka here—Dora——

Goose-fleshing ecstasy, that would send the old eyelids
behind their new glass fronts batting. Heart banging
out against torso. All there was to it. Looka here,
Dora! You know! I know! All is not gold that
glutters! Glutters! That would be a fine thing if his
tongue slipped up on him like that! All is not gold that
—all is not gold that *glitters*.

Then the figure, standing dallying behind the elm tree
and mysteriously plunging out every so often with his
right arm, jerked himself together and in a dash was up
the cinder-road to where the swell of millwork and
wooden rococo verandah came into view. And there,
blotting out the horizon, blotting out the universe, on
the patch of front lawn before the house, was Dora,
crouched on her knees beside the open hydrant, an iron
arrangement about two feet high, with a tin drinking-cup
dangling from a chain, and engaged in the precarious
business of holding a fox-terrier under the faucet with one
hand and lathering him with a highly evasive cake of
soap with the other.

How beautiful she was as she crashed upon his vision.
The sun was all caught in her hair, and stood off in a
little halo, like a soft-pencil mark when you smudge it
with your finger. To David, swallowing his heart, there

was something shameful and furtive, standing there with
his eyes positively seared to the back of her neck. Her
curls, with the single skewer of hairpins through them,
were on top of her head, obviously impaled there with
one soapy hand, when they interfered with the business
of lathering her dog.

Her neck was like a beautiful river full of sinuosities.
River full of sinuosities. Not bad. Or had it swung
itself into his memory from a line on a page in Henry's
Oxford Book of Verse? Her neck—her neck was like
the glide of one of those snakes, in his zoology, (the
Pythono morpha, found in Europe, North America and
South America), with the lovely power to move forward
in paddling grace.

Her neck—her neck was like a shower of star-shaped
clematis that covered the verandah.

Her neck was like—was like one of the unused white-
silk handkerchiefs in Henry's drawer, that were not bor-
rowable.

There was something shameful, standing there appraising that loveliness of neck, and yet it was like—
what new and as yet unplumbed beautifulness *was* it like?
There were, of course, other beautifulnesses that clutched
you by the throat like this. That time Stevey had swung
past with his company. Lying on your back, in the sheep-
pasture, watching Capella tremble in the heavens. Something about his mother's face, when he opened his eyes
suddenly and caught her regarding him above his bed.
Yet not one of them brought quite this identical hotness
into his throat and across his eyes.

Was it shameful to stand there tingling with this
beautifulness of Dora as she soaped her dog? The
sickening talk of farm-boys, which clung to his ear-drums
now and then, made gazing upon the beauty of Dora
seem something of desecration. The furtive snickerings

of hired-hands, seated with their backs against the barn and nibbling at blades of grass and spitting tobacco in long streaks. It made of Dora something to enshrine for his own private, sacred adoration. Even the thought of Kenneth, to whom the sickening talk of farm-boys would have been equally obnoxious, gazing upon the beauty of that pale curve of neck, smote him like a blow, and choked an exclamation from him.

Simultaneously, Dora and her dog became aware of David. With a leap that sent him slick and quick as a watermelon-seed from Dora's soaped and sopping clutch, "Prince Charley," crony of Dave's through many a star-specked dawn, met him with such a leap and a bound, that before he could dart back, the side of his face, from contact, was lathered with a burning brand of much-advertised flea-soap.

"Prince Charley!" screeched Dora, and darted after him with a great flapping old towel, as stunned David stood under the bombardment of suds exploding along his face. "Hold him, Dave! He'll get himself all muddy if you let go. Hold him, Dave! For goodness' sakes, Dave, if you love me, don't let go! Prince Charley!"

Slippery, oozy holy-terror! Four soapy paws frantic for clutch. Licking. Leaping. Yelping. Splattering. His eye-glasses became flecked. And his mouth painted with suds, in a mustache that tasted and stung. A great slab of lather began to sing somewhere under his collar, so that his chin sank into soft, popping ooze.

It was horrible, and it was glorious. "Davey, if you love me, don't let go!" Spat-splutter-plop. Davey, if you love me.

Spat-splutter-plop.

She had handed him the key of the world, and his eyes were full of soap. If only the blamed little old pup

—weren't so blamed old slippery —— Down, you!
Splup—Splu—p-p-p-p-.

The stinging taste of the soap. The splutterings of
sud-flecked lips. Horrible!

"I'm so sorry, Dave! Just hold him—plee-ze Davey,
while I lasso him with the towel. E—e-e-e. Don't let
go! Prince—Cha-a-arley."

It was no use! The squirting, slipping ooze! Time
and time again, clawing, grasping, snatching fingers all
but released their hold upon pawing gyrations. Blinded
now by the shower of lather up against his eye-glasses,
lye-bitten, lye-blinded, and smeared even to a great erect
peak of suds on top of his head, he held on bravely, to
the screeching tune of "Davey-if-you-love-me!"

"Davey, if you love me!" Wilderness of snapping
towel, spats of wet paw against eye-glasses, more taste
of lye and ooze of more wet fur.

"Davey, if you love me, don't let go, Dave. I've
nearly got him. Bad ittsie Dora's baby! Bad! Bad!
Bad! Mama spank! Bad naughty baby darlin' doggie!"

Spat! Yap! Guzzle! Ugh!

"Don't let go!"

Spat! Yap! Guzzle! Ugh! Snork-k—and some-
where in the distance, the purr of an engine, the grinding
of brakes, or was it only through the blindness, the roar
of encounter.

"Prince Charley! Bad! Stop it! Mama spank!
Um-m-m-m great big automobile wun over Prince Char-
ley. That's a good boy! That's muvver's good Charley
Prince."

Climbing out of the darkness, rubbing his spectacles
clear of blur, digging suds from his bitten eyes, fumbling
for a handkerchief that would not materialize, feeling
out toward the direction of the confusion of laughter, of
voices, of yapping, and the sound of the water still run-

ning from the open spigot, was a performance that took exactly one lifetime to accomplish.

There was Dora, with just enough of a smudge of suds across her curls to make her adorable, triumphant now, with Prince Charley captured and wrapped in the towel under her arm, and standing beside her, convulsed in the kind of laughter that gave them red, boiled faces from trying to restrain it, Kenneth Chipman and a new-comer to town whom Davey faintly knew by the name of Florine Kent.

They had arrived in Kenneth's roadster, which stood by, chugging.

One glance through his lye-bitten, belladonna-tortured eyes, and Dave knew. They had arrived in the "hub" and the "bub" of the scramble. In time. In time for the ignominy of his encounter through the suds. In time!

And there was Dora, with her free arm helping him to fumble for his wretched handkerchief, that would not seem to be anywhere, and trying, through the boiled look of her own face, not to give in to that impulse to laugh. That look in her eyes! The same look of Miss Simpson when she bit her lips. Of five intertwined girls, down Sycamore Street, and Odette who had seemed suddenly to explode of repressed hilarity.

Laughing world. There, Dora had exploded, too!

"Here," said Kenneth, with what evenness of voice he could muster, "take mine, old man!" and tossed him a gray-silk handkerchief with a wide border of purple pin-stripes. He was in white trousers. The universe became a pair of white trousers. Silk handkerchief! Meany Henry, who owned six non-borrowable silk hand-kerchiefs.

"Thanks!" sputtered David, and tossed back Kenneth's

handkerchief, and with his hand still fumbling for his own torturously evasive one, bolted down the path.

"David!" cried Dora, and darted after. "You mustn't go! We're going to have lemonade and cake on the porch, as soon as I change into something dry. Please, Dave, don't go!"

"Come on back, Dave!"

"Davey Schuyler, if you go, I'll never speak to you again! We're going to have lemon———"

"Mush go———"

"All right for you, Davey! If that's the way you're going to act, just because———"

"Mush go!" coughed David blindly. Blackly. Bleakly. "Mush!" And rushed off down the cinder walk, the one desire in his head for the relief of aloneness. A quick aloneness, into which he could crawl. For eternity.*

---

*   . . . at a dinner given at the State Mansion in honor of a legation about to depart for Russia on a tour of observation, Dora, telling this story to a group of old Middleton and Centralia friends, stopped short in the middle of it, heavy tears over her eyes, and regarded my brother, the then Governor, quite helplessly, unable to proceed.

With his usual alertness to emergency, and his unfailing understanding of her, he picked up the story where she had left off, concluding it in a gale of merriment shared by the entire company.

Later, Dora confided to me that suddenly, the pathos of the memory of that boy back there, battling for her so absurdly and so valiantly through soapsuds, simply rose and choked her, making it impossible for her to conclude an anecdote to which the Governor always listened with the relish of hearing it for the first time.

It is characteristic of him that he never again asked her to tell the story, or repeated it in her presence.

Chapter Thirty

THERE followed days and weeks, and then months, when the fervor for his father's patch of farm became an obsession. The security of long days, sunk up to the aching arm-sockets in chores that had to do with a clogged water-pipe, milking at dawn, currying for Nemo, sheep-driving by starlight, manure that steamed as he pitched it, pip among the wyandottes, new tin rain-gutters along the house, corn-shucking, sheep-dipping, hay-pitching, well-digging, sheep-herding.

Then long, secure evenings of further escape from the reality of humiliation. Flat on his stomach, his aching feet bare, his candle burning softly through hours of boring concentration on the book in hand.

During that winter, aided by Henry's shelves, the Centralia Public Library, the motley universes of land and sea and firmament jammed up that little slapsided room under the eaves. Prehistoric monsters out of Java, larger than the Igrotte house itself, performed the miracle of squatting within its walls. China seas swung within that room, firmaments wide as Galileo's, winds spiced in sandalwood.

Pages. Pages. Pages. *Wealth of Nations.* Spencer's *First Principles. Les Miserables. History of the Aztecs. Karl Marx.* Sinclair's *The Jungle. Uncle Tom's Cabin. Famous Speeches of Famous Men.* The "All-Boy" series. *Romance of Pocahontas. King Arthur's Round Table. Tales from Shakespeare. History of Colorado. Ivanhoe. Conquest of Peru. Tariff and Its Ramifications. Governors of Utah. The Growth of Illinois Transportation. Industrial Development of the Middle West. Territorial Period. Life of Anthony Wayne. Hiawatha. Vision of Sir Launfal. Sea Reptiles and Mammals of South America. Life of Cecil Rhodes.* Peary's *The North Pole. How to Build Your Own Hydroplane. Gem Collection of After-Dinner Stories. The Five Years Antedating the Russian Revolution. Compleat Angler. Vanishing Rights of the State. Raffles. Shandy. Japanese-American Relations. Two Boys and a Raft. Adonais. Cellini's Autobiography. War and Peace.*

He was sealed up that winter, all right. Silently. Something fierce about his kind of silence.

Henry, who sometimes sat abstractedly in his office or room thinking about it, said nothing.

Mathilda went up to him sometimes, as he sat at table finishing his meal, as if she would place a hand on his shoulder and get said the question that seemed perpetually hovering along her lips. Or often, as he was climbing into his reefer for his dash out into the sleet-bitten days of that long, cold winter, she would kiss him timidly on the forehead and bleat of castor-oil.

Strangely, the Old Gentleman, not given to reticence, and communicative enough, dear knows, on any number of controversial subjects those long evenings indoors, lapsed into a silence not only toward, but concerning his youngest. Not an ill-natured silence. Except suddenly the subject seemed to have lost the power either to interest or irritate him. Strange wisdoms sometimes were his.

There was about the box-shaped little house during this winter that lashed it constantly with high winds and blew the dry snow in tall, uneven drifts about it, a curious kind of abeyance. As if, by unspoken assent, the moments, as they passed, must be sufficient unto themselves.

Sometimes, usually with a book open to a chapter that had stumped him, David crept down to Henry's room, invariably sure to find him awake and reading, his feet wrapped in an old gray blanket against the creeping cold of the house, and his body hunched low in the chair beside his reading-lamp. Then, for more hours with David huddled alongside of Henry on the arm of the Morris chair, they pored, and sometimes read aloud, alternately.

Long, rich, slow evenings, without once a reference to anything except that which pertained to the world of ideas and homely chores into which David was so obviously and hermetically sealing himself.

If the family discussed among themselves this prolonged, this somewhat startling state of hiatus in the case of Davey, it was among themselves, and then usually not in the presence of Henry.

One day, Bek, striding into the Igrotte house in one of Winslow's ulsters, collar turned up and her skirts tucked down into her knee-high boots, inquired from her mother David's whereabouts, and then strode off into the barn, where her young brother was fitting an improvised rope halter across the horns of a young steer.

"Where are you going, Dave?"

"Down to Herkhimer's with this here steer. Father's traded him in for two red sows."

"Good! I'll hike along. Old Herk's got some money coming to him for putting those Howey red terriers to stud last spring. I've got two pretty sick ewes and a ram over at the farm, Dave. Mind coming back the long way and stopping to take a look at them? You've luck with them."

"Sure, I'll come."

They started off through an afternoon the color of wet slate. Banks of low snow-clouds, full-looking as udders, blew along. Gusts of damp air, like wet cloths, flapped against the face. A chilled gray waste of an afternoon, farmhouses, that could gleam in sun, absolutely shrunk and huddled-looking, and the back road writhing along in two frozen wheel-ruts.

Suddenly Bek stopped, and with a lack of diplomacy that characterized her, tilted back David's face with her large, mittened hand.

"What's the matter, Dave? Bilious or in love?"

He jerked away sore and hurt.

"Quit!"

"I'd much rather it was your liver than your heart, Dave."

"Fine way to talk."

"Why?"

"There's some things just aren't talked about."

"What? Livers?"

"No."

"Hearts?"

"For goodness' sake, Bek—honest—such talk makes me sick."

"But, at least, if it's the liver, you can talk about it in terms as definite as calomel. Is it, Dave?"

"Honestly, Bek, if that's what you've come along for . . ."

"I'm a great believer in preventive medicine. But if it's heart, there's not much to do about it but let it run its course, and kill or cure. My own experience, and my children's, have taught me that."

"Well, then—well, then—it's a good thing to profit by experience."

She touched his cheek lightly with her mittened hand. Poor old Dave!

The rushing sensation was immediately behind his tonsils again, and the appalling fear that, behind his high-power glasses, tears would spurt; and, that they might not, he broke into a laugh. A laugh that cut against the grain, because it was so absurd and young and pain-addled. It moved his sister to want to put out her hand and tuck him somewhere close inside Winslow's ulster. But she did nothing of the sort. Instead, she swung a little ahead, level almost with the steer's lightly roped horns, looking quite away from him across the stubble of corn-fields that were stiff with old runts, and rattled.

"Life isn't so black as it can sometimes seem at seventeen, Dave. As a matter of fact, fellows like your brother Henry and Phil were pretty confirmed misanthropes before they were twenty. Are you at that stage, Dave?"

"You're always tabulating people, Bek. A fellow can't pass an ordinary remark without you trying to fit him into one of your pigeonholes of life."

"Adolescence pigeonholes rather easily, Davey."

"I'm not talking about adolescence, I'm talking about life."

"It's adolescence makes you talk that way about life."

"Well, any blamed fool can sing a song of sixpence about it. What's it to sing about, anyways? The poets are your truly sensitive spirits. 'Things are not what they seem, life is but an empty dream.' Know that one? It's by ——"

"And you're the boy who used to talk to me about the men who fly and the men who explore and the men who rule and the men who do! Why, you used to act as if everything mattered to you so terribly, that you couldn't make up your mind which mattered most."

"Then and—and now are two different matters."

"How different?"

He turned on her a pair of scarred-looking boyish eyes that scowled and blinked behind their glasses.

"Don't!" he said.

"Don't what?"

"Quiz—please ——"

They marched through the soupy gray in silence, except for the clopping hoofs of the steer and the low moan of wind rattling the corn-runts.

At the Herkhimer farm, a mean one, of squat building and outhouses, Gramaw Herkhimer, a furiously old walnut of a woman, in a perpetual gray head-shawl against neuralgia, came limping around to the barn at sight of Bek; and nothing short of coffee in her small and spotless kitchen, and chunks of corn-bread, just from the hot stove-top, would do. Dave, and one of the Herkhimer boys, a great loutish fellow of twenty, of the group who told sickening stories about country-bumpkin girls, must come in too, and take their coffee out of great, ironstone, thick-lipped cups, into which the corn-bread "dunked" deliciously.

A coal-range of magnificent draught roared in one corner, and a huge pan of Gramaw Herkhimer's dough, rising to the yeast, overflowed its sides like a fat pig. A warm, sour-smelling little old kitchen, which Bek seemed to cram to the raftered ceiling with her enormous presence.

Her incredible capacity for detail with these people! No subject too small to snag her interest. Gramaw Herkhimer's tatting. Old man Herkhimer's chilblain. Chest-protectors for Herkhimer babies. There were three of them lying asleep alongside her ailing daughter in another room. Woolen wristlets. Geranium-cuttings. Drunken son-in-law. First-communion veil for little Maggie Herkhimer. Bacon-cracklings. Then nothing would do but a jar of apple-butter to be wrapped and sent home to Winslow. Back in the old days, High Ridge Farm had practically fed the Herkhimers. Maggie Herkhimer, gaunt and pale, and interminably tall in a mother-hubbard that hit her above breast, elbows, and ankles, came in, all rumpled from napping, to thank Bek for the loan of a small crutch for her second boy, who had broken a leg, in almost the identical position Steve had at that same age. They had gone to school together, Maggie Herkhimer and Bek. They both looked their age. The one rather magnificently. Maggie, as if the years had hamstrung her.

It was a warming, heartening, little interval. It made the walk back to Bek's farm silent, this time, because facing the wind, it caught at the breath and shortened it, seem not so penetratingly damp and cold.

The two ewes and the ram, sunk in clean straw, were in the smaller of the two splendidly-equipped barns. Their nozzles came up softly; and just as Dave was putting aside the medicine-dropper, after having ministered to the shivering creatures with a curiously adhesive touch of hand that was never to desert him, this overwhelming thing happened:

Bek, who had gone directly up to the house, came into the barn, Winslow's reefer removed now, and a white sweater hanging across her shoulders.

"Dave, I wish you would wait a minute."

"Mother needs wood——"

"—— and walk Dora Tarkington home as you go back. She's spent the day here, helping Winslow paper the dining-room in that pretty grass-cloth they're using now. Paula sent it. I wouldn't let him touch the Howey walls, so between the two of them, they've made a set of panels that fit on. They say at school, Dora's that tasty she ought to take up interior decoration. It's a

long walk, and those snow-clouds make it seem dusk so
early. Here she comes now, Davey. Walk her home."

The figure of Dora, in a woolly white sweater and
woolly white cap, and her short, pleated skirts flying,
came down the walk.

"Why!" she said, and stopped short, the light popping
out in her eyes and her cheeks, "I didn't know—Dave
was here."

"Didn't you?" said Bek drily. "Well, he is," and
walked off toward the house, and slam, bang, into it.*

---

* My brother and Dora have often accused me of conspiring
to bring about a certain encounter which took place between
them at the farm one blustery November afternoon, and out
of which meeting one of the first really formative events of
my brother's life was to take shape.

Be that as it may, the simple facts stand duly authentic.
Paula, home for her father's birthday, happened to remark
upon Dora's reputation at Tallahassee High for taste and skill
at decoration. Winslow jumped at my suggestion that we
ask her over to spend a day and help us stencil the grass-cloth
panels for the dining-room. Certainly anyone with a pair of
eyes in his head could judge for himself that David was looking peaked, of a complaint easily diagnosed. That same day,
calling over at Mother's, I did, it is true, ask him to walk back
home with me to tend some ailing stock. Also, the evidence
is that there were two sick ewes and a ram at the farm that
day, and Dave's skill with them was common knowledge.
Further than that, as they say in legal phraseology, I do not
feel called upon to elucidate.

Chapter Thirty-one

Even at this stage Dave was a good two inches taller than Henry. It smote him, as he stood there, facing Dora, in an old office-coat of Henry's, and trousers covered with the shine of long contact with Henry's swivel-chair, that he had never in his life worn a suit designed for his figure. That was why, in those rare moments when he had occasion to think about his appearance at all, he felt precisely as if he were dangling by the middle of the back of his coat from a nail. Short sleeves. Short trousers. Protruding knobs of ankles and wrists.

He confessed to Dora, countless of the reminiscent times in which they loved later to indulge, that it seemed to him for long moments after the loud crack of Bek closing the house-door, as if he had hung there in the clean, sweet-smelling barn, dangling from the middle of the back of his coat, like a cat when you hold it by the scruff of the neck.

"I'll race you," cried Dora suddenly, and on a flash of her unfailing ability to rise to the exigencies of the moment, sped, a flicker of white sweater and cap, down the path toward the open road.*

---

* I have never seen the like of Dora for her unfailing tact and ability to rise, or for that matter fall, to an occasion. No wonder they used to call her Madame Cherchez-la-Femme. Her memory for faces, for names, for circumstances, was of the most incalculable value to my brother, who had none of Roosevelt's genius for that sort of thing. Time and time again, I have seen her win for herself and my brother, the deathless loyalty, for instance, of a lumberman from Nebraska, whom she could recall having met five years previously at the

That dash along down the road released him, as it were, from that moment of hanging impaled in her presence. They caught up a quarter of a mile down, in flurry of quickened heartbeat, and impulsively she hooked her arm into his, without preliminaries.

"Davey," she said, "why have you been so mean to me?" And, incredibly, there were bright and beautiful tears against her eyes, that dried even as he gazed, giving him a feeling of mirage. "You're a meany, you are, David!" she said and a red pompon, on its string, dangled from her white and woolly cap.

The ground thus immediately cut from under his feet, down he went into the abyss she had opened for him.

"Gee, Dora," he said, almost borrowing her tone, "I won't be—mean—any more!" And then, overwhelmed by the realization of what her winding voice had done to him, stopped suddenly and burst out, red and redder of face, "You mean you're the mean one!"

"Why, Davey Schuyler, I never was!"

"Weren't, weren't you?"

"You know I—weren't."

"Oh, all right. Won't argue—with a lady."

"Wouldn't start something I couldn't finish."

"Start something I can't finish! Honest, I don't know what you mean."

"Well, if—if a girl was as meany as you say I'm meany—funny you couldn't tell her—how meany."

Sesquicentennial at Philadelphia, or recognize by name, the wife of someone they had probably shaken hands with from the platform of a moving train.

I was not present at the famous Franco-American banquet, where she averted what promised to be a fistic encounter between Ambassador Toussain and Leopold von Mark, by tilting a dish of raspberry ice into the lap of her canary-colored velvet gown, just as those two gentlemen were about to fly at each other's throats.

"How meany? Huh, as if you didn't know. Huh!"
(How beautiful she was, and he had just said "huh" to her.)

"Huh!" he said again.

"Well, if I felt that way about a girl, I wouldn't walk home with her," she said, and flopped like an adorable, beautiful little minnow. A minnow on the end of some bait too delectable to even conjure. Bait would have to be ambrosia for Dora's lips to nibble. Only one didn't nibble ambrosia. The Greeks musta drunk it ——

"Well, if I felt that way about a girl ——"

"Oh, Dora," he said, and reached out a long gawk of a bare-wristed hand, "I—I guess I feel every way about you, I guess."

"Well then—well then—well then, why the dickens don't you say some of the good ways," she cried, and stamped her foot, and let the clear bright tears pop out in her eyes again, and shook her head, and gritted her small white teeth.

"I never thought you'd listen, Dora. Honest!"

"Oh, you know well enough I'd listen, all right. You've always just kind of tried to make me feel little. I—I should worry!"

"Little?"

"Yes, little! My parties and all—your never coming, and you in our barn every morning—you never looking anywheres near the house where I might be. That day— that day—soap—Kenneth—the way you walked off on me—something I couldn't help. How do you think I felt that day—walking off on me—thataway——"

"Why—how do you think I felt?"

"As if I didn't know, Davey," she said and turned her eyes full upon him, as they stood face to face in the rutted road, a hard, windy, slate-colored twilight blustering about them. "I've cried and cried."

"You've cried, Dora?"

"You know I have," she said, and stamped her foot again, the bright, angry tears drying as soon as they formed. "You hate me—that's what I believe."

Hate Dora! Why, just as likely that he hate moon. Hate stars. Hate firmament encrusted in eternity. Hate Dora—why—why ——. Where were his words, to tell her? And so there he stood helpless before her indictment. And yet again, strangely, so strangely, there was something sweet about the indictment. There was something about hating—that was fiercely akin to loving.

"I've always tried," she said—"I've always tried —— tried ——"

"Tried what?"

The quivering would not let her get it said; and while he stood flaming with the same sense of exhilaration over her fumbling that the word "hate" had fired in him, he wanted to lie flat on his back before her, that she might walk over him with flaming heels. The trembling of her lips was cruelly pleasant to him, and yet he wanted to fling himself before her, because those lovely, trembling, pink ledges were trembling of his doings. Here was a hurt bird needing him. Here was a ewe with soft, sick eyes. Here were all the things in one that were tender and wounded.

"Well, well, tried what?"

"To—to—let you know I—how to let you know I—I wanted you not to—to hate me."

He could have bitten and ground the next words back against his tongue when they came. But there they were, said!

"Kenneth Chipman!" he barked.

"Silly! You silly! You silly of sillies!" (How lovely she was, as she grew pinker and her teeth whiter.) "You silly!"

Silly—silly—silly—why, there was even the same ecstasy in being that. To her.

"Haven't you eyes? Couldn't you see?"

"See what? See what?"

"That was part of the trying. Everything was. I—I don't care now. I might as well tell. An idiot might as well tell on herself."

(Idiot! Idiot! Blessed be idiots!)

"Why do you think I took all my lunches at Stevey's and Claire's? Huh? Huh? Huh?"

"Huh?"

"Didn't I have my own cousins, Essie and Tad, going home to their house every day right out of my same class and my aunt feeling offended, and all, because I went to Claire's and Stevey's?"

Gump! Gump! He hadn't thought of that.

"Don't just stare. Say something. Didn't I? Didn't I? And why? Why?"

"Why?"

"Because I thought sometimes you might be around at your relations. Then Kenneth—I—I—let Kenneth walk with me noontimes—thinking—oh, I'm not ashamed now —now that I wouldn't be friends with you for anything. Just not for anything. I let Kenneth walk with me noontimes, thinking—maybe you'd be there and see. Meany. Meany, you!" she cried, as the tears jetted and careened down to her lips. Then she broke from him and ran, down the rutted road, turning her ankle, lunging, and giving him run until he hurled himself around in front of the Tarkingtons', and blocked her.

"Quit now, stopping me. Papa gets worried if I'm out after six."

"Want to tell you something."

"No!"

"Dora!"

"No!"

"Dora! I like you! Terrible!"

"Well then—why'ncha say so?"

"You—you got so big, Dora. You got so big and so—so pretty. Us having to move away. You got so pretty on me, Dora; and I stayed—just me. Not even a look-in at High School—me—didn't dare. I wouldn't any more dared come near you. I thought, you see—slick-looking college-fellow like—like Kenneth. Patent-leather-haired. Dora—I like you so. I just can't seem to get my mind on anything. That's my trouble, Dora. Liking you. I'm full of always wanting to do a million big things that will make you look at me; and then, for thinking about you, Dora, I can't do a one of them. Crazy-like. Around in a circle. That's what's the trouble with me, Dora. I can't seem to think my way out of anything for seeing you. Just can't care about wanting anything unless it's got you in. Dora!"

They kissed timidly, lightly, there in the dusk. Wonder was out over them. "If only I'da known all along."

"If only I'da."

"You're so smart, Dave, and I'm just like everybody else."

"Smart, nothing! I haven't even finished County Grade."

"Alma Dreyfous's father says he walked a little way alongside of you on the road one morning, and you talked about airships and—and whatchamacallit—tariff, or whatever it is, and Woodrow Wilson, and where Ohio gets her water power from, like a Philadelphia lawyer; and Miss Weil, over at Tallahassee, told her class that the smartest boy in this county was a boy who'd never even finished county school, but put every single moment to cramming new ideas into his head."

"That wasn't me."

"Was so, because Efram Juss asked right out if it was, and she said yes."

"Shucks!"

"I like your being smart, Dave. So much smarter than me."

"Dora—if you like me—any way—at all—that's all I need."

"I do, Dave—only— You won't be mad?"

"No."

"Sure? Davey—that *isn't* all you need. Papa thinks it's awful, Davey—that—that you— You won't get mad, if I say it?"

"No."

"——— thinks it's awful that you're only a ———"

"Only a ———?"

"You won't get mad, Davey?"

"Only a farm-hand, is that it?"

"Yes."

"Huh, don't I know that? Sure. He's right, all right. Only I'm not going to be a farm-hand any more. Now. Fellow's got a reason to make something out of himself —all a fellow's got to do now is make sure of what he wants to be, and then—be it!"

"Davey, what do you want to be?"

"You know what, Dora? Know what I think I'd like to be?"

"What, Davey?"

"First of all, before we talk, we're engaged, aren't we?"

She turned him the fresh flower of her face.

"Yes, David!"

"Well then, Dora, how'd you like me to be something big for you?"

"I would!"

"I was thinking last night, as I was driving along a

flock of black-face sheep from the Howey stock—funny thing about that species—they're hornless, yet they belong to the hollow-horn family."

"But, Davey——"

"The interesting part is that you can't—exactly place where this species passes over into the goat family——"

"But, Davey—that's all right—about—about goats. But what about us?"

"That's just it, Dora. How'd you like for me to be a big-gun in the study of sheep-culture?"

"Pouf!" she said, and made a pink trumpet of her mouth. "Sheep! You're too smart for that!"

"Too smart! Huh! If I was smart enough to know everything there is to know about a great industry like wool—know what I'd be?"

"Wool. Woolen underwear. Sure enough. I never thought of that. I was just thinking of sheep. Only I hate woolen underwear next to my skin——"

"And you know what interests me a lot, too, Dora? I was talking it over with Henry the other night. Now, you take this here wool-industry, and then you take this here tariff-situation, and then you——"

"But, Davey—all that far-away, highfalutin' talk—what's the use? We're engaged. When a fellow's engaged, he can't stand around talking about whole industries. He's got to talk about a—job."

"Engaged! Oh, Dora!"

"Papa says the trouble with young people nowadays is that they have to have so much more to start on than they used to."

"Of course! A job. I'll tell you what, Dora, has always interested me a lot. I read a book on silk the other day. Dora, let me tell you something about this here little fellow, the silkworm."

"But, Davey—there you go again. Silkworms aren't —practical."

"Oh, I mean a job all right! Now, if I could get a job with some silk-firm. You see, now that the little old silk-worm isn't the whole silk-show any more, this here arti-ficial-silk industry is the coming thing in the whole industry."

"There you go again. Whole industry."

"But I'm talking about a job, Dora. If I could get a job, say in Chicago, with one of the big silk-firms, or in Springfield, where my brother Phil lives. There's a future to a job with a big mercantile house, Dora. Some day—maybe when I'm a big-gun in a silk-firm—I'll have to go to China!—you and me—China!"

"Oh, Davey!" she said and screwed her round little nose tighter into a button, and jammed down her cap more snugly over her eyes. "China! That would be heaven! Only—that would take so long, Davey—from now."

"How would Civil Service be, Dora? I could pass Regents' exams easy as anything. I like jobs that tie up the Government."

"Not a postman, Davey. I hate postmen. They're always being waited for."

"Naw. Wouldn't be a postman. Know what, Dora? I'd like to be a consul some day. That gives a fellow a chance to see the world."

"A fellow and—and—his wife, Dave. All consuls have wives. Or should have. Or got to have. Or just have."

"Wife! Gee, Dora! Wi-fe!"

On the magic of the word, they flashed face to face, their fingers feeling hungrily through the wool of mittens.

"I'd like that, Davey. You and me. Cleone Beal's father was consul once to a place called Uruguay."

"That's a republic in South America."

"They lived in a town called Mon—Mon—something."

"Montevideo. Oh, Dora, wouldn't I love to live in Montevideo with you!"

"And me with you, Davey! I'd entertain—them all—at balls in Montevideo."

"How would you like to go off exploring with me, Dora—and add new territory to the maps? Ever hear of Seward's Folly? Well, there's a fellow, 'course he didn't exactly go off and find it, but that fellow had an idea all right. He went to the Government one day, and said, 'Looka here, Government, here's a country called Alaska—that some day is going to ——' "

"Now, Davey—there you go again—some day! What about now, getting a job right now? Just thisaway—talking and dreaming and if-ing and and-ing, we'll never —get anywhere!"

Tears, that he wanted to snatch off with angry, frenzied hands, gleamed along her cheeks.

"Why—why—Dora—my brother Phil can get me a job in a wholesale grocery concern in Springfield right away! Twelve dollars a week ——"

"Oh, Davey, *now* you're talking!"

"You see, if I could send my father six out of that—we're so poor, you see, Dora—but even with six left—my brother can't afford to, but he'll board me awfully cheap, anyway. Then, Dora, if I went to evening law-school—there's something about law I like—suppose I was to do that?"

"How long?"

"I could do a four-years law-course in two. Nights. What do you bet? And then—a town like Springfield—Springfield's a capital. I could practice law there some day."

"Some day?"

"Law's the thing, Dora. Look at a fellow like Kenneth. He could marry now, and he's only been practicing a couple of years. I'm as smart as Kenneth—Dora."

The answering tug of her arm, closer, tighter, warmer, made his long legs seem to gallop over the frozen ruts of the road.

"How many years, Davey, before you could be ready?"

"It would have to be four before I could be a practicing lawyer, earning enough to ——"

"Four," she said, her eyes flattening as if they were contemplating four eternities.

"Dora—what's four years, when we'll have a secret—just ours ——"

"It'll have to be secret, Dave. You see, Papa—he ——"

"He thinks I'm a bum."

"He—he says you're not a go-getter."

"I'll go and get now, Dora."

"Just as I get you—I begin to lose you."

"Dora, the quicker I begin, the quicker ——"

"I know. The quicker you'll be ready."

"Dora—isn't it worth waiting for? Some day. You and me. A little old place of our own. One of those semi-bungalows. Springfield! Wholesale groceries—we could start together sooner—if we could count on getting our groceries wholesale. Maybe, if I get along in the wholesale grocery-business, I'll stay there and get to be a big-gun in the mercantile world."

"Oh, Davey—the sooner—the grander!"

The darkness was about them like a beatific cloak, except for two lights from the Tarkington place, which suddenly gleamed at them from the end of the elm-walk; and

some one was sounding a family-whistle of three staccatos
and a long, which Dora answered in fashion.

"That's Papa."

"We're engaged, Dora."

"Yes, Davey.   Say it again."

"We're engaged, Dora."

Parting, they kissed once more, in the light, startled,
pecking away.

Chapter Thirty-two

Every evening, after supper, Winslow started at carving his picture-frames out of an excellent grade of soft white pine that, for fifteen years, Bek had purchased from a lumber-dealer in Middleton. It was scarcely a purchase, but a trade in the literal sense. A two-gallon crock of Bek's piccalilli could keep Winslow supplied in picture-frame lumber for a year.

There was something grateful about the litter of wood-carving and the slithering little noise of the sharp knife rushing down into the pine and the clean, dry smell that rose off.

Over her account-books, at the green-baize desk in the corner of the dining-room, wanting her farm back, scheming for her farm back, contriving for her farm back, or poring over farm journals, with that same eye to winning her farm back, or darning heels of socks and stockings over the ridge of a great wooden ball, as she dreamed of winning her farm back, Bek liked the consciousness of Winslow, pipe drooping low, and absorbed in turning a difficult corner in the wood, or scooping out an ailanthus leaf.

Leslie liked it, too. He would sit among the litter of the curly white chips, splashing among them and letting the shavings cling to his beardless chin.

There was something so dreadful to Bek in this last. Leslie simulating manhood. She wondered if Winslow ever noticed, and contrived not to let him.

Sometimes Winslow leaned over to bestow upon Leslie a particularly handsome shaving. With sufficient of these he could weave a garland for his mother, which he placed across her brow as she sat at work, giving her the look of a tipsy Cæsar.

Dozens of Winslow's water-colors, prettily framed in the carved, gilded, and sometimes polychromed woods of his handiwork, adorned the walls of the house; and the attic-studio was hung in three rows of them, that touched edge on edge.

The copse of willows behind the barn, in every conceivable mood and perspective and light and shadow. The cow-pond, with Howey Holsteins standing knee-deep, in study after study of the same quiescence, same shadows draped painstakingly into their flanks and down into the water that opened about their knees. The distant rise of the hills that sloped toward the Igrotte house, with the magenta tinges woven into the purples, that no one in the family would dare admit never being able to discern. South Meadow in bright clover. The slant of red roof to old Jessup's shanty, showing through the stripes of the plane-tree boles. Sheep, at evening, meandering homeward, with their heads low. There was always a human figure injected somewhat timidly into these. A lanky gawk of a herdsman, with little more than the scissors-like attitude of the legs to distinguish him from the tree-boles. Indeed, the casual observer was scarcely able to discern at all this lone foray of Winslow's into the realm of human anatomy. To Winslow himself, this figure was Dave, to the eyelash.

The year that David was born, a water-color of Jessup's red roof, seen through the tree-boles, had been sold from the window of Hessy's art-store in Middleton, to a Sandusky bride and groom on their honeymoon. Eleven-seventy-five, framed. Ten per cent commission. On the strength of it, one or another of Winslow's had hung in that window ever since. Every Christmas, Bek sent a two-gallon offering of apple-butter to the Hessys.

And at Thanksgiving, a jar of mincemeat. But the Sandusky bride and groom remained Winslow's sole patrons. Dozens of his efforts adorned walls of Whittier and Wayne Counties. Birthday, wedding, Christmas, and anniversary gifts from the Winslow Renchlers. And meanwhile, undaunted in output, Winslow's power of production went on. There were rows of his pictures, in framed stacks, with newspaper in between, on the floor and shelves of practically every cupboard in the house.

Winslow still painted away the major portion of each day, the same technique, perspective, foreground, horizon, chiarascuro, overtones, scale, proportion, continuing to absorb him for long, squint-eyed periods over the top of a horizontal pencil.

Paula, who now taught history and first-year botany in Cleveland; belonged to a little-theater movement, and was secretary and treasurer of a large teachers' organization known as The Scribes, once winked at her mother across the top of a sheep-and-landscape her father was showing her, upon one of her Easter visits home. Such a scorching flame of anger and rebuke had leaped into Bek's face, that Paula's air of indulgence toward her father's work had been promptly nipped in the bud.

For over a period of twenty-two years, Bek had not seen to the impregnability of Winslow's art against any possible family-facetiousness, only to have Paula wink it down.

Even the Old Gentleman, torn between secretly despising the non-producer and admiring Winslow because he was Bek's choice, continued, in the years that one or another of Winslow's water-colors had been gathering dust in Hessy's window, to refer to his "artist" son-in-law.

Yes, Bek saw to that. Fiercely. Her subtle classification of Winslow held. Centralia, the family, the county, nailed by Bek's glittering eyes, came gradually to take Winslow at her valuation of him. A woman who marries an artist, she was fond of saying a little proudly, must learn to cope with nerves and temperament. Once you understand them, geniuses are the most lovable creatures in the world.

To listen to Bek, Winslow was that. A genius. Too indifferent to the world to reach out a hand to stay its heedless passing-by. A recluse. An inspired eccentric. Unappreciated by his contemporaries, but posterity to be his beneficiary.

Bek aided and abetted this psychology of her own building. Winslow's bottle-green velveteen coats, soft collars, and flowing ties were not his preference. On the contrary, in the beginning he had demurred.

"These long ties are a nuisance, Bek! They flutter and get in a fellow's mouth while he's trying to paint."

Bek knew better. They were not in the way of the special dispensation of public opinion that she sought for him, and missed but by an ell.

Even Paula, who belonged to the little-theater group in Cleveland that produced Synge, and who sent Christmas-gifts of *Jurgen* to her friends, returned from those Easter holidays with a couple of her father's framed landscapes in the top of her trunk.

One evening, in the large cretonned room in a "private house" that she shared with another school-teacher, she removed the chafing-dish from the cretonne-covered top of her trunk, unearthed them, and began showing them around as some "rather good bits of Dad's."

A young secretary of a philanthropic organization and a teacher of English in a High School regarded them with squints and slants, and secretly nudged each other.

Paula sensed rather than saw the nudges and with some of her mother's stubborn kind of indomitability hung one on each side of her dressing-table, but with discretion, so that they were out of line of vision of her roommate, who knew a Monet from a Manet.

Sometimes, covertly watching Winslow over the top of her mending or reading, a sense of the security into which her vigilance had tucked him, smote Bek with some of the warm thrill of gratefulness she felt when regarding Leslie. The sweep of her passion for Winslow had probably never been more or less than just that. He was someone whom she had tucked into the cove of her heart, to protect there, justify, elevate to a plane that however make-believe it might have been, was not make-believe to Bek.

Then, too, there was the curious compatibility of their opposing temperaments. His fastidiousness. His recoil from the sweaty chores to which she bent her wide and willing shoulders. His inability to cope with the conflicts in which she reveled. His spiritual distaste for barter, where she moved quick and sure through stockyard, cattle-pen, and sty, keeping to the shrewd side of the bargain. In Winslow, was something preciously apart. Hers. To be kept in its cotton wadding; to be mounted as you mount a jewel against the proper background.

It was the mother twice over, who sat these evenings, wanting back her farm, while her husband whittled, and Leslie, her perpetual baby-son, grown now, sat among the shavings, fashioning garlands with which he fantastically bound all three of their brows.

The lean years of servitude to the Howeys had squared Bek's face and grayed her heir. The lean years had scarcely touched those two there. Thank God! Nor Paula, who had flown the nest wisely and soon. Nor Steve. Again, thank God! Thank God! Safe in a nest of his own feathering.

How securely she had kept the world of mean detail from Winslow's reckoning. His face, with the soft smile, would have been a jerked and nervous face had she not kept it tranquil. His long, facile hands that she loved for recoiling at the chores she could tackle. His soft, fastidious air of isolation from the barn-and-sty—worlds through which she sometimes stalked knee-deep.

Bek would no more have permitted Winslow to behold her breaking open the mouth of a horse in the cattle-marts, or bartering in the clinical phraseology of the cattle-pen over bull or stallion or sow.

A secret sense of spiritual refinement at being the wife of an artist had been awake in Bek from the first, when as the smart, eldest Schuyler girl, she had gone off to Middleton one morning, with Henriette Simpson for companion and witness, and barn-and-sty worlds married Winslow Renchler, son of a Presbyterian minister up Ideola way, who, at twenty-six, had never done anything more than clerk in a haberdashery by day and dabble away his evenings in a rigged-up studio over his father's barn.

There had always been, to Bek, something a little Robert Louis Stevensonian about Winslow in appearance. The nervous kind of slenderness. The white, thin-skinned æsthete's brow. The full, rather beautiful lips, behind a brown mustache. Winslow had first pointed out the likeness. After that, she read *Treasure Island* and hung a print of Stevenson in the parlor.

There was so much one could do for Winslow.

Now with Paula, it had been so different. If there seemed to be between Bek and Paula a certain outward incompatibility, it was probably because of the too perfect similarity of the two. At bottom, there existed a passionate admiration of each for the other's power of dominance. In spite of it, they clashed constantly. Paula made no evasion of the fact that life in the same house with her mother was impossible for her. Their wills met and tilted. Since she had been seventeen, and out of Centralia Normal School, they had lived at sufficient distance to keep those strong wills in respectful leash in the comparatively brief periods of Paula's vacation-visits home.

There was so little one could do for Paula, who was so capable of doing for herself.

With Steve, it had been different. No one but Bek would ever know how much there had been to do for him.

For Winslow, sitting there in the lamplight, at his whittling, there had been so much to do. So much! And for Leslie.

Regarding her twenty-year-old son, with his delicate, listening, beardless face, and the look he had of knowing minute, woodland things, there was the old streak of pain across her heart, that could feel to her exactly as if it were bleeding. And then, combined with it, a secret sort of exultation that shamed her.

He needed her so.* She still undressed him at night, and sat on his bed-edge to tell him his choice of the legend of the Golden Fleece, the story of Esau, Peter Pan, and a folderol chant about Chanticleer which ended in a loud crowing that invariably sent Leslie off into long and repetitious mimicry. He played a flute, one that

---

* Leslie died yesterday. I suppose we were what you would call prepared for the end. Winslow closed his eyes. The President of the United States drew a sheet up over his face. He lies downstairs in a white coffin. At forty-eight Leslie's coffin would have to be white. He never had any age to him. Only youth. I can't realize that my boy who remained a child for me is gone. To think I must go on waking up every day and never again know what it is to be needed by him—my dear darling——

Winslow had improvised for him out of a reed, down where the cattails grew. He came crying to Bek when it became clogged, even though it was his father who had fashioned it. He cried to her when it rained, and looked to her to cause the sun to shine. She did, by a contrivance of electric light with a reflector behind, which she had rigged up in the attic, against the curious effect of depression and actually impaired digestion, which weather had upon him.

There was a tune, a concoction of her own that still sent him off on his afternoon nap, his hand in hers. She knew his sometimes bafflingly inarticulate names for favorite trees, and his bird-calls, and could sit patiently on the outside of the minute woodland life that could cause him to break into soft and private laughter.

How snug he was in that strange world where the tragedy of her life had tucked him. Sometimes, when her thighs flamed of fatigue, and the world of accounts and hoof-and-mouth disease and locust-scourge and drought, and the constant carping grief for her farm was too much with her, again and again the consolation of this thought smote and half-shamed her.

How secure Leslie was in the world back there in the hinterlands of maturity, in the land of fantasy from where he had never crossed the frontier into reality.

Leslie, whose eyelids were still hung with the shining scales of illusion. How safe he was from the realities that could beset and become grotesque, when she woke at night to find them sitting on her chest. Realities like her chronic dread of Winslow's deep-seated lungy cough. The never quite realizable calamity that the farm was no longer hers. Her parents scrimping themselves into old age. Paula, whom she loved, so strangely remote in her associations and preferences. That blighted potato-crop. Life-insurance policy to be met. (Heaven knew

how.)   Phil's apparent inability to regain his business
feet.   Strangely persistent adversity.   His first years
had shown such business promise.   Rita was looking
peaked, too.   Was another baby coming?   Of course, it
would be fine if the doctors had been wrong—except for
the strain—the financial millstone that seemed around
the neck of the family.   Sometimes Clara, off in St. Louis,
on the modest certainty of Sam's salary, seemed best
off of all.   But with her children growing up—what prospects, what future?   All the panorama of these realities
could seem so grotesque at night, or rather toward
morning, when she awoke, as was her wont, of a heavi-
ness at her chest.   The squatting realities.   David, a
curiously thoughtful boy in his slow, observant way.
What private panorama moved behind his square, calm
imperturbability of face?   If any?   Was the lethargy
into which David seemed locked just inertia that characterized the type of boy slow to get his bearings?   Or
was he the kind of boy, almost extinct now, who would
stick to the farm?   Or was here another Henry?
Dreamer.   Yearner.   Spectator.   Idealist.   Genius.
Failure?   Or just David.   Any boy.   Good boy.   Slow
boy.   Thoughtful, deep, rather intellectual boy.

The peaked expression that for the first time was
coming through her father's face!   That sunken area
about the mouth.   Almost the way he was going to look
in his coffin.   Ugh!

But it was only in that curiously corpselike hour before
dawn that such drearily hopeless thoughts could beset
her.   Sitting there over her accounts that evening, Bek
was scheming and contriving.   And now, after secret
years of the slowly planned project, the sudden return of
old Governor Howey from two years abroad, had ripened
the plan into action.

"I'm going to walk over to the Howey farm, Winslow. And see the Governor," she said, slapping a last account-book shut and pushing back from her desk.

"Better let the old man get his travel dust off, hadn't you?" he replied, without glancing up from his whittling.

"He's been home two days. Besides, I need to see him."

"I suppose he's holding you to an accounting for your loose management," said Winslow with an elaborate gravity.

"Why should he?"

"Oh, I thought he might be inclined to fire you for a more competent overseer."

"Stranger things have happened," she said, getting his point and smiling back at him.

"Maybe, but not much," said Winslow, whittling away on a staff of long, white-pine.

"The Governor has early supper same as always," said Bek, winding a knitted scarf over her head. "I'll get there just about as he's finishing. It's as good a time as any to buttonhole a man you've business with. Thursday's corned-beef night at the Howeys, and if I do say it, I've never corned finer for them than the piece he'll be cutting into this evening."

It was a good two miles to the Howey place, over country it would never have occurred to her to fear. Country which she had stalked, after dark, times too countless to record. And yet she stood waiting, wanting Winslow to fear for her. Wanting to be worried over. Secretly resenting not being feared for, and yet everything, in her bearing, forbidding solicitude.

"Think I'll need a lantern, Win? Looks like snow."

"Nonsense! There may be a flurry of sleet, but it won't amount to much. There's a moon due in an hour."

She walked over and kissed Leslie on his long, palish brow.

"Mother will be back in a little while, Leslie, to put you to bed."

He held up a half-finished garland to crown her.

"Father says there's a moon tonight, Leslie. I'll tell you the fairies-and-elves story when I come back. Bank up the furnace, Win, but keep the third flue open. Never mind! I'll go down and attend to it myself, on my way out."

She left them puttering among the shavings and at whittling in the warmly lit dining-room.

In the basement, the coals made a rumbling noise as she dove in with her shovel and lugged and relugged more shovels of them to the greedy, red mouth of the furnace.

"Don't bank her up too tight, Bek," called Winslow through the dining-room register. "Shouldn't be surprised if, after all, we do have a flurry of snow."

"Yes? Then maybe I'd better not—go?"

There was no answer to her pause, because Winslow, who had been at the window to peer, was out in the pantry pouring himself cider into a pewter mug.

"Oh, Win——"

"Yes?"

"Think I'd better not venture? Don't think I'm apt to be caught, do you?"

"Nonsense, you won't mind a flurry, even if it comes."

"No—I won't mind—but if you're going to worry about me——"

"Be sure and leave us plenty of heat, Bek."

"Yes."

Outside, a half-clear and listening kind of night met her, the same lowering beauty of snow-cloud edged in sunset that hung over David and Dora as they dallied together further along the same road. A moon, about to rise out of the cloud-mass, cast its brilliance ahead in a rim of silver.

There was a hog, with a rip along its flank from an encounter with a barbed-wire fence, to be glanced at as she passed down the cinder-path to the open road; and, for the life of her, Bek could not pass a barn door without a dragging-back of bolts for a precautionary look-in.

A chorus of whinnies met her, and the lowing sound of bulls. There was a new mare, with a vicious snapping-habit, standing muzzled in her stall. She loosened the strap slightly and rubbed a flank or two as she passed along.

It was full-dark, with the moon slid like a coin into a slot of cloud, as she fiercely struck her pace out on the road. A swinging pace as free as a man's, and with her heart beating high from the excitement of her purpose, the cold air beat against her face and left it flaming.

Chapter Thirty-three

FOR thirty years, the Howey family, with a wealth of social and intermarriage connections that extended beyond the state to the Eastern seaboard and Europe, had exchanged the niceties of Christmas puddings, cider at Thanksgiving, walnuts off the Howey trees, and mince-meat out of Mathilda's larders. And every fall, up to the year of her death, Kate Howey had sent Mathilda the first cuttings of dill from her kitchen garden. A custom which Shirley, the eldest Howey girl, Princess von Windigger now of Vienna, kept alive, along with others of her mother's homely habits, cabling instructions to the caretaker of the old homestead.

Every Christmas, the Governor, who was indebted to Henry on a hundred counts (not least among them the hushing-up of an ugly land-deal involving Loring Howey, the Governor's second son) sent him, whether from Madrid, Washington, Paris, or Buenos Aires, where Loring now had headquarters, a box of fifty Habana cigars and a gray-silk muffler.

The remaining two Howey boys, Tom and Weston, never failed to drop into the office above the hardware-store on their infrequent visits "back home."

There existed a rather formal *entente cordiale* between the home-grown Schuylers and the globe-trotting Howeys.

A Schuyler was always sure of a gracious reception from a Howey. A Howey was known to cater to a vote long after the immediate need for it was past.

This relationship had never been tested beyond this insular one of the neighborhood. Bek Schuyler and

Shirley Howey were within six months of the same age.
But while Shirley had been educated in Switzerland, Bek
had attended Centralia public schools. Henry had attended the state-endowed university, and Tom Howey,
who was also a lawyer, Yale.

The Howeys respected the Schuylers. Although not
one of them would admit it, except perhaps Emma, who
was a family-joke on the subject, and to whom a Howey
was a Cabot, every Schuyler secretly nourished a wistful
kind of admiration for the Howeys; an admiration that
dated back somewhere from childhood. The prepon-
derant magnificence of gubernatorial prestige. The fine
old Howey homestead. The debonair habits of wealth.
The comings and the goings of the Howeys in motor-
cars, years before the Ford and the tractor had inundated
the countryside with the fecundity of locusts. Shirley
Howey was the first woman in the county to ride a horse
astride. Loring Howey laid out a nine-hole golf-course
along the left flank of his father's estate, years before
the Whittier Country Club was even dreamed of. The
Howeys dressed for dinner. With the exception of
Henry, a Schuyler had never owned a dress-suit.

A Howey was perennially exciting to a Schuyler, exotic,
mysteriously and a little splendidly, alien.

Claire cut out *Spur* and *Vanity Fair* photographs of
Shirley von Windigger, and every other imaginable snapshot of her she could lay hands on, and tried, with her
own pale and fluffy hair, to imitate her sleek-groomed
coiffures, and from one photograph of her, with her two
little girls, charming in their Kate Greenaway dresses,
proceeded to dress her own little girls in like manner.

A Schuyler just naturally revered a Howey.

Another favorite family-joke was to get Phil, who
was Loring's age, started at defending the rather
notoriously black sheep of the Howey family. They

had been boys together during the period of a scrub baseball-team and swimming-hole days, before Loring was shipped off to Grout's Academy in Pennsylvania. Phil could be bitter with loyalty to Loring.

The Ex-Governor, who at eighty-seven still had the aggressive bison-like lunge of head that had crashed him through two of the most tumultuous terms in the history of the state's legislation, was seated, the night Bek arrived on her mission, in his small study of red leather and mahogany, that was dominated by an oil-panel of himself, painted by Sargent, the year of his election to second term.

It was little more than an anteroom, and smelled of camphor and slip-covers. Except his bedroom, it was in fact, the only room there had been time to unwrap for him on the heels of his wire, announcing his coming.

The old Ex-Governor who had dined alone off a small table drawn up before the fireplace, greeted her with his inquisitive, appraising eyes, in a face more shrunken than she recalled it, but their alertness and their shrewdness undimmed by the years which had got at his body so and gnarled it.

"By Gad, Bek, you haven't changed a hair in the last ten years," he said, and lied gallantly and with the politician's reflex for the diplomatic word at any price.

Bek had gained thirty pounds in that period. And knew it.

"Nor you, Governor," she lied back. "Where do you get your own special kind of immunity from the years?"

"Don't!" he said, with the shadow of almost his only fear flickering across the uneven surface of his face. "I'm a goner, Bek! Angina pectoris. Fatal as hell. Two years at the outside will see my finish."

"Nonsense!"

"How's your father?"

"Father holds his own, considering." ·

"Ever get a penny out of that hound Milliken?"

"He died two years ago, intestate, so far as we were able to find out."

"And his son?"

"One of the heaviest tax-payers in Toronto."

"One of the orneriest scoundrels ever came out of this state."

"They've made it hard sledding for us, Governor."

"Hit the whole gang of you, eh?"

"Yes, we seem to be like that. As my brother Phil puts it, united we stood and united we fell."

"Phil's the third one, isn't he? How's he doing?"

"Well, Phil's the kind of fellow, Governor, good head on him, but somehow always standing just on the verge of something big that never quite comes off. As a matter of fact, he hasn't done much more than make a living since—since our—crash. But I understand he's got some right good prospects now on some sort of an airship deal a group of Springfield business men are trying to negotiate with the Government."

"Wish it to him. And Henry? Still trapesing along, wasting himself on a one-horse town? There's a fellow could have brought himself and his state glory, if he'd had guts. I was never so fixed, you know that, Bek, what with conditions I had to contend with in office, that I could throw as much in his way as I'd liked to, but he knew, from me a-telling him, I'd have backed him for anything within reason."

"Henry Schuyler, Governor, is a big tragedy to everybody in this state except himself. And, possibly—me. No man is a failure, Governor, if he has eyes that er—a —as we say it in elocution—see the glory of the coming of the dawn. Henry wouldn't turn a hand to earn for himself some of that glory—but he sees it, all right."

"Well, all that's pretty fine for the hymn-books, but where's it got him? One-horse lawyer to every two-by-four case in the county. All right for a man to sponsor the under dog, so long as he doesn't weaken his power for helping by remaining one of the under-dogs himself."

"Lot in what you say, Governor. Here's Henry, who's probably handed out back-stair wisdom in every important case in this state in the last twenty years, barely eking out a living for himself and for the fund we somehow manage to keep going among us children for the old folks, without their knowing just exactly what it is keeps them going."

"Old Gentleman won't stand for any out-and-out help from his children, eh? I'll wager that. Great character, there. Stuff that the salt and the magnesia of the earth are made of. Old fellows like him are what the language-manipulators, down Washington, are always referring to as the bulwarks of society."

"If ever a man stood for just that, I guess it is Father. Pretty much of a crude proposition on the outside, but at heart, he's the most uncompromising idealist I know. Father's been a rich man and a poor man in his day, but the one quality in him that hasn't swerved with his fortunes is his integrity. He hasn't got much of anything to show for it in a worldly way, but Father's far from a failure in my eyes. He's lived what he believes."

"Well," said the Governor, with his eyes suddenly seeming to shrivel into two scars, "maybe he hasn't got much of anything to show for the years, and maybe he has. At least he hasn't got a brace of sons that have taken his life's blood. You don't need me to tell you, Bek, the pretty penny my two boys have cost me since the day they were born, to say nothing of—of—keeping one of them out of penitentiary."

Bek didn't. Her knowing it so well, and his referring to it at this time, made what she had come to ask the harder.

"I understand Governor, indeed I do. No, Father's not had what you'd call a particularly brilliant brood of us, but—well—our boys have spared father much of what you've been through."

"Spared. Your father has a fine bunch of men to show. How's the after-thought the Old Gentleman sprung on us some years back? That boy ought to be along in his teens now."

"Davey's—let me see—going on eighteen ——"

"You don't tell me! Lord, don't a fellow ever get old enough to get over surprise at the way time sneaks up on him. I remember meeting the Old Gentleman down at the bank, day or two after the boy was born—'Hi, Schuyler,' I said to him, 'hear you been doin' some tardy propagatin' of this here vale of tears. Don't you know there's a birth-control bill up in this state?' 'Birth control,' barks the Old Gentleman, 'birth-control poppy-cock! All that's the matter with propagation is the quality. More and better propagation is my slogan.' There's a card for you, if ever there was one. 'More and better propagation,' he says to me. 'Well, sir, I hope that last kid is more and better propagatin'.'"

"Davey—well, Dave's a peculiar child, Governor. Coming along as he did, so long after the rest of us—growing up alone, you might say—Mother, bless her heart, treating him more like a grandchild than one of her own, most of his uncles and nieces twice his age, war coming along right in the middle of his childhood, Father's reverses, well—somehow, never has seemed to me Dave's had a ghost of a chance."

"You mean he isn't . . ."

"Oh, he's got the levelest head of any child you ever

saw. Good bit of a dreamer, too. Dave's the kind of a child you can't tell much about while he's growing up, and, all of a sudden, he turns out to be—a something or just—just a kind of nothing. Know what I mean, Governor?"

"You mean, if he's a dog, he's a dog, or if he's a leopard, the spots haven't come through yet?"

"Sort of. I just mean Dave's what you might call still-water in a way, but I've the feeling about him that he not only runs deep, but that he runs wide. A regular little Mississippi."

"What's he doing?"

"Well, I guess you might say, not much of anything. That is—I think what I have just been telling you is why Dave isn't doing more than he is in a—a regular sort of way, I mean. Dave's had no schooling to speak of; but Henry's influence, I always say, is more than a college certificate. Dave's got curiosity, Governor. 'Intellectual curiosity,' Henry labels it. Nothing satisfies that boy short of learning everything there is to know about everything."

"What did you say he's doing now?"

"Oh, well—truth of it is—Dave's just around the farm yet. No job in the regular sense. The Igrotte place isn't much more than kitchen garden, but—well, it's just as I say, Governor, Davey hasn't had the deal the rest of us children had. He just growed, like Topsy. Father's needing him most of the time for herding and chores. Course he's had Henry. Even without what you might call proper schooling, that's an influence not one boy in a thousand comes under."

"Great deal in what you say."

"Except that Henry's not what you'd call, in this age we live in, much of a live-wire. It's made Davey kinda what you'd call a stagnant little fellow. Hope to goodness it don't mean he's going through life thataway. It's the wrong age to be born into, if you're slow-going. But unless I miss my bet, Dave's the kind that spends his time growing cone-shaped, and then watch your cyclone. Not that I mean—well, I guess about all I can out-and-out say to your question, Governor, is that, at present, Dave's tinkering around the farm."

"Humph!"

"Just the same, his information for a boy is surprising. He can tell you the distance of a star or recite the Fourteen Points, or, all of a sudden, tell you something out of Greek literature. He's got one of those curious combinations of conservatism and imagination, if you get what I mean."

"Humph! Guess you're about the pick of the crowd, Bek."

She sat before him, with the scarf fallen back from her large, capable face, her hair with the gray in it straggling a little from under the plait of it on top of her head, and her square hands clamping down tightly on each knee.

"Coming to that. Fact is, at this moment, I'm the failure of the family, Governor," she said, forcing his gaze to meet hers, squarely, "and you know why."

"I've never talked over our business arrangements with you, Bek, knowing that's all fixed between you and my overseer, but you know that I know, from what he tells me, that you've done as well with High Ridge as anybody could—considering two droughts, hoof-and-mouth disease, and bad crop-conditions the last five years—all things considered——"

How shrewd he was. As if he had not scanned to the penny the detailed fidelities of her annual reports. He knew to precisely what extent the High Ridge was a going-concern, and to what extent its expert first-hand

control had enabled it to yield richly on his investment.
Sly old rogue. He knew, and his old eyes slid under
her square gaze for the moment, but she captured them
fast again with her own.

"All things considered. You mean High Ridge hasn't
paid?"

"Not exactly that——"

"I can show you, Governor, a five-per-cent yield even
on your war years."

"Five per cent to a man who makes his money earn
almost twice that, isn't such a hell of a good investment,
my dear Bek, if you'll pardon my 'hell'."

"As a matter of fact, Governor, the average of the
last four years had been considerably over that, if you
figure——"

"In total, perhaps, but the alfalfa fiasco——"

"You know how I advised against that."

"Whatever the situation was—and mind you, in any
other hands than yours, there is no doubt but what the
case would have been much worse—the total results from
the farm haven't yet averaged a particularly good return for my money."

He lied down her own knowledge of her own figures
without as much as the batting of an old crocodile eye-
lid, and lying, knew that she knew he lied.

"You've averaged over six per cent on your money,"
she repeated, standing her ground with a cold and even
voice.

"Wrong, there. Can show you the figures. What with
the cost of upkeep. Now if we could cut down on the
expense of operation——"

So that was what made the old Governor so cagey.
Fear that she had come to demand an increase.

"Governor, you feeling as you do, listen to this. Here's
a proposition. I'll buy the place back."

"Eh?"

"I'll pay you seven per cent on your money."

With the lightning perception that his great age had not dimmed, he saw his trap almost before she had the words out, and with the same lightning perception, saw its cunning mesh.

What a woman! Damn fine shrewd old girl. Should have been a man. Worth the whole bunch put together. And as the situation flowed over him, he began to laugh until his bent old figure rippled along his blue brocade dressing-gown.

"So! So!"

"With that three-acre triangle just below Algahr's, and not counting the artesian well in the drilling, and the two tractors on order, and the electric milkers, I'll pay you—forty thousand dollars. Exactly twenty-five per cent more than the last mortgages I held from you on practically the same property. The matter of the slightly above the usual six per cent will be a private matter between you and me. Six-year term of mortgage, subject to extension for same period."

"By Gad, I——"

"It's my land, Governor. That farm's my child. My very roots are down in that soil. That's why, since I've lost the land, it has been as if an arm or a leg of mine were buried somewhere, and keeps hurting even though it is no longer part of me."

A curious, half-fanatical flame crept along Bek's face.

"Sell me back my farm, Governor," she said, and thrust her burning countenance closer and closer to his vision. "You've so much land. To you, land is just so much income. So many bushels of wheat. So many heads of cattle. So many mowing-machines to make it yield. But land, to me—that land, of that farm, to me—it's a bosom breathing, Governor!"

"Come, come, now, Bek. Not like you to talk business on a woman-basis. That's woman-bosh. If this farm that you know from A to Z is worth that much to you, why isn't it worth that much to me?"

"I'm glad you asked that Governor, because I can tell you why. It's because, with all the conscientiousness in the world, I can't make it worth that much to you. Why? Because I've lost the creative thing in me that made me mother to that farm. I'm just its wet-nurse now. God knows, I've given you just about one hundred and one cents on the dollar, Governor. No glory to me, but just on the principle that I'd go the limit for a child of mine, even though I'd given it out to another family for adoption. But just the same, Governor, I've lost the fire in me that made me the creator of that farm. I can't fight for her while she's not all mine. It's not in me. I'm hired. Sell me back my farm, Governor?"

"You are prepared to buy a forty-thousand-dollar farm?"

"Yes."

"How?"

She looked at him, aware that her face must be pulled to reveal a terrible state of eagerness which she did not want revealed to him.

"Right big business, Bek. Forty-thousand-dollar deal! What's your proposition?"

"I've given it to you."

"In detail?"

"I'll pay you out, Governor, barring the first year for breathing-space, on any—any conditions as to time and amount you think—fair."

"How much down?"

She captured his gaze again, squarely to the center of his eyeballs.

"Come now, Governor."

"Fair question."

"Nothing—down."

He drew on a beautifully colored but draughty old meerschaum pipe, with two ivory antelopes with locked horns on its hump, and laughed softly, so that the brocade rippled again.

"You're the best business man in this room, Bek."

"Wouldn't be surprised, Governor."

That tickled him more, so that he laughed out into a high thin, very old man's cackle.

"But it takes even a smarter man than you to get curd-and-whey out of water."

"You've nothing to lose, Governor, by taking a chance on my legerdemain."

"Why haven't I?" he barked.

"Why, if I don't meet my obligations—the mortgage is in your hands—as before ——"

"So you propose to meet those obligations on a zero foundation?"

"The moment I become even theoretic owner of my farm once more, my foundation ceases to be zero."

"How do you mean?"

"I'm a Samson shorn of my locks now, Governor. I'm tied hand and foot. I'm a hired-hand."

"Who tied you?"

"You, Governor. Not in so many words; but with somebody else's property, one goes safety-first. I've had half a dozen schemes in the last five years I'd have put into practice, if I'd been risking on my own. On one of my schemes alone, I'd be in a small fortune now. I'd have gone in for sheep-raising on a new scale here-abouts. I've an experimental-dairy idea that's been brewing for years. I see money in alfalfa. Not under the conditions you made me plant three years ago, but according to my own theories. Remember, I wired you and you vetoed? I've an idea up my sleeve that'll turn those acres of cornfields into quick-turn-over money. Experimental, perhaps, but a person will experiment with his own, when he won't take a chance for another."

"Something in that."

"As long as I'm working for you, Governor, I'll give you the best there is in me. But the very best isn't there. I'm a dead thing. My vision and my imagination and my courage are in my shoes. Sell me back my land, Governor. Take a sporting-chance on me and I won't fail you."

"I won't live to see whether you do or not," he said, drily, his eyes going dull, as if they were mirrors and someone had breathed on them.

"Sell me back my land, Governor. It's part of my state. It's part of my country. It's part of me."

"Don't know but what I will," drawled the Ex-Governor and sat back in his leather chair and pulled hard on his pipe with the two ivory antelopes. "Rotten bad business tactics, but, by Gad—don't know but what I will, Pek."

Chapter Thirty-four

It was at this precise moment that Dave, after Dora had dashed from him into the long row of elms, reached the little eminence of land, on his way home, from where he could see, on one side, the remote, low-lying roofs of High Ridge, and, on the other, the roof of the Igrotte place.

The moon had come out of its snow-bank, wafer-thin, and throwing a light the color of steel over the country-side. Fields billowed around him, as if under his very feet, he could feel the movement of their flow. Valley whose magnesia of the soil was the soil of his own make-up. He had that sense of oneness with the ground, as if the roots of him, like the roots of a tree, flowed down through layers of the curiously alive earth into sub-strata ———

Years of his dreams, dreamed from the flat of his back, had risen off that soil. Folded close to the deep, the loamy, the fructifying dirt, what countless times he had dropped his book on its face, to float off to worlds of pirate and raft, shark and Tartar. North Pole. Airship. Submarine. Dick Needham. Later, Ivanhoe. de Galis. Tom Brown. Cecil Rhodes. Galileo. Captain Kidd. Peary. Teddy! Marconi. Orville Wright. Othello.

Everyone of them had sat on the slope of his hill that slid down on one side toward Bek's and on the other side toward the Igrotte house.

Why, buried somewhere on the left slope of hillside was a copy of Darwin's *Variation of Animals and Plants under Domestication*. He had played at Captain Kidd

burying his treasure on damp spring afternoons. That
was his treasure. For months, it had lain moldering
there, waiting for him to find time to go searching the
spot, over which tufts of grass had grown meanwhile,
erasing trace of the ritual.

Dreams had been dreamed here, and now culminating
within him, in what seemed actual spurts of energy, came
the first concrete impulse to be up-and-doing he had ever
known.

Here was his soil flowing into a future that seemed
suddenly to draw aside one of its many thicknesses of
curtain for him. The future that was to be flecked with
the rise and dip of aeroplanes. The future when this
soil must run fertile and yielding as far as Stefansson had
been able to visualize in the *Northward Course of Empire*. The future that suddenly was something to arm
cap-a-pie for. That he must rush to meet. The future
that suddenly, amidst the vision, the dipping of the
planes, the onward rush of empire, had its nucleus under
his feet and stretched out to new horizons. Suddenly
that future became alive. A future of men whose ideals
must rise above the soaring of the planes, or who would
be crashed to earth by them.

A future that was suddenly luminous, because it contained him and Dora under the rooftree of a semi-
detached home of their own making, in a town called
Springfield.

How suddenly and gloriously alive this future, starting under his feet and radiating outward, chiefly toward
Springfield! Clerkship. Husbandship. Dora!

Something else, too. The something else that was part
of that future. Uncorrelated. The fields all about him
were soaked with his dreams; with his inchoate impulses.
To launch new ships. Dreadnoughts, with nothing to

dread, were the only kind of ships that ultimately must mark man's ability to rise above his mechanical age.

One thought a great deal about that. Henry said, what good is the telephone, the telegraph, the aeroplane, the motor-car, if man use these magnificences of his own inventive brain against himself. . . .

Henry said. Henry said . . . Henry said . . . somehow swam out of the vast ether of moving molecules —Henry said! Impulse to warn men lest the power of brain prove to be a boomerang. Impulse to jerk the world into compactness by quick navigation of air. To make men less strange to one another, less afraid of one another, by annihilating distance. Supremacy of the air must mean just that—not the power of poison-gas. Henry said ——

To tread new altitudes that back, through the ages, only eagles had dared. To seek new pastures. A world to be tamed by its mechanical magnificence, not made savage by it. A world to leap to the stars on the quick mechanical steeds of its achievement, not to hurl bombs from them—not to rush to intellectual, spiritual, idealistic destruction on them. Henry said—Henry said ——

The impulse to straddle the world as if it were Pegasus gone mad and check-rein it—Henry's words— Henry's words were kindling in one. To ride toward the stars, instead of into destruction, on a steed with mechanical entrails and seven-thousand-league hoofs.

And above all, to come back to Dora four years hence, with money in the pockets of a blue serge suit that was nattier than Kenneth Chipman's, and carry her back to a Springfield that had a shingle over his office door, a client on his books, and a first month's rent planked down on a two-family house! Dora!

Against the horizon, from the direction of the Howey place, her silhouette unmistakable, climbed the figure of his sister Bek, at enormous stride, even for her. A stride that seemed to spin the road, a little contemptuously, back from under her strong feet. A stride that somehow, as he stood on his eminence of small hilltop, with a rising wind flapping his shabby, baggy trousers, filled him with a curious and comforting sense of inheritance.

Some of that power that made his sister magnificent, and his father like a stanch old phaeton that would carry its burden even when the spring groaned; that made his brother full of a wisdom that seemed to begin far behind things and leap so far ahead of them—some of that power must be his!

There were new ships to launch—somewhere—airships! Dream-ships come true. Power!

Why, he had seen his mother, who was full of years and had fainting-spells, deny her chilblains and walk miles on feet that must have been fiery and icy furnaces under her. He had seen her, who sickened at blood, finish sticking a knife into a pig, when a farmhand cut himself. Even his nephew Stephen, whom he had seen kick in the side of a dog, had a valor that had pulled him through.

Some of that power, flowing like a mill-stream through his family, must be in him. Big wheels to turn. Why not? Half of a two-family house in Springfield—some day—who knows—there was a future to law—corporation law—if Kenneth Chipman could—well—if Kenneth Chipman could ——

His dreams must be struck into life, as one would strike a match into flame.

As Dora had struck the match of him into flame!

Chapter Thirty-five

LOPSIDEDLY, the rust-colored, pot-bellied stove in Henry's office had whirred through its twenty winters. Second-hand originally, in setting it up the fourth leg had come off, so that from the beginning, it had stood propped on two wooden blocks. Its hoarse, hurried whisper was indissolubly associated with that flimsy-walled room in one of the few frame buildings that remained on High Street.

It was probably the only coal-stove left in a High Street office. It had a gaseous, soft-coal breath that hovered over the place even when August crowded its humidity into the little room. Its soot lay along the mountain-ridges of the relief-map of North America that occupied one entire wall, like the grime in the wrinkles of an old gypsy's face.

There was never a time within Davey's recollection, when the Socrates on the bookcase had not grime in the curlicues of his hair or along the deep sills of his eye-sockets, or when the top of Henry's yellow oak table, that served as desk, was not gritty to the touch. Usually Henry sat in a swivel-chair, with one bony knee crooked against the table-edge, and foot dangling free of the floor. Except when a client was present. Then it was his idiosyncrasy to seat the client in the swivel-chair, where the hard light from the window fell upon his face, and himself occupy the casual straight chair alongside.

It was a motley, ill-ordered table-top. For as long as Davey could remember, a horseshoe had dangled from a nail at one end, and to which nail the countless zigzag rents in Henry's seersucker coat bore witness.

Briefs piled in stacks had slid down along themselves. A magnificent plaster-of-Paris Holstein-Friesian bull, of the vintage of a Nineteen-Hundred-and-One State Fair, browsed in the center of a litter of ink- and mucilage-pots. Above the table was a flecked picture of Abraham Lincoln, that had once been given away, on his birthday, with a Sunday edition of the *Kansas City Star*. An excerpt from his Gettysburg speech was pasted alongside.

. . . that from these honored dead we take increased devotion to that cause for which they gave the last full measure of devotion —that we here highly resolve that these dead shall not have died in vain—that this nation, under God, shall have a new birth of freedom—and that government of the people, by the people, for the people, shall not perish from the earth.

It might be said of Henry that he dallied for hours in his swivel to the rhythm of that segment of the speech. Not consciously. The text of it was almost part of his very texture. In that speech was Henry fluttering for flight. In that speech his cry, his plea, his dread, his hope, his passionate yet passive caring about men and their emancipations. Tilted in his swivel for hours, he could regard the bit of print, without actually seeing it, but soaked in its rhythm, which was the rhythm to which he swung his knee and tilted in his chair and passed his days. Alone. As much as they would let him be. Flies had specked it, and a celluloid campaign-button, from the first Howey campaign of 1896, was dug into one corner.

There were road-maps and wavy stacks of books, half-a-man high, staggering from the floor above the table-top; an engineer's map of the plan of a proposed spur-railroad off the main line from Centralia to Springfield; a blue-print of a thirty-mile stretch of a new state

highway; a plan of a negro-shanty, where a murder had
been committed in the name of chicken-thievery. A
black-and-white print of President Wilson. Charts for
a proposed clearing of a swamp known as Nigger Hollow. A hand-made map of the States of Ohio and
Indiana, with red-headed pins outlining sources of water-
power. A photograph of Phil Schuyler's one-time pretentious home in Springfield, with Phil and Rita and the
children seated on the porch rail.

A country-bumpkin of an office. Probably the only
one of its kind left in a small city that now boasted its
Chamber of Commerce, two ten-story, fire-proof sky-
scrapers, a Federal bank, the largest tool-works west of
Massachusetts, two five-and-ten-cents stores, a daily Blue
Plate Business Men's lunch served in the Rotarian Rooms,
two radio-shops screaming out onto the sidewalks, omni-
bus-service to Seven Mile, Cottage Corner, Tallahassee
Dam, and Middleton, and a bill pending for the inclusion
of Seven Mile within the city limits, thereby adding one-
fifth to the population.

And, curiously enough, in that antiquated office over
the hardware-store, from his tilted swivel up there,
where for hours on end he could make chapel of his ten
fingers, and gaze with mild, amused, sardonic eyes upon
the flow of High Street, it was Henry Schuyler who had
his long, lean finger in all of these pies of progress.

A finger that never bothered to draw out a plum.

There was something inscrutable in this smile with
which Henry surveyed the scene from his window. The
hurrying clang of bright new street-cars. He had been
instrumental in wrenching a franchise from political interests. The new concrete viaduct jerking Seven Mile
greedily closer to the flank of Centralia. The machinery
of the appropriation for that considerable piece of engineering had passed through his hands. The World War

Soldiers' Memorial Park that had threatened to take the form of a block of marble, until he had intervened. The distant shine of the Tallahassee aeroplane-field and hangars, which he had influenced old Hiram Tallahassee to endow in his will.

The town, bustling, banging, rattling in its small way with the things that mattered to it. Its increasing and growing canning- and foundry-industries, attracted by bonuses that Henry helped appropriate; its modern pressed-brick schoolhouses, with sunlight-factory exteriors and every modern device for the presentation of not-so-modern curricula. Its paved highways for easier and swifter mileage, its cinema-houses for surcease from the too crushing reality of days filled with the quest for more capital, more speed, more lust for water-power, horse-power, candle-power, man-power. All this spread itself before the mild, sad eyes of Henry Schuyler, like a satirical play in which he had unwittingly collaborated.

"These first twenty-five years of this century are undoubtedly the greatest in bulk of achievement in the history of the world," he used to say. "Of course, it is true that invention makes history. For lack of a telescope, Aristotle's astronomy is a tissue of childish romance. For lack of a microscope, his biology wanders endlessly astray. It was her low power in industrial and technical achievement that kept Greece below the general standard set by her unparalleled intellectual achievement. And yet, here we are in the age that excels along those lines, skimming under seas and over mountains, and annihilating distance with the jerking of a lever. What bothers me a little bit, though, is, whither? Is the aeroplane going to do as much for humanity as Socrates did, who sat on a coping in his home town most of his life, and thought out loud to folks who had the time to listen to him? Where are we rushing? Strikes me we're all dressed-up and no place to go."

Henry was not dressed-up. His office was pretty much his coping, in which he sat, in seersucker, intoning to his world, which he seemed to regard as infinitely younger than he. Inviting definition from all with whom he came in contact, but usually ending by giving it himself.*

In the swivel, before his brother's littered table, the light from High Street hard against his squaring young face, and Henry seated by in the casual attitude of visitor, David faced his brother, the morning following his encounter with Dora in the wind-swept twilight. They might have been father and son, but in the largely impersonal way that Henry somehow seemed paternal to the world he lived in.

There were small, rigid places at the edges of David's mouth, occasioned by a sort of misery at what he was doing. He was asking of his brother a loan; and knowing, as he did, his financial status, the moment was pretty obnoxious to him. Furthermore, sitting there stammering out his request, his eyes fixed unhappily upon

---

* To the great embarrassment of his elders, David, as a boy, was a great one to insist upon definition, urging detailed explanation of any subject which caught his attention. There is little doubt but what my brother Henry, who had one of the finest capacities for intellectual curiosity I have ever known, was largely responsible for this trait. Later, of course, he (David) came to be known as The Inquiring Mr. Question Mark, and in the memorabilia of the Museum of Baltimore is the original of the much-reproduced Glake cartoon, which is a most amusing likeness of my brother, entirely drawn in small question-marks.

It is said of him, and I think rightly, that it was his insistence upon definition that saved America from being party to the Allied International Peace fiasco at Moscow.

a sheet of paper sprawling on the table before him, suddenly, as he stammered along, the blur of typewritten letters shaped themselves into words, and the words into meaning.

It was a letter from a firm of solicitors in Middleton, holding to account Henry Stephen Schuyler for the sum of four hundred and fifty dollars, for which he had gone bond for a young farmer named Edwin Penwhistle, who had defaulted payment by disappearing from the state two days before said moneys fell due.

It made the hard, jade-white areas along the side of David's nose quiver and flatten as he limped along with his recital. The snagged places on Henry's shabby seersucker coat too, kept hooking onto his hot and tortured gaze. Not that under conditions of the most fantastic financial well-being could he imagine his brother in an unsnagged seersucker, but just the same, those little repetitious triangles kept jerking up his words, making him stammer and stumble, and finally end up by just sitting in the middle of a sentence and regarding Henry with stinging, miserable eyes.

"—hate like the dickens . . . come to fellow like you for a loan—but it's the poor help the poor—money don't seem to mean much to the poor."

"Something a little wise in that, boy. The poor remain poor, as a rule, because they spend easily. They've never known the gloating of watching a bank-account grow."

"It's asking a lot, Henry. Two hundred. You see, though, that could tide me over the winter-tuition. I can't very well ride Phil, the way he's got to hustle to make their ends meet—his kids and all. Looks like you're the only one, Henry, a fellow can sort of turn to. You couldn't see your way clear, could you, Henry, to let me have that coupla hundred? If I'm going to do the law nights, I'm already three weeks late for the beginning of the term."

"What determined you, boy, so all of a sudden?"

"That's why I caught the milk-truck in, so we could talk in town. Private."

"Quite right. But last time we tried to get anywhere, talking this matter over, Dave, you were all heated up about the Wheeler book and had decided to devote your life to zoölogy, and then *Arabia Deserta* and Stefansson got you het up about reclaiming the waste places of the earth, and it looked like engineering or Cecil Rhodes empire-stuff; then, if I remember rightly, Wilson's perplexities got you thinking about international law, and then forestry seemed a good bet, and then, 'long toward the last, wasn't it ovibos-breeding, Antarctic exploration, ornithology, banking, lumber-jacking, astronomy, shipbuilding?"

"Of course, if you're going to rub that in . . ."

"Now, old fellow, don't go getting sore. I think the idea of taking that job Phil can swing for you in Springfield with a grocery-firm, where you can dig into the law nights, is bully."

"Then why the dickens didincha say so?" said David, his dry lips lifted back off his dry teeth and his eyes seeming to push up close to the lenses of his spectacles.

"Well, I just do kinda say it now. It's a darn good decision. A job by day, and a law course to keep you out of mischief nights."

"Law's something a fellow can fasten his teeth into, Henry."

"Knowledge of the laws men live under, Dave, even if you never do much more with it than—well, I guess you'd have to do more with it than I have, or strike a mark below zero—me being the zero—but what I started to say, boy, knowledge of the laws men make for themselves to live under is one way of getting at the knowledge of the kind of fellows human beings are to have made them just that way."

"That's it, Henry. Even if I wasn't ever to actually go out and practice law——like you ——"

"God forbid!"

"Sometimes, Henry——know what?"

"No, what?"

"Well, just a little turn of the wheel, and, all of a sudden, a fellow's got his bearings. Know what I mean?"

"Think I do. All of a sudden, well, just all of a sudden, something hit you. That about it?"

"Exactly. Nothing so much in a grocery-job, but it's wholesale, and, anyways, Father's always said he didn't care so much whether he had all silk purses in the family, just so he didn't have any sow's ears." *

---

* I shall never forget that rather murky November evening, when I was out in what I always called Winslow's garden, wrapping a hydrangea-bush in straw, when, lo and behold, who should turn the corner of the porch, but Henry. A most unusual thing for him to show up at the farm.

"Bek," he said to me, without an ado or introduction, "Dave's made up his mind to go to Springfield and take that job polishing spittoons and the handles of the big front-door for a wholesale grocery-firm."

It wasn't anything to take on over, and yet I can never forget the curious feeling that shot through me. Like dropping suddenly in one of those thirty-story elevators I never can get used to.

"What on earth," I cried, "made him decide that? Couldn't he do that good here in Centralia?"

"That's just the fine part of it, Bek. The kid wants to go to Springfield because there's what they call an Extension Law Course he can attend evenings. Beat that?"

Maybe you could have beaten it, but to Henry and me, standing there grinning, in the cold, gray twilight, it didn't

"I'd like mighty much to see you surprise the Old Gentleman with a hundred-per-cent silk purse."

"He's a silk purse himself."

"No, the Old Gentleman is more like the honestest woolen sock in the world."

"A sock that Mother knitted."

Out of their laughter, a shadow fell across Henry's face, as if a shade had been lowered.

"Tenacious old folks, ours, Dave. Such old-fashioned and relentless ideals as toil and integrity and loyalty are pretty much out-of-date. Father yells and hollers about it all, but he's the tree and root and the sap of the soil all right. It's fine to be an acorn off that kind of oak. That's what you are at your age, Dave. An acorn crammed with future."

"Remember what you said to me once, Henry, when you were reading Aristotle to me? Inventions make history, but is history worth the making? That wasn't nice, Henry."

"Of course it wasn't, and of course history's worth the making. The hominy must have been scorched that morning for breakfast. What I probably meant was something like—well, to make history really worth the making, the age of invention should have preceded the age of thought."

"That's what I say, Hen. What could those Greek fellows be expected to know about some of the most or-

---

seem beatable. It lifted Dave's going, for us, out of the dreariness we associated with his job as grocer's handy-boy.

"Know what I think, Bek?" Henry went on to me. "He's sweet on some girl. Wonder could it still be the Tarkington girl?"

"I wonder," I said, smiling a smile that, as it stretched across my face, made me feel as if I looked exactly like an old gray tabby we had, called Sly.

dinary facts of the world they lived in, when they had no way of getting around it? No wonder old Aristotle was way off on his astronomy. Didn't even have a pocket telescope like mine. Know what, Henry?"

"No, what?"

"Well, sir—looka this country. If Greece could do what she did without inventions, what do you think we ought to be able to do, having them? Looka the aeroplane. Didn't we invent it? A pair of fellows right here in the Middle West? And here's France and all those countries getting more use out of it than we are. What's distance or cold or heat to us, or any of the things that have kept other nations down? Yes, siree, if I was practicing law in a live town like Springfield, living say in a little attached house with a front yard to squirt evenings with the garden hose, and plenty of time to think things out—oh, say—oh, say—well—just 'oh, say,' is all I got to say."

"Yeh!" said Henry, fumbling among the litter of his table and reaching across the body of the boy toward the far end. "Hand me that check-book, Dave ——"

It was a scrubby affair through which Henry's wetted forefinger rustled.

"How's a hundred and forty-three dollars and fifty-six cents on account, boy?" he said, after some figuring on a margin, "That's fifty-six dollars and forty-four cents shy of the two hundred, but ——"

"You mean, Henry—that's all you've got?"

"I mean nothing of the sort. There's always more coming in somehow. Fellow up here in Tole County blew in last week and paid me seventy-five dollars for a fee he's owed me nine years back ——"

"But ——"

"Take it or leave it," said his brother, scrawling on the check and jerking it testily out of the book.

There was always in Henry's manner toward his money-affairs, and in his response to any and everybody's inroads upon the notorious generosity, a manner apt to be embarrassing to even the most hardened collector off his bounty.

He treated money with the tip of a somewhat contemptuous finger.*

The canny, the meretricious, the sycophants, and the needy, who at one time or another passed in almost constant stream about that white-pine table, sensed it even when Henry himself was most unconscious of the trait.

His scorn for money. It made even the hardened recipient of his largesse shrink a little as he left his presence. It made Dave, to whom money had suddenly and for the first time loomed with importance, feel sticky-fingered at the savage generosity which made his brother, as if angrily forestalling more ado, thrust the check into his hand.

"Henry, you're just about the best friend a fellow ever had."

"I'm just about the best boob a fellow ever had. Keep me in front of you, boy, for your 'Don't' slogan. Look at me, and pretty nearly everything you see me doing,

---

* I have often wondered, in a practical family such as ours, reared as we were to know the value of a nickel, where my brothers Henry and Dave inherited their disregard for money. It is probable that each, in his own way, was responsible for vast fortune after vast fortune that was to fall into the hands of other men. While it is true that our family-fortunes were destined to rise on the wings of a winged invention, not one penny of that fortune was due to the business acumen of these two men. Where their imagination and vision soared, it took men like Phil and my Steve to capitalize the ideas from such minds as Henry's and Dave's as they fell to the ground like feathers from an eagle in flight.

don't do. And above all, don't laugh at the age you live in. Laugh with it. That's not my idea so much as the laughing philosopher's, Democritus. Whatever you do, don't, like gloomy Heraclitus, shed tears about it. Shed your illusions if you must, and then fight like hell to recapture them in terms of reality. Don't keep your tongue in your cheek. Just poke it in occasionally. The pupils of Socrates, you remember, were divided into cynics and Cyrenaics. Don't let the stale apathy of cynicism get you, ever. It takes a clever man to turn cynic, and a wise man to be clever enough not to."

"Is that one of those eppy-grams, Henry?"

"No, only a rather dull truth. A wise man lets his mind ferment, Dave, but never turn to vinegar. You've got a level head on your shoulders. Keep it there. Don't let it get caught in the rut between your shoulders. The sixth human sense, Dave, is a sense of humor. Care passionately about everything, Dave, using your sixth sense all the while, and see to it that almost everything is worth caring about. Then curb your passions."

"I can care all right, Henry—*now!*"

"Don't march ahead of the band-wagon. They'll stone you, boy, if you do. Ride with it, but keep your eyes ahead. If you see Light, guide them toward it, only in the name of Heaven, don't let them know they are not seeing it for themselves."

"You know what you should have been, Henry?"

"Yes, I know what I should have been, Dave. I'm one of those fellows who, by making a few wise cracks to the not-so-wise, gets the reputation of still water running deep. As a matter of fact, still water doesn't run at all. Yes, know what I should have been? I should have been Diogenes with a radium-lantern. I should have been Socrates with the wing of an aeroplane for his coping. I

should have been that fellow Teufelsdröck. Who was
Teufelsdröck? Quick!"

"Oh, I know! He's the old chap in *Sartor Resartus*
who ——"

"Good! Well, I should have been him, spending my
days in the tower of a two-hundred-and-ninety-eight-story
Woolworth skyscraper, playing marbles with the stars.
Or maybe, by Jove, I should have been a third-rate coun-
try-lawyer trying to sprinkle salt on the tail of the comet
I inhabit, and preaching to a small brother, to be able
when he reaches my age, to sum up his life in terms of
'I am,' instead of like me, 'I might have been.' "

"Well, allrighty, you mighta been—allrighty—you
mighta been ——"

"I mighta been, allrighty ——" said Henry, looking
out upon the tide of High Street, his eyes seeming suddenly to be the wise, tired, prophetic eyes of what he
"mighta been."

There entered, unannounced, as everyone entered that
office unannounced, the hurried, perspiring figure of Steve
Renchler. In spite of the fact that he had come in out
of the thin-aired bluster of November, there were moist
little places out under his eyes and along his upper lip;
and although he wore a sweater-waistcoat (a handsome
slip-over, of a variety which Claire could knit so skillfully
that a Springfield department-store purchased her output), his coat was jerked back, and his derby hat was
along the back of his head, pushed there by a mopping
handkerchief.

There was little resemblance left to the dark, tortured
boy and dreamer. It was a fed face. The face of a man
of strong, healthy appetites, and strong, healthy gratifi-
cations. If the mere smell of alcohol could turn Steve
pale and gone-at-the-knees, the delights of the table had

done their measure, and apparently were not without compensations. Steve's clothing bore the horizontal creases of a man whose legs bend heavily. There were dimples out along the backs of his hands, set in little cushions of fat. The tailor, in taking his measurements, had to throw the tape-line around his waist.

Right in the town of Centralia, hundreds of replicas of this derby-hatted Steve were meeting their life-insurance endowment-policies, being fairly true to their wives, reading their *Saturday Evening Posts, Literary Digests* and comic-supplements, mowing their front lawns, paying their installments on loud-speakers, eating their Blue Plate luncheons, dodging jury-service, reconciling themselves to bob-haired wives, driving their family sedans, having their children's tonsils out, purchasing Frigidaire ice-boxes in fourteen monthly payments, attending the cinema-houses, tuning-in before turning-in, struggling to relieve financial strain, staving off blood-pressure, subscribing to fifty bricks, at a dollar a brick, in the new municipal hospital, scheming to turn in this year's four-cylinder model for next year's six, dreaming of college education for the children, struggling for Country Club membership, "now that the children are growing up," hoping for that raise, dreaming of the trip to the Canadian Rockies, spoiling their children, hating, indulging, loving, or spoiling their wives, achieving nervous indigestion, joining the boosters' club, stifling another old dream, climbing after new dreams, voting the full Republican ticket, flying an "excuse my dust" pennant from off the old sedan, teaching son to salute the flag, doctoring income-tax.

The stamp of his times was on Steve. His was the rather flabby figure of a man with a body still fairly adapted to the lugging of water and the killing of game, but who finds himself instead, turning spigots, and pick-

ing up the telephone-receiver when he would eat red
meat. He read two newspapers a day. A local morn-
ing-sheet controlled by Republican interests and a Chicago day-old pink evening-sheet controlled by capital and
designed to meet the mammalian needs of who runs as
he reads the-syndicated-universities of Frank Crane and
Parkes Cadman, Eddie Guest, Beatrice Fairfax, Bud
Fisher, Glenn Frank, comic strip, and baseball brevities,
and such of the financial, industrial, governmental, international, and political fluctuations as were deemed diges-
tible for a barley-watered public. The newspapers were
as doped for public consumption as many of the food-
stuffs and drink-substitutes that found their way down
the naïve palate of Centralia. A press that was free to
mix, dilute, pervert truth to meet the demand of politics
and policies, hurled its vitiated and vitrioled facts in
twirled newspapers against the front doors of Centralia
as the carrier passed down the streets in a two-wheeled
cart, from which he was crack sure-shot.

Steve read his morning-paper propped up against the
sugar-bowl as he dipped up his nationalized cereal, and
then left it at home for Claire, who read the death, marriage, advice to-the-lovelorn, and Lost and Found De-
partments.

Claire, however, also read Mencken and Sherwood
Anderson and Cabell at her Saturday Morning Literary
Club, considered them terribly interesting, and "Mencken
a scream. I just love his way of writing. He sees right
through everybody—and don't hesitate to say so."

There was an uncut volume of *Prejudices, First Series*
on the center table of Steve's reception-hall, and an un-
thumbed edition of *Winesburg, Ohio,* inscribed "To
Claire Schuyler in recognition of her loyal presidency of
the Saturday Morningers," and in a neat row, between
bronze-elephant book-ends, such miscellany as Burns's

Collected Poems, The Winning of Barbara Worth, Girl of the Limberlost, Ingersoll's Collected Sermons, Stella Dallas, Guide to Bridge Whist, Motion Picture Classic, Watch Your Calories, Adult Book of Knowledge, Child's History of England, Kathleen Norris's *Mother,* Ben King's *Verse, A Thought a Day,* Owen Meredith, *Ethan Frome,* Papini's *Life of Christ, Innocents Abroad, The Iron Woman, Garden of Allah, Mary Page,* by Leroy Scott, *One Hundred Famous Quotations,* and *Friendship and Flower Book.*

When Stevey waited for his barber or dentist, or took a train to Springfield, the *Literary Digest* served him one news-concoction after another, as quickly as an Automat.

News-reels flashed to him, from his favorite motion-picture theater, such items of the day as were considered good for his American well-being. Such as the Soviet scenes that could instruct him only in the dangerous and unsuccessful aspects of the gigantic world-experiment. Political slogans put forth by this and that "interest." Propaganda. Publicity. Advertising.

If the thousands of half-doped Steves abroad over the land ever paused to think about Russia at all, it was in terms that had been doled out to them in careful rations from a careful Press, of a terror-ridden country lying prostrate under the savage and kicking heel of crazed and delirious labor.

At the same time, the headline-story of some creedist in Vermont being thrown into jail for protesting against jury duty, scarcely indented itself with any of its monstrous and satiric import into the anæsthetized brains of the Steves.

Birth-control, book-censorship, Eugene Debs in jail, Tea Pot Dome scandal, lynchings, child-labor, Lawrenceville Kansas, or any of the acid awarenesses of things current that had cut the lines of pain and cynicism around

Henry's mouth, flashed across the less-sensitized, half-doped Steveys who mutely accepting their God, their food, their censored motion-pictures, books, and politics in the tabloid form rationed out to them in the interests of the greatest good for the greatest number, were mute indeed.

The Steveys were the doers, not the thinkers. They bought their tinned propaganda, theirs not to reason why. They read the Tea Pot Dome scandal as news, and not an outrageous infringement upon their own rights. They let their propaganda-logged eyes skim Eugene Debs head-lines, and said "Serves him right." "Tarring and feathering is too good for those anarchist fellows."

They squealed a little when the shoe pinched their own particular foot, or when a case of local or municipal graft touched their particular pocket-nerves. But otherwise, except for nervous indigestion, the infernal high cost of living, the appalling and expensive precocity of children, the wife's mounting demands of budget, the daily grind of office and high blood-pressure and self-playing piano, the bad street-car service and the unendurable tax-burden, the growing difficulties of labor-unrest, the high cost of production and college education, of butter and life in-surance, coal, children's shoes, tires, tonsil operations and dining-room rugs, life was a charivari, merry enough in its way, of radios, electric signs, aeroplane-races, baseball series, Armistice Days, lodge meetings, and making ends meet.

Steve Renchler had been caught up by the rhythm of the machine. He ate his morning cereal and slightly-watered milk with the newspaper-spokesman of that ma-chine propped up against the sugar-bowl, and suffered no more than the normal indigestion due to overeating. Cereal and watered milk, news that the Ku Klux had tarred and feathered a negro, a college professor dismissed for free speech, Mexican unrest, Rockefeller's dime-gesture, private ownership of railroads, were as normal to the digestion of the Steveys as seal meat and frozen fish to an Eskimo.

The stomach and the brain can be trained to overcome any initial aversions to certain foods and learn to assimilate them.

Steve had assimilated. At thirty, he had practically passed the danger of thinking, hurting, or rebelling against any social, æsthetic or spiritual shortcomings of environment, except where personal struggle for existence, and sweet butter and life insurance, coal, children's shoes, tires, and dining-room rugs had kept the mind competitively keen as a blade. Due to the exigencies of the age in which he lived, the chief of his sensory organs which he had developed was the eye. The motion-picture, the rotogravure, the observation-car, the motorcar, had developed a visual age. Stevey thought mostly with his eyes.

What he beheld first-hand, with the evidence of his own eyes, stimulated him. The Tallahassee Aeroplane Field and Government experimental shops, practically adjoined the Tool Works where Steve was by now department-manager.

In the beginning, it had been necessary to use disciplinary methods with the foundry employees, and even with the office-workers, to keep them from flocking to the windows every time a flight or even the most casual hopoff took place.

The curiously exultant roar of a mounting machine had long since become a matter of course, scarcely causing the lifting of a head. Except to Steve. The excitement of that living, throbbing note of release, as steel and timber took flight, never ceased to thrill him. In spite of the need to be exemplary to his men, it was practically impossible for him to remain away from the window when the song of flight began to hum its way above the din of foundry.

Frequently, instead of lolling his lunch period at home with Claire and the children, or stretched on the flat of his back beneath his five-passenger sedan, he spent it among the men on the field. Government inspectors. Mechanics. Pilots. Once, unbeknown to Claire, he had made a short flight. He was even versed in the phraseology of a new, strangely buoyant, etheric world. Air-pockets. High-pressure areas. Angle-of-drift.

With something of the old inchoate yearnings which had stirred the dark and nervous boy, this present goose-stepping Stevey, snatched back to normalcy by what was probably an inherited capacity for it that was stronger than even his weakness was weak, must have felt something of those remote old stirrings. But felt them safely.

The air, particularly after his first flight, interested Stevey principally from the vantage of his two feet on the ground.

Here was a new world of navigation, of commercial possibility that soared beyond credulity. New un-dreamed-of lanes of transportation, unchartered. By Jove, the day those two Ohio fellows flew at Kittyhawk, had unroofed the world! There were fortunes in those new lanes up there as yet scarcely trammeled by competition.

Here was a means of communicability as yet unchartered to any appreciable extent by "interests."

Steve meant to be a ground-floor man, so to speak, in the new etheric zones of air commerce.

Men's creative brains had wrought the miracle of the flying-machine. The brains of practical men must launch it.

Air commerce. Air franchise.

Steve's dreams as a family-man began to weave about this idea. His ambition for position. A large and beautiful home for Claire. Heavy insurances. A new battleship-gray limousine with balloon tires. A thousand-dollar radio and loud-speaker. That see-America-first rail-trip, celebrated in a folder that he and Claire liked to pore over. Niagara Falls. Yellowstone Park. Seattle. Banff.

Suddenly, to Stevey, who paid forty-two dollars a month house rent; doctor, music, dancing, school fees for the children, clothing for two adults and three youngsters; laundry, gas, gasoline, fuel, lodge, fire, automobile, and life insurance, special tutelage for his child Henry, who stammered, and miscellany *ad infinitum,* on a salary of forty dollars a week, had come a chance which brought him pell-mell, and with a speed that caused the caves of perspiration beneath his eyes, to that haven of the needy and the desirous, his uncle Henry's office.

"Uncle Henry, must see you. Right away. Alone. Sorry, Dave—get out—there's a good kid. This is the only time I can get away from the office."

In a slow-mannered sort of indulgence, Henry regarded his nephew without uncurling his posture.

"Hold your horses, Steve. Me and Dave are having a talk here that about amounts to what you fellows would call a 'conference.' Everything in the world excepting time and a bad egg will keep on a day like this."

"I've only about forty minutes, Uncle. I wouldn't butt in this way, if it wasn't important."

His uncle rose, his great length of body unwinding in slow good-humor.

"Of course, if it's something special."

"It is, Uncle. As special as anything that has ever happened to me."

"I see. Well then, Dave, shall we give way to your nephew a bit? Guess we've about said it all for the present, anyway. We'll let the universe rest as is."

Dave rose and began rolling his cap. A conference was something inviolate. And here was Stevey crashing selfishly, inconsiderately, domineeringly, through the very warp and woof of an hour of interview with his brother, so privately his own.*

---

* . . . speaking of red tape, and his abhorrence of it, long after his (Dave's) official position would have given him precedence in any important man's anteroom, he never permitted himself to be ushered into the private office ahead of those waiting their turn. If there was no appointment, he insisted upon taking his place. I am in possession of an amusing incident that had to do with this characteristic quality of his consideration for others.

Once, while he was Police Commissioner of Springfield, and calling on the then Governor of the State (Canfield), he sat next to a garrulous old farmer in the anteroom, who, also waiting his turn, struck up a conversation with my brother. In the course of it, the old fellow, whom my brother had never seen before, began to describe to him the Police Commissioner, whom he professed to know intimately.

"Quietest fellow you ever seen. Square Dave, the boys call him. Kinda solid, square-looking fellow. Says a thing. Does that thing. Biggest fighter for what he thinks right you ever seen and never lifts his voice or his hand or his little finger so far's anybody around him can see. When them Russians and Pole factory-workers began copying them Soviets two years ago, I was standing within a stone's-throw of him. But believe me, I was behind a pillar. Yes sir, I coulda put out my hand and touched him. Well sir, I wanna say to you—I wanna say to you that he stood on the little old balcony outside the Civic Building window, square, plain-appearing fellow, full-blast where a bullet or even a fist could have done for him. Did he budge? Not a budge. Some pretty little lady, his wife, I

"Well, one thing," said Dave defiantly, folding his check and slipping it into his trousers pocket with the long down-gesture of a man now of pocket-affairs, "if I've got to shove my way in this world, I'm going to shove it with my head, and not my shoulders."

Stevey, far too hurried to be amused, cast a perspiring look at the rangy figure of his young uncle.

"Snap out of it, Dave, and don't be a fool."

"Dave's in nobody's way. Out with what's on your mind, Steve."

Steve slapped down his hat and, straddling a stool, jerked it to him until he was up face to face with the lean lantern from which Henry's eyes looked so humorously.

"I've got the chance of a lifetime, Uncle. And I need two hundred dollars to grab it."

It was Steve's pronouncement of himself as a crisp go-getter man of affairs. Bandier of no words. American business man tactics. Straight from the shoulder. Right to the point. Efficiency.

It was Dave who half leaped forward, not Henry, who

---

reckon, poking her head outa the window in back of his, was shivering all right, but never letting out a cheep.

" 'Attention,' he snaps out suddenly, when the brick hit his cheek that smashed his glasses. Not scared-like. 'Attention—' he says to the militia quiet-like, as if he was telling them to drink a cup of tea. 'It's between principle and the people now. Principle must save the people. Jerk them to their senses with three shots, and I'll hold them there. Attention—Fire!' Just like that! And darned if that's just what he did do. On three shots, mind you. Three shots, mind you, and them shots in the air.' "

And all through this, my brother, who had never seen the fellow before, listened gravely to this piecemeal picture of himself, mostly inaccurate, and evidently garbled from newspaper accounts of the opening explosion of the bloodless Springfield riots.

sat with his slow, contemplative thumb and forefinger, stroking his slow, contemplative jaw, and his other hand, with pipe that always smelled, held equally lax, as he tapped it against the table.

"That's not such a large order, Steve, provided the fellow you're striking for the loan has the two hundred."

"Well, you have it for every Tom, Dick and Harry, Uncle!"

"You may be right, Steve," drawled Henry, "but fact remains, I haven't got it—now."

"He hasn't," yapped Dave. "Henry's no mint."

"Keep out of this, Dave! It's the first time, Uncle, I've ever come to you for the loan of a penny! I've worried along on my own pretty steadily. You'll have to grant me that. But there's nobody I can turn to, between heaven and earth but you now, Henry."

"That's what we all say. That's why he's the hounded one of the whole fam ——"

"Shut up, Dave. I only need a couple of hundred dollars, Henry. My whole future depends on those few paltry dollars. If I'm ever going to be anything more than a two-by-four cog in the wheel of a man-eating iron-foundry, you've got to advance me the few dollars to pull myself and my wife and kids out of the rut that'll close us in, sure as fate, if I wait much longer. I'm borrowed to the hilt, as it is, on my insurance-policies. My Buick isn't even paid for. Let me have that couple of hundred, Uncle. You can. You must. I'll give you my note on any terms you say."

"That's not fair, Steve. Henry's not got it."

"For cripes sake, keep out of this, I say, Dave. It may do you some good to listen to some of the things I've got to say. They may help you to get a move on."

"Steve! That's no way to talk to the boy."

"Opportunity is knocking at my door, Uncle. Oh, I'm

not whining, but if you stop to look at my life for a minute, it—it hasn't been all beer and skittles, Uncle. I— I've had a fight every inch of the way through two or three kinds of hells that—for what I've got—out of it——"

"I appreciate that, Steve," said his uncle.

"You should, Uncle, because—you—helped." *

"I do understand, Steve, more, perhaps, than you realize."

"Well then, Uncle—you know better than anybody —the everything of what I've been through. I've worked my way along pretty steadily these last years, grant me that."

"Indeed I do. I've man-size respect for the struggle you've made and won, Steve."

"Well then, prove it. Opportunity bobbed up for me today. Out of a clear sky. Opportunity's knocking at my door. For two hundred dollars I can open it."

"I tell you he hasn't got it. Is it always going to be like this for him? First me. Then you. Tom and Dick and Harry? I've just borrowed his last penny off him. If you don't believe it—here—looka this check—then looka his stubs. What are we around him, anyway? A lot of bleeders? Henry hasn't got it!"

"Not so fast, Dave."

"He's got to have it. It's my whole life, Henry, getting my hands on this money today. There's a half a dozen can grab this chance away from me if I don't."

The narrowed look had come into Henry's face. A tired look. An old look.

---

* I have always had the feeling, although neither my brother nor Stevey ever referred to it, that Henry had more to do with the salvation of my boy than any of us were ever to know.

"Mighty 'fraid Dave's right, Steve. Fact is, I haven't got it."

"All you have to do is look at his stubs, Steve! If it was for anything else except getting me out of the way and started toward something, I wouldn't take it, either."

"Borrow me that money, Henry. For God's sake, get it for me."

"Why, boy, I can't borrow the price of a bus ticket from here to Middleton. Everybody in this town is onto my way of borrowing from Peter so Paul can borrow it off me."

With a quick fist flashing down over David's wrists, Steve jerked his young uncle toward him, so that his spectacles jerked off one ear-lobe and hung dangling across his face.

"Dave, let me have that money."

"Steve!"

"He's only a kid, Uncle. Whatever he's going to do with it now, he can do later. I'll make it up to him. This is my chance, Dave. You're eighteen. I'm nearly twice that and where am I? Tied to a snide job in a snide town. Opportunities like this don't come twice to a man like me in a town like this. You see, Dave, I've got a family and kids. I've got a mother—your own flesh and blood sister, who deserves, if ever anybody on God's earth did, to have me make good. All right, call it sniveling if you will, but let me have that money, Dave."

"Steve—shame!"

"Why, Uncle? A man with sense will go any length to throw a sop to opportunity, if she's pausing outside his door. I wouldn't ask Dave if I wasn't so sure. It's a turning-point in my life. It's now or never."

"What about Dave's life, Steve?"

"He's a kid."

"Yes, but Dave's been what you might call grist be-

428 A PRESIDENT IS BORN

tween the mills of poverty and war, pretty much since he was born. He came along just in time for his father's bad financial times to set in, and then what did he do but run into a world-war during the years he was growing up."

"He's got life before him."

"That's where it will remain for him, Steve, unless he begins to encroach upon it."

"My life's as important to me, as yours is to you, Steve."

"I know that, Dave. But what you've got to realize is this. You're a bright kid in your way. Maybe a slow way, but you've got something to you that I won't have, if I live to be a hundred. May not get you anywhere—much—unless you get a hustle on you. But you've the makings, Dave, of quite an unusual kind of fellow. Don't know just what kind—but—but life's full of opportunities for you. Scientific farming. Or maybe big business. I'm just a regular, every-day fellow, Dave, with a nose for the opportunity when it comes along. And I tell you this is opportunity."

"Might I ask," said Henry, tapping his dry teeth with a pencil, and regarding his nephew with a frown overhanging his eyes, "the nature of this er—a—mysterious opportunity?"

"Indeed you may! That's my best selling-card, the nature of the project. You'll be the first to see the thing, Uncle. The idea sells itself to a fellow with vision. . . ."

"Well?"

"The birth of the air-age is taking place right under our eyes. I want to capitalize that fact. I want to ride in on it. Me and a fellow at Tallahassee Field, Eugene Bymore, a crack pilot and a fellow that knows the air-game, A to Z, can buy up a plane out of that Smoothfield wreck you read about the other day for a song. This is all inside stuff that comes to Bymore, who's the Government aeronautic engineer. Took a fancy to me. Anxious to meet you, Uncle Hen. Knows about the family and all. This plane can be bought, Uncle, for the price almost of so much junk. Nothing much the matter with it that a fellow like Bymore, who knows the plane through and through, can't handle in a jiffy. Me and this fellow—funny, Uncle, the way he took a fancy to me—we've got an idea for starting a parcel-delivery service between here and Chicago. Over a known lane that Bymore's flown himself for off and on of two years in mail-planes. Idea looks so big to me, there's just no stopping it. Somebody's going to hit on it sooner or later, certain as fate, and it might as well be us. It's coming, just as sure as there's express trains this minute running between here and there. Only, it's coming in a bigger fashion than anything we've ever dreamt of."

"You're right there, boy, but many a good man and good plane have gone down to prove what you're saying."

"The way we've worked it out, on the principle of what Bymore calls the aerodynamic safety in transport-aviation, there'll be minimum chance of a good man or a good plane going down."

"It's gambling with tomorrow, Steve, but tomorrow's coming, sure as hell."

"I knew you'd be the one to see the can before the can'ts. That's what makes you the darnedest fellow, Uncle."

"You mean, Steve," said Dave, with his spectacles thrust forward along his nose, and his head thrust forward on his shoulders, "you mean you're starting in the aeroplane-delivery business?"

"Exactly. Parcel-delivery by air, just like the Centralia Parcel Delivery by wagon. When the Chicago Motor Company needs a bale of special screw eyes from the Giles Tool Works, double-quick jiffy, we supply the double-quick jiffy. When Cincinnati needs half a gram of radium for an emergency operation, and that half a gram happens to be on a shelf in Chicago at nine A.M., Cincinnati is going to have that tube beside the operating-table forenoon that same day. Let us deliver your ivory, apes, and peacocks by air! Express by air and save ten hours delivery-time between Centralia and Chicago. Nothing in time or space can stop us, Uncle."

"It's big, Steve. By God, nothing should stop you!"

"I won't stop you," cried Dave, and slapped down the check on the table. "Yes, sir. Looka. Looka what the Zeppelins are doing now! Why couldn't it be the same from Hamburg to New York and New York to Bombay? You can have this here check, Steve—reckon that's all right with you, Henry?"

"You reckon right, boy, only how are *you* going to tunnel out, boy? Dave was going to Springfield, Steve, on that money to commit the well-known turning-point-of-his-career act."

"You won't be sorry, Dave. You and Henry can regard yourselves as partners in on this enterprise—stockholders or anything you say ———" *

---

* I suppose it may be said that The International Aircraft Corporation virtually had its birth-pangs in my brother Henry's office whither Stevey had hurried that epoch-making day I have just described. Destined, as it was, not only to affect our family-history, but to become one of the great factors of its time in world-progress, how little the three of them, maneuvering among themselves over the raising of that tiny initial capital, could have foreseen the immensity of circumstances that were to unfold out of that hour. For years, my son Steve and Eugene Bymore vigorously contended that Henry and David were entitled to large parcels of stock in the company, a concession which both of my brothers consistently refused.

"Gee, Stevey, you fellows get the world small enough, and there's not going to be any more distance!"

"Righto, Kid! I'll be in a position to pay you both back, tenfold, some day—mark my word ——"

"Cut out distance—kinda get the whole world to draw up its chairs in a closer circle and get acquainted, and you cut out a lot of misunderstanding between fellows and countries, get countries to feeling friendlier, and ——"

"Righto, again, Kid! This here initial money doesn't mean capital—it just means if we can get enough fellows interested in the cost of laying an air-line between ——"

"What's that you were saying Dave—about drawing up chairs closer ——"

"What I was trying to say, Henry, was—cut out the strangeness between men, so's they understand each other better by sitting in closer, and there aren't going to be so many wars, and—and—now my idea is this ——"

"Yes, Dave!"

"Say, the kid's right bright! It's as Bymore says, Uncle, if we can go to a bunch of fellows and say, look here, we have the ——"

"You were saying, Dave?"

"Nothing, Henry, except ——"

"This check means more to me than you'll ever know, Dave. It's going to put a crimp in your plans, but ——"

"Crimp, nothing, I'm going anyhow." *

* Much has been made of the fact that David earned his first year's law-book money in Springfield by operating a sawing-machine for a lumber company during his noon-hours and Saturday afternoons. In fact, Elsworth Tappen in his monograph, goes so far as to say that he earned enough money, what after paying his board, his lodging, and sending money home, to pay for his law-books and accessories by sawing wood. One way, I suppose, of interpreting the act of operating a sawing-machine.

But, in any event, the American public loves to think of David as literally sawing the wood.

Chapter Thirty-six

IT WAS toward the evening of this day of cross-currents in the affairs of Schuylers, that Henry, shaking down his pot-bellied stove, climbing out of his seersucker into the gray herring-bone one with the shiny shoulder-blades, and wrapping a gray wool string of a scarf about his throat against the chill of the long ride home on the dairy-truck, was interrupted by a final visitor, old Dr. Dan Kiskadden, who brought him tidings that made the long, tired brackets around Henry's mouth cut grimly deeper.

For forty-five years, the Kiskadden brothers, like their father before them, had practiced medicine in Centralia. Two months before, Eli, the younger, had fallen over dead while he was writing a prescription for a patient in the office he shared at one end of the old red-brick double dwelling which the Eli and Dan families had occupied since the two brothers had married the two Dinwiddie sisters at a double wedding that had gone to make Centralia folk-lore.

"Doctor Dan," as five counties knew him, had a high comb of thin, black hair, which lay on top of his otherwise bald head in a fat finger-curl. On his pipe-like legs, that were too slender and short for the paunch of his torso, he did sort of a running-walk, his neck darting in and out after the fashion of a rooster pecking gravel. His voice, completed the analogy. It rose and fell in hollow clucks, with the dartings of the neck. A squeaky little voice, emanating shrilly from the bantam little body.

Sometimes Henry and Doctor Dan passed each other as often as three and four times a day along High or

Sycamore Streets, occasionally drifting to a standstill for an exchange of local gossip that had to do with business or politics.

The doctor was usually carrying on dietetic experiments with guinea-pigs and rats in a laboratory he had rigged up, by courtesy of the school board, in a small room adjoining the zoölogy laboratory of Tallahassee High School. Sometimes, on Sunday mornings, Henry walked or got a lift into town, to pore over the doctor's charts with him in the deserted, chalk-smelling school-building.

When Henry was seventeen, Doctor Dan had fought through a close case of double pneumonia with him. A warm, curiously impersonal friendship had persisted, although it was only the second or third time Doctor Dan had ever appeared in his office.

In an age of specialization in medicine, there was something as antiquated about the general practitioner as a horse-car. In the little cubby-hole behind his office Doctor Dan still pulverized with his own mortar and pestle, and measured out physic in an ungraduated glass. Sometimes, for weeks, his prescription-pad lay untouched.

Their experiments in the fields of biometrics and dietetics had from time to time brought one or the other of the Kiskadden brothers, usually Eli, before frequent conventions and in important contributions to scientific journals. An instrument for determining nerve-heat in connection with caloritropic observation, called the Kiskadden fork, is in common use.

But in the main, it was the older generation in Centralia still called in Doctor Dan. The younger sought out more modern outer-office, with white trained-nurse attendants and card-index systems. Those who could afford it journeyed as far as Springfield, Chicago or Rochester for diagnosis.

Doctor Dan still opened his own office door to the ring of a patient. He neglected to send bills, except occasionally a mussy one made out by his wife, when the exchequer loomed bare. He answered night bells. He seldom operated for a pain in the side. He had a range of instruments along the shelves of a glass case, but usually he preferred to probe about in that sore throat with the handle of an old silver spoon he kept lying about his desk. As a rule, but not invariably, he washed his hands, between patients. His little grandson Denny's kiddie-car had a habit of cluttering up his office, and it was not unheard of for Doctor Dan to commit the ethical breach of ministering to a sick dog or cat. It was town lore that he had once answered a midnight call for Harriet Forbes's three-legged cat, Timp. Doctor Dan kept no card-index filing-system and he never inquired deeply into a patient's history. Usually he knew it beforehand, or did his best to figure it out for himself.

He, and particularly his late brother, considered the wave of vegetarianism sweeping the country as pernicious, in its way, as the immoderate use of red meat. Rigorously ethical in his practice, he none the less openly advocated birth-control, and was one of the first physicians in good standing, in his state, to become actively affiliated with the movement, and still keep that standing.

Every once in a while, he packed his bag and went off to Rochester to watch the Mayos operate.

He entered Henry's office with curt preliminaries.

"See you a minute, Henry?"

"Sit down. Glad to see you, Doc."

"Henriette Simpson came to my office today after school. Have you seen her since?"

"No." A kind of pallor flickered along under the leathery toughness of Henry's skin. In streaks, as if it could not all get through. "Nothing wrong, is there, Doc? She was well as usual when I saw her Saturday."

"Wrong as wrong. Thought I ought to talk to somebody. Not asking too much, is it, Henry, but I guess you're about the first in line. Not a relative to her name, so far as I know."

"Right."

"She's a pretty sick woman."

"Seemed all right. Don't remember ever hearing her complain."

"Astonishing constitution. Nasty cardiac condition there. Chronic endocarditis. Enormously enlarged heart. Fluoroscope reveals half the chest-area covered. Valvular leakage. One of those cases where she can go any minute, or outlive us all. Seen it happen. Look at old lady Beattie, up Middleton way. They were writing her burial certificate twenty years ago, and she's outlived her grandchildren."

"You—didn't tell Henriette of this?"

"No."

"Right. Right."

"That's why I'm here. Told her there was nothing much to worry about, and I'd drop in to look her over again in a day or so. Nothing to worry about! There's damn plenty to worry about."

"What's to be done?"

"How's she fixed?"

"She's still paying off on that little old house over on Ludlow Street her father left mortgaged to the hilt. It sucks up her salary like blotting-paper."

"She's got to quit teaching. Every inch of strain on that little body of hers is to the bad. May outlive us all if she's handled right. What you say about her affairs don't gee-up any too good with the situation, but there it is."

"I see. . . ."

"What ever became of that old friend of the family, 'Liza Simpson, used to live with them so many years?"

"'Liza's out in Arizona, Doc, taking care of her brother's children. Henriette sends what little she can spare, out there."

"Nice woman, Henriette is," said Doctor Dan, and sat with his bandy-legs dangling, and his eyes, from which all fluids seemed long since to have been drained, as twisted-looking as water being sucked through a drain-hole.

"Leave it to me, Dr. Dan. I'll take the matter in hand."

"Thought you would. You understand the situation. Care, leisure, ease, and she can live to be a hundred. Maybe. Maybe not. School-teaching's out of the question."

"I'd rather you didn't tell her anything until after I drop by there this evening. And when you see her in the morning, just let her know enough to see to it that she realizes the care she must take of herself. I'll find a way to break the news to her about the teaching part myself. Telling her the truth would about kill her. Most independent temperament in the world."

"Sorry, Henry. Know what a friend—of yours, and of your family's, she's been."

"We'll take a hand, Doc. Don't worry."

"S'long, Henry."

"S'long, Doc."

Chapter Thirty-seven

FOR five or six years, at intervals that had grown from semioccasional to occasional, tiny black flashes of vertigo had been laying hold of Henriette. The first appreciable instance was once at a blackboard, as she was diagraming the genealogy of the Tudor family for a class of twenty-six girls and boys. Just for a moment, like one of her prankish boys yanking the plait of the little girl ahead of him, something had yanked one of Henriette's breaths. It was something at first too quick, and too slight, to feel quite sure it had happened. For all the world like the little girl of the yanked braid turning her startled head.

Then it happened once or twice in church, or at Saturday-morning teachers' meeting; and one Saturday, while lunching with Henry at the Blue Bird, she had been obliged to put down her coffee-cup and grip the table-edge to hold herself steady, smiling all the while, but unconscious of one word he was saying.

It was disquieting, but scarcely so disquieting as embarrassing. Her lean, fibrous body had never, in all the years she had inhabited it, so much as called attention to the frailties of its flesh. It was one of Henriette's rare boasts that she had never in all her life spent a day in bed, or had so much as a headache.

There was something lean and ascetic and brown and tough about Henriette's body at forty-nine. The fibrous body of a woman whose flesh had never dared to shimmer of those ecstasies that lay sleeping beneath its surface.

And just as there was something shameful to Henriette about the girls she passed on High Street, most of whom she knew by name and taught in school, who permitted their dresses to sag off one bare shoulder and their young breasts to tremble in outline behind their flimsy blouses, so there was something shameful in these vertiginous signalings of a body she had so rigorously held in subordination.

The one being for whom desire could awaken in that prim flesh, had by the very decorum of all his years of friendship with her, held it so in abeyance, that at forty-nine, the sight of Henriette to herself, undressed before her mirror, would have been shock and anathema to her.

Nice Henriette.   The chilled niceness of a little tomb.

Vertigo and that irrepressible rise of the nap of her flesh that the sight and too often the mere thought of Henry could inspire, were equally to be dismissed and despised.

For five years, Henriette, ashamed of the frailty, contemptuous of it, unwilling to admit that the attacks were anything more than "nerves," had fought the panic of these moments of black suffocation and ignored their recurrences.

Then one evening, seated at her little table in the tiny living-room of her frame house on Ludlow Street, correcting examination papers on fractions, proper and improper, she fainted suddenly down into them.

There was no ignoring it this time, because it so happened that when Henriette sat down to the table and picked up the first sheet of foolscap, with "Martin Giles, Grade four E, Class B, Arithmetic," written across the top in the monotonous, vertical chirography of stubby fingers, the small, gilt shepherdess-clock on the mantel was striking seven, in the bleating little fashion it had. When Henriette struggled back out of the overwhelming kind of tight blackness that had flowed over and seemed to drown her, the index finger to her right hand still lay against Martin's rather dreary conclusion and $3\frac{1}{2} \times 6\frac{1}{4} = 18\frac{1}{2}$, and the shepherdess-clock on the mantel was now pointing to twenty-two minutes to eight.

The next day, after school, she paid her visit to Doctor Dan. The cruel grilling before the fluoroscope had been a harrowing experience. The baring of her breasts to the stethoscope. The close, personal questions that made her lips quiver and recede back against dry teeth, as she tried to answer them. The proddings and the punchings that only the enormously impersonal procedure of Doctor Dan, whose eyes were frighteningly attentive, but whose lips kept smiling, made endurable.

It had been a little awful, too, that moment before he called her back into his office, after she had climbed back into her waist and hooked the high-necked dickey close about her throat.

Not exactly awful with fear. Suppose, after all, there should turn out to be something seriously wrong with her. Well, suppose. Henriette had her God. A precious Presbyterian one. There were Simpsons, notably her parents, who had been dear to her, gone on to a peace more vast than anything finite she could hope to find. There were compensations, even if Doctor Dan's closely scrutinizing eyes should make findings. Most of the time Henriette believed in her soul's immortality. It behooved her that this be one of those times. There was something about the loneliness of stalking back into that office, to hear about the possible death of a life that had not been lived, that made Henriette need terribly to believe in her soul's immortality.

But after all, she had stalked back in, and Doctor Dan had only tilted in his swivel and made a church of his ten fingers and talked of run-down condition—too close application—general overhauling—and here she was at home again in her own chromesque sitting-room that you entered by two short steps straight from the small bricked yard, feeling a little sheepish after the frightening kind of aloneness of that moment of waiting until Doctor Dan called her back into his office after the examination.

Of course she was run down. Mid-year examinations. One of the most nervous classes of youngsters she had had in years. Must cut down on her Saturday Morning Club work. Resign from programme-committee. Dinah, an old family-washerwoman, might be induced to come in once a week for the general going-over of the little house. Yes, run-down. Doctor Dan had been clever. Fortunately, it was Friday. She would sleep an hour later tomorrow, and possibly pass up the Club, although Miriam Chipman was to read a paper on Leonardo da Vinci she particularly wanted to hear. Still, it might be a good idea to lie abed until time to meet Henry at the Blue Bird.

Part of the appalling sense of loneliness, in that moment before her re-entry into Doctor Dan's office, had been so complexly interwoven with Henry. Thoughts that she beat back from coming to life. . . .

On Monday she was to call back at Doctor Dan's for drops and further instructions. Run-down. Nothing much to worry about. But served her right for her absurd assurance, all these years, that her tough, lean body somehow had exemption from decay.

Well, anyway, it was sweet and normal and cozy to be back home again after the peep over the precipice into the abyss of loneliness that had yawned so suddenly at her feet. It left her a little weak and woefully in need of a cup of tea, which, somehow, she had not quite the energy to go into the kitchen and brew for herself.

Instead, Henriette just sat in an unwonted kind of idleness in the small sitting-room that smelled of dried grasses and chalk-powder, rocking away in a low chair with sawed-off legs, when, by routine, she should have been washing and peeling her usual two potatoes and pounding herself a bit of round-steak to lay in the skillet to fry, or fluffing up a pair of eggs into omelette. She just sat on, while the twilight began to pour around her, and the footsteps of Henry, who semi-occasionally of a Friday, stopped by to exchange a word about Saturday's plans, drew up at the door.

It was particularly nice to have him come this evening. It was part of her grateful return to a world of warm normalcy that was safely remote from the cold-steel curve of instruments and the odor of iodoform and frightening kind of loneliness that had so suddenly pervaded her heart. Yes, it was particularly nice to hurry across to light the gas and draw the shades and drag the stiff-backed rocker with the cane inset that Henry always occupied in a sitting-forward attitude, closer to the table.

The dear delight of living, it flashed over her suddenly, was like a flame, unbreakable, though it bend and double upon itself.

It was good and warm and all right to be opening the door for Henry. They were always of few words together. She drew out his rocker and took a bisque wheelbarrow from the mantel, into which he could rap his pipe from time to time, and placed it on the table beside him. While he lit up, she lighted a lamp on a small stand in an opposite end of the room, that had a white china rose-painted shade, and drew up her own chair primly opposite him.

"Getting right nippy," she said, narrowing her shoulders.

"Is it? I've been thinking, Henriette," he said.

She hoped he had not trumped up some afternoon excursion for their tomorrow. It would be difficult to evade it without telling him of Doctor Dan's dictum that she take it easy for the next few days. She would no more have told Henry of the ripple across the face of the tranquillity of the routine he had learned to expect from her!

"Here's an article, Henry, I cut out of *The Nation*. It's right in line with some of your ideas about the debt-cancellation. Bankers, it goes on to say, are beginning to realize the idiocy of the Versailles programme ———"

"Nonsense! Neither Democrats nor Republicans will face the fact yet for a while that the War was a colossal failure ———"

"But this article goes on to say that we are asking a country to mortgage not only itself but its children for two-thirds of a century—it's as if we were pledging all the little unborn babies to give us their note for a war that took place in this world long before they had ever arrived in it from the land of the unborn."

"Well, Mr. Mellon and Mr. Hoover know that, and will doubtless let their European friends know they know it; but no man out to get his votes is likely to dare talk such commonsense. But all that's beside the point. I—I've been thinking, Henriette."

Oh, dear—there *was* something he must be wanting to do tomorrow!

"Yes?"

"Henriette, something hit me between the eyes today."

For the moment, she seemed to take him literally, peering forward anxiously.

"What?"

"A realization."

"They do hit one—that way—sometimes," she said, and, for no reason she could diagnose, began to tremble.

"Life, Henriette, is passing us by."

"Why, Henry Schuyler, what *are* you talking about!"

"It's been my fault. Twenty years of the rather despicable, detached inertia of a man who thinks so long before he leaps, that by the time he's ready, the opportunity to leap has passed him by, that's me. Henriette, I hope the opportunity hasn't really passed me by."

"Why, Hen-ry Schuyler, what on earth are you talking about? Why, Henry Schuyler!"

She had to say something. Anything. Because all of a sudden, around Henriette's brain was racing and racing the excitement of her lifetime.

"Let's catch on to what there's left of life. You and me, Henriette."

"Why, Hen-ry—I believe you're proposing to me."

"I am."

She looked at him in a little short-of-breath fashion that was to become, from then on, a mannerism resulting from her ailment, as it settled, but which made it appear as if life were suddenly too large and delicious a gulp for her to swallow down easily.

"I think I'm going to giggle, Henry. It's funny."

"Let's make it funnier, Henriette."

"I never did!" said Henriette, and sat with her bony hands held up against her breast, and her mouth slightly open with the thirsty-bird look.

"You never did what?"

The impulse for hilarity was suddenly like a gale in Henriette. She began to laugh.*

---

* . . . I do not pretend to be adept at the psychology of human beings, but to even the most astute it must have been obvious that in the sunshine of her happiness with my brother Henriette Simpson's personality blossomed out into something almost unrecognizable from the Henriette we had known before. All her self-assurance, her prim restraint, her inhibited, timid little ways dissolved. She basked frankly and even a little lazily in the warmth of her new estate. She delivered herself

"I like to hear you do that, Henriette."

"Oh, Henry! It is funny!"

"Let's make it funnier! Marry me!"

"When?"

"What's the matter with now? Good a time as any. Let's walk over and rout out Ed Sykes for a special license and carry it around to the parsonage."

She reached out suddenly and caught him by the arm.

"Henry Schuyler, look at me!"

"Yes?"

"Look me in the eye. Who've you seen today? Are you being noble?"

"No more so than usual."

"Nobody's been telling you I'm run-down or anything? And need a little rest?"

"If they had, Henriette, I wouldn't be proposing anything so arduous as married life."

"Sure you haven't been talking to Doctor Dan ———"

"Doctor Who?" he said, with a bland prevarication he was never known to achieve before or after.

The sweet, eager look flowed back into her face.

"They won't let me teach—married, Henry."

"Dumb of them," he said; "but it suits me exactly. My bank-account for the moment is the shape of a hen's

---

up to the luxury of permitting her husband to wait upon her. She became a purring, pussy sort of little person, glorying in the relaxation of her happiness.

My daughter Paula always used to say that mirth was born in Henriette the day of her wedding. For a positive fact, it did seem to all of us that there rippled through her, dating from that time, a stream of good-humored and irreverent levity that was to amaze and delight Henry for the remainder of what was to be their singularly happy and by no means brief life together.

egg, but we can indulge in the amiable hallucination that two can live as cheaply as one."

"I haven't a thing to wear."

"Take my coat, if you think it's going to be damp walking over to the Sykeses," he said, and took his flimsy top-coat off a peg.

Her own was hanging on the same peg beside the door, but she slid into his.

"Come."

"Coming."

Chapter Thirty-eight

AND so they were married.*

---

*. . . that evening, when I arrived home from having supper with Steve and Claire, who were both in a great state of excitement over my son's impending aeroplane venture which Henry and David had just made possible, I was met at the door by Winslow with the overwhelming news that Father had just telephoned out that Henry and Henriette had been married. And indeed you must add, lived happy ever after. With a chivalry that almost passeth the telling, and at a time when under the conditions, it almost amounted to foolhardiness, my brother took over what had hitherto been the prim little life of Henriette Simpson. While she was never again to be robust, and all the remainder of her life was to be subject to fainting-spells, against which my brother was on constant guard, she was destined to outlive many of those of her own generation about her.

For four years subsequent to their marriage, they remained in the home of my parents, the Igrotte place, which has since burned to the ground.

After the death of my parents, my brother and his wife spent the greater part of each year in Washington, where they had an apartment in H Street.

It was in this apartment that my sister-in-law Henriette died of a singular and distressing accident.

Leaning out of the thirty-ninth-story window of the fine building in H Street, Level II, one morning, to wave my brother au-revoir, as was her invariable habit, she turned in the window-frame to look up at him, as his little two-passenger aeroplane slid from the hangar atop the building, just as the heavy window-sash gave way and fell across her chest, killing her instantly.

446

Chapter Thirty-nine

THANKSGIVING again. A decade and a half since a sheepish-faced Old Gentleman had faced the bombardment of eyes most immediately concerned with the impending event of another Schuyler about to be born.

There were Schuylers assembled again about the board of the Old Gentleman. This time, a far more meager board in the sagging old house set into a patch of scrubby farm-land that was all shot with rock-stratifications which every so often came to the surface suddenly in sparkling little micaceous platforms.

The latter years of her life were to witness a recrudescence of power in Mathilda that amazed her children and husband even while it dismayed.

She continued to outdo in menial labor any hired-hand that came to the place. As her face paled and shriveled and certain diabetic tendencies began to manifest themselves, the iron power of her hands——at scrub-and-rub over a washtub, at churning, at lugging, at beating rugs, which she flung single-handed across a sill, at red-washing the brick walk that led from the kitchen, at calcimining hen-houses, sawing, smoking hams, salting pork, rendering geese, even to cooking lye in vats for its use about the barns——seemed to mount with the years, rather than decline.*

---

*. . . for a wiry kind of power of endurance, I have never known Mother's equal. The least-robust member of all her husky family, it seemed to us as if, at sixty, her capacity for hard work had reached its peak. Remonstrate as we would, Mother began her day somewhere between four and five of

It kept her full of miseries that asserted themselves in backaches and swollen joints and the effects of chilblains which shriveled her valiant face into knots of pain for winter months on end. But there was no restraining the stern flagellation of toil that Mathilda had imposed upon herself, even back in the days when prosperity sat upon her house. Her hands and face were horny with it. In an age when grandmothers had silhouettes and stalked on tall heels, Mathilda was as gray as a moth. A moth with shriveled wings.

Strangely enough, in a way her children hoarded this horny-handed grayness of hers and the faded little streaks of her hair only barely covering the scalp, the corded hands and neck, the furiously wrinkled eyelids, like dried leaves, and the pointed basques she wore all inset with whalebones.

"Thank goodness, Mother has had the sense to grow old honestly," was one of Bek's frequent explosions. "If Mother looked like some of the freak old women one sees around, with their puttied-up faces and their diddering about all over the place with swollen ankles that sag down over their French heels, well, I—well, I just don't know *what* I'd do."

"Mother's got too much sense to make a caricature of herself," was Phil's invariable contribution.

---

the sleetiest, bitterest mornings. It was the only subject upon which I ever knew Father to be ugly with her. It angered and dismayed and humiliated him, as it did us all, for that matter.

Perhaps if Mother had taken better care of herself, she might have lived to even a riper old age. And yet, who knows but what the very rigors to which she subjected herself, were not the secret of her endurance. Thank God again and again that she at least lived to see the first of the great days for us that were to be followed by one epochal event after another.

"Why, I just wouldn't feel like I had a mother if I had to fumble around for an unpainted spot to lay a kiss on, the way the Whittier girls do their mother," trebled sweet Emma.

"I wouldn't change her for fifty thousand of the green coupons it takes to get a covered vegetable-dish," was the caliber of the Old Gentleman's summing it up. Pleasantries like that hit Mathilda right across her hungry heart. He could be so outrageously inconsiderate of her in the trifles. He could have kissed her small, tired feet, out of reverence for her, and yet the slightest compliment he ever paid her was a mocking one, in the key of the covered vegetable-dish.

She regarded him unsmilingly most of the time, sitting mute and unamused at his effulgences.

There was something of a fierce, lean look of hunger in Mathilda's eyes when she regarded her husband. She adored him. She wanted his caresses. Instead, he gave her persiflage, of this variety, and always in the hearing of others, which cut her even more.

She wanted something else, and the Old Gentleman, who gave so freely, and who would have cut off his right hand rather than hurt her, went on hurting her and did not know.

Forty years of being hurt and feeling herself on the rim of the life of a man by nature more intense, more gregarious, more boisterously alive than she, had taken any semblance of smile out of Mathilda. She regarded her husband, her children, her grandchildren, with solemn, worshiping, terribly concerned eyes. Concern for her husband's loose, easy ways with what sparse moneys came his way and which he brought to her, except when someone intercepted him first, and placed in her hands like a child. Money she used with frugality and wisdom. Concerns of this sort kept Mathilda's face a little stern.

Concern for a grandchild's first tooth, a daughter-in-law's watery damson-preserves, Bek's astonishing deal with the Governor, the incredible happening of the bringing-home of Henriette Simpson, a bride.*

Except for the eighteen-pound turkey gobbler, a basket of grapefruit and oranges which Phil and Rita had brought down from Springfield, Emma's usual offering of five pounds of hard candies from the St. Louis Busy Bee, and Claire's candied apples for the children, every dish of that Thanksgiving-dinner-to-eighteen, had been personally prepared by Mathilda.

There were two tables rigged up in the dining-room, another one in the kitchen, and the sewing-table spread in the hall for Rita's youngest two children and Clara's twelve-year-old, whom she had brought from St. Louis

---

* Coming into the home of my parents as she (Henriette) did, on the eve of Dave's departure for Springfield, was nothing short of a blessing for Mother. From the first, Henriette fitted herself helpfully and synthetically into the life of the Igrotte farm. Mother was by no means easy to live around that winter. While you might never have guessed it from any outward demonstration, indeed, I doubt if she guessed it herself, my mother's dependence upon Dave, what with all of us in homes of our own with interests of our own, was perhaps the motivating force of her whole existence. It was Henriette, I feel so sure, who saved her that winter from the throes of a nervous breakdown. I remember Father coming over one blustery winter evening, when he should never have ventured out, and begging me with ill-concealed tears in his bewildered old eyes to try and coax Mother to consent to a visit from Doctor Dan. As a matter of fact, all of us knew, Dave most of all, whose letters came to her regularly as clockwork, that what ailed Mother was heartache for Dave, who had never been absent from her side more than an overnight, in all his life.

this time. Even then, neither Bek nor Claire nor Rita nor Mathilda sat down.

Henriette, with high red spots in her lean cheeks and a blue-checked apron on over her spotted-silk foulard (net dickey out!), was eager to join the brigade of the serving women. But the family, all of them aware of what she was unaware, would have none of it. After all, in a way, it was her day, only the seventh after her marriage. And Henry, who was already displaying what were to be, with him, chronic symptoms of concern at tiring her, forced her down into a chair beside the Old Gentleman, who took immediately to serving her with enormous helpings that overwhelmed and indeed defeated the prim appetite of one long accustomed to preparing her own solitary snack-like meals, and then sitting down to table for the lusterless business of dining alone.

And yet, to Mathilda, who drank her mug of felicitous cider to Henriette and Henry, the most outstanding figure of all that Thanksgiving day was the figure of Dave, there among the in-laws and the cousins, the nieces, the nephews, and the aunts; grave and courteous, in the solemn, detached way he had.

There was a lead pendulum to the beat of Mathilda's heart. David, light of her wintry years—boy who had come to her long after she had ceased to smile, and could only dote silently—boy, who was so strangely, doubly dear with the dual preciousness of child and grandchild. To have begot a child again, after the climactic birth-throes of grandchildren—there was in that something beyond the telling. Not one of her big women daughters, who had borne and borne again, could quite sense that. And what was further beyond the telling, indeed almost beyond the admitting even to herself, was her sense of

failure toward David.   Her secret fear that she had been
a wintry, distant mother to him, full of a sense of embarrassment toward him, the same embarrassment that had
flooded her face at another Thanksgiving years before.

He had grown up around her tired old knees. The forest of the knees of the grown-ups. And of all the grown-
ups, Mathilda had been the most timid with, and of, him.
Sometimes a fierce flame of jealous anger flared in
Mathilda toward the Old Gentleman. His ability to
synchronize with youth. To lean out of years that had
never got him in their clutch. Life was not the serious
business to the Old Gentleman that it was to Mathilda.
Never had been. He was on back-slapping terms with
it. It was to his father that Dave brought a joyous and
adoring kind of irreverence that Mathilda coveted, in
place of the timid kind of tenderness he had for her.

The Old Gentleman and Bek and Henry had somehow,
each in a special way, got better acquainted with her boy.

And now, scarcely had she become accustomed to this
late visitor into a household that had turned a lean
shoulder to him almost from the very year of his birth,
than here he was, like all the rest, turning his young face
outward and away. Almost before she had begun to
know him; begun to dare to know this boy, to whom
books and long silences and heavy chores had been the
order of his days.

In the same pale, secret way that she had endured the
somehow less poignant passing of Phil and Clara, Emma
and Bek from the nest of her household, so now must
she endure the going of the last of them.

This last of them, who had been born so curiously into
two worlds. One foot, as it were, straddling a pre-war
and strangely remote universe, the other on a soil that
was forever to remain strange to Mathilda. A mad,

horrid, fascinating kind of world. A world thumbing its nose at most of the things Mathilda held dear.

David was going out now into it. In a half-dozen ways, he had been the least assertive of her children. Denied practically all of the advantages of the nicely-moderate wealth her others had enjoyed, there was something about his acceptance of the lean, menial days of his youth that could grip Mathilda by the tonsils any time she dared to let her mind dwell upon it.

How denied he had been. Denied even the warm, full breasts at which her other children had suckled. The founts of her being had been dry and runty to the pulling lips of the infant Dave.

He had been her only bottle-babe.

It had cost her secret shame before her husband and family every time she had inserted the viscid rubber nipple of a milk-bottle between his lips. He had not demurred, but had taken even his weaning gratefully. That was Dave all over for you. Had not demurred, but had drunk gratefully.

Then the long, arid days of pasturing, when her other children had enjoyed the advantages of the Centralia schools.

Squalid, pinched boyhood, spent mostly at such past-times as the flat of his back over Henry's books, or dickering about over his ant-hills, or whooping at the game of Indian-in-the-corn, in a mangy little suit left over from Stevey, or exploring the Pacific Ocean from the top of a knoll in the cow-patch that overlooked the dry, cracked bed of an old duck-pond.

Many an afternoon, gazing from her window, Mathilda had watched him climb, while his handful of sheep grazed, to the mock eminence of the knoll, and there peer with much magniloquence of gesture, and occasionally with an old, lenseless pair of Henry's field-glasses, out over the Pacific of the duck-pond.

She had never known its exact meaning, except that it was one of the toyless games of her lonely and deprived youngest.

All the others seemed to understand better. Henry. Bek. Even Phil, to whom he was now going, would get to know him better. *She* wanted to know him better. That way. It was to her that he turned with tenderness that was like the laying-on of hands. A diminished-seventh of a difference in his voice. A little bitterly, Mathilda did not want that diminished-seventh. With his father, he was a play-boy, wary alike of the Old Gentleman's digging humor and the stern old eye of rebuke. To Bek, the boy turned for the swift sure quality of her understanding; and with Henry, this boy of hers was a new boy. Hero worshipper. Climber of mountains. Balboa overlooking the Pacific of his duck-pond. Star-struck with the swimming beauty of planets and the red lamp of Antares. Gripped by the communism of ants. Led by this older brother of the strange wisdoms and the half-smile, into intellectual tourney and jousts long before he knew that they were that.

It was, of course, priceless to have his tenderness. Perhaps, after all, it would have been her choice of the gifts he had to bestow. But, cruel paradox, it neverthe-less kept in her heart, ache over David. Ache over what he was to her and over what she could never be to him. There was no time. Her life was too well burned along the wick. And now he was going. . . .

Life was a pecking jackdaw, after her precious morsel.

Dora Tarkington was a pecking little jackdaw after her precious morsel. Mathilda knew! Well, so had she known long before Bek and Phil and Emma and Clara had quite seemed to know these sorts of things for themselves.

Mathilda had known this from the days when, beside her back window of the spacious house on Sycamore Street, she could see David shinny his way through the hole in the hedge.

In all the years of his very young boyhood, during the months and whole winters that he had never so much as clapped eyes upon Dora, Mathilda had known. She knew it now on the eve of his going-away. She knew it bitterly, jealously, longingly, lovingly.

Mathilda loved Dora where Davey was not concerned. But as one of the daws at the precious morsel of her boy, she dreaded her jealously.*

All through the whirl of that crowded Thanksgiving in the quarters that were so woefully too small; all through the national performance of the dishing-up the mucilaginous miscellany of stuffed gobbler; jellied cranberries; candied sweet-potatoes; creamed cauliflower; hot biscuit; strained honey; pumpkin, lemon-meringue, and

---

*. . . nor was Dave an exception. Mother reacted toward Dora, even back in her childhood, precisely as she had reacted to all of her "in-laws," Sam, Rita, and Winslow. A dear, darling kind of jealousy of these pirate persons who came to carry off her children. There came a time, of course, when Mother would laughingly relate all this to Dora. Her jealousy of the little girl in pigtails, even back in the days when she had watched the squirmy form of her son, his blue-denim trousers-seats usually patched, wriggling through the hedge. Her prophetic awareness of these two, long before the boy and the girl had yet come into their rapture! I always say of Mother, she knew about Winslow and me before I had ever even clapped eyes on him. Oh, my dear Mother, sometimes, when I think back, it seems I must tear away this veil that divides you in your hereafter from me, and make up to you in sweetness what I fear me I may have failed in during your life. . . .

Boston cream-pie; candied apples; crystallized ginger; quince-preserves; nut-fudge, and cider—the eyes of Mathilda were like scars.

"Blessed are the meek in spirit," intoned the Old Gentleman, from a tome with all of Mathilda's multi-colored ribbon book-marks dangling from the end. "For they shall inherit the earth."

"For they shall inherit the earth," mumbled Mathilda, and the comings and goings of her big-shouldered daughters, eager to unburden her frail hands, began again.

"Blessed are they which do hunger and thirst after righteousness; for they shall be filled.

—Sing unto the Lord with Thanksgiving. Sing praises upon the harp unto our God."

Thank God for Henry! Years of the unreasoning jealousy, born of possessive instinct, that had rankled against Henriette, were dissipated already. It was good that Henry should have taken to himself Henriette as wife. It was right and it was good, and the heart of Mathilda, that had been sore, was rich with an honest gratitude that was fitting unto the day.

Thank God for Henriette to round out the wise, thoughtful years of this strangely practical, absolutely improvident eldest child of hers.

Thank God for the vigor and the grandeur of Bek and the plodding energy of Phil and good Clara and sweet Emma. Thank God for the radiance of grandchildren and great-grandchildren. Thank God even for Leslie, whom Bek had somehow managed to keep in the sweetness and the light of childhood, until God had taken him back.

Thank God for the flesh of her flesh that crowded the Igrotte house that day.

Thank God for the man with whom she shared all this living, vigorous splendor. Thank God for the vigorous,

living splendor of the Old Gentleman himself, whose
sense of duty was drawn along his mouth, making it
straight as a bolt, and whose sense of humor shimmered
in his eyes and made them like hospitable windows inviting the intruder to ignore the bolt and climb the sill.

Thank God—even—for Davey—going away. Thank
God, of course, for vesting him with vigorous manhood,
the pale, square face, the clear and seeing and sometimes too brilliant eyes. But the Old Gentleman's
mouth of restraint was Dave's, too. Thank God for
that. The time had come— Thank God, of course,
for this man-child about to flutter from the sparse, old
unfeathered nest. Thank God—of course—ah, yes
—Thank God——

It seemed to Mathilda, glancing up over her mumbling
lips three or four times as he read the blessing at table,
that Thanksgiving Day, that the Old Gentleman's voice
might give out.

It must have seemed that way to Henry, too, who
shoved him a glass of water.

Chapter Forty

THE impending event of conclave shone in the Old
Gentleman's eyes all through the hours of serving, of
eating, of the rushing of the women hither and thither,
of the tilting of the pitchers of cider, the ladling of the
gravy and the vegetable-dishes, of the high, querulous
voices of the children, grand and great-grand; through
Mathilda's fluty voice, importuning her young, her very
young, and her middle-aged to partake more freely, or
not too freely, of the bounty she quivered and fussed
and rushed to place before them. Platters, held high
to avoid spill and collision, clicked with narrowness of
escape. Rose the rich, hot smells of winter foods that
had simmered in their juices. The spice of cider. The
flicker of blue flame across the dome of suet-pudding.
The popping of the toy balloons that Winslow had
ordered Bek to order by catalogue. And through all this
charivari of the Schuylers, the Old Gentleman, his grandchildren from time to time crawling over his legs and
matting up his beard, looked out upon the scene and
waited. Waited while he joked with his daughters, rebuked, dandled, teased the youngsters, put out a sly foot
to trip his Bek, as she slid her large frame into the narrow
gauge between tables to remove plates.

"Father, that's just terrible to do a crude thing like
that! Bek might have fallen. Besides, I don't think it's
a bit funny to do before the children either," remonstrated sweet Emma in her treble.

"Aunt Emma is mad at great-grandpa," said the Old
Gentleman, mushing his lips against the soft, yellow hair
of Steve's eldest little girl.

"Puppa," quavered Mathilda faintly, "a little dignity before the children, please!"

"Dignity comes cheap. Cigar-store Indians have it."

"Well, we won't argue it, Father," said Bek, "only please don't trip up your stout, middle-aged daughters as they try to serve you candied yams. It just isn't done."

He leaned back in his chair to regard her, his sly old face foreshortened and his eyes creased into a sucking swirl of wrinkles.

"My daughter's been a good son to me."

Almost without precedent for her, she leaned over and pecked a kiss on the wrinkled old mat of a face.

"Not one of us is good enough, Father! Hadn't you better clear out the youngsters? They're getting restless."

It was then that the Old Gentleman brought down his fist as if it were a gavel.

"Clear out the children and close those folding-doors. Dave, sit over here."

Conclave was on. Not a Schuyler but knew the call. A Schuyler about to be born. About to be praised. About to be rebuked. About to be reminded that the stern ideals of the House were the stern ideals of the Mosaic Law. Commandments. To be written on the tablet of the heart. A humble house, but one that already had plunged root deeply and proudly into three generations of the soil. The same soil that had first fostered the Old Gentleman with the straight bolt of duty for a mouth, and the pallid Mathilda, whose eyes were no less steadfast than the straightness of that mouth.

Bek bundled off the last of the grandchildren.

Finally, the doors closed, the shades drawn, the ugly little Igrotte dining-room cleared of the extra table and jammed with the Schuyler faces, every member of the family knew, without the first word having been spoken, that this wasn't really Henriette's and Henry's day at all.

This was David's conclave.

He sat on the arm of Henry's chair, a lank fellow of square, white face that flickered behind his spectacles with a nervous batting of his eyes; and, above the soft, blue collar of the adult shirts he was beginning to inherit from the well-worn stock of Henry, his Adam's-apple rode like a buoy.

By now, there was a marked Schuyler-cast to his face. The something in the bone-structure of it that made it four-cornered. Cheek-bones strictly vertical above jaw-bones. Brow that was set across with the perfectly horizontal adjustment of a key pediment.

The Old Gentleman and most of his offspring—with the exception of Steve's little boy, who was Mathilda all over again, and Emma, who was like a big, flowering Viking out of nowhere—had that rectangular type of face.

A great-grandfather, named Hans Milton Schuyler, who had been his own plow-ox on a Swiss farm sixty-eight years before, had been known as far as Engeborg and as wide as Saalsberg, as "Breitgesicht," which in Swiss means "square-face." It was just about now that David, ceasing to gangle his way upward into greater height, was to begin to settle tightly into the squat hewn and thewed look of face and figure that was to make him even more susceptible to cartoon and caricature than Roosevelt.*

---

*. . . a young and enormously talented fellow named Donald Wight, who graduated from Harvard with my grandson, has done some of the most delightfully eloquent caricatures of my brother that have ever been made. The originals of these are in the portfolio collection of Paula's second daughter. The strip of cartoons which I am pasting on this page is by no less

He might easily have been the son of Henry, as he sat there on the arm of his chair, dangling a long, loose leg and batting his nervous eyelids under the circling buckshot of Schuyler eyes that were slowly swinging into tribal circle.

Conclave was on, and it was characteristic of the Old Gentleman not to bandy words.

"Dave, come here!"

His mother flung up a protesting flutter of hand against her throat, as if a pain had smote her.

The boy strode immediately beside his father, the dignity of his swift, sure obedience blurred a bit by the batting eyelids and that violent thing, his Adam's-apple, beating relentlessly against his collar.

"Phil," said the Old Gentleman, taking his youngest's hand and swinging his quizzical old head round to where sat his rotund second son, "Dave's made up his mind to go to Springfield."

"That's all right with us, Father. Isn't it, Rita?"

"Indeed it is, Father Schuyler."

Rita, who always wore large, pink pearls in her ears and against her soft and fat white neck, had an invariable gesture of seeming to protect the beads against the tugs of her youngest child. She was a soft, voluble little person, prematurely gone fat, given to a certain amount of self-pity but outstandingly generous in her sympathies

---

an artist than the celebrated Nea. The one at the end, right, done in exactly six strokes, suggests in masterly fashion the square, rather pugnacious qualities of my brother. The second, with those quick, exaggerated quirks to the eyebrow and corners of the mouth, suggests, in uncanny fashion, the winged, visionary look that was characteristic of him in certain moods. The last, perhaps, is the most wittily characteristic of all. The four-square solidity of a man whose feet are to the ground and whose nose is sniffing stars.

toward others. The too-ready tear, the too-ready laugh,
hung on the brink of Rita's eye and lip. All her life,
small partridge of a person that she was, she was destined to be interrupted in the middle of a sentence.
They came so volubly. In such quick succession. So
sure-fire commonplace. Even her children had a way
of chopping her off along about the middle of the pre-
dicate.

"As I always say to Phil, we haven't got much but,
what we have got is . . ."

"I think Dave has made a pretty good decision,
Father. Maybe you wouldn't judge so from my present
performance, but what I said to him a year ago, holds
today. Springfield hasn't licked me yet by a long shot.
It's a live town for a live fellow."

"St. Louis is a good town," interposed Clara into this
concatenation of family-events. "If Sam had only had
the gumption when he was a younger man! Why, most
of the men in the big wholesale-shoe crowd on Washington Avenue started in as city-salesmen!"

Years of bitterness on this subject had worn down
Clara's voice to a whine when she broached it. St.
Louis, which she chose to denounce upon every occasion
as a city which had throttled her dreams and initiated
her into the scrimped existence of the wife of a city-sales-
man, had long since shed its first years of strangeness to
her. Now, after eighteen years, it was secretly near and
dear to her. But she still nagged persistently to Sam,
that life there, so remote from her home and parents,
was a meager and thankless affair.

As a matter of fact, at the close of the first few days
of her annual visits home, an actual nostalgia for the
scenes and friends of the city of her constant denuncia-
tions began to set in. Her eldest daughter was already
a prize pupil in the third grade of the St. Louis public

schools and Sam practically a pillar, by now, of the Second Presbyterian Church. They shared the upper floor of a "St. Louis flat" with a family who owned a Buick sedan and was generous with it. Clara herself belonged to a sewing, a bridge, and a window-garden club, and was beginning to enjoy contacts with the wives of men who were in business for themselves.

Clara's Mecca. Business for themselves! Sometimes to Sam, who was a steady, plodding man of modest desires, that phrase could close like a tomb around his contentment. "Business for himself." That phrase was a din in his ears.

"I'm a great believer that the boy who starts out in life with his eye on getting himself into business for himself as soon as possible, is the one who will escape the rut."

Clara's relationship to David was something as baffling to her as it was abstruse. Eight years after her marriage to Sam and her subsequent removal to St. Louis, David had been born.

He was a perpetual shock to her on her return visits. For the life of her, she could not associate him with her girlhood background.

Her own children were full of curious questions about him that she could not quite answer. It smote her one middle-of-the-night that he would be great uncle to her first grandchild, and she wakened the snoring Sam at her side to put the fantastical idea before him.

It is doubtful, if in all, Clara and Dave had ever exchanged an hour's talk, and that never sustained beyond the casual. And yet here he was, this remote brother of hers, who might have been son, needing something she felt it part of her tribal responsibility to be able to give him, and feeling somehow, a smoldering anger against the absent Sam.

"If only Sam were in business for himself, instead of a man on a small salary, Dave could come to us and learn the wholesale shoe-trade. Sam says St. Louis is the coming shoe-center of the—whole world!"

"Know what I was thinking the other night, Henry? S'pose you double the grazing-area of this country by raising reindeer in Alaska. Well, double the grazing area and see how it affects the leather-industry ——"

"Well, I don't know anything about that, but I do know that if Sam had been the man to push himself ——"

"Your point is well taken, boy," said Henry, and the large, slow smile began to shoot in wrinkles from his eye-corners—"well taken, but out of order, I should say."

With a sensitiveness to the slightest rebuke or poke of fun from Henry that was never to leave him, the sides of David's head seemed to lighten suddenly with the flash of two pink ears, and a flooding flush of embarrassment ran down into the soft, blue, attached collar of a shirt that had already served Henry and served him well.

"It just kinda came to me, all of a sudden, is all I meant."

"That's exactly Dave's difficulty," said Bek, her eyes, that always flowed beneficence for him, full of a mock despair. "I'm sure that right now he's standing there trying to decide at the last minute whether he's starting out to be an astronomer, a taxidermist, or a ——"

"God forbid!"

"A policeman, a Senator, a veterinary, a bank teller, a sheep-herder, an explorer, a wholesale shoe-merchant, a doctor, a lawyer, a merchant, a chief, or a ——"

"Many the good veterinarian that has been sacrificed to the United States Senate."

"Hennery!"

"Well, we don't need any veterinarians in the family."

"Better in the family, Bek, than in the Senate!"

"Nonsense, a veterinarian in the Senate is worth two in the family."

"What's all this talk about a vegetarian in the family?"

"A veterinarian, Father!"

"What's the difference, they are both for letting the animal live, aren't they?"

Paula, who outside of her teaching had started a batik, painted-shoe-trees, character-doll, telephone-doll, hot-muffin, jasmine teas, book-ends, art-smock, and candied-praline shop in Cleveland, in partnership with a teacher in night school (who had advanced the initial two hundred dollars), leaned over to her brother Steve.

"Isn't the darling priceless? I could get him big time in vaudeville."

"Or Sing Sing," laughed Steve and laid a friendly and conservative wallop across his grandfather's shoulders.

"At my age," said the Old Gentleman, "I don't expect big time any more. In Sing Sing, or out of it."

"Puppa!"

"Guess, Mother, why my life is like a tail."

"Puppa!"

"Because it's all behind me. Sometimes I think it's ahead of Davey, but like a tail, too, and one that he's trying to put salt on."

"Father—don't tease!"

"But, Father—my mind's made up for sure—this time!"

"That's a fact, Father, all joking aside. Dave's been over this thing with me same as he has with you. That's the hurry idea of putting it up to Phil and Rita now. Dave's missed three weeks of the evening law-session down Springfield now, as I understand. Dave's come through about this present plan on his own voluntary decision. Isn't that about it, Dave?" said Henry, fixing on him the eye of an ally.

"That's it, Father," said Dave, on a gulp, and looking around at the fortress of friendly faces, began to bat his eyes. "Not much to herding—is there—for a fellow like me ——"

"There's not much to herding except to a fellow that was born to be a herder."

"Be surprised, though, Father—fellow learns a lot about how ants and sheep and butterflies and chipmunks and field-mice and skunks manage their world."

"Skunks," said Phil, "that's a mighty helpful part of a fellow's education!"

"Mebbe, if it helps you recognize a human skunk when you meet one. The world's full of them without the smell."

"Puppa!"

"Yea, and watching butterflies—they'll get you pretty far, Kid, in the world you happen to be born into. Try concentrating on cream-separators or garbage-incinerators. They'll get you further."

"Oh, Phil," cried Rita, with a ripple across a face that was seldom marred by petulance. "What's funny in that? Can't you let the boy alone?"

"I knew a fellow once, up St. Louis way," said the Old Gentleman, "made a fortune out of some sort of a dredging-machine. Got the idea from lying on his back in the park zoo Sunday afternoons, watching the rhinoceros dig himself out of some Missouri mud they'd spilt in his tank."

"Dave's got more information," said Henry, "up there in that kinda blockhead of his, than you'd think, offhand, Phil."

"Don't I know it? Can't anybody around here stand a little kidding?"

"Cut it out, Henry. I don't need anybody tooting my horn."

"You see, Phil, the boy's idea in going to Springfield is a sound one."

"Sure it is. I've been after him to come to us for a year. Springfield is a live town, and a boy in a wholesale grocery-firm can work his way either in or out of it."

"Exactly, and as Dave has figured it out, what with your offer to roof him, it's as good a place as any, and maybe a little better, to—get his start in."

"Better, I'll say!"

"Exactly. To get himself a law-education evenings and at the same time scrape together his meal-ticket on a daytime job. That about it, Dave?"

"Yes," said David, and stood up suddenly with a click of his muddy heels, in the attitude that was to be so characteristic of him on rostrum and lecture-platform. A rather defiant, inelegant throwback of figure, elbows hugging his sides, head tilted, and his legs in the attitude of a trained runner about to swing into motion.*

"You see, Father, I'm no good at inventing or engineering or exploring or any of those things that some fellows have done to move the world along. But Henry and I know that as sure as we're standing here, the time is coming when aeroplanes are going dipping around

---

* . . . Henry Gothard says of him (David) that half of his platform-power (my brother was not a fluent speaker) lay in that almost eccentric pose of a squat, low, tight-sinewed man, self-flailed to endurance. Blierot's statue of him, which stands at the head of Hudson Boulevard and Three Hundred and Thirty-sixth Street, suggests that dogged quality. The painting by Rockwell Bosworth, which hangs in the National Gallery at Washington, is still my favorite, however. Incidentally, it was while he was posing for that portrait that he is said to have dictated his Conciliation Message to Russia. I know that to be erroneous. That document was composed six months later, in the summer White House.

the world just as plentiful as trains. No man-control at all, but operated by wireless. Well, that's the way I feel about a job. I'm no good at inventing the wireless, but if I could get a job where I'm the wireless-apparatus itself . . . that's where I'd come in."

"Times are better for a young fellow now than they were when I first went to Springfield," said Phil, with sagging, disappointed lines springing about his mouth. "It's the age of nerve and it's the young have the most of it. Take the building-trade in my town. I took my plunge just ten years too soon."

"I think I'd like the building-business, Phil! You know what? Henry, I was thinking. Take the lay-out of towns today. The whole system has got to change in the next twenty years. People ten miles out won't be in the suburbs any more. They'll be ten minutes by plane from . . ."

"The building-business, eh? Well, how would you like to go into the automobile, Oriental-rug, the ladies'-wear, the coffin-manufacturing, the vacuum-cleaner, the banking, the baking, or the breeding-of-tadpoles business? Or would you compromise on taking a twelve-dollar-a-week job licking stamps for a fellow named Ox White, whose got a *mail*-order business, selling radios?"

"I'd like that fine, Phil! Funny thing, but I was thinking to myself last night in bed, know something that will save a lot of time and money for the Government? Get before them, so they see what you're talking about, the idea of the further development of the C.O.D. mail-delivery and it's going to revolutionize ——"

"Save it, or try it out on Ox. He's a great one for ideas and cigar coupons!"

"Phil!" called Rita, and looked with her sweet eyes at Dave, as if she could cry for him.

"Oh, let me alone, can't you, Rita? The kid's got to get practical sooner or later, doesn't he?"

"Oh, I know what I'm up against, all right."

"I wonder!" said Bek. "I wonder!"

"He's never had advantages like my other children," suddenly bleated Mathilda, coming up behind the chair of her youngest. She was like a wraith of hunger, of yearning, and of torment of self-indictment. "He's had just scraps all his life."

"Nonsense, Mother!" said Henry, frowning. "What the rest of us had in advantages, he's made up for in his way, and don't you forget it! The boy's all there—a little nutty on the speed-age, it's true, without ever asking himself where all this speed is going to take us!"

"But, Henry, you're the one who sees it as much as I do. More!"

"What if I do? Whither, is what I'm asking—now that we've got it, what are we going to do with it?"

"Davey!" There was his mother's hand on his shoulder again. It was light as a leaf. It was lighter. It was as veined and as palsied as if a wind were trembling it. It made him want to cry. The lightness, the timidity and the fact that even with its frailty, its callous places hooked onto the nap of his coat. How doggedly and persistently, ever since he had known those small, claw-like hands, they had poured out twice the strength of which they seemed capable.

Her children like to tell of her, a little wistfully and a little humorously, how she had once lugged a kicking calf who had poked his luckless head into a hornet's nest, moaning and plunging, the two miles from the ravine where she found it, back to the Igrotte house, where she deposited it in the barn and fainted.

The odor of lye and soft soap hung chillily about Mathilda. Every day that Davey had ever known her, the gray wisp of her figure had lumbered through the dawns, bent at some chore too heavy for her. The bluish smoke of frying foods enveloped this sudden heart-hurting procession of his memories of her, as her hand lay like a flake upon his shoulder. She was forever at doing things that curved her thin back into a hook. Winding a windlass to raise a bucket of water. Stooping to draw her pans of well-risen bread out of the oven. Sweeping out a hen-roost, her head wrapped in the blue bandanna kerchief that hung behind the kitchen door, waiting for her.

The bandages she had wound! Not only around Davey, but around the quinsy sore throats, the cut fingers, the twisted ankles of farmhand, neighbor, man, woman, and child. The liniment she had rubbed! The ducklings, the bulls, the rams, the ewes, the kittens, the colts, the calves, the chickens, she had ministered to, moving through the soft or freezing dawns, as the case might be, barn and barnyard flickering to the swinging of her lantern.

Once, when Dave was eight and had a diphtheritic sore throat, and hoof-and-mouth disease was among the cattle, and a cow with calf was giving dangerous and premature birth, she had fluctuated, the night through, between helping the Old Gentleman in the barn, returning to the house every so often to strip off her clothing for garments that had not been exposed to the cattle; then to the swabbing of David's throat and back into the gray slip of a cotton dress with the blood-spots on it; out once more into a blackness that seemed to cut her in two as it struck her on the walk from the kitchen across the chicken-yard to the low, red building that was filled with the sobbing of a cow in labor.

There was no attitude of a human being in toil or fatigue that all through his life was not to suggest to

David, his mother. A figure lugging a pail of water across a field as his train sped by. A sway-back woman with her arms filled. A head lolling on tired shoulders. A pair of knotted hands that, in repose, were stiff and ill-at-ease looking.

How frequently she went about her service, drawing on the secret spring of her strength, her large, milky eyes tired, yet full of the strange exultation of self-torture.

The way she pressed food upon her menfolk, almost with the fanatical zeal of one whose own hungers could be vicariously assuaged by the sight of their indulgence.

For years the Old Gentleman had wailed, "Mother, stop watching me eat! Come eat with me!"

When her children, including Dave, had grown in years and weight to an age where she could scarcely bear up under the burden of lugging them in arms, she had continued to carry them, glorying with perhaps the inner exultation of sacrifice, in the burdens that her Lord had seen fit to bestow.

She was like a stone at the heart of her family, Mathilda was. Every one of her children, and the Old Gentleman as well, was sooner or later to come to know the bitter sweetness of heartache for Mathilda.*

---

* The morning of the day of my dear mother's death, on one of those telepathic and not quite explainable impulses, I drove over to the Igrotte house in the forenoon, although it was my usual custom to arrive there about four in the afternoon in time to lift Mother, who was so dreadfully crippled of inflammatory rheumatism that winter, from her couch into her bed.

To my horror, I found her this day (it was actually the day of her death, dear darling) trying, with her pain-crammed fingers, to knit a blue neck-scarf for Steve's eldest daughter, Pauline.

I shall never forget the stab of pain with which I beheld

Her relentless industry. Her fanaticism for service. Her mute power of reproach. Not reproach against those she served, but because under her very feet, as it were, her world, that she labored so to conserve, ran away from under her like sands.

Her hands were not only horny, but empty. She had gathered a harvest by their productivity, and the reproductivity of her body, only in order that she might lose it.

The granaries of her house and her heart were continually emptying themselves faster than they were restored. And now David, who had come into her autumn and was leaving her in the dead of her winter.

It was not merely as if the hand on Dave's shoulder pressed against the nap of his coat and the nap of his flesh, it was more as if it melted and ran along through his veins, into their stream and pumping through his heart, made it ache.

Bek knew precisely what David was feeling then. That same pain racked her most when she woke up during the low-ebb hours of the night, with a troubled awareness of that small, shriveled figure of her mother lying two miles away in the Igrotte house.

Henry knew the ache that went with contemplation of his mother. It made him sometimes brusque with her.

Clara too, to whom events back home, as she viewed them from St. Louis, were somehow as through the wrong end of the opera-glasses, and Phil, who took the background of family too much for granted to notice, did regard his mother, once in a rare while, with something of an indefinable pain for the manner in which the years had gnarled her.

Mathilda somehow had grown old in the way of a fruit tree that had borne long and richly.

those tortured fingers working their laborious way along the needles. . . .

Emma sometimes frankly cried to Bek, asking passionately and rebelliously what Mother ever got out of it, she'd like to know.

Why—why—nonsense, Mother got plenty out of it.

The Old Gentleman, who loved her, and who was slightly afraid of her terrible meekness and the hint of hurt disapproval that it shrouded, thought too, when he thought about it at all, which was seldom, that Mathilda had got plenty out of it. Love and fear of her Protestant God. A good wifehood. A superb motherhood. A family consistently striking deeper and deeper root into a soil that had fostered it.

The Old Gentleman could strut of this sense of his Americanism. Probably once a year he got his yellowing citizenship-papers out of a drawer in his desk he kept locked, and with his steel-rimmed spectacles low on his nose, reread them. It pleased him to think that his children had never one of them set foot out of America. Americans all.*

Henry was the only possible exception. But as the old Ex-Governor had once put it, he was perhaps the best American of them all. That he dared, benignly, to challenge the cardinal virtue of patriotism, one-hundred-per-centism, Protestantism, Rotarianism was Henry's way. Not to be taken seriously.

Mathilda herself never challenged. She was only hurt, deep down into the very sinews of her being, with the

---

* . . . the first member of our large family to go abroad, was my son Steve, who flew to England, *via* Newfoundland and Ireland, the year he became president of the International Air Corporation. During his lifetime, Father, for some curious reason, was never sympathetic to the idea.

For a while, Phil and Rita were extremely anxious to send their second daughter to school in Switzerland, but out of deference to Father's wishes, abandoned the idea.

pain that she carried about with her into her barnyards.
To her churning. To her perpetual task of laying patches
against men's clothing, and opening the squeaking beaks
of poultry to the medicine-dropper.

It was as vague, this pain, as her sense of the surface
of her body. She could not have analyzed it. But it was
what her young son, standing there in the abashed throes
of family-analysis, seemed to feel melting in the shape of
her hand through his coat, into his blood, and washing
painfully around his heart.

"It's not easy for a boy with no advantages these
days. Our Dave hasn't had them. . . ."

"Mother," he cried, and turned passionately toward
the hovering gray of her figure—"quit saying that, can't
you? I'll get on all right. I'm going to get me a good
job in a good town."

"Attaboy, Dave," cried Phil, "the boy that starts right
in that town today, can clean it up and run it—I came ten
years too soon."

"Sure I am, Mother."

"Attaboy," cried Phil, and whacked him on the back
so that his spectacles jumped.

"Quit!"

Mathilda regarded her youngest with eyes that seemed
to crawl out toward him with their love and gratitude.

"I've got you ready, son. Six as new shirts as a boy
ever left home with. Flannels and middle-weights.
There's a patch had to be laid on the blue serge, Dave,
but it's an excellent suit for every-day—with overalls, for
sweeping out office of a morning. You can travel in it,
son. The patch won't show up, son, if you're right careful about your stoops."

"Mother," cried Dave and sprang back from the
stroke of her thin hand, "not that old serge to travel in!
What if Dor—what if somebody's down at the train to

see me off.   Wouldn't I be a pretty sight—backing away? Gee, a fellow's got to look right, traveling, Mother."

"You can have my middle-weight gray pants," said Henry, rising as if to conclude the occasion.   "You're right.   A fellow on his way to the conquest of Springfield is entitled to a pair he is not ashamed to turn his back on his home-town in."

"Hen-nery!" fluttered Mathilda, "be refined!"

Chapter Forty-one

T HE sleet came down and hopped off shoulders and blew
and bounced along the streets and then finally formed a
coating of ice that shellacked the windward side of buildings and trees and made walking a matter of balancing.

High Street wore its coating promptly away into a
mucilaginous ooze of mud, but the tributary streets, except where housewives leaned from the top steps of their
porches and threw out handfuls of ashes, or ice-cream
salt, glittered in an armor of thin ice, and the naked
branches of the double rows of maples along Sycamore
Street shone like a regiment of fountains with their orna-
mental waters frozen in action. Shrubbery in front yards
sagged under ice. Horses pedaled for footing and struck
sparks. In front of the Five and Ten Cent Store, one
was down, with a driver sitting on his head, while they
shoveled ashes under his plunging hoofs. The pair of
iron stags on the Court House lawn had ice beards.

In winter, Henry Schuyler persisted in wearing a veteran coon-skin cap with ear-flaps, probably the only one
still extant in Centralia.

When he came down out of his office to emerge into the
sleet, these flaps were tied down over his ears in a little
bow of black tape under his chin. In his short reefer,
coon-skin mittens, and goloshes that he lashed closer to
his thin legs with a winding of hemp, there was a lanky
Ichabod-look to him, as he strode surefootedly along the
perilous streets.

David was leaving on the one-forty-nine. Henry had
left Senator Jim Kearney, who wanted unprofessional advice on an extradition case he was handling in Cincinnati,

waiting with his feet up against the base-runner, while he made the dash around to the station. As the Senator put it, he had just dropped in. As a matter of fact, Henry knew, and the Senator suspected that Henry knew, that he had made the trip to Centralia for the express purpose of the interview with Henry.

The one-forty-nine was due in ten minutes.

Henry hurried.

David, and his father, and Mathilda in an outlandish-looking dolman cape with ball fringe that gave her coachman's shoulders, and Dora Tarkington in her white wool cap, were standing around a stove in the waiting-room, with their clothes steaming and smelling.

Tom Willets had raised the ticket-window grating and was leaning along the outer sill to talk with the Old Gentleman.

Katie, old Trina's niece, who before her marriage had done day-work in the House on Sycamore Street, getting wind of Davey's departure, had driven in on her husband's dirt-cart from Ideola with her three-year-old twins, who kept up a constant trekking across the room to the water-cooler, Katie constantly after them for keeping the spigot open.

There were two other passengers for the one-forty-nine. A salesman with his sample-case and a shawled woman with a live chicken in a chip basket.

The sleet beat against the smoke-smeared windows in a monotonous tattoo.

"It's a bad day for travel, son," said Mathilda for the fourth time.

"Oh no, Mrs. Schuyler!" cried Dora. "I just love to travel on a rainy day. There's something so cozy about being right out in the middle of the weather and not a bit of it able to get at you. Don't you think so, Dave?"

David thought so.

"Of course, I know what you mean, Mrs. Schuyler. There's something depressing about people going away in the rain. Sad-like."

Dora's voice was too high. It had a nervous pitch to it from talking to David's mother. She was not quite herself. They were a little fierce together, these two, a rush of excitement out over them just from being in each other's presence. Mathilda, without quite knowing it, full of unease, as if something were rubbing against the grain of her very being.

Pretty Dora. David's shy eyes these last moments were furtively for her.

Mathilda knew it by the tight feeling behind her eyes.

Dora, by that same token, knew that Mathilda knew. With all of her astonishing capacity for rising to the demands of almost any sort of moment, Dora, even with her throat so hot and dry and nervous-feeling, knew that there must be just one right sort of kindness to make this moment more endurable to Mathilda.

In a way, she almost accomplished that miracle. Except for the overstrain in her manner, which David wanted passionately not to be there.

It kept her too eager. Too high-voiced. Too voluble. And not more than once did she let her glance be caught and pinioned by David, whose eyes ached to be caught and pinioned.

"Don't you think it fun to travel in the rain, Dave?"

"Dora isn't really this way, Mother," he wanted to shout. "She's sweet and neat and cozy. She isn't really this way, Mother."

"You do think it's fun to travel in the rain, Dave?"

"You bet!"

He had a dry throat that kept breaking his sentences into gulps. There was even one between the "you" and the "bet."

How beautiful she was in that woolly cap that shone against the dirty morning. And she had cut her hair. The curls that had romped through a thousand of his fancies of her, were gone now from their yellowish riot along her shoulders. And strangely, incredibly, the little bang of yellow that escaped her cap, and the short, straight line of yellow that lay along her cheeks, and the furry little peak where it petered out in the back of her head, like a boy's, were just as goose-fleshingly lovely as the curls had been.

How beautiful she was. The secret thing between them that he had whispered to his mother a thousand times with the secret lips of his heart, was obscured for the moment by the enormous casualness of her manner. Too casual. Too obviously casual, he thought. Even strangers could be expected to meet eye-to-eye. The eyes that must serve him as lamps now. Two shining lamps down in his heart.

Yet there they stood, scraping their feet along the fender of the stove, dilly-dallying through the infinitesimally small talk of waiting for a train.

"When Father took me to Springfield when Aunt Genevieve died, we ate in a dining-car!"

Gabble. Gabble. Dora's tongue was like the hum of his mother's sewing-machine. Gabble. Gabble. Dear gabble, gabble.

"Of course, with local trains, it's different. . . ."

It made all the commotion of his emotions somehow subservient to just her nearness and dearness.

Once it seemed to him that something shining lay along her lashes as she half raised them to him. Only half, but it swept the plunging excitement higher and dryer into his throat.

"Only ten minutes, Dave," said Mathilda, her words seeming to collapse against the rim of her lips.

"Yes, Mother."

How beautiful she was. Dora.

"You'll remember, Davey, to make a package of your dirty wash every-other-week and parcel-post it home."

Dirty wash! At least she might have put it "soiled linen." Mother!

"Rita's got her hands full with her own family. Besides, son, it will be almost like having you back. The clothes—you've worn—close—to you. Don't forget to change regular, son."

"Mother." What if he should cry. His throat ached so.

"I've put in two weights, Dave. The ones with the little red 'D' embroidered on the drawers are the heavies, son."

Drawers! How terrible. How Terrible. How TERRIBLE. In front of Dora. Dora, whose sweet eyes were almost looking into his now. Dora, whose sweet eyes were violets. Red "D" on the belt of his drawers. Ignominy drenched him. It made red signals of his ears. It made a throttle of his Adam's-apple.

"Mother!"

"Dora knows, son," said Mathilda, and fixed her ineffably tired eyes upon the two of them, standing flaming in the murk of the clogged air of that waiting-room which they enchanted for each other. "Dora knows such things have to be thought about. No right-thinking girl, Davey, is ever above thinking about those kind of things," said Mathilda, and began to cry miserably and in sniffles that screwed her face cruelly because she tried to hold them back.

"Oh, Mother, Mother, Mother!" cried Davey to himself, as if his heart were turning to sand and running away from him.

And yet he only stood and gulped the Adam's-apple that would not stay gulped.

"Dear Mrs. Schuyler," cried Dora, and stepped over the impediment of Dave's cheap, light-yellow suit-case and neatly-wrapped shoe-box of lunch, which he had consistently tried to keep kicked out of her sight, "look what I've brought him, if he thinks you're kind of fussy about—about little things. I knitted it myself. All but the orange stripe. Mary Chipman was sleeping with me one Saturday night, and she knows the zigzag stitch— she did the stripe."

"A muffler! For me—all but the stripe—gee, swell— fellow needs muffler—all but the stripe—gee ——"

"He—wouldn't let me put the one I knitted for him in," sobbed Mathilda, the words tumbling off her lips like coals, and then making a forward jump as if she would scrape them all back again.

"Why, you darling, of course he wouldn't. No son in the world ever would."

"He—he—said—no ——"

"Mother, I didn't mean ——"

"You did!" said Dora, who had an armful of Ma-thilda, and stamped her foot. "You did! You were horrid! You did!"

"He didn't!" cried Mathilda. "You see, it was a gray one. Of a bit of wool left over from his father's socks. He was always a child liked color. It's the orange in this one. He didn't!"

"That's exactly what I meant, dear—he did—I mean he didn't—I— mean—of course I mean he did."

Oh, Dora—Dora—sweet, appeasing, ever-ready Dora ——

Things began to happen then, starting with the faint shivering of the timbers under their feet and a blast of whistle. A door blew open on a gust of sleet.

Tom Willets slammed down the ticket grating and the straggle of travelers made stooping dives for their luggage. Katie hoisted her babies. Henry strode in, and as if shooed, the group began to move out to the ice-sheeted platform.

"Got your ticket, Dave?"

"Yep, Henry."

"Remember us to the folks down Springfield, Dave."

"Yep."

"Don't forget to give Rita that strip of red flannel, son. It's packed under your shirts. Phil writes baby had quite another spell of croup."

"No'm."

"Write a body, son, and come home by the first holiday they give you. Don't bang that shoe-box, Dave. There's a jar of cole-slaw in it. Don't throw the glass away. Take it to Rita for her jelly-time. There's mustard in a separate paper for the sliced bologna, son. Plenty of it the way you like."

How terrible. How Terrible. How TERRIBLE. Dora's eyes laughing—at him!

"Mother!"

"I hope you put in a good dill-pickle, Mrs. Schuyler. He used to steal them for me out of your crocks and squirm through the hedge with large, green, luscious beauties for me."

"Two of them are in there, Dave. And a bit of corned-beef to munch with the cole-slaw. He's a great one for corned-beef and cole-slaw, Dora. Queer combination. Never saw the like." *

---

* The night of his (David's) election to second term (the most overwhelming landslide in the history of our country), he and Dora spent the larger part of that exciting evening quietly in my brother's private study, viewing the street scenes of New York, Chicago and Denver through the television.

"Corned-beef and cole-slaw," in front of Dora, when his heart was bursting to tell her that her eyes were violets! Tears would come. Humiliated hot ones which he kept swallowing back. Corned beef ——

"Goodby, Dave! I'll be waiting."

"Dora! Dora! goodby, Dora!"

"Goodby, son! God bless you!"

"Mother, goodby!"

"Boy! Boy! Boy!"

"Yes, Mother!"

"Goodby, son! God bless you!"

"Father—oh, Father!"

"Carry your own torch, son, for what you think is right, even if it's a torch no bigger than a lightning-bug."

"Yes—Father—goodby!"

"Goodby, Davey—Trina sends word, goodby, too."

"Goodby, Katie ——"

"Tell my twins goodby, Davey!"

Henry and Henriette, Winslow and I, and Stevey's eldest daughter, the Senator, had flown over to New York to see the returns come in at Phil's, who was bedridden at the time, with a broken leg, at his home in Upper Level, Park Avenue. We were all invited, however, upon our return from New York that midnight, to join Dora and David at a late snack of supper.

While wires hummed and buzzed around us, and messages the world over were pouring in, there we sat cozily sealed against it all, watching scenes in Nome, Alaska, and Bangor, Maine, through the television, and talking among ourselves. It was over corned-beef and cole-slaw, personally prepared by Dora, that my brother practically thought aloud, Henry taking it down shorthand and interpolating here and there, the first draft of an idea long discussed with Henry and which was beginning to take concrete shape in his mind.

It was his Superstate World-policy, which needs no explanation here.

"Goodby, youngsters!"

The train dove in then, parting the sleet like a curtain, and Charlie Herkhimer sprang up out of nowhere, in furiously greasy overalls and a torch, and began poking in and out of the day-coach entrails.

"So long, Dave! Luck!"

"S'long, Charlie! Well, well! Guess I'm off, Henry!"

"Yep!"

"All aboard!"

"Oh, Davey—there comes Bek!"

"Goodby, Dave! Catch! It's a sack of chestnuts. Roasted them for you this morning."

"Thanks, Bek! Goodby, Bek!"

"Don't eat them, son; they're bad for your headaches. Take them to Phil."

"Mother—Father—all—Bek—Dora—Goodby!"

"Your shoe-box, son! Don't crush! It's lunch!"

"Wave goodby to my twins, Davey!"

" 'By, twins!"

"Oh!"

Sleet bounced down against the shoulders of the little group on the platform, as the train that bore David Schuyler out of the years of his childhood, wound like a snake around the end of the old South Meadow of the now historic House on Sycamore Street.

FINIS

This book is set in Caslon Old Style *and* Caslon Old Face *types, following the lines of those originally designed by* WILLIAM CASLON *in the early part of the eighteenth century. Working at a time when type designing had fallen into a state of uninspired mediocrity,* CASLON, *by the beauty of his new types, did much to revitalize the art of printing. After two centuries of constant use, they are still considered the finest faces for book composition, embodying, as they do, both pleasing grace of line and maximum readability.*

The text is printed on Lorette laid stock from Perkins & Squier Company, *bound in glazed black Holliston vellum, stamped in art gold with linoleum - block printed sides designed by* A. W. Rushmore. *Set, printed, and bound by the* Haddon Craftsmen *in Camden, New Jersey, for the publishers,* HARPER & BROTHERS

THE HOUSE OF HARPER

NEW YORK
Publishers of BOOKS and of
HARPER'S MAGAZINE
Established 1817